Dilly Court

The Christmas Rose

HarperCollins*Publishers*

HarperCollins*Publishers* Ltd
1 London Bridge Street,
London SE1 9GF

www.harpercollins.co.uk

First published by HarperCollins*Publishers* 2018
1

A catalogue record for this book is available from the British Library

ISBN: 9780008199678 (HB)
ISBN: 9780008199685 (PB b-format)

This novel is entirely a work of fiction.
The names, characters and incidents portrayed in it are
the work of the author's imagination. Any resemblance to
actual persons, living or dead, events or localities is
entirely coincidental.

Set in Sabon Lt Std by Palimpsest Book Production Limited,
Falkirk, Stirlingshire

Printed and bound in the UK by
CPI Group (UK) Ltd, Croydon CR0 4YY

MIX
Paper from
responsible sources
FSC™ C007454

This book is produced from independently certified FSC™ paper
to ensure responsible forest management.

For more information visit: **www.harpercollins.co.uk/green**

Chapter One

Royal Victoria Dock, London, October 1882

Rose leaned over the railings, peering into the fog that had crept up on the steamship as it entered the Thames Estuary. It was even thicker when they arrived in Bow Creek, and as the vessel slid gracefully into the dock they were engulfed in a peasouper, making it impossible to distinguish the faces of the individuals waiting to greet the passengers.

'Is he there, love?'

Rose turned to give the small woman a weary smile. 'I can't see very far, Mrs Parker. But I'd know him anywhere, and I can't spot anyone who looks remotely like him.'

Adele Parker laid her gloved hand on Rose's arm.

'Don't worry, dear. I'm sure your young man is there somewhere.'

'Max promised to meet me.' Rose could not quite keep a note of desperation from her voice. 'We planned it all so carefully.'

'Then I'm sure he'll be here soon. It'll take a while for the crew to put the gangplank in place and unload the luggage.' Adele wrapped her shawl more tightly around her plump body. 'It's so cold and damp. We've been away for five years and I've almost forgotten what the English winter is like.'

'I was only nine when we left for Australia,' Rose said, sighing. 'But there's nothing to keep me in Bendigo now.'

Adele gave her a searching look. 'How old are you, Rose?'

'I'm eighteen, ma'am.'

'I do worry about you, dear. I sympathise with you and your young man, but you do know you can't marry without your parents' consent, don't you?'

'I'm an orphan. Ma died when I was very young and Pa was killed in a mining accident a year ago. He gave up the sea because he thought he could make more money in a gold mine. It was a bad move.'

'You didn't tell me that, you poor dear.' Adela gave her a hug. 'You're a brave girl, Rose. I wish you all the luck in the world.'

'Thank you.' Rose returned the embrace. Adele had shown her nothing but kindness during their time at sea, and, despite the difference in their ages, they had become good friends.

'We'll be staying with my mother-in-law, who lives in Elder Street, Spitalfields,' Adele said gently. 'I forget the number of the house but it has a black door with a lion's head knocker. Ma-in-law is very proud of that.'

Rose smiled vaguely. 'That sounds nice.'

'If you need anything just come and see me.' Adele craned her neck at the sound of the movement from a lower deck. 'The gangplank is in place. I must find Mr Parker.' She started off in the direction of the companionway, but she hesitated, glancing over her shoulder. 'We'll be catching the next train from Canning Town. You're more than welcome to travel with us if your young man doesn't put in an appearance.'

Rose was acutely conscious of the need to watch the pennies, but she managed a smile. 'Thank you, but Max will be here. He promised.' She strained her eyes as she peered into the thick curtain of fog, hoping to catch sight of the man for whom she had given up her home and her adopted family. A feeling of near-panic made her clutch the wet railing until her knuckles turned white. If Max, for whatever reason, could not meet her, she would be in a terrible fix. The possibility had not occurred to her during the voyage from the Australian port of Geelong to London. She had lived in a haze of romantic visions of what her life would be like as the wife of a dashing cavalry officer, but something as simple as a London particular was in danger of shattering her hopes and dreams.

Sadie, the woman who had become a second mother to Rose, had uttered dire warnings and these came flooding back to her now. Perhaps she ought to have listened, but she had ignored them and had allowed Max to purchase a berth for her on the *Bendigo Queen*. Sadie had been quick to notice the deepening affection between Rose and Max. He was five years Rose's senior and she had been slightly in awe of him when they first arrived in the mining town of Bendigo, and it was Jimmy, his younger brother, who had been her particular friend. Two years later Max had been sent back to England to attend Sandhurst Military Academy, and it was on his first trip home that they had met again. Rose closed her eyes, conjuring up a vision of Max, his gleaming blond hair waved back from a high fore-head, his classic features, piercing blue eyes, and his newly acquired military bearing. It had been love at first sight when she had met him then, even though they had known each other since childhood, and, to her surprise, the feeling was mutual. What a handsome young man from a wealthy family had seen in a skinny green-eyed girl with wildly curling copper hair she had never been able to fathom, but Max loved her and she loved him. Unfortunately his mother and Raven Dorincourt, his aristocratic stepfather, disapproved, and Max was promptly packed off to England to finish his training, but his parents could not prevent them from corresponding. Rose had a bundle of Max's letters tied with pink ribbon, stowed carefully in her luggage. Reading them at night before she went to sleep had kept her going through the long days of their separation and during the voyage home to England.

'Rose, dear. We're leaving now. Are you coming with us?'

Adele's voice brought Rose sharply to her senses, and she was left facing a wall of thick pea-green fog and an uncertain future. There was nothing she could do other than to follow Mr and Mrs Parker down the companionway to the lower deck. Everyone was pushing and jostling for position as the passengers disembarked. The level of sound from the dock grew in intensity as people called out to each other, whistling and shouting to attract the attention of those who had come to meet and greet them.

Festus Parker disappeared into the crowd, telling his wife to stay where she was while he went to retrieve their baggage. Rose could only stand there, damp, cold and increasingly panic stricken as she searched the crowd for the young cavalry officer who had stolen her heart in such a dramatic way.

Adele tugged at her sleeve. 'Maybe he was delayed by the fog. Come with us, dear. We're going to stay in Elder Street until we get out next posting.'

'Thank you, but I'll wait. Max will be here – he promised.' Rose's voice caught on a barely suppressed sob, but she held back the tears of desperation that threatened to overwhelm her as she struggled against a wave of homesickness. Sadie would tell her to keep a stiff upper lip, whatever that meant, but Rose was beginning to wish she had never left the noisy, often chaotic house attached to the school in Bendigo.

Adele fumbled in her reticule and brought out a pencil and a religious tract. She tore it in half, pulling a face as she did so. 'I'm sure the Good Lord will forgive me, but this is the only piece of paper I have.' She wrote something and passed it to Rose. 'This is where we'll be for the foreseeable future. If you get into difficulties, you know where to find us.'

Rose put it in her pocket. 'Thank you, Mrs Parker. I won't forget your kindness to me during our voyage.'

'Nonsense, Rose. You've been a delight and you helped to alleviate the boredom of the long days at sea.' Adele moved aside as her husband emerged from the gloom, carrying a large valise and Rose's carpet bag.

'You travelled light, Rosie,' Festus said cheerfully. 'I wish my wife could limit herself to so little in the way of clothing.'

Adele beamed at him. 'It's my one weakness. I know it is pure vanity, and I should try to overcome my love of pretty gowns and lovely colours, but we are as the Good Lord made us.'

'I'm sure you make up for it in kindness, Mrs Parker.' Rose leaned over to kiss Adele's round cheek.

'You can still change your mind and come with us, Rose.'

'Thank you for your offer, but I will wait here for Max. He'll come, I know he will.'

Adele and her husband exchanged worried glances. 'Have you anywhere to stay in London?' Festus asked abruptly. 'Has your young man found suitable accommodation for you?'

'Oh, yes,' Rose said airily. 'We'll be lodging at the Captain's House in Wapping. I lived there for a while when I was a child.'

Festus nodded gravely. 'Do you know how to get there, should your friend be delayed by the fog?'

'Max gave me instructions, so you really need not worry. But I am grateful for your concern, really I am.' Rose stood her ground, despite the Parkers' continued questioning. She knew that their concern for her was genuine, but she trusted Max. She had given up everything to be with him, and she was certain that he would not let her down.

After a tearful farewell the Parkers melted into the crowd and were immediately lost from sight. The peasouper seemed to be getting thicker with each passing minute and still there was no sign of Max. Rose picked up her luggage, edged her way towards a pile of wooden crates and perched on one, preparing to wait even if it took all night. Max had promised – he would come.

The crowds thinned and soon Rose was the only passenger left, but the busy life of the docks went on around her and she sat there, largely unnoticed. At one point a fussy man wearing a bowler hat demanded to know her business, and when she explained that she was waiting for someone he advised her to move on. She did not argue, but she ignored his advice, and an hour or so later a man wearing workman's clothing approached her with a mug of tea in his hand.

'Here, love. You look as if you could do with this.'

Rose took it and drank thirstily. The hot, sweet tea burned her tongue but she could feel its warmth seeping down to her empty stomach, and she realised that she had not eaten since breakfast. 'Thank you, sir.' She handed back the empty cup.

'Sir, is it? I don't often get treated with such politeness. Anyway, I got daughters of me own at home, and I wouldn't want to see them sitting there all day, waiting for someone what is obviously not going to come.'

His words brought her abruptly to her senses. She had lost all track of time but it was getting dark and the fog was thicker than ever. She struggled to her feet. 'Ta for the tea. Perhaps I'd better go.'

'That's right, love. You go home. Whoever it was that should have met you ain't worth nuppence, leaving a young lady like yourself on your own.' He lowered his voice. 'There are some strange types to be found in a place like this.'

'Can you direct me to the station, please?' Rose tried to sound casual, but she realised suddenly that she was chilled to the bone and she was shivering violently.

The workman frowned, pushing his cap to the back of his head. 'I've finished me shift, love. You'd best come with me. I'll see you safe to Canning Town station, but you're on your own from there.'

'Thank you. You're very kind.'

'I'd hope someone would do the same if any of my girls was in need of help. Follow me.' He loped off, leaving Rose to carry her heavy bag, but she was more than grateful. It was obvious that something momentous must have occurred to prevent Max from meeting her, and she would have to find her own way to the Captain's House. Sadie always spoke fondly of the old house on the wharf that was now owned by Max's older sister, Caroline, who had married well. Rose trudged after her protector, glad of his presence as she received whistles and indecent proposals from some of the men who were loitering around the dock gates.

At the ticket office her new friend turned to her. 'Got your money ready, miss?'

Rose had her purse in her hand, but it felt very light and she knew that the money in it would not take her very far. She took out her last silver sixpence. 'How far will this get me?'

The man in the ticket office seized the coin. 'Fenchurch Street, miss.'

'That's where I'm going,' Rose said firmly. She had no idea where Fenchurch Street was in relation to Wapping, but she had a dim memory of hearing the name and it seemed familiar. Anything was better than being stuck out here in the cold and dark.

'I'll leave you to it, then. Good night, miss.'

She turned to thank the man but he had vanished into the fog. 'I didn't even know his name,' she said out loud.

The railway clerk handed her a ticket. 'What did you say, miss?'

'Nothing. Thank you.'

'Platform one, miss.'

'Thank you.' She made her way to platform one, walking as fast as her cramped and tired limbs would allow. At least it would be warm on the train and she could sit down in comfort, for a little while. But where was Max? Why hadn't he been there when she needed him?

She had only been able to afford a third-class ticket, and when the train arrived it was overcrowded, with standing room only, and the passengers were crammed in shoulder to shoulder. After nearly two months at sea, breathing in the fresh salt-laden air, Rose felt that she was suffocating, and the smell of sweaty bodies and unwashed clothing was almost too much to bear. When the train eventually pulled into Fenchurch Street station she was forcibly ejected as her fellow travellers pushed and shoved in their efforts to leave the compartment.

Standing on the platform, a small island in the midst of a swirling sea of people, Rose had never felt so alone in her whole life. She grabbed the first woman who was about to rush past her.

'Excuse me, please. Can you tell me how to get to Wapping?'

The pale-faced woman, whose brown eyes were blank with fatigue, pulled her arm free with an angry twist of her thin lips. 'You should have got off the train at Leman Street.'

'I didn't know that,' Rose said humbly. 'Where do I go from here?'

The woman pointed vaguely. 'Head that way until you get to the Minories and then walk down Little Tower Hill and turn into Upper East Smithfield. You'll have to ask directions when you get there, but keep going towards the river and you'll get to Wapping High Street. Be careful who you speak to, girl. There's some odd sorts round there.' She wrapped her shawl around her head and dived into the crowd without giving Rose a chance to thank her.

There was nothing for it but to start walking. Rose tried to remember the woman's hurried instructions, but the fog was even thicker here than it had been in the Royal Victoria Dock, and she had to keep stopping to ask the way. Sometimes her enquiries were met with a helpful answer, but more often than not people ignored her and walked past.

It soon became obvious that she was lost – the landmarks were obliterated by the fog and her breathing became more laboured with each step she took. She had lost all sense of time, but it felt like the middle of the night. The occasional cab lurched past her, but the horses moved at a plodding pace, and it was not until they were almost upon her that it was possible to gauge how close they were, making it necessary for her to leap out of the way. Rose's nerves were shredded and she was exhausted and very hungry. Desperation was making her reckless, and, as she felt her way from wall to wall, she was suddenly aware of a shaft of light and the sound of raucous voices. The smell of ale and spirits wafted out of the pub in a cloud of tobacco smoke. Rose was about to go inside when someone grabbed her by the arm.

'I'd steer clear of that place if I was you, dearie.'
Rose struggled but she was hampered by her heavy

carpet bag and the woman had a grip of steel. 'What's it to you?' she said crossly.

'Up from the country are you?'

Rose dumped her baggage on the pavement. 'Who are you?'

'I'm a friend, love. But you're not from round here, are you? You wouldn't want to go in there if you was up to snuff.'

Rose sighed. 'I was born in London, but my pa took me to Australia when I was a nipper.'

The woman leaned forward to peer into Rose's face. 'I'm Cora Smith, and if you've got any sense in that noddle of yours you'll take my advice and move on from here. What's your name?'

'I'm Rose Munday and I'm trying to get to the Captain's House on the wharf at Wapping.'

Cora threw back her head and laughed. 'There's lots of wharfs at Wapping, love. D'you know which one?'

'No, but it wasn't far from the dock police station. I remember that.'

'Well, that's a start. Come on then. Seems to me this is my night to be a good citizen, for a change.'

'What do you mean?'

'My, my, you are a persistent little thing. What did they teach you in Australia, Rose Munday? Didn't they have women like me, with painted lips and rouged cheeks, what earns their living by any way they can – mostly flat on their backs or—'

'Yes, I understand,' Rose said hastily. 'I grew up in a mining town so I know how it goes.'

'Tell you what, Rose. I was going to point you in the right direction, but I don't want your dead body floating downriver on me conscience. I know this part of London like the back of me hand and I'll see you safely home. Is someone waiting for you?'

'I hope so,' Rose said fervently. 'Max was going to meet me – he gave me his word.'

'Men and their promises.' Cora tossed her head. 'Come on, this peasouper ain't going to clear before morning. Let's get going.'

They seemed to have been walking for hours. Rose could feel blisters at the point of bursting on her heels, and she was just beginning to think she would drop from exhaustion when Cora came to a sudden halt. 'Watch where you go.'

Slowly and painfully Rose followed Cora down a steep flight of steps, and she was in familiar territory at last. Despite the sulphurous stench of the fog mixed with the smoke from thousands of chimneys, the smell of the river mud took her back to her childhood. In her mind's eye she could see the run-down boatyard where her father had struggled to make a living. It had been her home and she had forgotten the hardships, remembering only the hot summer days when she had paddled in the shallows and picked wildflowers on the river-bank.

'This must be it,' she whispered. 'The Captain's House can't be far now and Max will be there waiting for me.'

'I wouldn't bet on it, love.' Cora reached out to clutch Rose's hand. 'Keep close to me. There'll be coils of rope, chains and all sorts waiting to trip you up and fling you into the river.' She paused. 'Can you hear it? The water is lapping the wharf and that means it's high tide.'

'Yes, I remember now.'

'Good. Then you know that if you fall in you won't stand a chance. No one will see you and they won't hear your cries for help. The current will suck you under and you'll be a goner.'

'Why are you doing this for me, Cora? Why would you want to help someone you've never met before?'

'You ask too many questions. Come on. I'm dying for a smoke and a drink, and the sooner I deliver you, the sooner I can find a nice warm pub.'

'All right. I'm coming.' Rose tried not to drag her feet as she followed Cora, who seemed to have limitless energy. Then, just as Rose was about to give up, she was aware of a different smell and one that was very familiar. It was a mixture of burning sugar, roasting coffee beans and spices emanating from the warehouses surrounding the docks.

'This is it,' she said excitedly. 'We must be very

near. I remember how it smelled when the wind was in a certain direction.'

'There ain't no wind, duck. It's your imagination.'

'You're wrong. I know this is the place.' Rose dropped her bag and, holding her arms outstretched, she walked slowly, feeling the way until she came to the wooden steps. She ran her fingers over the rail and there it was. 'This is the house,' she cried triumphantly. 'Max carved his initials on this piece of wood the day before we left for Australia.'

'Then there's only one thing to do.' Cora pushed past her and marched up the steps to hammer on the door. 'I want to meet this young man of yours and give him a piece of my mind for leaving a kid like you to find her way home in the middle of a London particular.' She took a step backwards as the door opened and a pale shaft of light pierced the fog.

'What d'yer want?'

Rose hesitated. It was not Max's voice and a shiver ran down her spine. 'I've come to see Max Manning,' she said nervously.

'Who?'

'You heard her, mister,' Cora said angrily. 'Have you got cloth ears or something?'

'Less of your lip.' The man held the lantern close to Cora's face. 'Ho, touting for business, are you? You'd best come in then.' He reached out a skinny but muscular arm and yanked Cora over the threshold before she had a chance to argue.

Rose dropped her carpet bag and ran to Cora's aid. 'Leave her alone. We just want to see Max.'

'There ain't no one of that name here, girl.' The man shoved Cora so hard that she stumbled and fell in a heap with a flurry of red flannel petticoats, exposing legs clad in black stockings.

'What have you done with Max?' Rose demanded, standing her ground. 'Where is he?'

'What's going on, Sid?' A second man staggered out of what Rose remembered to be the front parlour. 'What's all the din?'

'We got company, Wilf. Two ladies of the night to warm our beds. It must be our lucky day.' Sid slammed the front door and leaned against it, folding his arms across his chest. 'Nice of you to come calling, ladies. I think I'll take the younger one. You can have the old tart, Wilf. Let's get to it before the others come to.'

'No,' Rose cried. 'There's been a mistake. We're looking for someone.'

Cora scrambled to her feet. 'Move aside, cully.' Before he had a chance to argue she had a knife to his throat. 'I don't go out at night without my chiv, so get away from the door.'

Terrified, Rose held her breath. She had seen plenty of brawls in the streets of Bendigo, but she had never encountered danger at such close quarters.

'Get out, Rose,' Cora hissed. She twisted the knife so that it nicked the flabby skin at the base of Sid's scrawny throat, and she gave him a hearty shove that sent him cannoning into Wilf. The pair of them fell to the floor in a tangle of arms and legs. 'Run for it, Rose,' Cora screamed. 'Run.'

Chapter Two

Rose wrenched the door open, but in her hurry to escape she misjudged her footing and tumbled down the steps, landing on the carpet bag, which served to break her fall. Unhurt, she scrambled to her feet and Cora leaped to the ground, grabbed Rose by the hand and headed off into the fog. She did not stop until they reached the relative safety of the High Street.

'That was a close one,' Cora said breathlessly. 'I knew I should have walked on when I spotted you outside the pub. This is what I get for doing a good deed.'

'I'm sorry, Cora.'

'It's not your fault, young 'un. Coming here at night in the middle of a peasouper weren't the best idea I ever had.' Cora brushed a strand of unnaturally brassy hair from her forehead. 'What am I going to do with you now? Do you know anyone in London?'

Rose bent double, holding her side in an attempt to relieve a painful stitch. 'There's Max's sister.'

'Well, why didn't you say so in the first place? Where does she live?'

'I don't know.'

'That ain't no help. What's her name? Maybe I knows her.'

'She's called Caroline and she married Phineas Colville. He owns—'

'He owns the biggest shipping company in England. Well, I'm blowed. Who'd have thought it?' Cora put her head on one side, narrowing her eyes. 'You're not making this up, are you? It ain't funny.'

'No. On my honour, it's true.'

'On your honour.' Cora hooted with laughter. 'Where'd you learn to talk stuff like that?' She held up her hand. 'No, don't tell me. I ain't sure if you're genuine or the best little liar I ever met, but I ain't hanging around here a minute longer than necessary.' She walked off, heading back the way they had come.

Rose grabbed her bag and hobbled after her. 'I'm sure that Mrs Colville will vouch for me, Cora. I just need to find out where she lives.'

Cora paused, glancing over her shoulder. 'Maybe she'll offer a reward. I mean, a girl has to earn a living. I could have been working instead of traipsing round the docks with you.'

'I really am sorry.'

'Of course you are.' Cora stopped and turned to give Rose a searching look. 'What am I going to do with you, Rosie? I can't abandon you, even though common sense tells me that I should.'

'Maybe I could spend the night at your lodgings?' Rose suggested tentatively. 'I haven't got much money, but I think I have enough to pay my way – for one night, anyway.'

'Oh, all right. I suppose I ain't got no choice. You'd best come with me.'

Rose could hardly put one foot in front of the other by the time they reached the run-down building where Cora lived. Rose was completely disorientated and she could not have said where they were, except that she was glad to stumble into the relative warmth of the building when Cora ushered her inside.

'It ain't much, but this is where I doss down,' Cora said firmly. 'My room is upstairs.' She mounted the narrow staircase, trailing her hand casually on the banister rail, which was blackened from years of grease and dirt. The flickering yellow gaslight popped and fizzed, adding its own pungent odour to the general fug, but Rose was too tired to be critical. It felt good to be safe from the outside world, even if some of the stair treads were rotten and several of the banister supports were broken or missing.

She had barely reached the first landing when a door opened and a man lurched out, ramming his cap on his head as he pushed past her and thundered down the stairs. A young woman poked her head out, grinning when she spotted Cora.

'Had a good night, duck?'

Cora jerked her head in Rose's direction. 'Got a visitor, watch what you say, Flossie.'

'Ooh, hark at her, girls.' Flossie took a drag on her cigarette.

'Shut up, you silly tart,' Cora said affably. 'Poor kid's just got off the boat from the back of beyond and been let down by her bloke.'

'We've all been there, luv.' Flossie exhaled a plume of smoke at the grimy ceiling. 'Did you see Regan hanging around downstairs?'

Cora shook her head. 'No sign of him. I should take a break if I was you, girl. There's not much doing out there tonight – it's a real peasouper.'

Flossie's throaty laugh echoed off the walls. 'Good advice. I could use some beauty sleep.' She stubbed her cigarette out on the doorpost, eyeing Rose curiously. 'What's your name, luv?'

'It's Rose Munday, miss.'

'Nice to meet you, Rose. And it's even nicer to have someone in the house what has good manners.

Charmed, I'm sure. My name's Flossie Boxer, and you can call me Flossie.'

'Don't listen to her yakking on and on.' Cora opened a door further along the narrow passage. 'Come on, Rose. This is where I hang out.' She ushered Rose into a small room that contained a brass bed, a chest of drawers and a washstand. A single chair, draped with woollen stockings and a pair of stays, was placed in front of a fire that had burned down to nothing, and an overfull ashtray spilled cigarette butts onto the hearth. Cora tossed her feathered hat onto the bed, followed by her shawl, and she sat down to unlace her boots. 'You can stay here tonight, but you'll have to take the chair or sleep on the floor.'

'Thank you.' Rose glanced at the Windsor chair, which would not have been out of place in Sadie's kitchen. 'I'm so tired I could sleep almost anywhere.'

Cora gave her another searching look. 'You're whiter than the sheet on my bed. When did you last eat?'

'Breakfast,' Rose said, closing her eyes in an attempt to stop the room from spinning out of control. 'I didn't eat much because I was so excited at the thought of seeing Max again. It's almost two years since we last met.'

'That's a long time to be apart. Are you sure he hasn't changed his mind?'

'I've known Max since I was a child. He wouldn't behave like that and he wrote beautiful letters.'

Cora tossed one boot on the floor and began to unlace the other. 'You've got more faith in men than I have, kid. In my experience they're rats, all of 'em.'

Rose moved the grubby stays from the chair and sat down as another wave of dizziness threatened to overcome her. 'I thought he'd be at the Captain's House.'

'Well, he weren't, and you'll have to get used to the idea that he's changed his mind.' Cora picked up a pillow and threw it to Rose. 'Here, get your head down, love. You'll have to wait for morning to get some grub. I don't keep food in me room because of rats – the four-legged kind.' Cora chuckled and turned on to her side with a creaking of bed springs. 'There's a spare blanket under me bed,' she added sleepily. 'Night-night.'

Rose slid off the chair, lifted the trailing edge of the coverlet to look under the bed, and found herself staring into the beady eyes of a huge spider. She retreated hastily and curled up as best she could on the chair, resting her head on the pillow. Cramped, stiff and cold, she thought longingly of her old room in the school house, and the tantalising aroma of baking that floated up from the kitchen where Sadie was undoubted queen. She and her husband, Laurence, ran the school that Max's stepfather had built for the local children. Rose was in awe of Raven Dorincourt, but both Max and Jimmy thought the world of him. Even so, she preferred gentle, unworldly Laurence, who believed strongly that girls ought to be as well educated as boys, and she had benefited from his teaching.

As she struggled with the cold and damp of an English winter and the discomfort of trying to sleep in an upright chair, Rose was beginning to doubt the wisdom of her actions. Had she been carried away on a romantic dream, fuelled by ardent love letters from Max? More to the point, what would she do now that she was on her own in London? The questions kept coming but there were no answers. Eventually, she fell asleep from sheer exhaustion.

'Wake up.'

Someone was shaking her and Rose opened her eyes to such an unfamiliar scene that she thought she was dreaming.

'You was dead to the world,' Cora said cheerfully. 'Put your boots on, Rose. We're going out to get some breakfast.'

Rose stretched her cramped limbs, wincing with pain as the feeling came back to her hands and feet in the form of pins and needles. 'Where are we going?'

'There's a coffee stall on Tower Hill.' Cora sat on the edge of her bed and pulled on her boots. 'How are you off for readies?'

'I've got some money,' Rose said warily. 'But it

won't last very long. I was counting on Max meeting me at the docks.'

'You said your Max was related to the Colvilles. Is that true?'

'His elder sister married into the family. I was at her wedding.'

'So she knows you.' Cora tied the second bootlace into a neat bow and stood up, reaching for her hat. 'Then after we've had breakfast I think we should pay a call on this lady. The Colvilles are rolling in money.'

'I don't want to go begging,' Rose protested. 'I'm sure Max has a good reason for not coming to meet me. Anyway, I told you, Cora. I don't know where Caroline lives.'

'But I do.' Cora thrust a hatpin into the feathery creation on her head. 'Don't argue, kid. Food first and then we're going to Finsbury Circus. I know that's where we'll find them because one of their footmen was a client of mine, if you get my meaning?' She winked and opened the door. 'Come on, don't loiter. I'm dying for a cup of coffee.'

Having eaten a ham roll and drunk a mug of hot, sweet coffee, Rose was beginning to feel more optimistic. The fog had lifted, leaving a sooty smell lingering in the air, and it was bitterly cold, but at least they could see where they were going and Cora set off at a brisk pace with Rose hurrying after her.

The blisters on her heels had burst and were painful, but she was feeling more positive and the thought of receiving news of Max, or even finding him at home with his sister, made the walk to Finsbury Circus seem less arduous. But it was a nerve-racking experience as they had to dodge in and out of the traffic and push their way through crowds of pedestrians. Rose was uncomfortably aware of the withering looks that Cora received from respectable matrons, who had their maidservants in tow, and the knowing grins from the costermongers and road sweepers. Whistles, cat calls and scornful glances accompanied them, but Cora herself did not seem to notice and she marched onwards, head held high, and the black and red ostrich feathers on her hat fluttered in the breeze. She swung her hips and twirled her reticule as if performing on stage, to the obvious delight of small urchins, who mimicked her shamelessly. In daylight the colour of Cora's hair was even more remarkable – almost white at the tips, darkening through every colour of yellow to bronze at the roots – but beneath all the paint and rouge Cora's good nature shone out like a beacon, and Rose was well aware that she owed her new friend a huge debt of gratitude. What might have befallen her last evening without Cora's timely intervention was anyone's guess.

'We're here,' Cora announced, coming to a sudden halt.

Rose just managed to avoid colliding with her as she stopped, staring up at the grand façade of what was undoubtedly a mansion. Sadie had often mentioned the old days, before Mr Manning's premature death, when the family lived in Finsbury Circus, and she might have been describing this very house.

'What do we do now?' Rose whispered.

Cora marched up the steps and knocked on the door. 'I ain't going to the tradesmen's entrance. The blooming servants are worse than their masters when it comes to looking down on people.' She moved a step closer as the door was opened by a liveried footman.

'Go away,' he said through clenched teeth. 'This is a respectable household.' He was about to shut them out when Cora put her foot over the threshold.

'I dunno what makes you think I ain't respectable,' she said boldly, 'but I'm as good as you, Jem Wilkins, and I don't think your superior would take very kindly to one of his men frequenting a—'

Wilkins opened the door a fraction wider. 'Shut up, Cora. Don't let the world know my business.'

'Then let us in. This young lady is a friend of Max Manning. She wants to see him.'

Wilkins rolled his eyes. 'She can't be much of a friend if she doesn't know that Captain Manning's regiment sailed for Alexandria nearly two months ago.'

'No,' Rose said faintly. 'I don't believe it. Max wouldn't do that to me. He would have let me know.'

Cora turned on her in a fury. 'You was miles out at sea, you silly cow. Why didn't you think of that? You never said he was a soldier.'

'Let me shut the door, Cora,' Wilkins said urgently. 'Go away and take her with you.'

'No.' Rose found her voice. 'If Captain Manning is away I need to see Mrs Colville. She'll remember me.'

Wilkins folded his arms across his chest. 'Well, that's going to be a bit difficult, miss. Because Mr and Mrs Colville are away from home.'

'Stop smirking, you smug devil,' Cora snapped. 'I can still peach on you to the butler or the house-keeper. Either will do.'

'The master and mistress left on a business trip to Australia six weeks ago,' Wilkins said stiffly. 'Now go away, please. I can't tell you anything else.'

'Just a minute,' Rose cried anxiously. 'Do you know how long Captain Manning will be away?'

Wilkins gave her a pitying look. 'According to the newspapers the war in Egypt is over, but I doubt if the generals themselves know when the troops will be sent home. Sorry, miss, but there it is.' He gave Cora a push that almost overbalanced her and slammed the door.

Rose sank down on the top step. 'I can't believe this is happening to me,' she murmured, shaking her head.

29

'A pretty pickle you got yourself into, kid.' Cora stared down at her, frowning. 'Sitting there, feeling sorry for yourself, ain't going to help either.'

'I need to think,' Rose said slowly. 'I'm sure that Max would have made arrangements for me to be provided for until he returns.'

'If he comes back at all.' Cora threw up her hands. 'Don't look at me like that, young 'un. He went to fight in a war. If the bullets don't get him he might have fallen sick from them foreign diseases. You got to face facts, love.'

'Then I'll travel to Egypt so that I can be near him.'

'Oh, really! You said you got no money, and it's a long way to walk.'

Rose stood up, bracing her shoulders. 'I'll get work and I'll find a way.'

'Well, I can't leave you here, but I got to earn a living, too. You'd best come home with me.' Cora gave her a calculating look. 'Regan would take you on. He's always looking for fresh faces and young bodies, especially virgins.'

Rose felt the colour flood her cheeks and she turned away. 'I'm not that sort . . .' She broke off, too embarrassed to finish the sentence. Cora had been kind to her, and how she supported herself was nobody's business but her own.

'It's all right, love. I'm used to having my profession thrown in my face. It bounces off like rain on a pigeon's feathers.' Cora hitched her shawl around her shoulders as she negotiated the steps. 'Come on if you're coming. You can stay with me for another night or two, but you got to make yourself scarce when my gents come to call. D'you understand?'

Rose followed more slowly. 'Thank you, Cora. I won't impose on you any longer than necessary. I'll look for work of some sort and a place to live.'

'You ain't going home then?'

'I was happy in Bendigo, and Sadie and Laurence were kind to me, but they aren't family. I have no ties there now.' Rose fell into step beside Cora.

'What about Max's mother? Don't she approve of you or something?'

'She said we were too young to marry, and her husband agreed with her. They said that Max should establish himself in his career before thinking of marriage.'

'Maybe you should write and tell her that he's let you down. She might send you money.'

Horrified, Rose almost lost her footing on the uneven pavement. 'I wouldn't think of asking for charity.'

'Suit yourself, but your young man got you into this mess, so it's up to him or his family to get you out of it.'

Tears stung Rose's eyes but she was determined not to cry. 'I have only myself to blame, Cora. It's up to me to find a solution.'

Cora shot her a sideways glance. 'You're obviously well educated, Rose. But without references you won't find it easy to get work.'

'I can cook simple things, and I can look after small children. I can scrub floors and wash dishes.'

'Put us two together and we'd make someone a perfect wife,' Cora said, chuckling. 'Walk faster, Rose. I got work to do, even if you haven't.'

Regan was hanging around outside the house in Black Raven Court, and Rose took an instant dislike to him. Despite his thickset physique and aggressive expression, his scarred face and broken nose suggested that he had come off worst in a good many fights. His unsavoury appearance, and the stench of his unwashed body made Rose shrink away from him, but his beady eyes lit up with interest the moment he spotted her.

'You can forget it, Regan,' Cora said firmly. 'She's not for sale.'

'Pity. I could find plenty of work for someone like her.' Regan smiled at Rose, putting her forcibly in mind of the Big Bad Wolf in the fairy tale, except that the teeth he displayed were broken and hideously decayed.

Cora turned to Rose with a warning frown. 'You'd best go about your business, Rosie. I'll see you tonight, but knock three times on the door or you won't get an answer.' She turned away, proffering her arm to Regan. 'What pleasures have you got for me today, cully?'

Rose shivered as a chill east wind rushed up from the river. The sky was heavy with cast-iron clouds that threatened rain. She wrapped her shawl more tightly around her body and started walking, although she had no idea of where she might be going, but it was too cold to stand still. Her bright dreams for the future were fading fast, and she had very little money. She closed her eyes, praying silently for inspiration, and then she remembered what Adele had said just before they parted. Acting on impulse, she hailed a passing cab.

'Elder Street, cabby.' Rose climbed inside and closed the half-doors with fingers that were numbed by the cold. Sadie had warned her to pack more warm clothes, but she had travelled as light as possible, hoping to purchase a more suitable wardrobe in London. She wished now that she had paid more attention to Sadie, and had not allowed herself to be carried away by rash promises from Max. She took her purse from her reticule and counted the coins. There would be precious little left after paying the cab fare, but she had no idea where Elder Street was situated in relation to the Tower, and the pain in her feet was crippling. Perhaps Adele could find some kind of work for her that would pay enough to keep body and soul together until Max returned home. One thing was certain, there was no way she could raise enough money to buy a passage home, but she was not prepared to give up her dream, not yet anyway. She would wait for Max and they would marry and live happily ever after, just like the princes and princesses in the story books.

Adele rushed into the front parlour holding out her hands in welcome. 'It's good to see you, Rose. I've been thinking about you and your young man.' She turned to the maidservant who had let Rose in and was now hovering in the doorway. 'Bring us tea and cake, please, Bridget.'

The girl, who could have been no more than thirteen, acknowledged the instruction with a vague nod of her head and backed away very slowly.

Adele closed the door on her. 'She's still learning,' she said by way of explanation. 'But what brings you here today, Rose? Is everything all right?'

'Not exactly.' Rose clasped and unclasped her hands, suddenly nervous. It was one thing to be told that Max had been called upon to fight for his country, but quite another to put it into words.

'To tell you the truth, Adele, I am in a very difficult situation.'

Chapter Three

Despite interruptions from Bridget when she brought in the tea tray, and another when she returned with a plate of small cakes, and yet again when she came back with the plates that she had forgotten in the first place, Rose managed to explain the circumstances that had brought her to Spitalfields.

Adele sipped her tea, frowning thoughtfully. 'I am so sorry, Rose. You were looking forward so much to seeing Max again. It must have been a bitter disappointment.'

Rose nodded, swallowing hard to prevent herself from bursting into tears.

'You were lucky to have been befriended by such a good woman,' Adele added earnestly. 'I've never believed in judging others harshly, and Cora seems to be very kind-hearted.'

'She is, and I don't know what I would have done had she not taken me under her wing, but I can't expect her to look after me. I need to be able to support myself.'

'Surely your family in Bendigo would make the necessary arrangements for your passage home?'

'I'm sure they would, but I've come this far, Mrs Parker. I want to be here when Max returns from war.'

'I don't think you've thought it through, Rose, but I can see that you've made up your mind.' Adele replaced her cup on its saucer. 'Maybe Festus would have some useful suggestions.' She eyed Rose thoughtfully. 'You are well-spoken and ladylike. I suppose you could try for a position as lady's maid or companion.'

'I haven't any references, and I wouldn't know where to start if someone wanted me to put up their hair or wash their fine lace, but I'm not afraid of hard work.'

'Wait here, Rose. I'll go and speak to Festus – he's attending to his correspondence in his study.' Adele jumped to her feet and left the room without giving Rose a chance to argue.

She reached out to take another slice of cake, but, tempting as it was, she decided that it would be greedy, and she folded her hands in her lap waiting for Adele to return. The room was quite small and the heavy velvet curtains seemed to absorb what little light filtered through the small windowpanes, but a fire burned merrily in the grate and the air was filled with the aroma of tea and chocolate cake, furniture polish and just a hint of old books.

She stood up and went to examine the leather-bound books on a shelf in one of the chimney recesses, but they were all academic works on philosophy and religion, nothing that would remotely interest her, despite her love for reading. A stuffed green parrot seemed to be glaring at her from the inside of a glass dome, and she wondered why anyone would want such a keepsake. Its eyes appeared to follow her and she moved on to study a photograph of a much younger Festus and Adele in their wedding finery, but at the sound of approaching footsteps she returned to her chair and sat down, folding her hands primly in her lap once more.

Adele entered the room followed by Festus, who gazed at her soulfully. 'I understand you are in a sorry predicament, Rose,' he said in sepulchral tones. 'Rash actions often end in disaster.'

'It's not exactly a disaster, my dear.' Adele laid her hand on his sleeve. 'As I just told you, Rose has come to ask our advice.'

Festus went to stand with his back to the fire. 'You are a well-educated young lady, Rose.'

'I think so, sir.'

'Living on your own in a big city is not to be recommended.' Festus stroked his chin, something he did when he was thinking deeply, which was a habit that Rose had noticed during their time at sea. 'If you want my honest opinion,' he said at length, 'I think you ought to go home and wait there for your young man.'

Rose knew that this was good advice and probably the most logical thing to do, but somehow logic and common sense seemed to have flown out of the window, and a stubborn streak that she had not known she possessed had taken hold of her.

'Thank you both, but it isn't as easy as that. As I explained to your wife, I haven't enough money to pay for a passage home.'

Adele glanced anxiously at her husband. 'We would lend it to you if it were possible.'

'Which I'm afraid it is not,' Festus added quickly. 'Our means are limited, Rose. But your young man is related to the owners of the largest shipping line in the country, isn't that so?'

'It is, but Mr and Mrs Colville are away on a business trip. There is no one in London who could help me, and, if I'm honest, I don't want to return home, not yet anyway. What I need is a job so that I can support myself until Max returns from Egypt.'

'Young ladies do not go out to work.' Adele's eyes widened and she pursed her lips. 'What would your sainted papa say if he knew?'

'My pa was a practical man, Mrs Parker. He

worked hard for his living and he would expect me to do the same.'

Adele raised a hanky to her eyes. 'Oh dear, this is very distressing. I wish we could help.'

'You must get away from that place of ill repute,' Festus said firmly. 'We would offer you sanctuary here, but this house is quite small and it belongs to my mother. We have to respect her wants and needs.'

Rose jumped to her feet. 'Thank you, but all I wanted was some advice as to what sort of work I might do. I didn't mean to put you in a difficult position. I think it best if I go now.'

'Festus, we can't allow Rose to leave without at least trying to help her.' Adele clutched her husband's arm, gazing up at him with imploring eyes.

'My dear, we've been out of the country for five years. I expect things have changed significantly since we left.'

'I really should leave now,' Rose said hastily. 'It's a long walk back to Black Raven Court and I left my things there.'

'Oh dear.' Adele's eyes filled with tears and she pulled a crumpled handkerchief from her sleeve. 'Don't let her go like this, Festus. There must be something we can do to help poor Rose.'

'I was planning to visit the office of the *London Leader* today. It's owned by a friend of mine, and he might be in a position to give you advice. They used to run a Situations Vacant column, unless things have changed greatly.' Festus fixed Rose with a meaningful stare. 'Will you come with me?'

Rose nodded emphatically. 'Yes, gladly.'

Adele clapped her hands. 'Splendid. Do have some more cake before you go, Rose. I made it myself.'

'There's no time for that.' Festus opened the door. 'Come along, Rose, best foot forward. We'll see if Cosmo has anything helpful to say.'

The cab dropped them off outside the *London Leader* offices in Fleet Street and Rose alighted to the pavement while Festus paid the cabby. This was a part of the city that Rose barely knew, but immediately it felt like the beating heart of London. The traffic was so dense that it hardly seemed to be moving and the coachmen, cabbies, draymen and carters shouted and bellowed at each other, flicking their whips in seemingly useless displays of bad temper and impatience. The pavements were equally crowded, and people pushed and jostled as if reaching their destinations was a matter of life and death. Festus hurried Rose into the building, stopping at the desk where a harassed-looking man was dealing with an irate person who was complaining bitterly about the size and positioning of his advertisement. Eventually the bald, bespectacled clerk held up his hand.

'If you will give me a moment, sir, I'll see if I can find someone to deal with your query.'

'Query? It ain't a query, my good man. I want my money back. I paid in good faith for—'

Festus cleared his throat noisily. 'If you will excuse me for interrupting, might I suggest that you allow this man to do his job, sir?'

The irate advertiser turned on Festus with an angry snarl. 'And who are you, mate? Did I ask you to interfere?'

Rose had had enough of this senseless arguing and she stepped forward. 'I suggest you sit down, mister. We've all got business here and you're not helping anyone, least of all yourself.'

The man stared at her, shocked into silence.

'Precisely,' Festus said firmly. 'And I wish to see Mr Cosmo Radley.'

'I'm sorry to say that Mr Radley senior passed away four years ago, and his son, Mr Arthur Radley, took over the editorship.'

'That's all very fine.' The angry man spoke up again. 'I want to see Mr Radley and put my complaint in person.'

'Even if he's in the office I can't guarantee that he'll see you, sir. Mr Radley is a very busy man.' The clerk edged out from behind the desk and scuttled across the tiled floor.

'I'm not leaving until I've had words with him,' the man said huffily. 'I've got a genuine case.'

Rose had to curb the sudden desire to laugh. There was a childishness about him that made him look like an overgrown schoolboy, but he was still grumbling when one of the office doors opened and a tall man emerged into the foyer. At first sight, with his dark hair and neatly trimmed beard and moustache, he reminded Rose of a pirate or a dashing musketeer, and there was certainly a hint of a swagger in the way he strolled over to the desk.

'May I be of any assistance?'

'This man is being attended to,' Festus said quickly. 'I came to see Mr Cosmo Radley, but I've been told he's no longer with us.'

'Yes, sadly that is the case, but I'm his nephew, Eugene Sheldon. How may I be of service?'

'Festus Parker, and this is Miss Rose Munday. Might we talk in private?'

Eugene's gaze rested on Rose for the briefest of moments and she noticed that his eyes were the colour of amber rimmed with jet. 'Of course,' he said smiling. 'Come this way.'

Rose followed them into a small office where a large desk dominated the room. Piles of newspapers were scattered in seemingly random heaps on the floor, and the walls were lined with shelves crammed with files.

Festus claimed the most comfortable chair. 'Your uncle was a close friend of mine, but I never saw Arthur as being suitable to run the newspaper. He was always a rather dull boy.'

Rose held her breath, waiting to see if Eugene had

taken umbrage at this tactless remark, but if he thought that Festus was being a little too frank, his genial expression did not falter. He pulled up a chair for Rose before taking his seat behind the desk. 'I was only twenty and still at university when Uncle Cosmo died. Arthur had been subeditor for years and it was only right that he should step into his father's shoes. I joined the staff when I left Cambridge.'

'People can change, I suppose.' Festus sighed heavily. 'I'm sorry that I didn't have a chance to say goodbye to my old friend.'

'I understand, of course, but you are here now so how may I be of assistance?'

Festus steepled his fingers, eyeing Eugene thoughtfully. 'I came, as I said, with the intention of renewing my acquaintance with Cosmo, and I brought Miss Munday with me because she finds herself in a difficult situation.'

Eugene turned his attention to Rose. 'I'm sorry to hear that.'

She felt her cheeks redden. 'I need a job, Mr Sheldon. It's as simple as that. I arrived in London recently to find my situation had changed, leaving me stranded with very little money and in desperate need of finding cheap lodgings.'

'Might I ask how a young lady like yourself came to be in such a plight?'

'You're not going to write about me in your paper, are you?'

Eugene's lips twitched. 'I promise that this is strictly between ourselves.'

Rose met his amused gaze with a frown. Her situation might seem funny to someone who led a comfortable existence, but it was no laughing matter. 'My fiancé, Max Manning, sent for me,' she said coldly. 'However, when I arrived in England I discovered that his regiment has been sent to Egypt.'

'Dashed bad luck, but surely he has family here in London?'

Festus leaned forward. 'Suffice to say that we've been through all this, and Miss Munday is in a bit of a pickle. We met on the boat travelling back from Australia and we only landed yesterday, so you can see that Rose hasn't had time to look around. You, however, must run a Situations Vacant column.'

'And you were hoping that my uncle might put the lady in touch with a prospective employer. Capital idea, but too late, I'm afraid.'

'Do you treat everything as a joke, Mr Sheldon?' Rose asked angrily. 'I lost my pa a year ago and I don't find it as hilarious as you do.'

Eugene's smile faded and he shook his head. 'Of course not. Some of us disguise our feelings with humour, finding it the only way to deal with the difficulties that beset us. I am really sorry about your father and the predicament in which you find yourself.'

'So can you help?' Festus demanded. 'I really can't

spare much more time on this. Rose needs to find lodgings and she has to have work so that she can pay for her bed and board.'

'Have you considered returning home, Miss Munday?' Eugene chose to ignore Festus, focusing his attention on Rose. 'The war in Egypt might be at an end, but the unrest could go on for years.'

'I don't care,' Rose said stoutly. 'I'll wait here for Max to return regardless. I'll wash clothes or work in a kitchen. I'll do anything legal to earn my own living.'

'Rose has received a good education.' Festus glanced at the grandfather clock standing in the corner. 'Oh dear, I had no idea it was so late. I have other business to attend to this morning. You may remain here, Rose, or you can accompany me, but I will be going about my own affairs.'

She realised that this was his way of saying that she was on her own, and yet she could not blame him. The Parkers were shipboard acquaintances, nothing more, and it would be unreasonable to expect them to go out of their way for a relative stranger. She managed a weak smile. 'Thank you for everything, Mr Parker. I'll be quite all right.'

He stood up abruptly. 'Well, if you're sure, I'd better be on my way.'

Eugene was already on his feet, as if anticipating Festus' sudden departure, and he went to open the door. 'Goodbye, sir. It's always a pleasure to meet my late uncle's friends.' They shook hands and Festus nodded to Rose as he left the office.

Eugene closed the door. 'Well then, Miss Munday. It seems as though you've been left in the lurch, yet again. Does this mean you have nowhere to sleep tonight?'

'It would have been so, but I met a lady who helped me last evening. She didn't have to go out of her way to assist a stranger, but she allowed me to share her lodgings and bought me breakfast. There are some generous people, if you're lucky enough to meet them.'

'Will you be able to stay with this person until you find work and a place of your own?'

'I expect so.' Rose raised herself from the chair. She was still stiff after spending an uncomfortable night in Cora's room, although she was not going to admit that to Eugene, who, despite his claim to be sympathetic, still appeared to find her situation amusing.

'If you would like to give me your address I'll contact you should anything come up.'

'The house is in Black Raven Court – I didn't notice the number – but I think most people there know Cora Smith.'

He frowned. 'I know the name from somewhere. It will come back to me. As to Black Raven Court – it's not the most salubrious neighbourhood, especially for a young lady like yourself.'

'I'm hardly a lady, sir. I spent my first nine years living in a hut in my father's boatyard in Chelsea, and then we went to Australia and I grew up in a mining town. I think I know how to look after myself. Anyway, I'm sorry to have wasted your time. It really wasn't my idea to come here.' Rose walked to the door and reached out to clasp the handle, but Eugene moved swiftly and laid his hand on hers.

'I'm sorry. I didn't mean to offend you, and of course I'll do anything I can to help. It's time for luncheon, by my reckoning, and I'd be honoured if you would join me for a meal at the Cheshire Cheese where they do excellent chops and steaks.'

Rose was going to refuse, but her stomach rumbled – it was a long time since breakfast and the slice of cake at the Parkers' had been very small. It would be foolish to turn down the offer of a free meal, and the cab fare to Elder Street had depleted her dwindling supply of cash yet further.

'Thank you,' she said stiffly. 'That would be nice.'

Outside the cold air hit her like a slap in the face. She had left Bendigo on a warm spring day and, even though she had known that it would be late autumn when she arrived in London, she had not been prepared for such a stark contrast. The clothes she had packed were not really suitable for a spell of wet and chilly weather, but Max had promised to buy her a whole new wardrobe, one befitting the wife of an army officer. She had imagined elegant gowns and smart riding outfits, although at this moment she would have given anything for a waxed drover's coat and a pair of woollen gloves.

'It's not far,' Eugene said cheerfully.

'I should have brought some warmer clothes with me. But I left in rather a hurry.'

'You're a very plucky young woman.' He shot a sideways glance at her. 'I look forward to hearing about your travels, and the man who inspired you to come halfway round the world on your own.'

Rose's teeth were chattering and she needed all her breath simply to keep up with him. She nodded and managed a smile, but it was the thought of a hot meal that kept her placing one foot in front of the other, and fortunately it was not far to Ye Olde Cheshire Cheese. The pub was situated in Wine Office Court, a narrow alleyway off Fleet Street, and the interior, as Eugene had said, was warm and welcoming, with whitewashed walls, beamed ceilings and a roaring log fire. The enticing aroma of roast meat mingled with the fragrance of wine and the sturdy smell of ale and tobacco smoke. But the main thing as far as Rose was concerned was the warmth, and the flickering firelight was both comforting and homely.

The waiters greeted Eugene like an old friend, and they were shown to a secluded table behind a pillar. 'I can recommend the steaks they do here.' Eugene waited until Rose was settled before taking a seat.

'Or perhaps you would prefer chops or pie – everything is well cooked and tasty.' He turned to the waiter. 'A bottle of claret, if you please, and I'll have my usual. What about you, Rose? I may call you Rose, mayn't I?'

She nodded. 'I'll have what you're having.'

'A good choice.' Eugene dismissed the waiter with a wave of his hand and a friendly smile. 'You'll feel better when you've eaten.' He sat back in his seat as another waiter hurried over to pour the wine. 'Now tell me about yourself, Rose. I've never met a young lady adventurer before.'

Rose eyed him suspiciously, but the twinkle in his eyes was irresistible and she began to relax. Sipping the warming red wine she found herself telling him everything from the time when she had first met Max at her father's boatyard on the Thames, through her childhood to the moment when her relationship with Max had changed for ever. Then, of course, there was the pressing matter of the Captain's House and the men who were living there with, or without, Mrs Colville's permission.

'So, you think these people are squatters,' Eugene said slowly. 'There must be someone at Colville Shipping who handles the family's private affairs. It shouldn't be too difficult to track him down, and persuade him to evict the trespassers. You would certainly be better off living there than in one of Regan's brothels.'

'You know him?' Rose could hardly believe her ears.

'He's notorious,' Eugene said calmly. 'The authorities close him down and take him into custody, but somehow he gets away with a fine and he just starts up again at a different address. There are plenty of men like Regan in London.'

'Oh!' Rose was at a loss for words, but by this time the food had arrived and she ate hungrily, earning praise from Eugene, who said that he liked to see a girl enjoying a good meal, instead of young ladies who picked at their food like birds. He questioned her further but managed to do so without seeming to interrogate, and she found it surprisingly easy to tell him how she had come to be in such a difficult situation.

'But,' she said, replacing her knife and fork on the plate, 'I want to prove myself and not just to impress Max. I realise now that I want to be someone in my own right. I didn't choose to go to Australia; it was decided for me. I didn't ask to be raised by Sadie and her husband, that just happened, and I didn't expect to fall in love with Max. It was always Jimmy, his younger brother, who is now in the navy, who was my special friend while we were growing up.'

Eugene drained the last of his wine. 'And you haven't seen Max for two years?'

She eyed him warily. 'I know that sounds a very

long time, but we've corresponded regularly. He writes the most beautiful letters.'

'Hmm,' Eugene said slowly. 'A soldier and a poet.'

'Now you're laughing at me again. You seem to find my situation very comical.'

'No, indeed I do not. In fact, I regard it as extremely serious.' He nodded to the waiter, who appeared suddenly to clear the table. 'Now, more importantly, Rose. Would you like to sample the treacle pudding? I can recommend it.'

'Oh, yes, please. Sadie used to make lovely suet puddings with either jam or treacle.' Rose hesitated. 'I will, but only if you will, too. I don't want to be a glutton.'

'Excellent. That will be two treacle puddings, please, waiter. And a jug of custard, too.'

The pudding was so delicious that Rose could have licked the plate, and at one time she might have done so, but not, of course, if Sadie had been looking. Sadie was very particular about table manners, although Laurence was much more relaxed about such things. However much the temptation, Rose was not going to let herself down in front of Eugene, but she was glad that he seemed to enjoy his food as much as she did. She sat back in her chair, replete and feeling much more optimistic. However, Eugene seemed to have forgotten why she had come to see him in the first place and had been amusing her

with descriptions of his life as a subeditor and some-
time reporter. But all too soon it was time to think
about leaving the cosy interior of the pub and to
venture out once again into the cold unknown. Rose
plucked up the courage to interrupt before Eugene
embarked on another risqué tale.

'You've been very kind,' she said earnestly. 'But I
have to get back to reality. Do you think you could
help me to find paid work? I have to earn my living,
and, as I told you, I've very little money left and
nowhere to go other than Cora's room in Black
Raven Court.'

'Yes, of course. I was enjoying your company so
much that I almost forgot.' Eugene eyed her thoughtfully. 'You've never worked in an office, have you,
Rose?'

'Not really. Unless you count helping to sort
Laurence's papers and keeping accounts. I did help
with all that, especially when Sadie was too busy to
do the books.'

'Do you know what a typewriter is?'

Rose shook her head. 'No, I've never heard of
such a thing.'

'It's fairly new in this country, although gaining
popularity in America. It's the modern way of writing
letters and documents. I purchased such a machine
on a recent visit to New York, but I haven't found
anyone who is willing to learn to use it, as our clerks
prefer writing documents by hand.'

'Are you offering me a job, sir?'

He leaned back, giving her a calculating look. 'Would you consider working for me? It would mean learning how to use the typewriter, keeping files and doing general office work.'

'And you'd pay me?'

He threw back his head and laughed. 'Of course I would. It wouldn't be a fortune, but it would be enough to live on.'

'I'm in no position to refuse – not that I would, anyway. It sounds really interesting. When do I start?'

'Tomorrow morning at half-past eight. I like to get in early, although, of course, the printers are working most of the night to get the paper out first thing in the morning, and sometimes you might be required to work late, if there's a particular rush on.'

'I wouldn't mind that at all.' Rose stood up, swaying slightly as the effects of the wine made the floor seem even more uneven than it was. 'I'll start looking for a room somewhere nearer.'

Eugene was already standing and he proffered his arm. 'A breath of fresh air will blow away the cobwebs. I think you'd best come back to the office with me and I'll show you round. Then I'll get one of the boys to see you to Black Raven Court.'

The fresh air had a sobering effect and by the time they reached the offices of the *London Leader* Rose was back to her old self, or very nearly. She decided that drinking wine in the middle of the day was not a good idea, and it had left her with a slight headache, but she was buoyed up by the fact that she had found employment.

She was not quite so confident, however, when faced with the brand-new Sholes and Glidden typewriter, and she was uncomfortably aware that her presence in the office was provoking furtive glances from the rest of the staff. Eugene did not seem to notice anything untoward and he sat her in front of the strange machine, inserted a sheet of paper and struck a few keys.

'There,' he said triumphantly. 'That's not so difficult, is it? I saw women in New York who could use both hands, as if they were playing the piano, but they were actually typing documents.' He picked up a file and pulled out a typewritten letter. 'This is how it should look. What do you think? Could you work this machine?'

'I don't see why not.' Rose perched on a chair and studied the keyboard. Tentatively at first, but with growing confidence, she tapped out a series of words.

'You'll soon get used to it,' Eugene said confidently. 'What do you think, Rose?'

Chapter Four

The mere fact that an important man like Eugene Sheldon was asking for her opinion and treating her as an equal sent a warm, fuzzy glow rushing through her veins, which had nothing to do with the glass or two of wine she had drunk with her meal. Suddenly, from feeling like a displaced person, an alien in her own homeland, Rose felt wanted and needed.

'I think it's a marvellous invention,' she said enthusiastically. 'I've spent hours and hours writing letters for Laurence to sign, but if I'd had a typewriting machine I'm sure it would have saved time and a lot of effort.'

'It's good that you're open to change, Rose.' Eugene turned away as one of the clerks rushed over to him waving a piece of paper.

'Guvnor, this has just come in – an affray in Eastcheap. It could be the gangs are tearing each other apart yet again, but there's no one here to send.'

'I'll go. I enjoy a good scrap.' Eugene grabbed his hat. 'Come on, Miss Munday. You can see what we do first-hand, and it's not too far from Black Raven Court. I'll see you safely home as soon as I've got a story.'

A bubble of excitement swelled in Rose's chest and she leaped to her feet, grabbed her shawl and reticule and hurried after Eugene. Standing on the edge of the pavement, he hailed a passing cab.

'Eastcheap, cabby.' Eugene leaped into the vehicle. 'You'll have to move faster than that, Munday, if you want to get to the scene of a news story in the shortest possible time.' He reached out to grab her hand and heaved her unceremoniously onto the seat beside him as the cab lurched forward. 'Sorry, Munday,' he said with a rueful smile. 'Manners fly out of the window when the matter is urgent.'

'I understand,' Rose said breathlessly. 'Do you think I could train as a reporter?'

'First things first, Munday.'

Rose clutched the seat as the cabby urged the horse to a trot and they careered along at an alarming rate, veering this way and that through the busy traffic. Rose was certain that at any moment they would overturn or be thrown from the cab, but Eugene remained calm, as if this mad ride was an everyday occurrence.

'It's all right, Munday,' he said calmly. 'The cabby knows what he's doing. This chap has taken me on many an assignment. I always tip him handsomely, which is probably why he's always lurking in Fleet Street.'

'I'm not scared.' Rose turned her head to study his profile. 'Why are you using my surname? You called me Rose in the pub – why the sudden change?'

'Ah, but that was pleasure, Rose. If you're going to venture into the male domain of newspapers, you'll have to be treated like a man. When we're working you'll be referred to as Munday.'

'Oh, I see.' Rose stared straight ahead. 'I am grateful to you . . .' she hesitated. 'What do I call you?'

'When we're working you call me Guvnor.'

'Yes, Guvnor.'

'That's right – you're learning. But when we get to Eastcheap, keep out of the way. Don't expect me to look after you. You're just a bystander.'

'I understand.'

'Good. Then we'll get along well. I think it must have been pretty rough in the goldfields, but I doubt if you'll have experienced anything like the violence of some of the street gangs that still exist in the East End. Although what we're heading for is probably just a brawl between rival costermongers, which won't make the front page.'

'I'm not scared,' Rose repeated stoutly and, to her surprise, she realised that she was more excited than anxious.

The cab slowed down and the trap door in the roof opened suddenly.

'We're here, guv.'

Eugene handed the driver some coins without bothering to ask the fare, and made ready to spring out as the cab drew to a halt. Rose was left to alight on her own and she found herself at the back of a jeering, bellowing crowd. Eugene had disappeared and she experienced a moment of panic, but she was also curious and, forgetting his instructions to stay back, she pushed her way through the bodies until she had a view of the fray.

As Eugene had suspected, the fight was between a group of burly costermongers who were throwing punches, kicking, shouting and swearing. It was a mêlée of fists, feet and bleeding noses, and her heart missed a beat or two as she saw Eugene wade in, accompanied by two police constables armed with truncheons. The sound of running feet preceded the arrival of their colleagues, and the ear-splitting sound of their whistles momentarily silenced the onlookers.

Rose craned her neck in order to get a better view and saw Eugene pulling two men apart and holding them at arm's length, even though they struggled to break free. She had put him down as a bit of a dandy at first sight, but the man she saw now was a completely different person. And, as if joining in a brawl was not bad enough, Eugene was grinning broadly as if he were enjoying the fracas.

Suddenly it was over, and the police had taken control of the street. The antagonists were bundled into a Black Maria and driven away, and there was a general scramble as children and adults alike fell on the fruit and vegetables that were strewn over the cobblestones. Rose waited until Eugene had finished speaking to the police sergeant who had brought the reinforcements, then she hurried to his side.

'Are you hurt?'

As he met her anxious gaze she could tell by the fire in his eyes and his triumphant smile that he had enjoyed the altercation.

'Are you all right?' she asked. 'Your nose is bleeding, and I think you'll have a black eye by morning.'

'Have you got a handkerchief, Munday? I seem to have forgotten mine.'

She took a small cotton hanky from her reticule. Sadie had embroidered it with her initials and rose-buds, but within seconds it was covered in blood. 'Maybe you should sit down, Guvnor,' she said hastily.

He clamped the hanky to his nose. 'I'm not a little girl, Munday. It's just a spot or two of blood and it'll stop soon. Come on, let's get you back to your friend in Black Raven Court before another scrap starts.' He nodded towards an irate costermonger, who was berating a gang of young boys for helping themselves to the apples that had fallen to the ground.

'You can put your arm around my shoulders if you feel faint,' Rose insisted. 'You're very pale.'

'Good grief, are you my mother now, Munday?' he said laughing. 'I want to see you safe and then I've got a story to write up.'

Rose fell into step beside him and she realised with a sense of fulfilment that she was beginning to recognise landmarks as they made their way along Great Tower Street. They were closer to Black Raven Court than she had supposed, but when Eugene saw the house he was obviously unimpressed.

'This is worse than I remembered,' he said angrily. 'This isn't the sort of place for a young woman like you, Munday.'

Rose knocked on the door. 'I was lucky to be brought here. I could have spent the night sitting on a crate in the station yard.'

'This won't do. There must be a way to get in touch with your fellow's relations. They're responsible for you in his absence.'

'I'll be fine, Guvnor. It would have been so much easier if those men hadn't taken over the Captain's House.'

'You mentioned that place over luncheon,' Eugene

said, frowning thoughtfully. 'You might not be able to make enquiries, but I can. Leave it to me, and—' He broke off as the door opened.

'Oh, it's you.' Flossie drew her wrap up to her neck, although Rose was uncomfortably aware that Eugene must have seen her state of undress. 'Who's this with you, Rosie? Have you brought your fancy man home with you?'

'No! I have not,' Rose protested angrily. 'Shame on you, Flossie.'

'A very natural mistake,' Eugene said, bowing. 'A pleasure to meet you, Miss er . . .'

'Flossie Boxer, sir.'

Rose glared at Eugene. 'Thank you for seeing me home, Guvnor. Hadn't you best get back to the office?'

'I'll see you at half-past eight in the morning, Munday. Don't be late.' Eugene walked away, waving the bloodied hanky like a flag.

Flossie leaned out of the door. 'Where'd you find a chap like that? I'd do him favours for nothing.'

Torn between laughter and annoyance, Rose shook her finger at Flossie. 'He's my guvnor. I've got a job and I can pay my way, or I will be able to when I get my wages.'

'Some people have all the luck.' Flossie glowered at a passing youth who whistled at her and offered a penny for her services. She retreated into the house. 'You'd best come in, although what Cora will say when she sees you is another matter. She needs her room for business, and Regan will want his piece of you if you choose to stay here. None of us gets a free ride, so to speak.'

'I haven't much choice at the moment.' Rose made for the stairs. 'Is Cora in?'

'Dunno, love. I ain't seen her today. She might be in the pub, touting for business, but she don't lock her door. We're an honest lot in here.' Flossie followed Rose up the stairs, her stays creaking like the masts on a tea clipper at every tortuous step. 'I'll be in my room if you need me, duck.'

'Thanks, Flossie.' Rose tried the door to Cora's room, and, finding it unlocked, she went inside to wait for her friend's return. She sat on the unmade bed for a few minutes, gazing round at the disarray, and suddenly, unable to bear the mess any longer, she leaped off the bed and began to tidy things away. She ventured down to the basement where Cora had told her there was a communal kitchen, although, judging by the thick layer of grease and dust, not many took advantage of the facilities. There was a stone sink in a small scullery and a pump out in the yard close to the privy. Rose filled a bucket with water, but there was no means of heating it as the ancient range was covered in rust and it did not look as if a fire had been lit for some time. Rose hefted the bucket upstairs, together with an empty flour sack she had found in the larder.

Back in Cora's room, she set about a cleaning project that took all her energy and ingenuity. She swept the grate and put the cinders into the sack together with the contents of the overflowing ashtray and the paper wrappings of past meals, which were green with mould. It took a couple of trips down to the back yard to dispose of the rubbish, and she scraped together enough coal and kindling to get a fire going. With the kettle on a trivet, and the room beginning to look almost homely, Rose was folding the last of Cora's discarded clothing when the door opened and Cora herself breezed into the room. She was followed by a burly person wearing soiled workman's clothes and muddy boots.

'Blimey! What's going on here?' Cora demanded, gazing round in horror. 'What d'you think you're doing, miss?'

Rose smiled proudly. 'I'm just trying to repay your kindness, Cora.'

'I thought you was on your own,' the man growled. 'I ain't into twosomes.'

'Wash your mouth out, you great oaf,' Cora snapped. 'As for you, girl, make yourself scarce and leave my things alone. I don't want no one poking about in my room.'

'I'm sorry, Cora. I was trying to do you a favour.'

'Get out and find yourself somewhere else to kip. A girl has to earn her living.'

'I thought I was helping.'

'Out, now.' Cora advanced on her, hands fisted.

Rose snatched up her things and backed towards the open door. 'All right. I said I'm sorry.'

Cora bent down and picked up the carpet bag and tossed it out onto the landing. The door slammed in Rose's face and she found herself once again with nowhere to go. Perhaps Cora would change her mind later, but Rose could not afford to take that chance. It was getting dark outside and rain had started to fall during her last trip to the back yard.

'I warned you.' Flossie popped her head round her door, appearing suddenly like the cuckoo in a Swiss clock that Rose had possessed when she was a child. 'Where will you go now?'

'I don't know,' Rose said slowly. 'I haven't had time to think.'

'Regan is hanging around downstairs.' Flossie opened the door wider, glancing up and down the corridor as if afraid that he might suddenly appear. 'He's got his eye on you, girl. Steer clear of him, that's what I say.'

'How do you stand it here, Flossie?' Rose asked urgently. 'What brought you to a place like this?'

Flossie folded her arms beneath her ample bosom. 'I suppose you want to know how I became a fallen woman. Well, love, for your information, I was born on the pavement outside the London Hospital. My ma couldn't walk no further and she collapsed – I popped out kicking and screaming and she croaked.'

'Oh, dear! She died giving birth to you?'

'No, girl. She died from a mixture of jigger gin and laudanum. It was lucky that one of the nurses found me and took me into the hospital. They saved my life and dumped me in the orphanage. I consider meself to have risen above the pavement, and I don't touch alcohol nor drugs, but I do love chocolate. That's my biggest sin.'

'I shouldn't have judged you. I'm sorry, Flossie.'

'You got a lot to learn.' Flossie glanced at the carpet bag. 'You can't go looking for a place to stay in the dark – not round here, anyway.'

'I haven't got much choice.'

Flossie emerged from her room, tying a sash round her waist in an attempt to secure her loose robe. 'Don't tell Regan I said so, but there's a boxroom on the next floor. Regan uses it to store things because it's too small to take a double bed, if you get my meaning, so it's no use for any of his girls.'

'I just need a roof over my head for tonight. I start work early in the morning.'

'You can buy me a bar or two of Fry's Chocolate Cream when you get paid,' Flossie said, grinning. 'Follow me but don't make a noise. We don't want any of the nosy bitches in the other rooms to know what's going on – some of 'em are all right, but one or two would snitch on their grannies if they thought they'd gain anything by it.' Flossie's bare feet padded on the wooden treads as she negotiated the steep stairs to the second floor. She tiptoed along a narrow passage and at the far end she opened the door to a small room with a tiny window set high in the wall. 'You'll be all right here tonight, but don't make a noise,' she said in a stage whisper.

'Thanks, Flossie.' Rose peered into the gloom. 'I don't suppose you could let me have a candle and some matches, could you?'

'I can probably find you a stub or two, but you'll have to come and get them, and don't forget me chocolate.' Flossie headed back the way they had come, leaving Rose to stow her bags away before going downstairs to collect the candles.

Two hours later, aided by the flickering light from the two candle stubs, Rose had managed to pile up the various packing cases and boxes, and to her relief she had discovered an ancient campaign bed. She had also found some moth-eaten blankets and a stained pillow, which she did not inspect too closely. She unpacked the plain linsey-woolsey skirt and white cotton blouse she had worn when helping Laurence in the schoolroom, and shook out the creases before laying them carefully over one of the crates in the corner of the room. She must look smart and business-like when she presented at work, even if she knew very little about the new typing machine. She was both nervous and excited at the prospect of being employed in a busy newspaper office, and, once she had solved the problem of somewhere to live, she would settle down and wait for Max to return from war. He had warned her that a soldier's wife must expect an unsettled existence, and she was prepared to follow the drum, if necessary. After all, she had travelled this far to be with the man she loved and, if it had not gone too well at the start, she now had the chance to make something of herself. Rose lay down, fully clothed. She could hear scrabbling and scratching sounds coming from behind the skirting boards, but she was too exhausted to care and she closed her eyes.

'You're late, Munday.' Eugene glanced up from the pile of proofs on his desk. His expression was not encouraging.

'Yes, Guvnor. I'm sorry,' Rose said breathlessly. 'It took longer than I thought to walk here.'

'You should have taken a cab.' Eugene gave her a searching look. 'You're shivering. Haven't you got anything warmer to wear?'

'I'm all right, thank you. It's wet and cold outside.'

'You didn't answer my question, Munday? Haven't you got a warm jacket or a cape or even a pair of warm gloves? How do you propose to type with fingers that are clawed like that?'

'I'll soon warm up.'

'Have you had breakfast?'

Rose shook her head. 'It's a bit difficult where I am at present.'

'Did you have supper last evening?'

'I'm sorry, Guvnor, but that's my business.'

'Not if it affects the way you work, Munday.' Eugene sat back in his chair. 'Does Regan know you're lodging there?'

'Have you met him?'

'I don't have to – the chap is notorious. Anyway, don't evade the question. Have you eaten since I took you to luncheon yesterday?'

'No, Guvnor, but—'

Eugene jumped to his feet and went to open the office door. 'Scully, two teas. Chop chop.' He returned to his seat. 'Now, Munday, let's get this straight. You are on probation here, and I'm going to treat you just the same as I would anyone working for this paper. You need to get yourself some suitable clothing, and if there's a problem with your accommodation, we'll try to sort it out.'

'Yes, Guvnor. Thank you.'

'Don't thank me, Munday. I'll expect you to work damned hard for your wages, and you can't do that if you catch lung fever or if you're weak from hunger.'

'It's difficult,' Rose murmured, looking down at her clasped hands.

'Surely the girls in Black Raven Court have to eat. There must be a kitchen of sorts.'

She raised her head to give him a withering look. 'You obviously haven't seen how these women live. The place is disgusting and I've seen pigs kept in better conditions.'

A wry grin twisted his lips. 'That's better. Meek and downtrodden doesn't suit you, Munday.' He pulled open a drawer and took out a cash box. 'I want you to buy yourself some more suitable clothing.'

'I can't do that.'

He tossed the coins onto the desk. 'Give me one good reason why not.'

'You're not responsible for my wellbeing. I can look after myself.'

'This is strictly business. Call it a loan, if it makes you feel better, but the weather is set to get worse. You're no damn good to me if you're sick, so when you've had your tea I'll get the office boy to take you to the nearest second-hand clothes shop. And buy yourself a cup of soup or a cheese roll from the stall on the corner of Chancery Lane, and you can get me one while you're about it. I didn't have time for breakfast either.'

Rose tossed her head. 'Sadie would say that's the pot calling the kettle black.'

'She sounds like a sensible woman, but a bit of a bore. Anyway, I enjoyed a good supper last evening in the company of a very attractive young lady, so there's no comparison.' Eugene beckoned to the office boy, who was hovering in the doorway, clutching two mugs of steaming tea. 'Thanks, Scully.' He waited while the spotty-faced youth placed them carefully on two mats. 'When Miss Munday has finished her drink I want you to take her to the nearest dolly shop, and you can wait and bring her back. We don't want her to get lost.'

Rose reached for the tea and took a sip, glowering at Eugene over the rim of the mug. Maybe this was a mistake after all. She had been more or less free to do as she pleased at home in Bendigo, and she was not sure whether she could stand being ordered about by anyone, let alone a man she barely knew. The warmth and sweetness of the tea was already having an effect, but her fingers and toes were tingling painfully as the feeling returned to her extremities. She did not want to accept charity from Eugene, but she had underestimated the severity of a British winter, and she was in desperate need of warm clothing. However, when she received her first week's pay she would start repaying the debt. If Pa had taught her anything, it was never to owe money to anyone. She glanced at Scully, who was waiting for her to finish her tea and he winked at her, but she turned her head away. She was used to cocky boys.

But Scully's attitude changed the moment they left the office and he dropped his self-assured swagger, becoming almost deferential in the way he behaved.

Rose discovered that he was the eldest of seven children and his meagre wages went to his widowed mother, who worked as a charwoman in an attempt to keep a roof over their heads. Rose was sympathetic and Scully grew shy and blushed to the roots of his mousy hair, and he was clearly smitten. It might have been amusing to be the object of puppy love, but Rose was wary of hurting his feelings and she managed to bring Max into the conversation early on, describing him as her fiancé, even though their engagement was unofficial.

Later, having scoured the second-hand shop for clothing that was not too worn or dirty, Rose felt smart and warm in a grey flannel coat and a woollen hat, which was only a bit shabby with just a couple of moth holes. She stopped at the coffee stall and bought two cheese rolls with the last of the money that Eugene had given her. She could tell by the way Scully was eyeing the food that he was very hungry and his stick-thin limbs told a tale in themselves. She handed him one of the rolls.

'I'm not hungry, Scully. Do me a favour and eat this before the guvnor sees it.'

Scully licked his lips. 'It's yours, miss. I couldn't.'

'No, really. The guvnor told me to get two, and I can only eat one, so you'll be helping me out. Eat it now and he'll never know the difference.'

'If you're sure.' Scully snatched the roll from her hand and bit off a huge chunk. His pale blue eyes watered as he chewed and gulped the food down.

Rose turned away and walked on slowly, giving him time to eat and digest before they reached the office.

'Where's yours?' Eugene demanded when she placed the food in front of him.

'You were right,' Rose said airily. 'I was so hungry I ate it on the way back. Ta, Guvnor, and thank you for the outfit. I'm warm and dry, so now I can sit down and have a go at that machine in the corner.'

Eugene pushed back his chair and stood up. 'I've got to go out now, and I'll probably have luncheon in the pub, so I won't need the roll. You have it, or feed it to the birds if you don't want it.' He took his overcoat and hat from the clothes stand. 'Write up an account of the affray in Eastcheap. Let's see if you can master the typewriter and write a good article. I might slip it into tomorrow's edition if you do well.'

'Right you are, Guvnor.' Rose waited for a minute or two after he left the office and when he did not return she snatched up the roll and bit into it, demolishing it in a speed that matched Scully's. The food gave her the spurt of energy she needed to sit down and take on the new machine. This, she realised, was a test of her ability to master a new skill and her way with words. Her job depended upon both and she sat for a moment, admiring the floral decoration on the front of the machine. Then, controlling her shaking fingers with difficulty, she took a sheet of paper, slotted it behind the platen and wound it into position. She took a deep breath and began, using two fingers, to type out her account of what she had witnessed the previous day.

Chapter Five

It was not as easy as Rose had first thought, and it would have taken her less time to write the article by hand, but she persevered. Eventually, after wasting several sheets of paper, she managed to turn out a piece with only a couple of mistakes. It was slow going, but she was beginning to learn the layout of the keys, and she was studying the result when Scully put his head round the door.

'I'm sorry, Miss Munday, but Nicholls wants to see you.'

Rose stared at him in surprise. 'I'm busy doing the work that the guvnor set me.'

'You don't want to get on the wrong side of Old Nick.'

'What does he want?'

'I dunno, miss. But you'd best find out.' Scully

74

lowered his voice to a whisper. 'He'll make your life a misery if you don't do as he says.'

Rose placed the sheet of paper on the desk and stood up. 'All right. I'm coming.' She followed him into the main office and marched up to Nicholls' desk.

'You wanted to speak to me.'

'You can stop playing with that new machine and do something useful.' He jerked his head in the direction of a pile of documents. 'Those need filing in that cabinet over there, but first I want you to run these proofs down to the print room.'

Rose faced him angrily. 'I wasn't taken on to work as a filing clerk or to run errands. I take my orders from the guvnor.'

'You're a novice, and a woman at that. If you don't like it here you know what to do.' Nicholls pushed the pile of papers towards her. 'Now get on with it or I'll have a talk with Mr Radley, and you'll find out who's boss round here.'

Rose glanced round at the other clerks, who immediately bent their heads and pretended they were too busy to take any notice. She met Nicholls' hostile gaze with a straight look.

'As it happens I've finished the task that the guvnor set me, so I'll do what you ask, but we'll see what he says when he returns.'

'I suppose you'll flaunt your titties and flutter your eyelashes like all females do when they want to get their own way. Well, it won't wash with me, miss. If you want to work here you'll have to do as I say.'

Rose tossed her head. It was not worth arguing with someone like Nicholls, but she had a feeling that the other men in the office were not on her side. In fact, her only friend was Scully, who was hopping from one foot to the other in an attempt to catch Nicholls' eye.

'I got nothing to do, Mr Nicholls,' he said, blushing. 'I could take the proofs down to the print room.'

'Did I speak to you, Scully?'

'No, sir.'

'Then shut up and fetch me a cup of tea, a dash of milk and two sugars.' Nicholls waved Scully away as if he were an irritating insect.

Rose felt sorry for the boy, but she knew that any attempt to stand up for him would only make matters worse. She took the proofs from Nicholls and made her way to the print room, where the men seemed to share Nicholls' opinion of women in the workplace. No one spoke to her, and it was becoming obvious that surviving in a man's world was not going to be easy. It would be so simple to quit in the face of such opposition, but she needed the money and she was determined to stay and prove them all wrong.

Eugene returned from his luncheon appointment in the middle of the afternoon and he was in a good mood, if slightly tipsy. His overcoat was pearled with raindrops and he created a minor storm as he shook it before hanging it on a peg.

'Did you enjoy your meal, Guvnor?' Rose asked, trying not to chuckle as he aimed his hat in the direction of the stand and missed.

'Very pleasant, thanks, Munday.' Ignoring the fact that his expensive topper was lying on the floor, Eugene went to sit behind his desk. 'How did you get on with the typewriting machine?'

Rose placed the sheets of paper in front of him. 'It will take a lot of practice, but I think it looks good.' She waited anxiously, crossing her fingers, while Eugene scanned her work.

He looked up at last. 'Not a bad attempt. In fact it's very promising.'

'Thank you, Guvnor.'

Eugene eyed her speculatively. 'We might make a reporter of you yet, Munday. As to the typing, it could be better. I want you to work at it every day.'

'Mr Nicholls thinks I'm here to run errands, Guvnor. I'm not complaining,' Rose added hastily. 'It's just that I need to know exactly what my duties are.'

Eugene leaned back in his chair. 'You're paid to do as I tell you, Munday. You take your orders from me.'

'That's what I thought, but I think it might be best if you tell him so.'

77

'When I want advice on running the paper I'll ask you, Munday.' Eugene took a notebook from his drawer and tossed it to her. 'Type that up for me – I want to get it to the print room before five o'clock.'

'Yes, Guv.' Rose picked up Eugene's hat and placed it on the stand before she took her seat.

'Scully.' Eugene raised his voice to a shout. 'Get me a cup of coffee from the stall before the chap packs up.'

'You could have tea and save him from going out in the cold,' Rose said crossly.

'Less of the cheek, Munday. It's started to rain and I could have sent you instead of Scully.' Eugene rose to his feet and marched into the main office. 'Nicholls, I want a word with you.'

Rose worked hard all afternoon. She ventured into the outer office to get a fresh supply of paper and was met with silence and stony stares, especially from Nicholls, who glowered at her beneath lowered brows. She knew it was only Eugene's presence that saved her from a verbal assault, but she did her best to ignore Nicholls and the other two clerks, who had obviously taken his side. She collected the paper and returned to the safety of her desk, earning praise from Eugene for finishing the document quickly and with the minimum of errors.

'Take it to the print room,' he said, nodding. 'They'll sort out the mistakes. That's their job.' He glanced at the clock on the mantelshelf. 'It's nearly six. Time you weren't here.'

'But you're still working.'

'I keep on until I'm finished, but you're just an office junior, so you get to go home.'

'Thank you, Guvnor.'

'And don't be late tomorrow morning.'

She unhooked her coat and laid it over her arm. 'I'll be on time,' she said, smiling. 'Good night, Guvnor.' She plucked her hat from the stand and was just about to leave the main office when Nicholls jumped out at her from behind the door.

'Just because you've got the boss wrapped around your little finger, don't think you can get away with anything, girlie. I've got my eye on you and the first wrong step you make you'll be out on your pretty little ear. D'you understand?'

Rose faced up to him. After everything she had suffered in the past twenty-four hours she was not going to allow a man like Nicholls to bully her.

'I'm here to do a job of work,' she said angrily. 'Keep your distance and I'll keep mine.'

'Or what? I'm your superior.'

'No, Nicholls, you're wrong there.' Eugene emerged from his office. 'I'm the boss and you take orders from me. I heard what you said to Miss Munday and you'll treat her with the respect due to any colleague, or I'll want to know the reason why.'

Nicholls turned away, saying nothing, but Rose knew that she had made an enemy and she would have to be very careful. She left the office and was about to let herself out in the street when she realised that Eugene had followed her.

'Just a moment, Munday.'

'Yes, Guvnor?'

'You'll be paid at the end of the week, but I could let you have an advance if you need it.'

Her first instinct was to refuse, but she had been wondering how she might eke out what little money she had until she was paid, and the only food she had eaten that day was Eugene's cheese roll.

'Thank you. It would help.'

Eugene took a handful of coins from his pocket and dropped them into her outstretched palm. 'Make sure you eat properly. An employee fainting from lack of nourishment is no use to me.'

'Yes, Guvnor. Thank you. Good night.'

'And you need to find somewhere to live nearer the office.' He followed her to the door and opened it. 'Are you still sharing with Cora?'

'No, Guvnor. I'm camping in the boxroom.'

'You'll be in trouble if Regan finds out,' Eugene said, frowning. 'He's often up before the magistrates and so is Cora. You ought to get away from there as soon as possible.'

'I will, of course. I'd best be on my way.' She left the building and stepped into a large puddle.

'Wait a minute, Munday.' Eugene followed her into the street. 'Take a cab.' He pressed a couple more silver coins into her hand.

'That's not necessary,' Rose protested.

'Don't argue. I'm your boss.' Eugene waved down a hansom cab. 'Black Raven Court, cabby.'

The decision having been taken out of her hands, Rose climbed into the vehicle. She was grateful to Eugene for his thoughtfulness, but he seemed to think that he owned her, and that was both frustrating and irritating, even if it was partly true. She did depend upon him and his newspaper for her living, at least for the present. She sighed and leaned back in an attempt to avoid the rain that was slapping her cheeks. First of all she had faced a peasouper and now she was in the middle of a rainstorm. It seemed as though London was trying to tell her something, and the city was not making her feel welcome.

Rose clutched the hot potato she had purchased from the stall on Tower Hill, stopping for a moment to lick the melted butter from her fingers. The mug of coffee she had drunk standing on the wet pavement had helped to warm her, giving her the energy to walk the last few yards to the house. She slipped inside and was able to get to her room without being seen. Sounds of activity from behind closed doors left little to the imagination, and the inclement weather did not seem to have affected the business of the house, or perhaps Regan had been drumming up trade in the local pubs. At least she was safe for another night, and she looked forward to a quiet evening, although huddled on the canvas bed with a single blanket was not exactly the height of luxury. She sat down and savoured each mouthful of the baked potato, trying not to compare it to the hearty meals that Sadie had cooked each evening. When she was in Bendigo she had been homesick for London, and now the situation was reversed. If the return fare had not been so exorbitant she might seriously have considered going home to wait for Max, but if she did that she would have to face the displeasure of both families. Better to wait in London, and she had to admit that Eugene was right – her first priority must be to find somewhere to live. The last stub of candle guttered and went out, leaving her in a dark room with just the reflected glow from the streetlights on the cracked window-panes. Still fully dressed and with her overcoat laid on top of the blanket, she curled up and closed her eyes, but it was not easy to drift off to sleep when her feet felt like blocks of ice. If she caught pneumonia in this draughty room she might lie here for weeks before anyone found her body. It was not a happy thought, but it made her even more determined to find proper lodgings, preferably a room with a fireplace and a decent bed. The potato lay heavily in her stomach, but she was still hungry and she thought longingly of the meal she had shared with Eugene. The delicious taste of the pudding and the creaminess of the custard were a distant memory that tormented her, and when she did fall asleep she dreamed she was enjoying the well-cooked food all over again.

The man at the coffee stall was beginning to recognise her, and he was there next morning looking as cheerful as ever. Rose stopped for a mug of sweet coffee before walking to work and she bought a ham roll, which she tucked into her reticule to eat later. The money that Eugene had advanced on her wages would not stretch to three meals a day, so the coffee would have to carry her through until midday, if she could last out that long.

'I'll see you tonight then, duck,' the stallholder called after her as she walked away. 'I'll save you a meat pie – if I gets any today, that is.'

She acknowledged him with a nod and a wave as she set off on her way to work. She had made a point of leaving early and by the time she reached the office in Fleet Street she was glowing with heat, and extremely hungry. The advantage of being early was that Nicholls had not yet arrived and the two other clerks ignored her, which was preferable to barbed remarks and scornful glances. Eugene was not in his office, but Rose still had the notes he had given her to type and she set to work with a will, picking out the letters one by one using her index fingers.

Eugene was still absent when the editor walked into the office later that morning. Rose stood up, not knowing quite how she was supposed to greet him. She had seen Mr Radley in the distance, but they had never been formally introduced, and she wondered if he knew of her existence. If he had not done so before, he did now, and he was staring at her with a perplexed look on his doughy features. Short, thin and balding, Arthur Radley was a middle-aged man with a permanently worried look and a bizarre taste in clothes. His purple velvet waistcoat did not go well with his florid complexion, and his pinstripe suit and ruffled shirt would have been more appropriate for evening wear. Such outlandish garb on a small insignificant man was the stuff of pantomimes. Rose tried to look serious, but inwardly she was laughing.

'Miss er . . .'

'Munday, sir. I'm Rose Munday.'

'Yes, Eugene did mention that he'd taken someone on to work that infernal machine.' He gazed at the typewriter as if expecting it to burst into flames. 'We've managed perfectly well without one.'

'Yes, sir.'

'Where is Mr Sheldon? I want to speak to him.'

'I believe he went out early on a story, sir.' Rose

had no intention of making trouble for Eugene. He might, for all she knew, be following a story, although from the little she knew of him she suspected that he might have had a late night, with all that entailed, and be sleeping off the excesses of the previous evening.

'Oh, very well. What a nuisance.' Radley fingered some papers on Eugene's desk, losing interest almost immediately. 'Tell him I need to see him urgently, Miss er . . .'

'Munday,' Rose said, but she was talking to thin air as Radley had already left the office. She shrugged and returned to the task of deciphering Eugene's scrawl, correcting his spelling as she went. By midday she had placed the finished article on his desk and was moderately pleased with her efforts. Her stomach was rumbling and she was about to eat her ham roll when Eugene breezed into the office, tossing his hat on the coat stand and missing yet again. Rose got up automatically and rescued the topper, placing it safely on the highest peg.

Unabashed, Eugene took off his greatcoat and draped it over a chair. 'Is everything all right, Munday?'

She gave him a searching look. His dark hair was curling wildly round his head and there were bruise-like smudges beneath his eyes. The woody, citrus scent of bay rum could not quite conceal the smell of garlic, wine and cigar smoke that hung about him like a fine mist.

'Mr Radley has been looking for you.'

'What did you say to him?'

'I said I thought you were chasing up a story.'

A slow smile lit Eugene's eyes with golden glints. 'Well done, Munday. I was in fact asleep until less than half an hour ago. A bit of a late night. I think I had a good time, but I can't remember much about the last part of it.'

Rose stifled a chuckle. 'You should be ashamed of yourself, Guvnor.'

'Oh, I am. Deeply.' Eugene sank down in the chair behind his desk. 'Send Scully to fetch me some coffee, please, Munday. My head is pounding.'

'The editor wants to see you urgently.'

'I can't do anything until I've had a mug of strong black coffee. No sugar. Cousin Arthur will have to wait.'

Rose gave him a pitying look and went to find Scully, who dutifully braved the rain to fetch the coffee. He returned having filled a jug with the steaming brew.

'It'll take more than one mug to sober the guvnor up,' he said, grinning. 'We go through this regularly. You'll get used to it.'

Rose said nothing, but she filled a mug, and took it to Eugene, who was sitting back in his chair with his eyes closed.

'Here you are,' she said coldly. 'There's more if you want it.'

Eugene opened his eyes. 'Don't look so disapproving, Rose. It's not a crime to enjoy oneself.'

'I never said it was, but I've seen men take to drink and it doesn't end well.'

'Heaven help me, your missionary friends haven't encouraged you to join the Temperance Movement, have they?'

'I've never heard of it,' Rose said truthfully. 'Men in the goldfields often drink to excess, but it's a hard life out there.'

'My dear Munday, I enjoyed an evening out with friends, a good meal and fine wine. You can hardly equate that with the hard-drinking mining community in the State of Victoria.'

Rose could see this conversation going nowhere and she hastily changed the subject. 'I've typed out the article you wrote. If there's anything you want to change, just say so and I'll retype it.'

Eugene drained the last dregs of coffee and handed the mug to her. 'Excellent coffee. A refill, please, while I take a look at your latest effort.'

Rose did as he asked and waited patiently while Eugene pored over the article. He reached for the coffee and drank deeply.

'Excellent. Not many errors and a masterly piece of reporting, even if I say so myself. My talent is being wasted writing such paltry items of news. I need something I can really get my teeth into.'

'Like a war?' Rose said, smiling. She meant it as a joke but Eugene seemed to take it seriously.

'By Jove, yes. I've been trying to persuade Arthur to send me to Egypt to cover the war, but it seems to be over. Although I gather the situation is still tense.'

'Best finish your coffee, Guvnor.' Rose took the sheet of paper from him. 'Shall I run this down to the print room?'

'Give it to Scully. I've got an assignment for you, Munday.'

Rose could hardly believe her ears. 'Really? You're sending me out to do a report?'

'Yes and no. I'm taking you to the Savoy Theatre this evening to see *Patience*, the latest opera by Gilbert and Sullivan. Do you like opera?'

'I love music,' Rose said slowly. 'But I thought you said I was going on an assignment.'

'You will be. I can hardly send you to the theatre on your own, now can I? I'll take you, but you will be the critic.'

'I can't.' The reality of what he had said brought her back to earth with a jolt. 'I haven't got anything to wear. I don't know about London, but people at home dress up to go to the theatre. You'll have to take someone else – I'm sure you have lots of lady friends.'

'I'm not disputing that, Munday, but their talents lie elsewhere – you, on the other hand, show promise and I am giving you the chance to prove yourself.'

'It still leaves me with the same problem,' Rose said impatiently. 'I only brought the minimum of luggage because Max promised me a whole new wardrobe. Maybe I was naïve, but there it is.'

'I think I have the perfect solution. My sister, Cecilia, has dozens of elegant gowns, far too many, in my opinion. She'll lend you something suitable.' He stood up and reached for his coat. 'Get your outdoor things on, Munday. We're taking a cab to Tavistock Square.'

'Is this where you live?' Rose stepped out of the cab, looking up at the grand façade of the four-storey house with wrought-iron balconies on the first floor and tall windows interspersed with Ionic columns.

'It's my parents' house,' Eugene said, sprinting up the steps to the front door. He rapped on the knocker. 'Cissie should be at home, although knowing my sister she's probably still in bed.'

'At this time of day?'

'Cecilia loves parties that go on into the small hours.' Eugene stepped over the threshold. 'Come in, Rose. Don't stand there dithering.'

She eyed the footman warily as she entered the house, but he was staring stonily into the distance and he closed the door after her. Eugene shrugged off his coat and gave his hat and gloves to the servant who was standing to attention, arms outstretched like a human coatrack.

'Giddings will take your things,' Eugene said impatiently. 'Come on, Munday, we haven't got all day.'

Rose took off her coat and handed it to Giddings. It might be her imagination but she sensed his disapproval, and she suspected that the servants would view her second-hand garments with contempt. But Eugene was striding across the black and white marble-tiled floor, heading for the graceful sweep of the staircase. She was inexplicably nervous and she shivered, despite the warmth from a fire blazing at one end of the entrance hall. Until now Eugene had been her boss and mentor, but this was his home and she realised that he came from a family where money seemed to be no object. As she mounted the stairs she had visions of being scrutinised by his wealthy parents, and if the footman looked askance at the girl from Bendigo, what would Mr and Mrs Sheldon think of her?

Eugene opened one of the double doors at the top of the staircase. 'Ah, you're up and dressed, Cissie. That makes a change.' He beckoned to Rose. 'Come and meet my sister.'

Rose entered a room that was even grander than the Dorincourts' mansion in Bendigo. The crimson and gold upholstery of the ornately carved mahogany sofas and chairs glowed like hot coals in the cold light that filtered through the tall windows. The cream background of the vast carpet was adorned with an abundance of pink roses and white daisies, wreathed in green leaves. The warmth in the Sheldons' drawing room was such that it might have been a summer's day, and the effect was heightened by a roaring coal fire and the light from two gasoliers with glass shades shaped like waterlilies.

'Of course I'm up. I'm not a lazybones like you.' A young woman rose from the sofa nearest the fire. 'Who is this, Eugene?'

'Rose, ignore my sister's bad manners.' Eugene gave Rose a gentle push. 'I want you to meet my sister, Cecilia.'

Remembering what Sadie had drummed into her, Rose bobbed a curtsey. 'How do you do?'

'Cissie, this is my protégée, Rose Munday. She is learning to use the typewriting machine I purchased in America and I'm giving her a chance to prove that she has it in her to become a reporter.'

Cecilia looked Rose up and down. 'How do you do, Miss Munday? I must say, I'm impressed. I don't suppose you realise how honoured you are.'

'I don't know what you mean.' Rose glanced at Eugene, who shrugged and went to stand with his back to the fire.

'My brother is a typical man, Miss Munday. He thinks that we have nothing on our minds other than fashion and marriage, in that order.'

'That's not fair, Cissie. I never said that.' Eugene

gave Rose an apologetic smile. 'Well, I might have thought that way once, but times have changed. I met several lady journalists in New York and I admired them greatly.'

'So what makes Miss Munday a suitable candidate?' Cecilia demanded. 'I want to know.'

'Maybe she'll tell you her story one day, but that's up to her. For now all I want is for you to lend her something suitable to wear to the opera this evening.'

Cecilia turned to Rose with a curious look. 'What's this all about, Miss Munday? Because if you think that my brother is a good catch I can assure you that he's the last person I would recommend as a prospective husband.'

Chapter Six

'You couldn't be more wrong,' Rose said angrily. 'Such a thought never occurred to me.'

'Yes, that's a bit strong, even for you, Cissie.' Eugene strolled over to a side table and selected a cut-glass decanter. 'Would either of you like a drink?'

Rose shook her head. 'No, thank you.'

'It looks to me as though you had enough last evening.' Cecilia shook her finger at him. 'You're turning into a rake, Gene. What would Papa say?'

'Father was in Cairo last time I heard from him, so he's not here to judge me.'

'Your father is in Egypt?' Rose was suddenly alert. 'Is he in the army?'

Cecilia raised a delicate eyebrow. 'Heavens, no! Papa is in the diplomatic service, and the last letter

I had from Mama said that the consulate had been relocated to Alexandria.'

'That's the last place I'd want to visit at the moment.' Eugene poured himself a generous tot of brandy and swallowed it in one gulp. 'Anyway, that's beside the point, Cissie. Are you going to help Munday, or not?'

Cecilia shot him a scornful look. 'How patronising you are, Gene. The poor girl has a name. Either address her as Miss Munday or Rose, but don't treat her as if she were on the cricket pitch at your old school.'

Rose looked from one to the other. She felt like a tennis ball, being batted to and fro between the brother and sister, each trying to score points off the other. 'Really, it doesn't matter,' she said hastily. 'You can find someone else to go to see *Patience*, Guvnor. I don't want to cause a fuss.'

'There, Cissie. Now see what you've done.' Eugene refilled his glass and took a sip. 'You've embarrassed Munday.'

'The only embarrassing person in this room is you, Gene.' Cecilia turned her to Rose with a concil-iatory smile. 'I'm sorry, Rose. We're being very ill-mannered, and of course I'll lend you a gown.' She glanced at her brother. 'On one condition, Gene.'

He drained his drink and placed the glass back on the tray. 'Go on. How much is this going to cost me?'

'Another ticket to the opera. I'm dying to see *Patience*, and Rose needs a chaperone.'

'Munday is a working woman,' Eugene protested. 'The stuffy rules of etiquette don't apply.'

'They do in the real world,' Cecilia said firmly. 'You live in the make-believe land of those who purport to tell us the truth, when half of the things you print have no bearing on reality whatsoever.'

'That's a bit harsh Cissie.'

Cecilia placed her arm around Rose's shoulders. 'Take no notice of him. We'll go to my room and find you something to wear tonight, and I'll choose my gown so that we don't clash.'

'My sister is a harpy,' Eugene said, throwing up his hands. 'Don't listen to her if she says things about me, Rose.'

'Shut up, Gene.' Cecilia held her hand out to Rose. 'Come with me. We'll do very well without my brother's assistance.' She glided from the room and Rose hurried after her.

Cecilia's bedroom was spacious and elegantly furnished with a peach and gold colour scheme that created a feeling of everlasting sunshine. Cecilia ushered Rose into a dressing room lined with cupboards. The doors were faced with mirrors, creating a kaleidoscope effect, and Rose could see several versions of herself. She had to stifle a childish urge to pull faces, but Cecilia was in deadly earnest and she opened the first cupboard to reveal shelves packed with neatly folded garments. Another was crammed with ornate gowns hanging from brass hooks. Yet another revealed sets of drawers; some of them filled with lace-trimmed undergarments, while others were overflowing with gloves, scarves and stockings. There were open shelves filled with hats of every description, trimmed with flowers and feathers in rainbow hues. Rose was both dazzled and impressed, but also slightly bewildered.

'As you can see, I love clothes,' Cecilia said happily. 'My maid takes care of everything, but you may have your pick, providing I approve.'

Rose had never seen such a collection of garments belonging to one person – in fact, she had never been in a shop that was more comprehensively stocked. 'Are you sure about this? I mean, you were pushed into it by your brother.'

'Gene might try but he could never force me to do anything against my will. You have to treat him like your boss, but he's just my brother. I'll leave you to choose, try on anything you take a fancy to and come out and show me.' Cecilia left Rose alone in the dressing room surrounded by finery that took her breath away. She was beginning to realise that the fashion in London differed from what was considered *haute couture* in Bendigo, and she began her search for something that was suitable, but not too elaborate.

When she finally emerged wearing a pale-blue silk

gown, with a modest neckline and a small bustle, Cecilia shook her head.

'That's an afternoon dress, Rose. You need something a little more dashing for the opera, and I think I know exactly which one would suit your glorious copper hair and milky complexion.' Cecilia jumped to her feet and returned to the dressing room, reappearing moments later with a shimmering armful of gold silk brocade trimmed with delicate tulle roses. 'Try this one on.'

It was a command rather than an invitation and Rose retreated into the privacy of the dressing room and changed into Cecilia's choice.

'Oh, splendid.' Cecilia clapped her hands when Rose re-emerged. 'Take a look in the mirror and you'll see that I was right.'

Rose stepped in front of the cheval mirror, staring in astonishment at her own reflection, although to her eyes it was a stranger who gazed back at her. Cecilia came up behind her and dragged Rose's unruly curls away from her face, piling them on top of her head so that they fell in a cascade, framing her face and elongating her neck.

'What a transformation. I can't wait to see Gene's face when he sees you dressed up to the nines. That might make him treat you more like a colleague rather than an office boy.'

Rose moved away, allowing her hair to fall back into place. 'I am very junior at the newspaper, Miss

Sheldon. The other employees don't want to work with a female, and your brother has given me a chance to prove myself. I don't mind if he calls me Munday. In fact I think it's a good thing.'

'Well, well, so you have some spirit after all, Rose. I was beginning to think that you were a doormat, but I can see that I was mistaken.'

'Don't think I'm ungrateful, but I can't wear this,' Rose said desperately. 'This gown must have cost a fortune and I'd feel terrible if it got marked or I caught my heel in the hem.'

Cecilia stood back, frowning. 'You and I are the same size and height. I wonder if my shoes would fit you, because you can't wear those ugly boots tonight. They don't go with that gown.'

'You aren't listening to me, Miss Sheldon. You're just like your brother.'

'I am not at all like Eugene, and don't call me Miss Sheldon. I'm Cissie to my family and friends, and I want you to be my friend, Rose. I like you and I admire you for standing up to the beastly men in Gene's office, and I see in you a kindred spirit. We'll have no arguments about the gown. It doesn't suit me anyway. In fact I don't know why I bought it. Gold is your colour, not mine.'

'You do have lovely dark hair and a beautiful complexion,' Rose said, nodding. 'You're right to wear bright colours – they suit you.'

'Yes, I know they do, and tonight I'll wear my

crimson shot silk. We'll turn every head in the Savoy Theatre. I doubt if anyone will be looking at the stage when we're there.'

Rose was not so sure, but she found herself trying on shoes that were a surprisingly good fit, although ultimately it was Cecilia who made the final choice. Then, having listened intently to Rose's account of her reasons for leaving home, Cecilia insisted on turning out a quantity of garments, including daywear, underwear and nightwear, all of which she insisted she had not worn for ages, and had no intention of wearing again. She threw in several pairs of shoes and boots, a velvet bonnet and a warm mantle, which she said was last year's fashion and fit only for the missionary barrel at the local church. She became so enthusiastic that Rose had to put a stop to her burst of generosity, gently but firmly.

'Oh, very well,' Cecilia said sulkily. 'But I rarely do anything for anyone else, and you've probably saved my eternal soul from hellfire.'

'I think you have a lot of living ahead of you, Cissie,' Rose said, laughing. 'I don't think hellfire is waiting for you just yet.'

'You can laugh, Rose. But I'm serious. I was spoiled by my parents and shamelessly overindulged. Just look around you.' Cecilia encompassed the room with a wave of her hands. 'Of course, Papa doesn't earn a great deal working for the Foreign Office, but Mama inherited a fortune when my grandfather died a few years ago.'

'You're very fortunate,' Rose said smiling. 'And very kind. I don't know what I would have done without your brother's help, and now you're doing something splendid for someone you've only known for an hour or so.'

'Yes, that does make me sound much nicer than I really am.' Cecilia picked up a silver-backed brush and began to rearrange Rose's hair. 'You shouldn't wear your hair scraped back into a bun, my dear. That style went out years ago. You're lucky to have natural curls. I have to sleep with rags in my hair every night because my hair is as straight as rainwater.'

'You're very elegant, Cissie. I don't think you need to worry about your looks.'

'I don't really. I know I'm beautiful, everyone says so, but sometimes I feel quite plain and dull. Maybe I should think of going out in the world and earning my own living.' Cecilia pressed Rose down on a stool in front of a burr-walnut dressing table. 'I'm going to try a much more flattering style, and you can tell me more about yourself.'

'I thought I'd told you everything.'

'You told me about your life in that far-off place, but you must know some people in London, apart from the ones you've met recently. I don't think missionaries or prostitutes are going to help you establish yourself in society.'

'I was hoping that Max's sister would help me, but she and her husband are away on a business trip to Australia.'

'They're in trade?' Cecilia's tone was anything but enthusiastic.

'The Colville Shipping Company is one of the largest in Britain,' Rose said stoutly. 'At least that's what I was led to believe.' She could see Cecilia's reaction in the mirror, and it was obvious that there were degrees of what branch of trade might be considered acceptable.

'That does make a difference,' Cecilia said grudgingly. 'The Colville family are well known for their philanthropic work. In fact I met Caroline Colville and her half-sister, Maria, at a charity function about a year ago. Maria is a few years my senior, but she and I got along so well that we've become friends.'

'Maria Colville?'

'That's her maiden name, she married a seafarer and she's Mrs Barnaby now.'

'She's Max's half-sister.' Rose twisted round on the stool, facing Cecilia with a tremulous smile. 'I was only nine years old when I attended her wedding, but I remember it well. Do you know where she lives?'

'Yes, I do. I visit her quite often and we help to raise money for seamen's charities. Maria's husband is away at sea for months on end, sometimes a year or more, and I think she gets lonely with just a housekeeper and her children's nanny for company.'

'She might be able to help me,' Rose said excitedly. 'Max was going to arrange everything, so he must have told Caroline about us. Maybe she left a message for me with her sister.'

'There's only one way to find out. As it happens I'd arranged to have luncheon with Maria next Tuesday. I'll make Eugene give you time off so that you can join us.'

'Maybe it would be better if I asked him nicely.'

'You'll have to learn how to handle the male of the species, Rose. Especially those akin to my brother, who is as stubborn as the proverbial mule and can be very contrary. I'll tell him of our arrangement and heaven help him if he refuses to allow you to accompany me.'

Rose turned to the mirror and her reflection gazed back at her with doubtful eyes. She did not share Cecilia's confidence in her ability to manipulate Eugene. 'I don't want to cause trouble between you and your brother,' she said.

'Believe me, I'm used to dealing with Gene, and I'm not stupid, Rose. I'll wait until this evening when he is in a sunny mood and then I'll ask him.' Cecilia smiled and nodded. 'You have to have a strategy when dealing with men like Gene, as you will discover if you're going to work together with any degree of success.'

* * *

Eugene was seated by the fire, reading a copy of *The Times* when they finally joined him. He folded the newspaper and rose to his feet. 'At last. I was beginning to think I'd have to send a search party for you two.'

'Very funny,' Cecilia said, smiling sweetly. 'We were just sorting out some of my things for Rose and we lost track of time.'

'Did you find her a gown for this evening? We need to cut a dash. I don't want to be outdone by the chaps from the other dailies.'

'So we're there for decorative purposes, are we, Gene?' Cecilia was smiling, but there was an edge to her voice.

'I'm there to work,' Rose said quickly. 'Aren't I, Guvnor?'

'Of course you are. Don't take any notice of my sister. She can be a virago when she wants to be. You are going to write the article, Munday, and we'd best be getting back to the office, or poor Arthur will be having forty fits.'

'What about tonight, Gene?' Cecilia demanded. 'Will you bring Rose here to change?'

He frowned. 'I hadn't thought that far ahead.'

'I can't very well get ready in the office,' Rose said thoughtfully.

'I'll bring her home with me.' Eugene made for the door. 'Come on, Munday. We'll grab a bite to eat on the way to the office.'

'Why not stay a while and have luncheon with me?' Cecilia followed them onto the landing. 'Another hour or so won't make any difference.'

'Sorry, Cissie. We have a deadline to meet,' Eugene called over his shoulder. 'Hurry up, Munday. There's work to be done.'

Cecilia was dressed in her finery, waiting for them in a considerable state of agitation when they returned to Tavistock Square that evening. Eugene had been working on a last-minute addition for the morning paper, and there had been several hold-ups during the cab journey when a sudden downpour had caused chaos. An argument between a carter and a hackney cab driver had held up traffic for what seemed like forever, until a police constable strolled up and threatened to arrest both of them. Then a barrel had fallen off a brewer's dray and had hit the cobblestones with such force that it split, spewing out a fountain of ale. People appeared from nowhere, attempting to catch as much of the amber liquid as they could in mugs, jugs and even bowler hats, while others simply opened their mouths to gulp down the free beer.

It had not been a dull cab ride, but now they were late and Cecilia was fuming. She rushed Rose upstairs and with the help of her maid managed to get her into the tightly fitting gown, coiffed and ready in less than an hour.

'Wait a moment,' Cecilia cried as Rose was about to escape. 'You look splendid but you need some jewellery.'

'I'm a very junior reporter,' Rose protested. 'Who's going to look at me?'

'Never say anything like that in my hearing. You have to make the best of yourself whatever the circumstances, Rose Munday.' Cecilia caught her by the hand and dragged her back into the room. 'Lindon, fetch my jewel case.'

The harassed maid stopped picking up hairpins that were scattered on the floor and hurried into the dressing room, reappearing seconds later with a rosewood box inlaid with mother-of-pearl. She set it down on the table and stood back while Cecilia rifled through the contents.

'Sit down, Rose. Let's see if pearls look best, or maybe a simple velvet choker.'

Rose had learned that to argue with either of the Sheldon siblings was a waste of time and she sat down as obediently as a schoolgirl. She could hear Eugene calling to them from the top of the stairs, but she allowed Cecilia to select several necklaces, settling in the end for a gold chain with a pearl and peridot pendant and matching earrings.

'There, that's absolutely splendid. The peridots are virtually the same colour as your eyes.' Cecilia stood back to admire her handiwork. 'What do you think, Lindon?'

'Very nice, Miss Cecilia. Just right for a young lady who isn't out yet.'

Rose looked from one to the other. 'That sounds as if I've been in prison.'

Lindon raised her eyebrows and Cecilia stifled a giggle.

'Don't you know anything about the London Season?' Cecilia threw up her hands.

'Maybe you should explain later – the guvnor is growing impatient.'

'Stop calling him that silly name. He's Eugene or Mr Sheldon, and for tonight I suggest you use his first name, or it will make a mockery of the whole evening.' Cecilia turned to Lindon. 'Fetch our wraps, please. We'll miss the first act if we don't hurry.'

Cecilia had been right – heads turned to stare at the two elegant young women who accompanied Eugene Sheldon. Rose was embarrassed to be the centre of attention, but Cecilia was apparently accustomed to creating a grand entrance, and Eugene looked positively dashing in his black tailcoat, bronze silk waistcoat and pristine white shirt. Rose was acutely aware of the admiring glances he received from the ladies present, but Eugene himself seemed oblivious to the sensation he was causing. He stopped every now and then to exchange pleasantries with the men who were standing in small groups, chatting and laughing as if they had known each other all their lives.

'They're gentlemen of the press,' Cecilia said in a whisper as they took their seats. 'You'd think they were bosom friends, but they would cut each other's throats if it meant they could be the first to make the headlines.'

Rose was prevented from questioning her further as the orchestra began tuning up and the lights dimmed. Eugene made his way down the aisle and sat down beside her.

'You've created quite a stir, Munday. You polish up like new in that gown.'

'Hush,' Cecilia said sternly. 'The opera is about to start.'

Eugene pulled a face. 'Wake me up at the interval, Munday. I'm relying on you to get the gist of the story, because I can't stand this sort of thing.' He closed his eyes and bowed his head.

Rose glanced anxiously at Cecilia, but her attention was fixed on the stage as the curtain was raised and the overture commenced. As the story unfolded and the music swelled, filling the pale yellow and golden auditorium with mellifluous sound, Rose found herself entranced and enthralled. She barely noticed the gentle snores emanating from Eugene with the rise and fall of his chest, and it was only at the interval that she realised people around them were pointing and laughing. She dug him hard in the ribs.

'Wake up, Guvnor,' she hissed. 'Everyone's looking at you.'

Cecilia leaned over Rose to prod her brother. 'Gene, you're making a fool of yourself and a spectacle of us.'

Eugene opened his eyes. 'Is it over?'

Cecilia smacked him with her fan. 'You philistine.'

'It's the interval,' Rose whispered. 'You were snoring, Guvnor.'

'I was just resting my eyes.' Eugene rose to his feet. 'I'm going to the bar for a tot of whisky. Would you ladies like to join me?'

Cecilia sat bolt upright. 'No, you've embarrassed me enough this evening.'

'What about you, Munday? You might hear a bit of gossip you could use.'

Rose glanced at Cecilia's disapproving profile. She was bound to offend one or the other, but if she wanted to be taken seriously as a reporter she knew what she had to do. She stood up, placing the programme on her seat. 'Yes, all right, Guvnor.' She was close behind him as he joined the stream of people making their way up the aisle.

'You might like to start the article with a few words about the splendid electric lighting,' Eugene said in a low voice as they edged their way towards the bar.

'It is amazing. Do you think it will catch on?'

'Almost certainly, and I'll install electricity at Greenfields, my property in the country, as soon as it becomes possible.' Eugene placed a protective arm around Rose's shoulders as they reached the crush at the entrance to the bar.

Rose glanced inside at the sea of male bodies and she refused to move. 'I think I'd better wait out here. It doesn't look as though women are welcome in the bar.'

'Nonsense, you're with me, Munday. You're a newspaper man now and you'll find yourself in places where other females wouldn't dare to tread.' He propelled her through the throng of men clamouring for drinks.

Rose tried to look unconcerned, but she felt the colour flooding her cheeks and the remarks she overheard were not flattering.

Eugene ordered a glass of champagne and a whisky and soda, ignoring the disapproving looks from the barman.

'There you are, Munday.' He pressed the champagne glass into her hand and raised his drink in a toast. 'Here's to your future success.'

'You shouldn't bring a lady into a place like this.' A distinguished-looking man with silver hair and a waxed moustache turned his head to glare at Eugene. 'We have to draw the line somewhere, Sheldon.'

'This young woman is a fledgling reporter on my newspaper,' Eugene said loudly. 'If anyone has anything to say, then say it to my face.'

A sudden hush seemed to suck the air from the crowded bar.

Rose could feel the undercurrent of resentment swelling like the incoming tide and she raised her glass. 'I drink to your health, gentlemen. I might be the first female newsperson to enter a predominantly male domain, but I won't be the last.' She downed a mouthful of champagne, placed the glass on the counter and marched out of the bar, but when she reached the foyer her courage ebbed and her knees threatened to give way beneath her.

'Well said, Munday.' Eugene had followed her and he gave her a brief hug. 'Maybe I should have patted you on the back as if you were a chap, but you're a sight for sore eyes. No wonder the fellows were confused.'

'I shouldn't have spoken out like that. I'm sorry, Guvnor.'

'Nonsense, you've just written your own headline. Wait there, I'll fetch my sister and we'll take a cab to the office. This story will be on the front page in the morning, I can see it now.' He paused, smiling ruefully. 'Sorry, Munday, I was forgetting – this is your story. You can call it what you like. Think about it while I get Cissie and retrieve our coats from the cloakroom. You and the redoubtable Millicent Fawcett have a lot in common, but this is your big moment.'

Rose waited anxiously, trying hard to look unconcerned, but she knew she was attracting attention for all the wrong reasons, and she tried to ignore the salacious remarks she received from one man who had obviously drunk far more than was good for him. It was a relief when Eugene appeared, followed by a sulky-looking Cecilia.

'This is ridiculous, Gene,' Cecilia snapped. 'Walking out in the interval is stupid and very bad manners.'

'Nonsense. This is Munday's chance to get her piece in the Monday morning paper. The other chaps will do the same thing. Wait there, I'll get a cab.' He hurried out into the street.

'You shouldn't encourage him,' Cecilia said, sighing heavily. 'Gene always manages to create a stir wherever we go.'

'Then perhaps you should be used to it by now.' Rose was in no mood to take the blame for something that was beyond her control.

Having taken Cecilia back to Tavistock Square, Eugene and Rose returned to the office where, despite the fact that it was late evening, Rose worked on her review of the opera for Monday's edition. When both she and Eugene were satisfied with the result, it was left for the typesetters to put into print, and Eugene saw her safely back to Black Raven Court.

'We must address this problem urgently, Rose,' he said as he handed her from the cab. 'I don't like leaving you here.'

'I'll be all right, Guvnor. I've got Cora and Flossie looking out for me.' Rose hoped she sounded more

positive than she was feeling as she stepped inside
and closed the door.

Having slept for most of Sunday, Rose was up early
on Monday morning. She dressed hastily and rushed
out to buy a copy of the *London Leader* from a
stall outside Fenchurch Street station. To see her
words in print for the very first time would be a
thrill, and she could scarcely wait to get back to her
room. In her excitement it was even possible to
ignore the pangs of hunger that gripped her stomach
and the chill of a late autumn morning. With her
shawl wrapped around her head and shoulders she
trudged back to Black Raven Court. She did not
notice Regan until it was too late.

Chapter Seven

Rose came to a sudden halt at the sight of the man who ruled the lives of the women in his house, and was about to turn and run when he grabbed her by the arm and dragged her inside.

'Cora is a poor liar,' he said, pressing Rose up against the damp wall. 'She told me you'd gone, but Nat Regan is nobody's fool.'

'I won't be here much longer. I can pay rent.'

Regan curled his lip. 'Only girls who work for me are allowed to live here, sweetheart. I got plenty of clients who would pay good money for your favours.' He glanced at the newspaper she was clutching to her chest. 'And you can read, too. I ain't sure that's a good thing.'

'Let me go.' Rose glared at him, too angry now to feel fear. 'I'm leaving today.'

He pinned her to the wall with surprising strength for a small man. 'That's up to me. This is my place and what I says goes.'

'I've got a job, Regan,' she said boldly. 'I'm a reporter on this newspaper, and if you don't get out of my way you'll find yourself headline news in the next edition.' It was a vain boast, but it had the desired effect and Regan released her, taking a step backwards.

'You're lying, you little bitch.'

Rose leafed through the newspaper, searching desperately for the article that bore her name. She found it, even though it was tucked away beneath a list of other social events. The print was small, but her name was there and she waved it under his nose. 'There's the proof in black and white. And if you don't let me go I'll be late for the office.'

Regan stared at her in disbelief, his mouth working silently. Rose seized the moment and slipped past him. She raced down the steps and kept running until she was out of breath and had to stop and take shelter in a doorway. One thing was for certain: remaining in Black Raven Court was not an option. Thanks to her bragging, Regan knew her name and where she was working. She had made a tactical error, but the main thing now was to get to the office on time.

* * *

Nicholls was already at his desk and he looked up, his expression hardening when he spotted Rose. 'You're late again, Munday.'

'I'm sorry, Mr Nicholls. I was unexpectedly delayed.'

'No matter what Mr Sheldon says, I'm the head clerk, and, if you're late again or you don't do as I tell you, I'll report you to Mr Radley.'

'Yes, Mr Nicholls.' Rose decided that arguing with Nicholls was a waste of time and she forced herself to answer meekly.

'Get to work, Munday,' Nicholls snapped. 'Your days are numbered, so make the most of your five minutes of glory.'

Rose could hear the two more junior clerks sniggering, but she ignored them as she marched into Eugene's office, resisting the temptation to slam the door. They were determined to make her life as difficult as possible, but Eugene had given her a chance to prove herself and she had no intention of letting him down. That aside, her most pressing problem was where she would sleep that night, and how she would retrieve her things from the boxroom in Black Raven Court. It was fortunate that the clothes given to her by Cecilia were still in Tavistock Square, waiting until she had found more permanent accommodation.

Rose sat down in front of the typewriter, running her fingers over the keys. The night before last she had felt proud and elated when Eugene allowed her to write her piece about the theatre, and seeing her name in print for the first time was undoubtedly a thrill, but working in a man's world was going to be an uphill struggle. She took a sheet of paper and inserted it in the machine. There was work that Eugene had left for her and it must be done; even so, she was finding it hard to concentrate, and she was still sitting there when he breezed into the office half an hour later.

'What's the matter with you, Munday?' he demanded. 'I thought you would be beaming all over your face this morning.'

'I've got a bit of a problem, Guvnor.'

Eugene made to throw his hat onto the stand, but seemed to think better of it and placed it on a chair together with his overcoat and scarf. 'Anything I can help with?'

'I have to find somewhere else to stay.'

'I could have told you that living in a house of ill repute was not the best address for a budding reporter. However, joking aside, I agree with you wholeheartedly.'

'I bumped into Regan again and he's being difficult.'

Eugene took his seat behind his desk. 'I imagine that's putting it mildly. I suppose he wants you to join his happy band of workers.'

'That's it exactly, and I daren't go back to collect

my things in case he sees me. Besides which, I've nowhere to go.'

He turned his head to give her a long look. 'Then you must stay with us in Tavistock Square, and I'll try to find out if those men have the legal right to be in the Captain's House.'

'Thank you, Guvnor. But your sister might object to having me as a guest, even for a short time.'

'Cissie? Why would she? My sister isn't a bad sort when you get to know her, Munday. Her main problem is ennui. Cissie is an intelligent woman and she hasn't got enough to occupy her mind. She doesn't particularly enjoy balls and soirées, and, in my opinion, she needs a cause to fight for. You might find you have a lot in common.'

'Maybe,' Rose said doubtfully. 'She's been very kind to me, but I don't want to foist myself on her.'

'I don't think Cissie will have any objections to you staying with us until you find something more suitable. You seemed to get on quite well at the theatre.'

'She did invite me to join her when she has luncheon with Maria Barnaby. Maria is half-sister to Max Manning, my fiancé.'

'There you are then. Maria might be able to give you some information, so stop worrying and type out that article I gave you yesterday. You're still an office junior, Munday, so get back to work.' Eugene tempered his words with a smile. 'And don't worry about your possessions. I'll come with you when we finish work this evening. I'd enjoy sorting Regan out.'

Rose shot him a sideways glance. 'You'd take him on?'

'I can handle myself in a fight. You'd be surprised.'

It was dark when they arrived in Black Raven Court and Rose was nervous. It was not only feral cats that lurked in doorways and down dark alleys. There was danger in the back streets even in daytime, but when the shadows deepened after dusk it was a brave person who walked there alone. Rose had learned this much already, and she kept watch while Eugene marched up to the front door. He turned to her and beckoned.

'It's not locked – the girls are obviously expecting to do a good trade tonight. Come on.'

Rose hesitated on the bottom step. 'Maybe it would be best if you keep watch outside. I'm used to creeping up the stairs.'

'All right. Go ahead, but be quick.'

Rose entered the house on tiptoe. The nauseating smell of unwashed bodies, damp rot, cheap perfume and tobacco smoke hit her with almost physical force. The familiar sounds of laughter and creaking bed springs were punctuated by raised voices and the occasional scream. Rose broke into a run, taking the stairs two at a time, but in her haste she trod on the step that everyone tried to avoid and the loud creak brought Cora to her door.

'Blooming hell, Rose. You gave me a fright – I thought it was Regan come to collect the rent.' Cora took a drag on a cheroot and then stamped it out under the heel of her boot.

'I'm sorry,' Rose whispered. 'I've come to collect my bag. I'm moving out.'

'Good for you, nipper. I wish I could do the same.'

'What keeps you here? Haven't you got any family who would take you in?'

Cora gave her a pitying look. 'You might have good people waiting for you, but some of us ain't so lucky. My pa is in the clink and Ma only wants to see me if I give her money for gin. Go on, kid. Grab your things and make a run for it before his nibs turns up. Flossie says he's got his eye on you, so don't hang about.'

'I will, and thanks, Cora. I'll miss you and Flossie, will you tell her that for me?'

Cora nodded emphatically. 'Good luck, kid.' She retreated into her room, and closed the door.

Rose hurried up the second flight of stairs and collected her things, but as she made her way downstairs she heard a door open and Regan's loud voice berating one of the girls. It was dark on the landing, but peering through the banisters she could see him standing in a shaft of light. He was shaking his fist and using foul language that would have made the toughest gold prospector blush. Rose shrank into the shadows, hoping that he would visit another of the rooms on the ground floor, and she sighed with relief when she heard the sound of his booted feet stamping towards the back of the house. She hurtled down the remaining stairs and out into the cold night, almost falling into Eugene's arms as he waited for her.

'You'd think the devil was after you,' he said, relieving her of the heavy valise. 'Come on Rose, let's go home.'

Cecilia was not over-effusive, but she made Rose welcome and sent a maid to light a fire in one of the many bedrooms. Giddings relieved Rose of her outer garments and she could feel his silent disapproval, but she smiled and nodded graciously, taking Cecilia as her model for ladylike behaviour as she handed him her valise. If this was how a lady was expected to behave she could do it with ease, even if she had to resist the temptation to tell the footman that she might be poor, but she was just as good as him, and she did not judge people by outward appearances.

'I've got some correspondence to deal with. I'll be in the study.' Eugene hurried off without giving his sister a chance to object.

'Come with me, Rose,' Cecilia said calmly. 'We'll wait for Gene in the drawing room.' She led the way up the gracefully curving sweep of the staircase to the crimson and gold drawing room, where she motioned Rose to take a seat.

'So what happened to bring you here this evening?' Cecilia selected a cut-glass decanter from a side table. 'Would you like a glass of sherry?'

Rose nodded. 'Yes, please, Miss Sheldon.'

Cecilia filled two delicately engraved glasses and handed one to Rose. 'I thought we'd agreed that you would call me Cissie.'

'Yes, I'm sorry, but you didn't invite me to stay. It was the guvnor who insisted that you wouldn't mind, given the circumstances.'

Cecilia moved to a chair by the fire and sat down. 'What were they exactly, Rose? Gene didn't stop to explain, which is typical of my brother.'

'Nat Regan is the man who owns the house in Black Raven Court. I think you know what sort of place it is.'

'I have a vague idea.'

'Well, he discovered that I was dossing down in the boxroom, and he wanted me to work for him, if you know what I mean.'

'I'm not so naïve that I don't know what happens in a brothel, although Gene probably supposes that I am innocent in such matters. I'm a woman of the world, or at least I'm not entirely ignorant of what happens outside my own door.' Cecilia sat back, sipping her drink. 'Tell me what happened.'

It was a relief to talk freely and Rose did not spare the details of the filthy conditions in which the girls lived, or the violence that Regan used to control them. Cecilia appeared to be more saddened than shocked and she shook her head.

'If only there was something that could be done to save women from being exploited in such a way. This man Regan ought to be locked up in prison and they should throw away the key.'

'I agree,' Rose said earnestly. 'But I'm afraid that society would have to change its ideas, too.'

'Whatever do you mean, Rose?'

'I travelled from Australia in the company of two missionaries, Mr and Mrs Parker. Adele Parker is a kind and lovely person, but she talked about "fallen women" as if they were a different species. From what I saw in Black Raven Court, the girls there had little option other than to sell the only thing they have – themselves. It's poverty that drives them to that way of life, and men like Regan who take advantage of their misfortune.'

'I'm afraid there is a lot of prejudice among good, honest people, and it will take years or even decades to bring about a change in public opinion.'

'One day, when I've had more experience, I'll write an article about their plight,' Rose said with feeling. 'Cora and Flossie helped me when I was lost and alone with no one to turn to. That isn't the act of bad women, and I was sorry to say goodbye to them.'

'I understand, although I've never had direct dealing with ladies of the night.' Cecilia looked up as the door opened and Eugene strolled into the room. 'We were just talking about Rose's friends in Black Raven Court. She wants to write a piece about them for your paper.'

Eugene poured himself a drink. 'That would make Radley sit up and take notice, but we need to wait for the right time. At the moment I'm trying to persuade him to send me to Egypt to cover the aftermath of the war. The bombardment might be over, but it's a sure bet that there will be trouble later on.'

'No! Are you really going to Egypt?' Rose almost spilled her drink as she placed the glass on a nearby table. 'How exciting.'

'Come on, Gene,' Cecilia said, chuckling. 'You just want a holiday, admit it. You could stay in Alexandria with Mama and Papa and attend the balls and parties that I'm sure still continue even now, as they seem to do when the army are involved. I believe, if the history books are correct, that there was a ball on the eve of Waterloo.'

'I wasn't very interested in history at school.' Eugene went to sit by the fire, taking the decanter and a glass with him. 'Anyway, the last thing I want is to squire the plain daughters of generals and naval captains at stuffy soirées.'

'So you really want to go to a place ravaged by

war?' Rose stared at him open-mouthed. 'Won't it be terribly dangerous?'

'Maybe, but that's what makes it so attractive. I wanted to be an explorer when I was a boy, but Papa wanted me to join the army or the Civil Service. I was at a complete loose end when I left Cambridge and then Arthur offered me a job on the paper. I don't think Papa has quite forgiven me for going into journalism.'

'Poor Gene,' Cecilia said drily. 'You'll have us both weeping into our hankies in a minute.' She turned to Rose with a mischievous smile. 'My brother is all talk. He truly believes that the pen is mightier than the sword, and much safer.'

'Thank you, Cissie. I'll prove you wrong one day.' Eugene sipped his drink, eyeing Rose thoughtfully. 'Your fiancé is in Egypt, so I might well run into him. If you want to give me a message, I'll pass it on.'

'Do you really think you'll see Max?' Rose asked eagerly.

'Who knows? But it's possible, I suppose.'

'Don't give her false hope, Gene,' Cecilia said sharply. 'That's unkind.'

Rose jumped to her feet. 'You could take me with you, Guvnor. I don't want to stay in the office without you, and Nicholls would make my life impossible.'

'That's ridiculous.' Cecilia rose to her feet. 'That

was the dinner gong. Let's put a stop to this conversation before it becomes even more outrageous. Whoever heard of a woman reporter, let alone one travelling abroad to report on a conflict?'

'You're forgetting that Mama is in Egypt, supporting our father in everything he does, and Miss Nightingale went to the Crimea with her nurses . . .'

Cecilia held up her hand. 'Stop now, Gene. Don't fill Rose's head with such nonsense. We have to find her somewhere safe to live and a regular source of income that does not involve guns and bloodshed.'

'No, really, Cissie.' Rose hurried after her as Cecilia left the room. 'The thought of travelling to Egypt doesn't frighten me. When I marry Max I'll follow the drum, or whatever they call it.'

Cecilia turned to give her brother a black look. 'See what you've started, Gene. This is all your fault.'

'It always is,' Eugene said, chuckling. 'Who knows? Rose might make an excellent war correspondent. At the very least her presence would cheer the men up.'

'Idiot.' Cecilia tossed her head and continued downstairs to the dining room in affronted silence.

That evening, after a delicious meal and two glasses of wine, Rose went to her room. A fire burned brightly in the grate and the chintzy curtains had been drawn to shut out the cold night. The coverlet had been turned back and the pillows plumped up so that the brass bed seemed to beckon to her with the promise of her first good night's sleep since she had left the ship. Her feet sank into the soft pile of the blue and pink carpet and the highly polished mahogany furniture gleamed in the firelight. She sat for a while in a chintz-covered chair, warming her feet on the brass fender. Wild imaginings of travelling to Egypt with Eugene made her dizzy with excitement, but the voice of common sense told her that it was just a dream and unlikely to happen. But if Eugene were to go abroad, it would leave her alone in a man's world, where the inevitable outcome would leave her jobless as well as homeless.

The euphoria created by excellent wine and good food evaporated as the events of the past few days crowded in on her, and she dragged herself away from the comforting warmth of the fire. A nightgown in fine lawn, trimmed with broderie anglaise, had been laid out on the bed, and she marvelled at Cissie's thoughtfulness. A quick look in the clothes press revealed that the garments that had been given to her were neatly folded, waiting for her to take her pick next day, and there was warm water in the jug on the washstand. To be made so welcome by relative strangers brought tears to her eyes, and she knew she could never repay such kindness, but she also knew that she must not get used to living like this. Tomorrow she would meet Maria after a gap of nine years, and she hoped that she would be able to give her some information about the tenants of the Captain's House. Eugene, under the influence of several glasses of claret and an excellent dinner, had given Rose permission to take the time off next day, and the prospect of meeting Max's half-sister again after so many years was daunting and yet exciting.

Rose undressed and washed, using the expensive cake of scented soap, before drying herself on a fluffy cotton towel. The nightgown was cool to the touch but the delicate material warmed to her body in an almost sensual way as she climbed into bed and, having snuffed out the candle, she lay down on the soft feather mattress. The flickering firelight sent shadows dancing on the ceiling and she closed her eyes, allowing herself to relax and slide effortlessly into a deep sleep.

After an undisturbed night in a comfortable bed Rose awakened next morning, feeling ready for anything the day might bring. She raised herself on her elbow, realising that she had slept through the maid clearing the ashes from the grate, and a fire had been lit. The curtains were pulled back to allow a pale, watery sun to filter into the room and a cup of hot chocolate was ready to hand. The unlooked-for luxury of being waited on was delightful, but even as Rose sat back and sipped the sweet drink she kept telling herself that it would not last. She would have to face the real world sooner or later, and it was with this in mind that she joined Cecilia in the dining room for breakfast.

'Is Eugene still in bed?' Rose asked as she spooned buttered eggs onto a plate.

'Heavens, no. He left half an hour ago for the office. I think he's planning his campaign to persuade Arthur that a trip to Egypt is an absolute necessity.'

'Do you think he'll agree?' Rose snared a piece of crisp bacon on a fork and added it to her plate before taking her place at the table.

Cecilia filled a cup with coffee and passed it to her. 'Gene usually manages to get his own way in the end.'

'You don't mind him risking his life like that?'

'What I think doesn't matter as far as my brother is concerned. Gene does what he wants. Anyway, it seems that the fighting is over.' Cecilia reached for a slice of toast. 'Don't forget we're visiting Maria Barnaby later this morning.'

'I haven't forgotten,' Rose said earnestly. 'She's Max's half-sister and I don't suppose she'll know me now, but I remember her. She was a really beautiful bride and she had lovely blue eyes and dark hair.'

Cecilia slapped butter on the toast, adding a spoonful of marmalade. 'She's a nice person, and I'm sure she'll help you, if she can.'

'Where does she live?'

'Great Hermitage Street. It's not a particularly good area, but her brother-in-law gave her the house as a wedding present. I don't suppose her husband earns a great deal as a sea captain, at least nothing like the fortune that Phineas Colville has made for himself.'

'I hope she remembers me,' Rose said earnestly. 'I really need her help.'

Chapter Eight

The domestic buildings in Great Hermitage Street were dwarfed by tall warehouses, linked by bridges high above ground level to those on the far side of the road. Maria's four-storey house was sandwiched between a disreputable-looking pub and a ship's chandler, and yet more pubs were interspersed with small shops selling anything from second-hand furniture to exotic seashells, and curios brought back from far-off lands by generations of mariners.

Rose stood on the pavement, gazing up and down the cobbled street with the vague stirrings of childhood memories.

Cecilia brushed past her to hammer on the door. 'This is not the sort of place I would like to live,' she said in a low voice. 'I don't know how Maria can bear it here when she was brought up in Pier House, which is a palace compared to this.'

Rose was trying to think of something suitable to say when the door opened and a large woman with a florid complexion stood there, glaring at them. 'Yes?'

'Mrs Barnaby is expecting me,' Cecilia said coldly.

'What's yer name?' A wart on the side of the woman's nose wobbled when she spoke.

'I'm Miss Sheldon, as you very well know, Edna. I've been coming here once a week for the last six months at least.'

'Only doing me job, miss. Come in, and close the door. I don't trust the sorts that wander the streets round here.' Edna turned her back on them and waddled off, returning moments later to lead them along a dark, narrow passage, past a steep staircase and on until she thrust a door open at the rear of the house.

Rose stood in the doorway, taking in the details of the room that was crowded with old-fashioned furniture and a horsehair sofa that sagged in the middle. The heavy curtains seemed to absorb what little daylight managed to filter through the small windowpanes, but the flickering flames of a coal fire and a single candle set on the middle of a table revealed a young woman seated in a chair by the hearth with an overflowing workbasket on the floor at her feet.

'They're here, missis.' Edna stood, arms akimbo, as if ready to throw them out at a word from her mistress.

'Maria, how are you, my dear?' Cecilia sailed past Edna, giving her a withering glance. 'I've brought an old friend to see you.'

'I suppose you'll be wanting tea or some such thing,' Edna said gruffly.

Maria Barnaby rose from her chair, abandoning the small garment she was mending. 'I'll ring if we need anything, Edna. Tell Cook there'll be one more for luncheon.'

'My sister won't be best pleased,' Edna muttered as she backed out of the room. 'Jessie hates people what take liberties.' She slammed the door.

'I'm sorry to come uninvited,' Rose said hastily. 'Perhaps I ought to leave.'

'Don't take any notice of Edna. She's an old harpy.' Cecilia turned to Maria with a disarming smile. 'I knew you wouldn't mind if I brought Rose with me. You might remember her.'

Maria put her head on one side, eyeing Rose thoughtfully. 'I'm afraid I don't recognise you,' she said slowly. 'But I did once know a little girl with copper hair and green eyes.'

'That was me.' Rose studied Maria's face, comparing the thin, pale-faced woman with the beautiful bride she had been all those years ago. 'Sadie and Laurence took me in when my pa went back to sea. I was at your wedding, but I've grown a lot since then.'

Maria rushed forward to give her a hug. 'Rose Munday, of course I remember you. What brings you back to London? I thought you migrated to Australia with Sadie and Laurence.'

'It's a long story.' Meeting Max's half-sister again after so many years made Rose inexplicably tongue-tied.

'Rose has come all the way from Australia to meet her fiancé, only to find that he's been sent abroad with his regiment.' Cecilia shrugged off her fur-trimmed mantle, laying it on a chair together with her gloves and reticule.

'Oh, dear. How awful for you, Rose. Who is the lucky young man? Might I know him?'

Cecilia lowered herself carefully onto the well-worn sofa. 'Tell her, Rose.'

'It's your brother Max,' Rose said slowly. She refrained from using the term 'half-brother', even though it was more accurate. The story of the brief affair between Grace Colville and Jack Manning, which had resulted in Maria's illegitimate birth, was well known in the family, but still a raw subject for Jack's widow, Esther, and was rarely mentioned.

'Max must be a handsome young man,' Maria said, smiling. 'I wish I'd known him better.'

'Max, Jimmy and I were at school together in Bendigo, and then Max returned to England to attend Sandhurst. When he came home after a couple of years' absence we met again and fell in love. It was as simple as that.'

'I'm a little confused.' Maria shot a questioning glance in Cecilia's direction. 'What is the problem? I never had the chance to get to know the boys properly, but I remember Max as being a charming young fellow, and James also.'

'The family objected,' Cecilia said, nodding. 'You know how that feels, Maria.'

Maria returned to her chair and sat down with a sigh. 'I thought the old scandal would be forgotten after Jack died, but it's lived on to haunt me. Now it seems that you and Max are suffering because of it, Rose.'

'I don't think it had anything to do with you or your mother,' Rose said hastily. 'Mrs Dorincourt, Max's mother, doesn't think I'm good enough to marry her son. She made that perfectly clear.'

'I can't see why Esther would take against you, Rose,' Maria said, frowning. 'She came from a very humble background, even if she has married into the aristocracy, but I faced much the same problem when I fell in love with Theo.'

'But you married him anyway, and it's worked out well for you.' Rose gazed at her hopefully, waiting for confirmation.

'We've been very happy, even allowing for Theo's long absences. My grandmother was very much against our marriage and I was determined to prove her wrong, but being married to a seafarer isn't easy.'

Cecilia had been listening quietly, but she was suddenly alert. 'Is the old lady still as intransigent?'

'Grandmama has never forgiven me for being born, let alone marrying a man she considers to be unworthy, which is ridiculous. I visit her once a week, but we have very little to say to each other.'

'I'm surprised that she is still alive.' Cecilia raised her delicate eyebrows. 'She must be getting on in years, Maria.'

'She would never admit her age, but she's quite infirm now and confined to her bed, which hasn't improved her temper. She has servants to wait on her, but she is very much alone.'

'That's hardly surprising, considering the way Clarissa Colville has treated you and your mother,' Cecilia said, pursing her lips. She sat back on the sofa, and the springs creaked ominously. 'Let's not talk about her any more. You have two delightful children, Maria. Where are the little ones now?'

'They're in the nursery with their nanny.' Maria's sad expression melted into a tender smile. 'She'll bring them down after we've had luncheon and you can meet them, Rose. Do you like children?'

'Yes, indeed I do. I used to help in the schoolroom, and I loved it.'

Cecilia gave her a calculating glance. 'You didn't tell me that, Rose. Perhaps you could earn your living as a teacher, or a nursemaid.'

'I'm getting confused again,' Maria said, frowning. 'You said that you are engaged to Max, so why would you need to work, Rose?'

'That's the nub of the matter, Maria.' An impatient note crept into Cecilia's voice. 'Max's regiment was sent to Egypt, and he doesn't seem to have made provision for Rose, which is why I brought her here today.'

'Max told me that should he be prevented from meeting me, for any reason, I was to go to the Captain's House and wait there for him,' Rose said eagerly. 'But I found it occupied by some really horrible men. They didn't seem to me to be the sort of tenants that anyone would want.'

Maria reached out to put more coal on the fire. 'I believe the house was rented out to a perfectly respectable family who fell on hard times and had to move out. It seems likely that the men are squatters and should be removed.'

'Do you think I would be allowed to stay there?' Rose asked eagerly.

'Caroline owns the house and I know she adores her brothers. I'm certain she would be happy to have you as a tenant.' Maria frowned thoughtfully. 'But we would need to find out if those people are there illegally, and I have no influence whatsoever in my cousin's business. If Phineas were here it would be different.'

'He must have left someone in charge of the day-to-day matters.' Cecilia shifted her position on the sofa, and once again the springs protested with loud pings. 'You are part of the family, Maria. Who is the head of the company when Phineas is absent?'

'I believe our grandmother is still a major share-holder, although she would have nothing to do with the actual running of Colville Shipping.'

'Do you think she would help?' Rose asked anxiously.

'I very much doubt it.' Maria gazed into the fire, her whole body tense. 'I spent my early years a virtual prisoner in that beautiful ice palace. It holds only unhappy memories for me, but Max is my brother and if he loves you that's good enough for me, Rose. I'll visit Pier House, but I can't promise anything.'

'I can't thank you enough. Maybe I could come with you so that she can see I'm not a bad person and that I would be a suitable tenant.'

'I'd be grateful for moral support, but don't mention Max. Grandmama won't allow the name Manning to be mentioned in her presence.' Maria tugged at a bell pull. 'I'm sure you both must be hungry. Cook must have luncheon prepared by now, although to be honest she's not very good, but she's

Edna's sister and I daren't sack her or Edna would go too.'

'I wouldn't stand for that.' Cecilia tossed her head, causing her perky little hat to slip over one eye and she adjusted it hastily. 'You ought to be firmer with your servants, Maria. Sack the pair of them, I say.'

'I took them on to save them from the sort of lives they were forced to endure,' Maria said sadly. 'If I turn them out they would have little option but to return to their former ways, and I would never forgive myself.'

'It was a good thing to do.' Rose could see that Cecilia's forthright tone was upsetting Maria. 'I arrived in London to find myself lost in a peasouper. Max wasn't there to meet me and if Cora hadn't taken me in I don't know what would have happened to me. She is one of the unfortunates you mention, but she's a good person.'

'If I were to sell myself I would make sure I only slept with very wealthy men, who would set me up in style,' said Cecilia with a wry smile.

Rose stared at her open-mouthed. 'You wouldn't?'

'Of course not, silly. But I might consider taking a lover at some time in the future, should the man I marry turn out to be an utter bore.'

'You should see your face, Rose.' Maria burst out laughing. 'Don't believe a word Cecilia says. She loves to shock.'

The door opened before Rose had a chance to

reply and Edna poked her head into the room. 'Grub's up, ladies. Come and get it.' She withdrew quickly.

Maria merely rolled her eyes and sighed. 'Don't say anything, Cissie. Believe me, I've tried to teach her the basics, but Edna insists on doing things her way, and she is better than a guard dog when it comes to drunken sailors knocking on the door.' She jumped to her feet. 'Come on, I'm hungry. I just hope the food is edible, and when we've eaten I'll send for Nanny and my babies. You'll love them, Rose. They are so adorable. I can even bear the loneliness of being separated from Theo when I have them with me.' She opened the door and led them into the next room where a small table was laid with what Rose assumed had once been a white cloth, but it was now grey and covered in stains.

Maria took her place at the head of the table and rang a small brass bell. 'When I lived with my grandmother we were summoned to dine by a gong. It rang once five minutes before the meal and that meant we had to be seated at the table in readiness for her arrival. Grandmama disliked unpunctuality, especially for meals.'

'It sounds like boarding school to me.' Cecilia unfolded her napkin, gazing at it with distaste as she laid it on her lap. 'Don't take this the wrong way, Maria, but your laundress isn't doing a very good job.'

'I know. She's another of the Spriggs sisters, although she's married with ten children and she takes in washing to make ends meet. I can't say anything for fear of upsetting Edna and Jessie. They're a very close family, and I admire them for that.'

Rose tried to ignore the fragment of squashed cabbage she found in the middle of her napkin. 'Is the nanny also one of the sisters?'

'Izzie is only thirteen – she's the youngest of the Spriggs sisters. She's not very bright, but she's very loyal.'

'So was my King Charles Spaniel,' Cecilia muttered. 'But I wouldn't trust him to look after children.'

A thud on the door echoed round the room as it flew open and Edna marched in carrying a tureen, which she slapped down in front of Maria. 'Cabbage soup. Ignore the burned bits, Jessie says. She was at the door chatting to the butcher's boy when the bottom of the pan caught.' She slammed out of the room.

The meal, as Maria had predicted, was barely edible and highly indigestible. The soup was awful and the roast lamb so overcooked that it was burned to a crisp, but the potatoes were raw in the middle, and the cabbage had been boiled until it was a greenish-brown mush. The pastry covering the apple pie was rock hard and the apples extremely sour, while the custard was so thick that it could have been cut with a knife. Maria was apologetic, but Cecilia laughed it off and Rose ate it anyway. If she held her breath while swallowing, the food did not taste too bad.

Edna bumbled in to clear the table, which was a signal for Maria to take her guests back to the parlour, and Izzie brought Maria's children, Polly aged five and Teddy aged two, to meet them. Cecilia and Maria chatted amicably while Rose went down on her knees and played with the little ones, but when the clock on the mantelshelf struck three, Cecilia rose to her feet and announced that it was time to leave. Maria rang the bell for Izzie, and Rose gave the children one last hug with a promise to return soon. Izzie burst into the room without knocking and picked up Teddy. She seized Polly by the hand and left the room with her young charges protesting loudly.

Maria followed Cecilia and Rose to the front door. 'I will go and see Grandmama, but I really would like you to come with me, Rose.'

'Of course I will. Just tell me when and at what time.'

'Would tomorrow morning suit you?'

Rose frowned. 'I'll have to ask the guvnor's permission, especially since he gave me time off to visit you today.'

'I'm sure Gene will allow it,' Cecilia said firmly. 'In fact I'll insist upon it, even if I have to go to the top and speak to Cousin Arthur. What's the use of being related to the editor if you can't pull rank occasionally?' She stepped onto the pavement and waved at a passing cab. 'Come on, Rose. Don't dawdle.'

Pier House overlooked the entrance to Wapping Basin with an uninterrupted view of the upper pool of the River Thames. Set in wooded parkland, it might have been in the country if it weren't for the never-ending cacophony of sound from the steam whistles of the river traffic, and the general hubbub of the docks. Rose was impressed none the less, but she was unaccountably nervous as she followed Maria into the vast marble-tiled entrance hall. The house was beautiful, but the atmosphere in the echoing hall made the hairs stand up on the back of Rose's neck, and the grim-faced maidservant made her feel even more uncomfortable.

'How is my grandmother today, Gilroy?' Mary asked pleasantly.

'She might see you or she might not.' Gilroy eyed Rose suspiciously. 'Who's this?'

'I don't think that's any of your business,' Maria said firmly. 'And there's no need to announce me. I know the way well enough.'

'Hold on. You can't go barging in on madam.' Gilroy barred the way but Maria sidestepped her with a skilful move.

'You may think you run this household, Gilroy, but you're very much mistaken, and if I report your behaviour to Mr Colville you'll suffer the consequences.' Maria walked off, head held high.

Rose ignored the black looks she was receiving from Gilroy and she hurried after Maria.

'You put her in her place,' she said when she finally caught up with her. 'Is she always like that?'

'Gilroy used to bully me when I lived here. She's managed to worm her way into my grandmother's confidence, but I don't like her and I certainly don't trust her.' Maria walked on until she came to a door at the far end of the passage. 'I'll introduce you to Grandmama, although she might not acknowledge you. I'm afraid her mind wanders.'

'I understand.' Rose followed her into what must once have been an elegant drawing room, but was now a sickroom shrouded in semi-darkness. Rose could just make out a figure propped up on pillows in the four-poster bed, and as she drew nearer she was shocked to see an old woman whose skin was drawn so tightly across her bones that she looked like a living skeleton. A few wisps of white hair hung down from her lace nightcap and her eyes were closed.

'Grandmama, it's me, Maria.'

The heavy, blue-veined eyelids flew open and Rose found herself being scrutinised by pale watery eyes, and a claw-like finger pointed at her. 'Who's that?'

Maria turned to Rose with a hint of a smile. 'She's alert enough when it suits her.'

'I heard that. I'm not deaf. What have you come to steal from me this time, bastard child?'

'I've never taken anything from you, Grandmama,' Maria protested.

'Things go missing whenever you've been in this house. Gilroy tells me so.'

'Then Gilroy is the culprit, not me. I've come to see how you are.'

'No, you haven't. You hate me as much as I hate you. You're an embarrassment, you and your little bastard children.'

Rose laid her hand on Maria's arm. 'You don't have to put up with this. I'm sorry I asked you to speak for me.'

'What did she say?' Mrs Colville demanded angrily. 'Speak up, if you've got something to say, girl.'

Rose cleared her throat nervously. 'I'm sorry you're not well, ma'am.'

'No, you aren't. You don't know me and I don't know you, nor do I want to. Where's Maria? Tell her to take you both back to that rat's nest she inhabits with a common sailor.'

'I'm Maria, Grandmama.'

'Send Gilroy to me. I want Gilroy. I need my medicine.'

'All right, I'll fetch her now. Don't upset yourself,

Grandmama.' Maria hustled Rose from the room and the old lady's screeches followed them as they retreated to find Gilroy waiting for them.

'What did I tell you?' She made a move towards the door. 'I'm the only person who knows what she needs.'

'Wait a minute.' Maria stared at the brown glass bottle that Gilroy had clutched in her hand. 'What medicine are you giving her? She's much worse today than she was last week.'

'She's having what the doctor ordered, and that is peace and quiet without being bothered by the likes of you.' Gilroy disappeared into the drawing room, slamming the door in their faces.

'Are you all right, Maria?' Rose was alarmed by Maria's sudden pallor. 'Do you feel faint?'

Maria shook her head. 'No, I'm fine, thank you. I'm just anxious and I don't know what to think. I don't trust Gilroy, and I'm afraid she might be giving my grandmother too much laudanum or some other drug in order to keep her quiet.'

'Surely she wouldn't harm Mrs Colville. After all, if your grandmother dies Gilroy will lose her job.'

'I can't prove anything but I've noticed that small objects, quite valuable ones, are missing, and I think Gilroy is stealing things. Maybe she's selling them and putting the money aside because she knows that my grandmother cannot last for many more years.'

'Then you must tell someone. Your cousin Phineas should know.'

'But he and Caroline aren't expected back for some time. It might be too late by then.'

'Have you spoken to Mrs Colville's doctor?'

'No, but perhaps I should.'

'Let's go. We can't do anything here at this moment, but if it were my grandmother, even if she was a hard-hearted old woman, I wouldn't want to see her taken advantage of and cheated out of her belongings, let alone watch her being destroyed by drugs.'

'You're right. I'll go and see Dr Tucker right away.' Maria shot Rose a sideways glance. 'I'm sorry, I'd almost forgotten your predicament but, as you can see, my grandmother isn't in a fit state to do anything about the tenancy of the Captain's House.'

'Don't give it a thought. I'll manage somehow, and if I can do anything to help Mrs Colville I will because, whether I like her or not, she's Max's grandmother, and I know he'd want me to assist you in any way I can.'

Maria leaned over to brush Rose's cheek with a whisper of a kiss. 'Thank you, Rose. My brother is a lucky man, and now I don't feel so alone.'

Rose should have returned to Tavistock Square when she left Maria's house, but she had a mission in mind and she took a cab to the *London Leader*

146

office in Fleet Street instead. The fare took the last of her money but she was more concerned for Maria and her children than she was for herself, and she burst into reception, greeting the clerk with a cheery smile.

'Is Mr Sheldon in the office, Perks?'

'Yes, miss. At least, I haven't seen him leave.'

'Thank you.' Rose hurried up the stairs and raced through the main office, ignoring Nicholls' caustic remarks, as she flung open the door to Eugene's office.

'Where's the fire, Munday?' He stopped to stare at her with his overcoat draped over his arm. 'I thought you had the morning off to sort out your lodgings.'

'I did, but it didn't work out that way. I think I'm on to a great story, Guvnor, but I need your permission to follow it through.'

'It would have to be good, because you're supposed to sit behind that desk over there,' Eugene pointed to the typewriter, 'and you tap away on that machine, typing out letters and articles for me.'

'I know that, and I'm truly grateful for the job, but if I'm right, this is a story that will make the front page. Will you at least hear me out? Please, Guvnor.' She clasped her hands, meeting his cynical look with a tremulous smile. 'This means a lot to me and maybe life and death to someone who is old and helpless.'

Chapter Nine

Eugene listened, but it was clear that his mind was on other things. He tapped his toe and drummed his fingers on the desk while Rose told him, as briefly as possible, what had happened at Pier House.

'So you see,' she concluded breathlessly, 'I think Gilroy is stealing the old lady's valuables and slowly killing her off with large doses of laudanum, or whatever she had in that bottle.'

'From what I've heard of the redoubtable Clarissa Colville, it would take more than a few drops of laudanum to finish her off, and you are basing all this on pure supposition, Munday. If we printed a story like that we would face a libel suit and extortionate costs.'

'But Maria knows Gilroy of old, and she's a bad lot.'

'Maybe, but you have absolutely no proof of ill intent. As to objects going missing, it could be that Mrs Colville has put them away for some reason best known to herself. She's old, Munday, and it sounds as if her mind is wandering.' Eugene shrugged on his coat. 'Be a good chap and type those letters for me. I'm off to luncheon with a general and a senior government official.'

'Are you serious about going to Egypt, Guvnor?'

'I am, and I intend to make Cousin Arthur see the wisdom of getting the news of the unrest in that country direct from a trusted correspondent.'

'You might be risking your life.'

'My father always said I was a lost cause. I didn't shine academically and he didn't want me to take this job in the first place. Maybe I'll have a chance to prove my worth in Egypt.' Eugene plucked his hat from the stand and placed it on his head at a rakish angle.

'I've been reading some of your articles – you're really talented, Guvnor.'

Eugene flicked her a smile. 'You're just saying that to put me in a good mood, but it won't make me change my mind. The story about pilfering and poisoning is out, Munday. Do you hear me?'

'Yes, Guvnor.' Rose shed her outer garments and hung them up before taking her seat at the desk. She looked up to find Eugene watching her with an amused smile. 'You think I'm funny, don't you?'

He shook his head. 'On the contrary, I think you're sweet and charming, but very naïve. Now, I'm off, but I expect that work to be done by the time I return.'

'It will be. I'm getting used to this typing machine.'

'Excellent.' Eugene opened the door. 'You know you're welcome to stay with Cissie and me until you find something better. My sister has taken a liking to you, so you're honoured; she's very particular when it comes to choosing her friends.' He breezed out of the office, humming a tune that Rose recognised as a song from *Patience*, even though he had appeared to sleep through the first half of the performance.

She settled down to work, but the sickroom in Pier House and the ramblings of Clarissa Colville were never far from her mind. She felt deeply for Maria, who had obviously suffered greatly at the hands of the old lady. And then there was Mrs Colville's cunning maid. If Sadie were here she would know how to handle Gilroy. Rose had seen Sadie deal with drunken miners and belligerent ex-convicts with no other weapon than a sharp tongue. Sadie would see Gilroy for what she was: a conniving bully and a thief. The problem of squatters in the Captain's House paled into insignificance when compared to what was being done to a helpless old woman, even if she was a harridan. Rose was angry and however hard she tried, she could not put that cold, dark room and its frail occupant from her mind.

She spent what was left of the afternoon at her desk and stayed later than normal to finish off the letters that Eugene had scrawled in his appalling handwriting. She had not quite given up hope that he might change his mind, as a successful meeting, ending in a few drinks to celebrate the outcome, would mean that he would be in good spirits when he returned. The sound of the clerks in the outer office chattering and moving about signalled that it was time to pack up for the night, and Rose placed the finished letters on Eugene's desk. It was only when she was dressed in her outdoor clothes that she realised she had spent the last of her money on the cab ride, and she would have to go on foot to Tavistock Square.

It was dark when she left the building and the pavements were wet, but there was nothing for it other than to set off, walking as briskly as possible in order to keep warm.

Cecilia was seated by the fire in the drawing room and she looked up as Rose entered, closing the book she had been reading and placing it on a drum table at the side of her chair.

'Good heavens, what happened to you, Rose? You look as though you've been wading through puddles.'

'I have.' Rose sat down opposite her, resting her

booted feet on the brass fender, and almost immediately steam began to rise from her damp skirts
and petticoats. 'I didn't have any money for a cab
fare.'

'Where's my brother? He should have seen you
safely home.'

'I don't know,' Rose said truthfully. 'He had an
important meeting and he didn't return to the office.'

'I'll make sure he gives you an advance on your
wages. You ought not to be wandering about on
your own after dark, Rose.' Cecilia eyed her curiously. 'How did you get on with Mrs Colville? She
has quite a reputation, and from what Maria has
told me, the stories about the old lady are completely
true.'

'It would seem so, but she's bedridden and quite
poorly. There was no point in asking her for help.'

'So going to Pier House was a waste of time?'

Rose was tempted to take Cecilia into her confidence, but Eugene had made his opinion clear and
she was not to pursue the story. 'Yes, I suppose it
was. I don't know what I'll do now.'

'You're welcome to stay here for as long as you
like.' Cecilia reached up to give the embroidered bell
pull a tug. 'You look as though you could do with
some sustenance before dinner. Would you like a
cup of tea or something stronger?'

'Tea would be lovely, and thank you for saying I
could stay, but it doesn't seem right to burden you

with my presence when I should be living in the Captain's House. I'm certain those men have no right to be there, and I really should do something about it.'

'I've been thinking.' Cecilia eyed her thoughtfully. 'I might just be able to help you. I have a wide circle of friends, most of whom are on one committee or another, and Emily's husband is high up in the Metropolitan Police. If those men are known criminals it might be possible to have them evicted and then you could move in, although you really can stay here for as long as you like.'

'I'm very happy living here with you, Cissie, and I'm truly grateful for everything you've done for me, but I mustn't get used to this way of life. I'll have to be prepared for anything when I marry into the army.'

'You're a plucky girl, and I admire you for your attitude, but that sort of life wouldn't be for me.' Cecilia turned her head as the door opened and a young parlourmaid burst into the room.

'You rang, miss?

'Knock next time, Bertha.'

'Yes, miss.'

'Bring a tray of tea and biscuits for Miss Rose, and tell Cook there'll be two for dinner tonight, maybe three if my brother decides to grace us with his presence.'

Bertha nodded and backed out of the room, almost

knocking over a small occasional table in her haste.

'She's new,' Cecilia said, sighing. 'It's getting quite hard to find good servants these days. The lure of working in the West End department stores has taken away some of the brightest young girls, and they simply don't want to go into service as they used to in my parents' day.' Cecilia rose from her chair and went to the table where the decanters were set out amid a selection of cut-crystal glasses. She helped herself to a measure of sherry and returned to her seat. 'What was I saying?'

'You said it was hard to find good servants.'

'Yes, but before that we were talking about the house on the wharf. As it happens I'll probably see my friend Emily tomorrow at a meeting of the charity we both support. I'll mention your problem to her and we'll see what happens.'

'I might have to wait for months until Max returns, or even longer, so I have to be practical.'

'Indeed you do, and in the meantime I think you ought to change out of those damp clothes. It's usual to dress for dinner, even if it is just the two of us. We have to keep up our standards, as you will discover if you marry Max, and these will apply even if you find yourself in darkest Africa or the plains of India.'

Rose sighed. 'Would it be all right if I change my mind and have a glass of sherry instead of tea?'

'Yes, of course. Anyway, I hate drinking alone and

Bertha can take the tray back to the kitchen, that's if she even gets it this far without an accident. Help yourself, Rose, and we'll raise a glass to success in our campaign to free the Captain's House from squatters.'

Rose stood up and was pouring herself a drink when the door opened and Eugene walked into the room.

'You've started without me, ladies. I don't call that fair.' He moved to Rose's side and selected another decanter. 'I can see I have some catching up to do.' He poured himself a generous tot of whisky.

'Was your meeting successful, Guvnor?' Rose asked hopefully. If Eugene was going to Egypt she might yet persuade him to take her with him. It was a slim chance, but worth pursuing if it meant that she would be reunited with Max.

'I don't know yet.' Eugene sprawled in a chair facing them. 'I gave it my best shot and now it's up to the powers that be to grant me permission to work alongside the army, and then all I have to do is to persuade Arthur to let me go.'

'Maybe you should have done that first, you noodle.' Cecilia raised her glass to him. 'Anyway, good luck, Gene. I can't say that I want you to risk your life in the desert, but I know you'll go whatever I say.'

Eugene acknowledged the toast with a wry grin. 'I'm not sure whether that's a compliment or an insult, Cissie.' He shot a sideways glance at Rose. 'And if I do go to Egypt, I don't want you running around London, investigating imaginary crimes.'

'Then perhaps you should take me with you, Guvnor.' The sherry had warmed Rose's chilled bones and made her bold.

'What's this?' Cecilia was suddenly alert. 'What is he saying, Rose? What have you been up to?'

'I've done nothing wrong. I spent the afternoon trying to get to grips with that infernal machine.' Rose downed the remains of her drink. 'I think I'd better go to my room and change for dinner.' She jumped to her feet and was about to leave the room when Cecilia called her back.

'Not so fast, Rose. I think you owe me an explanation.'

'Let her go, Cissie,' Eugene said lazily. 'Rose is too intelligent to allow her imagination to run away with her.' He swallowed his drink in a single gulp and raised himself from the chair. 'I suppose I'd better change for dinner, too. Although why we have to be so formal is beyond me.' He followed Rose from the room, catching her up at the foot of the stairs. 'I meant what I said, Munday. Even if there is mischief afoot in Pier House, I don't want you to get mixed up in it. If I'm away you'll find it hard enough to keep your job without getting on the wrong side of my cousin. Arthur is a good editor, but he doesn't approve of women in the workplace.'

'All the more reason for you to take me with you, Guvnor.'

He gave her a slightly tipsy, lop-sided smile. 'You never give up, do you, Munday?'

'No, Guvnor. I don't.'

After two weeks waiting for Arthur to weigh up the situation and make a decision, Eugene was growing fidgety, and his changeable mood affected both Rose and Cecilia. At work conversations between him and his cousin were carried out in loud voices, audible through closed doors, and, although the words themselves were muffled, it was obvious that they were arguing fiercely. Rose was torn between hoping that Eugene would win and get his wish to report the political situation in Egypt, and the fear of what might happen to her if he did go abroad. It was obvious that Nicholls was waiting for an opportunity to have her dismissed, and the clerks in the main office seemed to agree with him. Try as she might to do her job well, she found herself subject to strong criticism and stern reprimands for the most minor mistakes. The men in the print room were easier to get on with, although she had to take some cheek from the apprentices, but she was used to dealing with boys and she knew how to respond to their teasing. Scully was on her side, but it seemed that he had to be careful not to show it in front of the other men.

Then there was the question of finding more permanent accommodation. Cecilia's friend had promised to make enquiries about the tenants of the Captain's House, and Rose waited anxiously for the outcome. And then, to make matters worse, Eugene received the news that he had been waiting for. He had been accepted as an official correspondent even though hostilities in Egypt had ended some time since in victory for Adjutant-General Garnet Wolseley, and the country was now occupied by the British in order to bring stability to the region. Eugene was still keen to go, and, somewhat unwillingly, Arthur Radley had given him permission. It was a bitter blow to Rose, despite the fact that she was pleased for Eugene, but she was keenly aware that her days at the *Leader* were numbered. She had done her best to persuade Eugene to take her with him, but without success, and after a flurry of packing and making travel arrangements, she found herself on the station platform, waving goodbye to her friend and mentor.

As the train chugged off, sending clouds of steam into the cold greyness of a November day, she knew that she would miss Eugene more than she would have thought possible. Standing on the dreary platform in the midst of a bustling crowd of travellers and people who had come to wish them on their way, she had never felt so alone and desperately lonely. There was nothing she could do other than to use the money Eugene had given her to take a cab back to the office, although she was certain of the outcome before she put a foot in the building.

Nicholls shot her a triumphant look as she walked past him and the clerks turned their backs on her, but she could hear them muttering to each other and she knew that they were making fun of her. The reason for this became clear as she entered Eugene's office to find Arthur Radley seated in Eugene's chair, and a quick glance at her desk revealed nothing but a blank space. The typewriting machine was missing.

'I've just seen Mr Sheldon off, sir,' Rose said hastily.

'You were absent without leave, Miss Munday. I've had nothing but complaints about your behaviour and your ability to do your work to the standard required. I'm sorry to say that your services are no longer needed.'

'But Mr Sheldon promised that my job was safe, sir.'

'Mr Sheldon was not in a position to say such a thing, and he will be away for some considerable time, so there is no place for you on my newspaper. You may collect your pay from the desk in reception, Miss Munday. That will be all.'

'What have you done with the typewriting machine?' Rose demanded angrily. 'Mr Sheldon bought that with his own money.'

'And he put it down on expenses, so it belongs to the company. Good day, Miss Munday.'

Rose was left with no option but to retrace her steps through the outer office. She came to a halt in front of Nicholls' desk.

'I suppose you think you've won,' she said in a low voice. 'But you won't find it so amusing when Mr Sheldon returns. I know you were responsible for this, Mr Nicholls, and I don't forget an injustice.' She stormed off without waiting for his response, although the sound of laughter followed her as she raced down the stairs, and, having collected her wages, she left the building. The sensible thing to do would be to take a cab back to Tavistock Square, but Rose was too upset to think logically and for some odd reason she found herself heading in the direction of Wapping. With her head bent she barely noticed the inviting shop windows filled with items to entice even the most pernickety customer to step inside and make a purchase. Not that Rose could afford to waste money on fripperies – she had been doing well, working in a man's world, but it had all come to nothing and she was now unemployed. She would have to find work elsewhere, and that was going to prove difficult for someone without any formal training.

The aroma of baking wafted out through the open door of a bakery, and the fragrance of hot pies and rich fruitcakes mingled with that of freshly baked bread. Rose's stomach rumbled, but she walked on, resisting the temptation to purchase a meat pie from a street seller on the corner of Farringdon Street and Ludgate Hill. She continued, battling against a cold east wind, but she came to a halt at the sight of a barefoot waif, standing in a shop doorway, offering sprigs of dried lavender for a farthing apiece. Rose stopped to take a threepenny bit from her purse, which she handed to the child.

'No, I don't want any lavender, thank you. Buy yourself some food.'

The girl, who could not have been more than eight or nine years old and was painfully thin and pale, tried to speak but her teeth were chattering so much that her words were inaudible. Rose took a silver sixpence from her purse, and pressed it into the little one's cold hand. 'Get yourself something warm to wear.'

'Me d-d-dad will take the m-m-money off m-me.' The blue eyes filled with tears, which ran down the girl's thin cheeks making runnels in the grime.

Rose hesitated. This poor man's child was one of thousands who tried to grub a living in any way they could, but there was something about this little girl that touched Rose's heart. She grabbed her by the hand. 'We'll see about that. Come with me.'

'I weren't doing nothing wrong, miss,' the child sobbed. 'Don't take me to the police station.'

'Don't be afraid. I'm going to get you some decent clothes and a pair of boots.' Rose retraced her steps to the second-hand clothes shop she had noticed a few doors down the street. 'Come inside, we'll sort something out. You don't want catch your death of cold, do you?' Rose lifted the child over the threshold and was appalled to discover how little the girl weighed, and the feel of her stick-thin limbs reminded Rose of a sparrow she had once tried to save after it had fallen from its nest. So long ago – she had been about this child's age then.

The dolly shop had the rank smell of garments well-worn and unwashed, but Rose had put her own problems behind her and she was on a mission to save a young life.

A blowsy woman with a pipe clenched between her teeth emerged from a back room. 'What d'you want, missis?'

'Clothes for this child. Anything would be better than the rags she's wearing.'

The woman reached out a claw-like hand to clutch Rose by the arm. 'You're wasting your time, luv. I know this nipper. Her ma is never sober and whatever you buys her will be back here before nightfall.'

'Surely a mother wouldn't do that to her own flesh and blood?' Rose protested.

'Not her, missis. Sid Piggin, the man this kid calls her pa, will strip her naked and sell her things to pay for a pipe of opium. There's no helping these sorts. Save your money.'

Rose looked down at the child, who was sobbing quietly. 'Is this true?'

'Of course it's true,' the woman snapped. 'D'you think I'd do meself out of a sale? I got six nippers of me own, that's why I'm telling you. Do the kid a favour and drop her off at the workhouse. At least she'll get clothed and fed, and won't be sold later for the pleasure of them what should know better.'

'What's your name?' Rose bent down, so that her face was on a level with the weeping child.

'S-s-sparrow, m-miss.'

'Is that your surname?' Rose shot a questioning look at the pipe-smoking woman, who was regarding her with a squinty smile.

'She don't know what a surname is, luv. I heard the man call her that, so it's probably the only thing she answers to.'

Rose fought back tears of sympathy, and forced herself to be practical. 'Please look out some decent clothes for her, and a damp flannel would help.'

'What are you going to do with the nipper? You ain't going to sell her down the market, are you?'

'Would you care if I did?' Rose took Sparrow's hand in hers and gave it an encouraging squeeze. 'I'm taking this poor child to a place where she'll be looked after and treated like a human being.'

'Not the workhouse then.' The woman stomped off and began rifling through a rack of small garments. 'Have a look at these duds. I keep them for special customers, but it'll cost you.'

'I don't care. She needs warm clothing and I'll

pay.' Rose fingered her reticule, knowing that her wages would not go far, but young Sparrow had touched her heart and she was not going to abandon her now.

Somewhat begrudgingly the shopkeeper provided a damp cloth, and Rose managed to clean the worst of the dirt from Sparrow's face and hands, but a warm bath was what the girl needed most and her lank hair, thick with grease and running with head lice, might prove to be mousy or blonde, it was impossible to tell.

Twenty minutes later, Sparrow was almost unrecognisable in a red woollen frock and thick black stockings, with only a couple of holes that didn't show beneath a red flannel petticoat. Rose helped her into a dark blue serge coat, adding a knitted woollen hat and mittens, and they had found a pair of boots that were almost perfect and fitted reasonably well. Sparrow had stopped shivering and if her cheeks weren't exactly rosy, her lips were losing the blue tinge that had made her look so ill. Rose paid the money without a second thought.

The shopkeeper tapped her pipe on the sole of her boot, sending a shower of dottle onto the dried earth floor. 'You'd best get her away from here before Piggin turns up to collect her takings, and watch out he don't send Regan looking for you, missis. You don't want to meet up with the likes of him.'

A shiver ran down Rose's spine at the mention

of Regan's name. 'Thanks for the warning.' She grabbed Sparrow by the hand. 'I'll make sure that man doesn't come anywhere near you again, you poor little soul.'

'Good luck, missis.' The shopkeeper slammed the door behind them.

'Where are we going?' Sparrow asked urgently. 'You ain't selling me body like the woman said, are you, miss?'

'Certainly not. You can forget about things like that. I'm taking you to a nice lady who has two little children, younger than you, and then we'll decide what's best.'

'He'll beat me black and blue when he finds me, and he will.'

'Not if I have anything to do with it. Fate must have guided my feet this way for a purpose,' Rose said firmly. 'Come along, Sparrow. I'm hungry and I expect you are too.'

'I'm bloody starving.'

'It would be better if you didn't say words like that in future. It's not very nice.'

'I know worse words than that.'

'I don't doubt it, but it's probably best to keep them to yourself.' Rose came to a sudden halt. 'Perhaps I should speak to your mother before I take you away from here. Do you know where she is?'

'In the pub. That's where you'll find her. I was to take me lavender money to her.'

Rose thought quickly. It would be a risk, but she did not want to be accused of kidnapping someone's child. 'Take me there, Sparrow. You don't have to go in with me, if you don't want to. I'll deal with this.'

The pub was situated in a narrow alley that stank of urine and animal excrement, and the interior was squalid, low-beamed and gloomy. The air was thick with tobacco smoke, and great puffs of soot billowed from the chimney, sending showers of black flakes falling like rain on the drinkers. Rose clutched Sparrow's hand as they moved from table to table, peering at the occupants in her search for the child's mother. Eventually, in the inglenook by the desultory fire, Sparrow pointed a shaking finger at a woman who was slouched on a wooden settle. Her chin was resting on her chest and her straggly brown hair was straw-like and matted with dirt.

'She's drunk,' Sparrow said in a matter-of-fact voice. 'You'll have to prod her hard or she won't answer you.'

Rose glanced anxiously at the woman, who looked as though she could handle herself in a scrap, if the bruises on her knuckles were anything to go by, although she was now semi-comatose. Rose cleared her throat. 'Excuse me, missis.'

A loud snore escaped the woman's lips and her large bosom lifted and fell like the incoming tide.

'Prod her,' Sparrow urged. 'Poke her in the ribs.'

Rose was not about to start a fight, but she needed

to get the woman's attention and she picked up the empty tankard and banged it hard on the table in front of her.

'Eh? What?'

'It's me, Ma.' Sparrow moved closer, tugging at her mother's sleeve with her small hand.

'What's your mother's name?' Rose whispered. 'What should I call her?'

'Bitch,' Sparrow said solemnly. 'That's what Piggin calls her. I calls her Ma.'

Rose could see this conversation was going nowhere. She leaned over Sparrow's drunken mother and shook her hard. 'Excuse me, but I need to speak to you.'

A pair of bloodshot, red-rimmed eyes opened, and the woman's bleary gaze fell on her small daughter. 'Where d'you get them duds? You don't go thieving unless I tells you to.' She shot a sideways glance at Rose. 'If she's stole them from you, lady, you can take her to the police station. I don't want nothing to do with her no more.'

'Is this your daughter?'

'I ain't saying nothing.'

Rose tried again. 'She says she's your child.'

The woman raised herself to a sitting position. 'I took her in after her ma threw herself off London Bridge. She ain't nothing to me, and I don't want no trouble. Take her and good riddance.'

'What did I tell you?' Sparrow said calmly. 'She's a drunken whore, that's what Regan says.'

'Shut your mouth or I'll shut it for you.' The woman's hand flew out to grasp Sparrow by the throat.

'No, don't do that.' Spurred on by anger and horrified to hear Regan's name on a child's lips, Rose grasped the woman's thin arm and prised the bony fingers apart until she released her hold on Sparrow. 'You're not fit to look after a child.'

'Take her – I can't bear the sight of her.'

'She might have relatives who would care for her. What was her mother's name?'

'If she had a family they must have thrown her out years ago, and then she got in with Regan. No wonder the poor bitch drowned herself.'

'But if you knew her well enough to take care of her child, you must have a name for her.'

'Ask Regan. He knows the names of all his girls. Now leave me alone and take the brat with you. I ain't telling you nothing more.' She glanced over Rose's shoulder. 'Talk of the devil. He's just come through the door and he's coming this way.'

Chapter Ten

Rose glanced over her shoulder and saw Regan heading towards the bar. Keeping her head down, she grabbed Sparrow by the hand and hustled her out of the taproom. They emerged from the pub to find that feathery flakes of snow had begun to fall from a cast-iron sky, and their breath curled around their heads as they ran.

'I don't think he saw us,' Rose said breathlessly when they reached the relative safety of Cheapside.

'It were a near thing.' Sparrow gazed up at her wide-eyed. 'Why are you doing this for me? What's in it for you, miss? I don't understand.'

Rose gazed at the small, pointed face and large blue enquiring eyes. 'I couldn't bear to see you so badly treated, but if you'd rather go back to that woman and your old life, I can't stop you.'

'Not bloody likely.' Sparrow's hand flew to cover her mouth. 'Sorry, miss. It just slipped out. I'll try to watch me tongue, just don't let me go back to Ma and Piggin.'

'That's all I wanted to know.' Rose raised her hand to hail a cab. 'We're going to Wapping to see a friend of mine. You'll like Maria, she's a very nice lady.' She waited until the vehicle came to a halt at the kerbside and lifted Sparrow onto the seat before climbing in beside her. 'Great Hermitage Street, please, cabby.'

Sparrow settled huddled up against Rose as the horse moved forward into the traffic. 'I ain't never been in one of these,' she whispered. 'I feels like a grand lady.'

Rose smiled and slid her arm around the small body, holding her close as the cab swayed and rattled over the snow-covered cobblestones. Was she doing the right thing? Only time would tell, but she could not have left this small scrap of humanity to the mercy of people who cared nothing for her. But the reality of her situation began to dawn on her with every hoofbeat and each spin of the wheels as the cab made its way through the crowded city streets. Rose glanced down at Sparrow, who had been lulled to sleep by the motion of the cab and the fact that she was warm and well dressed, probably for the first time in her short life. Rose held her close, protecting her from the more violent lurching as the cabby shouted curses at pedestrians and other vehicles that crossed their path.

When they eventually arrived outside Maria's house it was Edna who answered Rose's knock on the door. She stared pointedly at Sparrow. 'Is this your sister, miss?'

Rose shook her head. 'No, we're not related. Is Mrs Barnaby at home?'

'She's in the back parlour. D'you want me to tell her you're here?'

'No, it's all right.' Rose struggled to keep a straight face. The contrast between the well-trained servants in Tavistock Square and Edna's clumsy efforts made her want to laugh, but she did not want to hurt the woman's feelings.

'Shall I take your cape and gloves, miss?' Edna shifted from one foot to the other. 'And what about the nipper?' She bent down, grinning at Sparrow. 'What's your name, love?'

'Why d'you want to know?' Sparrow asked suspiciously. 'What's it to you?'

Edna straightened up, her smile fading. 'Pardon me, I'm sure. Hang your own coat on the hallstand if that's your attitude, young 'un.'

'Mind your manners, dear.' Rose sent a warning glance in Sparrow's direction as she took off her mantle and handed it to Edna.

'Spikey little thing, ain't she?' Edna eyed Sparrow

warily. 'I'll count the silver spoons and things when you've gone, nipper. So don't think you can get away with anything in Mrs Barnaby's house.'

'Thank you, Edna.' Rose snatched Sparrow's outer garments from her and passed them to Edna before hustling Sparrow along the corridor to the back parlour.

Maria looked up from the letter she had been writing, and her startled expression melted into a smile. She put her pen down and stood up. 'This is a pleasant surprise. I wasn't expecting you today.' She glanced at Sparrow, eyebrows raised. 'Who is this?'

'This is Sparrow – she doesn't seem to have another name.' Rose answered before Sparrow had a chance to speak for herself. 'I found her half-naked, selling lavender on a street corner. She was dressed in rags, blue with cold and I don't know when she last ate.'

'Last night.' Sparrow shot a wary look at Maria. 'They give me a bit of burned sausage to take the taste of the gin away. I hates the stuff, but they make me drink it so that I'll go to sleep.'

Maria and Rose exchanged horrified glances.

'But I seen what goes on,' Sparrow added with a knowing wink.

'Never mind that now,' Rose said hastily. 'Perhaps Mrs Barnaby's cook could find you something to eat.'

Maria nodded. 'Of course, and perhaps a bath wouldn't go amiss.'

'You ain't taking my clothes off. I ain't stripping in front of strangers.' Sparrow backed towards the door. 'What sort of place is this, miss?'

'Don't be scared, Sparrow. No one is going to hurt you, and you'll feel much better when you've had a good wash and a nice meal.' Rose spoke firmly, but she was beginning to wonder if taking this half-feral child away from her normal way of life was the wisest course of action.

'I'll ring for Edna.' Maria moved to the fireplace and tugged the bell pull. 'You're quite safe here, Sparrow.' She turned to Rose with a questioning look. 'Do you know where she comes from? She must have a family somewhere.'

'The woman she thought was her mother turns out to be a drunkard, and no relation. Her real mother was drowned years ago, and the people who were supposed to be her guardians are the lowest of the low.'

'They didn't want me, that's why they only give me one name, but mostly they called me the little b—'

Rose put her finger to her lips, shaking her head. 'They shouldn't have spoken to you like that, Sparrow. It was very wrong.'

A thud on the door was followed by Edna, who erupted into the room with an eager expression on her face. 'You rang, missis?'

'Yes, Edna. I want you to take this child to the

kitchen and tell Jessie to give her some food and a hot bath, and wash her hair thoroughly.'

Edna held her hand out. 'Come with me, nipper. Jessie and me will look after you.'

'My name is Sparrow.'

'Is it? Well, I'm Edna, so come along and don't lark about.' Edna held the door open, and Sparrow, clearly recognising a will stronger than her own, left the room, dragging her feet in silent protest.

Maria waited until the door closed on them before sinking down on a chair by the fire. 'What were you thinking of, Rose? That poor child has lived a life that you and I can barely imagine.'

'I know, but I couldn't leave her to freeze to death or die of starvation.' Rose took a seat on the opposite side of the fire, holding her hands out to the heat. 'I only intended to buy her warm clothes, but the woman in the shop told me that her mother was a hopeless alcoholic and the man she lives with is a brute. The fact that Regan is involved convinced me that I couldn't abandon her, and then I thought of you, and I wondered if you could help.'

Maria gazed into the flames, frowning. 'You can hardly take her to Tavistock Square. I don't know Cecilia Sheldon very well, but I imagine she might take exception to giving house room to a street urchin.'

'You could be right. I have to find somewhere to live, and I've lost my job at the *London Leader*. I still hope to move into the Captain's House, but I'm waiting to find out if those men are there legally or not.'

'What then? Would you take that little girl to live with you? How would you support yourself and Sparrow, and what would happen to her when you marry Max?'

'I hadn't thought that far ahead, Maria.'

'Your kind heart leads your head, but you need to think before you act.'

'I'm beginning to realise that, but I can't walk away from her. My pa left me with Sadie and Laurence, who were wonderful to me, but it wasn't like having a family of my own. I always felt the odd one out.'

'I understand, believe me. My grandmother made my life a misery. She kept telling me that I'd disgraced the family name simply by being born. I didn't find my mother until I was nearly twenty, and that was thanks to Caroline. If it weren't for her I would still be a virtual prisoner in my grandmother's house.'

'I haven't seen Caroline since her wedding to Phineas,' Rose said soulfully. 'I wish she were here now – it would make life so much easier.'

'Phineas would know what to do about Gilroy, too.' Maria sighed, shaking her head. 'I thought I hated my grandmother, but seeing her so frail and helpless makes me sad.'

'I'll come with you if you want to confront Gilroy. I tried to persuade the guvnor to let me investigate and expose her for the thief she is, but he wouldn't allow it, and now I've lost my job it's too late.'

'What did you do?'

'I did nothing wrong, apart from being a female. I went to the station to see Eugene off on the start of his journey to Egypt, and it made me late for work. Nicholls must have told Mr Radley all sorts of lies about me, and I was dismissed. I need to find another position so that I can pay my way.'

'Max is to blame for this,' Maria said angrily. 'He should have known better than to send for you when he was likely to be posted anywhere in the world at short notice, and to make it worse he doesn't seem to have made any provision for you. I know he's my flesh and blood, but I'm very cross with him.'

'I chose to come to London, Maria. I could have remained in Bendigo and waited for him there, but I didn't. I have to make the best of things.'

'We can only hope that Max will return unharmed, Rose.'

'Surely the family would have been informed had he suffered an injury.'

'One would hope so, but with Caroline and Phineas away I'm not sure that anyone would think to let me know,' Maria said gently. 'However, I have my own problems and Grandmama is one of them, whether I like it or not.'

Rose eyed Maria thoughtfully. 'That house is huge. Why don't you move in? Just as a temporary measure, of course, but then you could make certain that Gilroy isn't harming Mrs Colville or stealing from her.'

'Even if Grandmama was the worst person in the world I couldn't stand by and watch her being ill-treated. But the thought of returning to Pier House makes me shudder, and I doubt if I'd be strong enough to stand up to Gilroy. Unless I had someone to back me up,' Maria added pointedly. 'Someone who one day will be related to me by marriage.'

'Why are you looking at me?' Rose demanded. 'Oh, no, Maria. Surely you don't want me to go with you?'

'That's exactly what I would suggest. You said yourself that you can't remain in Tavistock Square indefinitely.'

Rose frowned thoughtfully. 'Cecilia has been very kind, but Eugene did foist me on her, and now I've got Sparrow to think of as well.'

'You might have to put her into the workhouse, Rose.'

'Never. I remember what people used to say about those places.'

'You need somewhere to live, and I need someone to help me get rid of Gilroy. You said you wanted a story, Rose. Maybe you could sell it to your editor after all, and he might take you on again.'

'I suppose it's a possibility, but what about Sparrow? I don't think Mrs Colville would be very pleased if I brought a waif from the city slums into her ice palace. From the little I know about Gilroy, I'm certain she would make trouble for us.'

'You could bring her, too.' Maria's eyes lit with a mischievous smile. 'I'd pit Sparrow against Gilroy any day, and Grandmama need never meet the child. I would have to keep my little ones out of her way, but the nursery suite is a long way from Grandmama's room. What do you say, Rose? You've nothing to lose and maybe something to gain.'

Rose stared into the fire, trying to visualise what life might be like in Pier House. The sound of the water lapping on the foreshore had served as a lullaby each night when she was a child, and her home on the river-bank was what she had missed most when she was taken to Australia. She broke free from her reverie and looked up to meet Maria's expectant smile.

'All right, I will. How do we go about it?'

'Really?' Maria's hands flew to cover her lips. 'I don't know exactly – I've only just thought of it. I suppose we could simply move in, because Grandmama isn't in a fit condition to turn us out, and Gilroy might think she owns the place, but she's just a servant. I'm my grandmother's next of kin while the others are away.'

'What about your mother?' Rose asked urgently.
'Might she object?'

'I don't think she's ever forgiven Grandmama for
casting her out, and I doubt if she has any feelings
left for her, which is hardly surprising.'

Rose was about to answer when the door flew
open and a small figure burst into the room. Sparrow
was naked except for the scrap of towel that she
held on to and her hair was wet and clinging to her
head. Rose jumped to her feet.

'What's the matter?'

'She's the trouble, miss.' Edna hurried into the
room red-faced and dishevelled. Her apron was
soaking and there were damp patches on her skirt.
'That little brat bit my finger when I tried to rinse
her hair in vinegar. She was running with vermin.'

'You hurt me.' Sparrow pointed a trembling finger
at her. 'I got stuff in me eyes and it stings.'

'You've got nits,' Edna said angrily. 'You'll pass
them on to Mrs Barnaby's little 'uns if we don't get
rid of 'em.'

Maria uttered a shriek of dismay. 'Oh, no. Look
what you've done, Rose.'

'It's all right. I'll deal with it,' Rose said calmly.
She took Sparrow by the hand. 'I'll come downstairs
with you and we'll sort it out together. Edna will
find a cloth for you to hold over your eyes and I'll
do the rest.' She turned her head to give Maria an
encouraging smile. 'Don't worry. I was used to doing

this for the children in our school at home. It's not as bad as it sounds.' She hustled Sparrow and Edna out of the room before Maria had a chance to protest.

Edna led the way down a long dark corridor to the back stairs and Rose followed, holding tight to Sparrow's hand.

The smell of something that had burned in the bottom of a saucepan hit Rose forcibly in a gust of steam when Edna opened the kitchen door. Jessie was seated in a chair by the range, fanning herself with a cabbage leaf. She jumped up when she saw Rose, and her thick brown eyebrows knotted together over the bridge of her beaky nose. 'Why have you brought that kid back here, Edna?'

'She didn't,' Rose said firmly. 'I did, and you've both done a very good job as far as I can see, but Sparrow needs to have the soap rinsed from her hair, followed by the application of vinegar to loosen the nits.'

Jessie puffed out her plump cheeks. 'I know that, but she wasn't having none of it.'

Sparrow growled at her like a feral dog, and for a moment Rose thought she was going to fly at Jessie and bite her. She slipped her arm around Sparrow's shoulders. 'Perhaps if I do it, Sparrow will submit to the treatment.'

'I ain't touching her again.' Edna retreated to the scullery and began splashing around in the stone sink.

Rose met Sparrow's rebellious glare with a smile. 'It won't take long, and you'll feel so much better when it's done.'

'If you don't let the lady do it, I'll get my scissors and cut the lot off.' Jessie unhooked a pair of scissors that had been hanging from a shelf and made snipping movements in the air. 'I ain't joking, nipper.'

Sparrow subsided without a murmur and allowed Rose to finish treating her straggly hair, which she towelled until it was almost dry. 'My goodness, who would have thought that you have such lovely golden locks, Sparrow?'

'I dunno. I never seen meself except in shop windows.'

'Then you need to look in the mirror.' Rose met Jessie's amused grin with a nod and a smile. 'What do you think, Miss Spriggs?'

'Very pretty, I'm sure, and you should call me Jessie, miss. I'm only the cook in this here establishment.'

'Thank you, Jessie. Although I think the kitchen is the heart of the house, and good food is very important.' Rose scanned the contents spread about in a higgledy-piggledy fashion on the pine table. It was obvious that whatever had been in the saucepan was burned to a cinder, and there did not seem to be anything else being prepared for their evening meal.

Jessie followed her gaze, scowling. 'I took me eyes off the saucepan for five minutes, that's all. I dunno what I'm going to give the missis.'

'Might I suggest that you make those vegetables into broth with that rather large beef bone?' Rose said tentatively. 'I don't want to interfere, but I can see that you've been very busy.'

Jessie mopped her brow with a duster. 'I should say so, miss. I got no help in the kitchen and her upstairs is very fussy about her food and what she gives to her little 'uns. We was brought up on bread and dripping if we was lucky and plain bread if times were harder than usual.'

'And if you had more help in the kitchen I dare say you would find life easier.'

Jessie let out a snort. 'That ain't going to happen, miss.'

'Oy!' Sparrow tugged at Rose's sleeve. 'Ain't you forgetting something or someone? Namely me. I want me clothes back and something to eat. You promised I'd be fed but all I can see are raw vegetables and something disgusting in that pan.'

'Of course you'll get something to eat, just let me finish what I'm doing.' Rose ran the comb through Sparrow's hair for the last time. 'We'll have to repeat this several times, but at least your hair is cleaner than it was.' She reached for the chemise she had purchased in the dolly shop and slipped it over Sparrow's head. 'There you are. You can dress yourself and maybe Jessie will be kind enough to cut you a slice of bread and butter.'

'She can have some cheese on it,' Jessie said grudgingly. 'But this ain't a home for waifs and strays. I hope the missis realises that I have to manage on what she gives me, which ain't that much.'

Rose could see a small cask of ale in the larder and a bottle containing some sort of alcoholic spirit. 'Yes, it must be hard.' She left it at that. There was no point in upsetting Jessie at this point in time, and it was Maria who needed a few lessons in managing a household. However, it was none of her business and she must not interfere. Rose fastened the buttons on the back of Sparrow's frock and waited while she put on her stockings and boots. 'Sit down at the table and I'll leave Jessie to give you some food. I'll be upstairs in the parlour when you've finished your meal.'

'You ain't going to run off and leave me, are you?'

'Of course not. Whatever gave you that idea?'

Sparrow took a seat. 'It happens,' she said darkly.

'Well, I won't abandon you, so don't worry on that score.' Rose hurried from the kitchen. She had made promises that it might be impossible to keep, and that was a worry, but she was determined to do her best for the child she had plucked from the gutter. She returned to the parlour to find Maria pacing the floor.

'You took your time, Rose.'

'I'm sorry, but I had to finish off what Edna had started, although Sparrow needs her hair to be treated daily if we're to rid her of nits.'

'Yes, well, that's not uppermost on my mind. I've been mulling over your suggestion about moving into Pier House.'

Rose sank down on her chair. 'What was your conclusion?'

'Theo won't be home for at least six months, and that leaves me free to take care of Grandmama, or at least to rid her of Gilroy and find her a more suitable servant and maybe a nurse.'

'So you're going to go through with it?'

'Yes, but only if you agree to come with me.'

'But what happens to Sparrow and me when things settle down?'

'You won't be any worse off than you are now, and maybe the Captain's House will become vacant. I do know one or two people in the office who might be persuaded to help.'

'I'll do it, but I have to make it right with Cecilia. She's been so kind to me and I know she'll miss Eugene even more than I will.'

Maria gave her a searching look. 'You weren't falling in love with him, were you, Rose?'

'Of course not,' Rose said hastily. 'I don't know what gave you that idea. The guvnor gave me a chance and he believed in me, that's all – and now he's gone.'

'You must make things right with Cecilia, but perhaps you'd best leave Sparrow here with me.' Maria picked up the small garment she had been darning. 'She'll be quite happy playing with the children.'

Cecilia took the news that Rose was leaving with a shrug. 'I thought this might happen when I saw how well you were getting on with Maria.'

'I am so grateful to you for everything, Cissie. You and the guvnor couldn't have done more for me.'

Cecilia held up her hand. 'Don't thank me, Rose. It was Gene who brought you here and he was the one who thought you had talent. I'm a social butterfly, darling. I pick people up and I drop them when they bore me.'

'I hope you don't think of me in that way, Cissie. I'd like to remain your friend.'

Cecilia threw back her head and laughed. 'You are an original, Rose. I would love to keep you here to alleviate the boredom of being rich and idle, but I will visit you in the slums from time to time.'

'Thank you, Cissie. I was afraid you might be offended.'

'Offended? Certainly not. I'm used to Gene and his flights of fancy, so this is nothing new to me. Good luck with your feral child and with the old lady, too. Clarissa Colville has a reputation for being a miser and a recluse. I pity poor Maria, but she will have you to stand up for her.'

The move, a few days later, went smoothly, largely because they took Gilroy by surprise, arriving in a hackney carriage with Sparrow and Maria's two young children, together with Izzie and two large carpet bags.

'I'll have my old room, Gilroy,' Maria said firmly. 'Izzie and the children will have the two rooms adjacent to mine, and Miss Munday will have my cousin Phineas' room, with a truckle bed for her charge.'

Gilroy's shocked expression would, in any other circumstances, have made Rose laugh, but it was replaced almost instantly by a sly, calculating look that confirmed Rose's previous opinion of the servant. Gilroy was a nasty piece of work and not to be trusted.

'Izzie will see to the children's meals,' Maria added. 'I'm going to speak to Grandmama now, and then I want to see Cook in the study.'

'Mrs Colville didn't say nothing about this,' Gilroy spluttered. 'I take me orders from her.'

Rose could see that Maria had exhausted the courage she had been summoning since they left the house early that morning, and she stepped in between them. 'It seems to me that you've been doing exactly as you please, Gilroy. You'll take your orders from Mrs Barnaby until her grandmother has recovered her health and strength.'

'The old woman's on her last legs,' Gilroy snapped. 'She needs me, not you.'

Maria took her small daughter by the hand. 'That's enough, Gilroy. You're frightening the children. Go about your business.'

Two-year-old Teddy had been quiet until this moment, but he buried his face against Izzie's shoulder and began to howl and Polly clutched her mother's skirts, staring at Gilroy wide-eyed.

Sparrow leaped forward and poked Gilroy in the stomach. 'See what you done? You do as the lady says or I'll set Regan on you.'

Twin spots of colour highlighted Gilroy's cheekbones and her eyes narrowed. 'Regan? What sewer did you crawl out of, you little brat?'

Rose placed a protective arm around Sparrow's thin shoulders. 'So you know him, do you, Gilroy?

'Everyone knows about him. You won't catch me out that way, miss. And we'll see what the mistress says about people who barge into the house and invite themselves to stay. This is Mrs Colville's residence.' She started off in the direction of the drawing room, but Rose had anticipated a rebellion and she barred her way.

'I think Mrs Barnaby made herself quite clear, Gilroy. You're to take the luggage to our rooms.'

Maria nodded. 'Either you obey orders or you pack your bags and find another position.'

Rose held her breath. Gilroy's expression would

have curdled cream, but then she bowed her head, mumbled an apology and picked up the carpet bags. She stomped off without another word.

'I think you won that round,' Rose said, chuckling. 'But if she knows Regan then she's in bad company. I think you ought to dismiss her, Maria.'

'I can't do anything without my grandmother's permission, but I wasn't going to say that in front of her.' Maria bent down to give her daughter a comforting hug. 'I'll take you to the morning parlour and you can wait for me there. I have to speak to my grandmama, who is a very old lady, and needs to be kept very quiet. Maybe you can meet her later.'

Polly sucked her thumb, eyeing her mother doubtfully, but young Teddy's tears had dried and Maria passed him to Izzie.

'Show us where to go and I'll stay with Izzie and the little ones,' Rose volunteered. 'Unless you'd like me to go with you?'

'I think it might be best if I go alone, but I may need you later. Grandmama's moods were always volatile.' Maria gave her a weary smile. 'I'll take you to the morning parlour first. Follow me, everyone.' She crossed the wide expanse of floor and led them to a large, chilly room where the furniture was draped in holland covers. 'I'll be as quick as I can and then we can set about making the place more comfortable.'

Rose nodded. 'We need to light the fire. I could do that, if you tell me where to find the coal and kindling.'

'I'll get Gilroy to do it after I've seen Grandmama. I won't be long.' Maria braced her shoulders. 'Wish me luck,' she said as she left the room.

Polly took her thumb from her mouth. 'Mama,' she wailed. 'I don't like it here. I'm cold.'

'Hush, Miss Polly. You'll make Master Teddy cry again.' Izzie jiggled the little boy up and down, making him chuckle.

'If you can look after them, Izzie, I'll go and find what we need to get a fire going,' Rose said, shivering. 'It's freezing in here.'

'I'll help you.' Sparrow was at the door before Rose had a chance to refuse. 'I'm good at finding things.'

'We'll be as quick as we can,' Rose said as she followed Sparrow from the room, closing the door behind her. 'I'll swear it's colder in this house than it is outside,' she whispered.

'Best go out the front door, miss.' Sparrow headed for the main entrance. 'We don't want to bump into that Gilroy. I've seen her afore, miss.'

Rose had to run to keep up with her. 'Are you sure?'

'I am now. She knows Regan and that's where I saw her – in the pub. They was together, drinking with Ma and Piggin. She's a bad lot, if ever there was one.'

Rose opened the door and they went outside into the cold and damp with a lowering sky that threatened yet more snow. 'Why do you say that, Sparrow?'

'I seen her hand something to Piggin. He's a fence, if you knows what I mean.'

'Not really.'

Sparrow gave her a pitying look. 'He deals in stolen stuff. I reckon she's been nicking things from the old lady and giving them to Piggin to sell on.'

Breathless from trying to keep up with Sparrow and gasping as the sooty air filled her lungs, Rose came to a sudden standstill. 'If that's true we have to tell Maria.'

Chapter Eleven

The flames took hold instantly and the kindling crackled and spat as it ignited the shiny lumps of coal, sending a warm glow into the morning parlour. Izzie sat on the sofa, cuddling the children, who were unusually silent as they took in their new surroundings, and Rose kneeled in front of the fire, adding nuggets of coal to build up the blaze. She needed to speak to Maria urgently, but first she must make sure that the children were warm and comfortable. With nothing better to do, Sparrow was roaming round the room, examining the rows of leather-bound books that filled the shelves in one chimney breast alcove. Appearing to lose interest, she went to inspect the porcelain figurines that were arranged on a rosewood pier table. She turned to Rose, frowning.

'I think some of these are missing, Rose.'

'How do you know?' Rose scrambled to her feet and went to see for herself.

'You can see the marks in the dust where they were.' Sparrow drew a circle around the clean patches with the tip of her finger.

'You're quite the detective,' Rose said, smiling. 'It doesn't look as if anyone has cleaned this room for a very long time.'

'I ain't offering.' Sparrow retreated to sit cross-legged on the floor by the fire.

'I need to show this to Maria. It might be important, or it might not. She suspected that things were going missing, and this might be the proof she needs.' Rose glanced anxiously at Izzie, but she seemed relaxed and was cuddling Teddy, who had fallen asleep with his head on her shoulder. Polly slid down from the sofa to sit beside Sparrow as if seeking comfort from an older child, and Sparrow pulled faces at her, making the little girl double up with laughter. 'Will you be all right for a few minutes, Izzie?' Rose said softly. 'I need to have a few words with Mrs Barnaby.'

Izzie nodded. 'Yes'm.'

'I'll be as quick as I can.' Rose left them huddled round the fire. There could be many reasons why the figurines were missing, but it might also be proof that Gilroy was pilfering small artefacts from the house. Standing in the draughty hallway, Rose was just getting her bearings when the deathly silence was broken by the sound of raised voices. She went to investigate and came across Maria and Gilroy in the middle of a fierce argument.

'What's the matter?' Rose asked anxiously as she hurried towards them.

'Everywhere is filthy,' Maria said angrily. 'My grandmother's room can't have been cleaned for weeks.'

'Me and Cook have to cope with everything since Mrs Colville took against the rest of the servants and sent them packing. You try looking after the mad old woman, running to and fro every time she rings the bloody bell, and I ain't paid to be a skivvy.'

'Don't speak to me in that tone,' Maria snapped. 'You forget yourself, Gilroy.'

'Why are you here, anyway?' Gilroy countered. 'I suppose you're waiting for the old girl to croak so that you can get your hands on her belongings.'

'How dare you?' Maria slapped Gilroy's face and the sound of skin hitting skin echoed off the high ceiling. 'You forget your place.'

Gilroy clenched her hands into fists, ready it seemed to fight back, but Rose stepped in between them. 'This has gone far enough. I think you have some explaining to do, Gilroy, and an apology to make.'

'Apologise?' Gilroy clutched her hand to her cheek. 'She struck me, damn her.'

'You deserved it for speaking to me like that,' Maria cried angrily. 'You're dismissed, and don't you dare ask me for a character. You are sly and untrustworthy, and I think you've been stealing from my grandmother.'

'I wanted to speak to you about that, Maria.' Rose lowered her voice to a whisper. 'It looks as though some things are missing from the blue parlour.'

'I heard that.' Gilroy held her fists at her sides. 'You can't sack me, missis. I'm going to tell the old girl what you just done.'

Before either of them had a chance to stop Gilroy she pushed past Maria and burst into the drawing room. Through the open double doors Rose could see Mrs Colville lying in the grand four-poster bed, and the old woman's mouth dropped open at the sight of Gilroy. She lifted her hand feebly, but let it drop to rest on the coverlet.

'What's happening?' Mrs Colville's voice was little more than a hoarse whisper but it echoed round the sparsely furnished room.

Maria rushed to her grandmother's bedside. 'Leave Mrs Colville alone, Gilroy. You've been dismissed, and I want you out of the house, now.'

Rose hesitated in the doorway, prepared to leap to Maria's aid if needed, but the old lady appeared to be anxious enough without adding to her distress.

'I've been falsely accused, madam.' Gilroy shook

off Maria's restraining hand. 'She's after your money, ma'am. She only came here to see you off.'

'How dare you?' Maria's voice cracked with emotion. 'Gilroy has been stealing from you, Grandmama. She's been giving you huge doses of laudanum in order to keep you quiet while she sells off your belongings.'

'All lies, madam. I've been your faithful servant for more years than I can remember. You ain't going to believe what that by-blow says, are you?'

'You've just heard how she speaks to me, Grandmama,' Maria said angrily.

'Prop me up,' Mrs Colville whispered. 'I can't see you very well.'

Maria pushed Gilroy out of the way. 'I'm here to look after you, Grandmama.' She lifted the fragile body while she plumped up the pillows. 'There you are. Is that better?'

'Who is that lurking in the doorway?'

'It's Rose, Grandmama. She's my friend and she came with me when I last visited you. Don't you remember?'

'They've come to bleed you dry, madam.' Gilroy moved closer to the bed, fixing the old lady with a hard stare. 'You can't believe ill of me, ma'am. Not after all these years of faithful service.'

Mrs Colville pointed a bony finger at Rose. 'What have you to say for yourself, girl?'

Rose approached the bed slowly. 'I came here to

support Maria, Mrs Colville. She believes that this woman has been keeping you drugged and that she has been stealing items from the house.'

'Lies, all lies,' Gilroy cried passionately. 'Don't let them twist you round their fingers, madam.'

With a sudden burst of energy, Clarissa Colville sat up and threw back the coverlet. 'Stop this haranguing at once. I won't have it.' She swung her legs over the side of the bed and attempted to stand. 'I want proof, Maria. You were a miserable little thing as a child, but unfortunately you are my flesh and blood.' She swayed and fell to the floor in a dead faint.

Maria went down on her knees beside the prostrate figure. 'See what you've done, Gilroy? You're responsible for this. Run and fetch Dr Tucker.'

'You've just sacked me, missis.'

'I'll go,' Rose said hastily. 'Just tell me where to find him.'

Maria took her grandmother's hands in hers and chafed them. 'Gilroy knows where he lives.' She looked up, her eyes reddened and brimming with tears. 'You'll fetch the doctor or I'll set the police on you, Gilroy. I have enough evidence to have you thrown in prison, and if my grandmother dies it will be your fault. Go now and hurry.'

Gilroy hesitated for a moment before stomping out of the room, muttering beneath her breath.

'Help me lift her, Rose.'

Together they managed to lift Mrs Colville onto the bed, making her as comfortable as possible.

'She's still breathing,' Rose said gently. 'But she does look very fragile, Maria. Do you think you ought to send for your mother?'

Maria slumped down at the foot of the bed. 'I'll wait and see what the doctor says.'

'What about Gilroy? You won't take her back, will you?'

'No, certainly not. I'd report her thieving ways to the police, but it would be almost impossible to prove.'

'Sparrow told me she'd been raised by a woman and a man called Piggin, who's a notorious fence. They spent most of their time in the pub and that was where she'd seen Gilroy having dealings with Regan. I think they're all in it together.'

'Sparrow is just a child. She might be mistaken.'

'It follows that if Gilroy has been taking things from the house she has to find someone who could sell them on without incriminating her. Sparrow might be young, but she's sharp and she has no reason to lie.'

'I can't think about Gilroy at the moment,' Maria said, sighing. 'I have to think about Grandmama, and do what's best for her.'

Rose pulled up a chair. 'Make yourself comfortable. We might have to wait a while for Gilroy to fetch the doctor.

*   *   *

After what felt like hours, although it was probably little more than thirty minutes, Gilroy rushed into the room, followed more slowly by a short, worried-looking man, wearing a frock coat.

'They brought the old lady to this state,' Gilroy said breathlessly. 'You know how devoted I've been, Dr Tucker. I've looked after her for years with little thanks from the family, and they're all too busy with their own affairs to care for their poor, dear ma.'

Maria jumped to her feet, her cheeks flaming with angry colour. 'Don't listen to her, Doctor. That woman has been drugging my grandmother with laudanum and she's been stealing valuables from the house.'

Dr Tucker placed his capacious leather bag on the chair by the bed and opened it. 'That is a matter between you and your maidservant, Mrs Barnaby. I'm here to examine my patient. I was told that she became agitated and collapsed when she attempted to stand.'

'That's more or less what happened.' Maria turned to face Gilroy. 'Get out of here. You're sacked and I never want to see your face again.'

'I take my orders from the mistress, not you.'

Rose met Maria's desperate glance with a grim nod. 'I'll go for a constable, shall I, Maria?'

'Take this argument outside, if you please, ladies.' Dr Tucker turned to examine his patient.

'Make sure she leaves the house, Rose.' Maria

remained standing at the foot of the bed, leaving Rose little choice other than to hustle Gilroy from the room.

'All right, I'm going, but you'll be sorry.' Gilroy stomped off in the direction of the back stairs.

Rose did not trust her to leave quietly. She waited by the window until she saw Gilroy trudging towards the main road with a battered suitcase clutched in her hand. The need to see Gilroy off the premises and as far away from Pier House as possible spurred Rose on, and she seized her shawl from the chair where she had abandoned it earlier, and wrapped it around her shoulders before letting herself out of the house. A sharp breeze slapped at her cheeks as she followed in Gilroy's wake. She had thought that Gilroy might make her way to the pub where Sparrow had seen her having dealings with Piggin, but to her surprise Gilroy headed for the wharfs.

The leaden sky seemed to merge with the gunmetal sheen of the river, and the snow had turned to sleet. Gilroy was marching ahead purposefully, but she came to a sudden halt on Black Lion Wharf, and Rose dodged behind a pile of wooden crates. Gilroy hesitated, glancing round as if she suspected she was being followed, and then, seeming satisfied that she was safe from prying eyes, she climbed the wooden steps that led up to a house that to Rose was now achingly familiar. It had been dark when Cora brought her to the Captain's House, but now recollections of childhood and long summer days upriver came flooding back, and she remembered the eccentric building where she had lived with Sadie and Laurence and taken lessons with Max and Jimmy.

Gilroy rapped on the front door, and moments later it was opened by a scruffy, unshaven man. The sound of raucous voices and a strong smell of alcohol and tobacco smoke filled the air as if a wild party was in full swing, even though it was not yet midday. A shudder ran down Rose's spine as she recognised Sid Piggin, who looked even more villainous by daylight. The rank odour of his body had lingered long after she and Cora had escaped from the house, and now the mere sight of him was enough to curdle her blood, but Gilroy seemed to have no such qualms. She flung her arms around his neck as he lifted her off her feet, kissing her greedily as he dragged her into the house. The door slammed and Rose stood there, momentarily frozen to the spot. She had suspected that Sid and his mate were part of a criminal gang, and now she was certain. Gilroy was a thief and the men occupying the Captain's House were there illegally. This was definitely a case for the Metropolitan Police. It would make headline news if she wrote up the story and presented it to Mr Radley, and he might be persuaded to reinstate her. Despite being wet through and chilled to the marrow, she hurried off in the direction of the pier head.

*   *   *

Rose rushed into Pier House, eager to share her news with Maria, but she came to a halt when she saw her friend's serious expression. 'How is Mrs Colville? What did the doctor say?'

Maria shook her head. 'It's not good, Rose. He thinks that it was apoplexy, which could have occurred at any time, but the scene with Gilroy almost certainly caused her collapse.'

'I'm sorry,' Rose said awkwardly. 'What needs to be done?'

'There's little we can do, apart from keeping her quiet and comfortable. She might recover, but Dr Tucker was doubtful.' Maria dabbed her eyes with her handkerchief. 'She was always hateful to me when I was growing up, but she is my grandmother and I must look after her.'

Rose took off her sodden bonnet as she glanced round the room. 'What have you done with the children and Izzie?'

Maria managed a watery smile. 'I haven't locked them in a cupboard. They were all starving so I took them to the kitchen, and Mrs Leary said she would find them something to eat.'

'I hope Sparrow is behaving herself.'

'I think she's a bit overawed by everything. It's been a sudden change for her.'

'That's true. It's been a bit of a shock to me as well. One minute I'm in Black Raven Court, and then I'm a guest in a grand house in Tavistock

Square, and now I'm staying with you in a mansion overlooking the river. Will you remain here, as planned?'

'Yes, of course. I can't walk away and leave Grandmama while she's in this state.' Maria hesitated, staring at Rose's wet hair and damp skirts. 'I should be asking why you're soaked to the skin. Where did you go when you rushed out of the room?'

'I followed Gilroy because I thought she would go straight to the pub where Sparrow saw her with Sid Piggin, but you'll never guess where she went?'

Maria shook her head. 'No, tell me.'

'She went to the Captain's House. I think it was Sid who opened the door, and they were obviously more than good friends. You should have seen them.' Rose shuddered. 'That first night when I arrived in London, and Cora took me to the Captain's House, we only just managed to get away from Sid and his mate. They're a bad lot and I'm going to do what I should have done in the beginning and report them to the police.'

'Don't do that, Rose. You can't prove anything, and it could have serious repercussions if Gilroy realises you were the one who pointed the finger at them. I won't risk my children's lives in order to get even with that woman. She's welcome to keep the things she stole, if she'll just stay away from here.'

'That house belongs to your family, and those men are squatters.'

'I know you want to be there when Max returns, but don't allow that to affect your better judgement. Those people are dangerous and best left alone.' Maria reached out to clasp Rose's hand. 'You can stay with me for as long as you like. In fact, I'd be very grateful if you would help me to get through this difficult time.'

Rose squeezed Maria's cold fingers. 'Of course I'll do anything I can to help you, but don't you think you ought to send for your mother? She should be here with you, and she might wish to see her own mother before . . .' Rose hesitated. 'Before, you know what.'

'Before Grandmama dies. You don't have to be tactful, Rose. Dr Tucker told me that she's unlikely to recover, and I will send for Mama. You're quite right – she should be here.'

'Perhaps you could send a telegram to your mother this afternoon, but in the meantime I suggest we go to the kitchen and see if there's anything left for us to eat – I'm ravenous.'

'You're right, of course. I've been too agitated to think about food, but I do feel a little light-headed.'

Despite Rose's efforts to bring warmth to the house, there seemed to be a permanent chill in all the rooms except the kitchen. The heat from the range hit Rose as she walked through the doorway, and almost immediately her damp skirts began to steam. Sparrow looked up and grinned.

'Mrs Leary makes lovely bread,' she said happily. 'And she cooked us some bacon.'

Polly nodded vigorously. 'I'm a good girl.' She demonstrated by holding up a clean plate, but Teddy was not so happy and he started to howl, holding his arms out to his mother.

'He ain't eaten much, missis,' Izzie said hastily. 'There ain't no milk, and I reckon he's thirsty.'

Mrs Leary bristled visibly. 'I wasn't expecting to have to feed hordes of people, let alone three nippers.' She shot a wary glance in Maria's direction. 'I mean, children, ma'am.'

'It's all right, Mrs Leary,' Maria said quickly. 'I know this is very sudden, but I wanted to look after my grandmother, and it's just as well we came today.'

'That's as maybe, ma'am, but I can't manage without help. The girl who comes in to clean hasn't turned up, although she'll be full of excuses when she does show her face again. And I gather that Gilroy has hopped it, so who will do her work? Not that she did much anyway, but she took care of the mistress.'

Rose glanced at Maria, eyebrows raised. 'What about Jessie and Edna? They won't have much to do if you shut up the house in Great Hermitage Street, at least for the time being.'

'You're right.' Maria took Teddy from Izzie's arms and he stopped crying immediately. 'Izzie, when you've finished your meal, I want you to go home and fetch your sisters. Tell them I need their help.'

Izzie stuffed the last chunk of bread and butter in her mouth as she leaped to her feet. 'I'll go at once, missis. Can they have nice rooms like me?'

'I'm sure they'll be very comfortable,' Maria said calmly. 'Tell them to pack up all the food in the larder that might go off, and bring it here.'

'I don't want no interference in my kitchen.' Mrs Leary stood, arms akimbo, glaring at Maria.

'There's no fear of that.' Rose spoke before Maria had a chance to answer. Jessie might have been popular with her clients when she walked the streets, but cooking was not her strong point.

'I'm sure you will be glad to have help,' Maria added, cuddling Teddy, who was falling asleep in her arms. 'We'll manage very well, and I'll look after my grandmother.'

'I'll do what I can.' Rose reached for a slice of bread and a chunk of cheese. 'I'll sit with Mrs Colville this afternoon when you go to the telegraph office, Maria. You're not on your own now.'

'What about me?' Sparrow demanded. 'I could wash dishes. I done plenty of that for Ma and Piggin. They was always too drunk to bother with keeping the place clean and tidy.'

Mrs Leary unhooked a pinafore and tossed it to

Sparrow. 'Make yourself useful and I might consider making a few jam tarts for tea.'

Despite Maria's reservations, Rose was determined to bring Gilroy and her accomplices to justice. As promised, she went to sit with Mrs Colville while Maria went to the telegraph office, but she had no intention of being idle. There was a dainty burr-walnut escritoire in the corner of the room and Rose pulled up a chair and sat down. She selected a sheet of writing paper and sat for a while, going over the wording in her mind before she put pen to paper. The words flowed easily, but she kept stopping to check on the sick woman lying corpse-like in the bed. At one point she thought that Mrs Colville had gone to join her Maker, but a shuddering sigh racked the slight body and Rose patted her on the shoulder, whispering words of comfort, although she doubted if she could be heard. Having satisfied herself that there was nothing else she could do, Rose returned to the desk and resumed work on the piece that she hoped Mr Radley would print in the next edition. She had just written the last sentence when she heard approaching footsteps. It would not do to worry Maria unnecessarily, and, if she could impress Radley enough to get her job back it would solve many problems. She slipped the paper into her pocket and went to stand at the bedside, getting there just a second before the door opened and Maria rushed into the room.

'How is she, Rose? Is there any change?'

Rose shook her head. 'No, none at all.'

Maria took off her bonnet. 'Dr Tucker promised to call again this evening, and I hope that my mother will come soon.' She unbuttoned her mantle and laid it over the back of a chair. 'It's still very chilly in here, Rose.'

A wave of guilt swept over Rose as she glanced at the fire that had died down to glowing embers. 'I'm sorry, I should have added more coal.'

'The scuttle is empty,' Maria said, frowning.

Rose hurried over to the fireplace and seized the empty copper scuttle. 'I'll fill it up now.'

'That's a job for the servants. Jessie and Edna should be here by now.' Maria was about to tug the bell pull, but Rose was already at the door.

'I'll go and see what's happening below stairs. Sit down, Maria. You look done in. I'll ask Mrs Leary to send up a tray of tea.' She left the room without waiting for Maria to answer and headed for the back stairs.

She could sense the tension in the kitchen even before she had entered the room. The door was opened and she could see Cook and Jessie standing on either side of the kitchen table, glaring at each other as if they were about to fight a duel, while Edna and Sparrow looked on. They turned with a guilty start as she walked into the room.

'We need more coal,' Rose said casually. 'Edna, I think that's your job. Sparrow will show you where it's kept.'

'It's in the cellar.' Sparrow folded her arms and remained seated. 'I ain't missing this for anything. There'll be fisticuffs in a minute.'

'What's the matter?' Rose asked angrily.

'I'm the cook in this house,' Mrs Leary snarled. 'I've been here for more years than I like to remember and I ain't having her tell me what to do.'

Jessie stood her ground, arms folded over the imposing bosom. 'I'm Mrs Barnaby's cook and she sent for me. I dare say you ain't up to snuff, you old witch.'

'I'll have you know I've cooked for the gentry, and been praised for my efforts. You can sling your hook, because I don't want you in my kitchen.'

Jessie bristled visibly and Rose could see things getting out of hand. 'That's enough, both of you. Mrs Colville is seriously ill and you two are brawling like fishwives.' She turned to Jessie. 'This is Mrs Leary's kitchen, but I'm sure she could do with some help, if you are prepared to swallow your pride.'

'I ain't taking orders from her, and that's that.' Jessie puffed out her chest. 'Come on, Edna, let's go home. We ain't needed here.'

Edna glanced anxiously at her sister. 'I don't want to upset the missis. She's been good to us.'

'You wouldn't say that if you was being bossed around by another housemaid. God helps those who help themselves and I'm standing up for my rights.' Jessie faced Mrs Leary with a belligerent set to her square jaw.

'Now wait a minute.' Rose held up her hand. 'You can leave here right away if you don't want to oblige Mrs Barnaby, but she might dismiss you out of hand, Miss Spriggs. I doubt if you'll find another position if you haven't got a good reference.'

'That's true, Jessie,' Edna said earnestly. 'We could end up in the workhouse.'

Rose turned to Mrs Leary. 'Are you willing to shake hands and start again? Miss Spriggs might be a great help to you at this difficult time, especially as Mrs Barnaby is expecting visitors.'

'Visitors?' Mrs Leary's expression changed subtly. 'Who's coming and how many? No one told me.'

'I don't know exactly but a telegram has been sent to Starcross Abbey in Devonshire, and Mrs Barnaby hopes that her mother and stepfather will arrive tomorrow or the next day, and they might bring a servant or two.'

'We'll need more supplies, and I haven't had time to work out menus.' Mrs Leary shot a speculative glance in Jessie's direction. 'I suppose I could use some help, providing the person realises that I'm in charge.'

Rose kept a straight face with difficulty. 'What do

you say, Miss Spriggs? Are you willing to work under Mrs Leary?'

'Say yes, Jessie,' Edna pleaded. 'We can't go back to Great Hermitage Street without Mrs Barnaby's say so, and I don't fancy sleeping in a shop doorway or under the railway arches.'

Jessie nodded reluctantly. 'I'll give it a try, but she'd better treat me like an equal. I've found the Lord and I've seen the error of me former ways – and I ain't no skivvy.'

'I don't care what you done in the past.' Mrs Leary drew herself up to her full height. 'But I think I know how to run a kitchen, Jessie Spriggs. I'll treat you with the respect you deserve – no more, no less.'

'That's settled then,' Rose said firmly. 'Sparrow, I'll leave you to show Edna where to get the coal and take it to Mrs Colville's room. I have to go out for a while.'

'Where are you going?' Sparrow demanded. 'I want to go with you.'

'Not this time,' Rose said gently. 'I have a very important errand to run and it won't wait, but I'll be back in an hour or so, and I want to find everyone working peaceably together, and no squabbling. I don't think that's too much to ask – is it?'

Chapter Twelve

Getting past Nicholls presented a problem, and the two clerks sniggered behind their hands when he met her request to see the editor with a snide remark, but Rose was not going to let them get away with such childish behaviour and she stood her ground.

'I want to see Mr Radley, and he will want to see me when he hears what I have to say.'

Nicholls shot a triumphant glance at his audience. 'Oh, well, then I'd better hold the press ready for this breaking news story.'

'I haven't got time for this play-acting,' Rose said angrily, and she walked round his desk to rap on the editor's door.

'Hey, you can't do that,' Nicholls protested.

'I can and I have.' Rose opened the door and walked into Arthur Radley's office.

He looked up from the copy he had been reading, peering at Rose over the top of his steel-rimmed spectacles. 'What is the meaning of this, Miss Munday? You no longer work here.'

Rose thrust the crumpled piece of paper under his nose. 'You might change your mind when you read this, sir.' She waited, hardly daring to breathe as he adjusted his glasses and smoothed the creases out with the flat of his hand.

'It's hardly the best presented piece of work I've ever seen.'

'Yes, I'm sorry about that, but I had to get it to you quickly.'

After a cursory glance he gave it his full attention, reading more slowly. Rose stood stiffly to attention, clasping and unclasping her hands – so much depended on his reaction. If she could get her job back she would be able to support herself and Sparrow, too.

Radley raised his head. 'Did you write this?'

'Yes, sir. I know I could polish it up but I had to write it under difficult conditions.'

'You surprise me, Miss Munday. This isn't perfect by any means, but it shows promise, and it's a shocking story. Are you sure of your facts?'

'I am, and I know that Gilroy has dealings with Regan, who is well known to the police.'

'How do you know about Regan?'

'He owns the house where an acquaintance of

mine has a room. Regan lives on immoral earnings.'

'It's a house of ill repute. Is that what you're saying?'

'Yes, sir. Circumstances made it necessary for me to stay there for a while, but Regan discovered me and he wanted to put me to work – if you know what I mean.'

'I see.' Radley took off his glasses and wiped the lenses on his handkerchief. 'I've been trying to get something on Regan for the last three years, but that man is as slippery as an eel. Get me evidence of Regan's involvement in the brothel, and if you can prove that he's handling stolen goods from the servant woman, I'll give it my due consideration.'

'Does this mean that you'll print my story?'

'If I have that information before the paper goes to print this evening, you'll earn full credit for the work.'

'Will you give me back my job?'

'One step at a time, Miss Munday. I can see that you have a way with words, but that's not enough for a reporter, especially a young woman like yourself. It's very much a man's world and I doubt if any woman is up to the rough and tumble of Fleet Street.' He held up his hand as Rose was about to protest. 'Having said that, I think the fact that most men would not consider you to be a serious threat might actually open doors that would normally be closed to someone like Eugene.'

'Have you heard from him, sir?' Rose asked eagerly.

'He cabled a brief account of his journey so far. His first article will be in tomorrow's issue. I suggest you buy a copy, Miss Munday. We need to boost circulation.'

'I will, of course, sir.'

'Now, if you're serious about getting your piece published you'd best go about your business. You have until seven o'clock this evening – I have a dinner engagement at eight, so I'll be leaving the office before seven thirty.'

'Yes, sir. I'm going.' Rose hesitated. 'But I need some money for expenses, sir. I'm a bit short of the readies.'

Radley's lips tightened and she thought he was going to refuse, but he reached into a drawer and took out a cash box. 'Here,' he said, extracting a few coins and handing them to her. 'Take this, but I'll need a note of how you spend the money. If you want to be treated as a professional you must learn to behave like one. Now go. You haven't got much time.'

Hardly able to believe the about-turn in her fortunes, Rose rushed from the office, barely noticing the muted cheers from Nicholls and his acolytes, who obviously mistook her hasty departure for defeat. But as she stepped out into the busy street she came back to earth with a jolt. It was all very well making rash promises, but she had just a few hours to gather the information that Radley required. It would soon be dark and danger would be lurking in every alley and unlit street.

What, she wondered, would Eugene do in such circumstances? Then, as if he were sending her a psychic message, she remembered Cecilia's promise to speak to her friend Emily, whose husband was something high up in the Metropolitan Police Force. If anyone could help her it would be Cissie. Rose raised her hand and hailed a cab.

Cecilia motioned Rose to take a seat by the fire. 'You look perished, and it will be dark soon. Haven't you anything warmer to wear than that thin cape?'

'I wouldn't have this if you hadn't turned out your wardrobe, and I'm truly grateful, but that's not why I'm here. I need your help, Cissie.'

'You can tell me when you've had a chance to get warm.' Cecilia reached for the bell. 'Tea or coffee? It's a little early for sherry wine.'

'Neither, thank you. I'm in a terrible hurry.'

Cecilia relaxed against the satin cushions. 'You haven't been near me for days and now you say you're in a rush. That's simply not good enough, Rose. I've been dying of boredom since Gene left and then you abandoned me.'

'That's not fair. You said you didn't mind when I told you that I was going to stay with Maria.'

'And I don't, in theory, darling. But I was enjoying your company and I didn't realise how much I'd miss you, especially with Gene in Egypt. He's staying with our parents and, if I know my brother, he'll be the darling of what society is left after that frightful war.'

'But he's well and not in danger?'

Cecilia eyed her curiously. 'You're very fond of my brother, aren't you? But he's a heart-breaker, Rose. Beware of men like Gene.'

'I'm engaged to Max,' Rose said primly.

'Tra la la. I've heard that song before.' Cecilia feigned a yawn. 'I'm sure you didn't come all this way from Wapping to tell me you miss me. So why are you here?'

Rose glanced at her anxiously and was relieved to see a mischievous smile curving Cecilia's lips, and a smile in her fine eyes. 'I do miss you, and I miss the guvnor, but the main reason I came this afternoon was to ask if your friend Emily has come up with any information about the men who have taken over the Captain's House.'

'So you still intend to live there until Max returns?' Cecilia put her head on one side. 'Is living with Maria not as much fun as you hoped?'

'We're staying in Pier House at the moment. Mrs Colville is very ill and Maria is taking care of her until her mother arrives from Devonshire. The truth is that I found a link between the squatters and Mrs

Colville's servant. Gilroy has been stealing from her, probably for years. It was Sparrow who gave me the clue.'

'Sparrow?' Cecilia raised her eyebrows. 'Who or what is Sparrow?'

Rose opened her mouth to explain but was interrupted by the arrival of the maid. 'You rang, ma'am.'

'Yes, I think we need sustenance. Coffee, please, and some cake.' Cecilia waited until the maid had left the room. 'A tot of brandy will keep out the cold. It's rather good added to coffee, as I discovered when staying with an elderly aunt who abhorred strong drink.' She stood up and went to the side table to pour two tots of brandy. 'Well, then, Rose, explain. Who is Sparrow?'

The fiery spirit was warming and Rose began to relax a little. Cecilia was a good audience, listening avidly as she sat on the edge of her chair, sipping her drink.

'Well, you have had an eventful time since you left here,' she said when Rose came to the end of her explanation. 'And in answer to your question, I saw Emily yesterday and, in the strictest confidence, she told me that the men who are squatting in the Captain's House are well known to the police. Unfortunately she didn't know, or couldn't divulge any names, but they are there illegally.'

Rose downed the last of the brandy and leaped to her feet. She rushed over to Cecilia and gave her a hug. 'Thank you, Cissie. The guvnor would be proud of you, and I am, too.'

'Where are you going now?' Cecilia asked anxiously.

'You wouldn't want to know.' Rose kissed her on the cheek. 'But I'll keep in touch.'

Cecilia rose to her feet. 'But you've only just arrived. Can't you spare me five minutes of your time?'

'I'm sorry, but this is really urgent. I have to hurry, or I won't catch Mr Radley before he leaves the office.' Rose left without giving Cecilia a chance to question her further, and, having declined Giddings' offer to find her a cab, she let herself out of the house, although she began to regret her hasty decision as she paced up and down. Several cabs went past but they were occupied. Just as she was giving up hope one drew to a halt at the kerb.

'Black Raven Court, please, cabby.' Rose climbed into the vehicle and the cabby flicked his whip, encouraging his horse to walk on. It was dark now and through lighted windows Rose caught glimpses of homes where families gathered for the evening meal and others where servants hurried about, laying tables and stoking fires. When the cab slowed down almost to a halt due to the heavy traffic, Rose could see into affluent homes where cut-glass decanters filled with wine and spirits glittered in the gaslight and uniformed maidservants fluttered past the windows as they laid tables, attended to fires and made ready for the evening meal. In one house Rose smiled when she spotted a maid and a footman embracing, and through another window children, who had most likely escaped the clutches of their governess, were snatching bonbons from a silver dish. These glimpses into family life made Rose feel homesick for her old home in Bendigo. In the State of Victoria their new day had yet to begin, but in her mind's eye she could see Sadie cooking up tasty dishes in the kitchen, while Laurence supervised the students as they pored over their books.

They reached the outskirts of the City where some shop windows were lit by gas and others by naphtha flares, but there were grim reminders of the hardships suffered by the poor. Huddled shapes, almost unrecognisable as human beings, crouched in unlit doorways and crippled beggars held out their caps to passers-by, but were largely ignored by the clerks and shop assistants who were hurrying home after a long day at work. Rose pulled her cape more tightly around her. She might have suffered a similar fate if Cora had not found her wandering about in the fog, and it was this debt of gratitude that she intended to repay in full. The contrast between the comfortably-off area of Tavistock Square and the squalor of Black Raven Court was even more apparent as she alighted from the cab.

'Do you want me to wait, miss?' The cabby leaned

down from his seat. 'This ain't the sort of place a young lady should frequent.'

Rose thought quickly, weighing up the cost against the advantage of a quick getaway. 'Yes, if you would.' She tossed a coin to him. 'I won't be long.'

He tipped his cap. 'I'll wait ten minutes, but it will cost you.'

'That should give me plenty of time for what I have to do.' Rose clutched her reticule under her arm as she made her way to the brothel. The door, as always, was unlocked and she let herself in. The familiar stench that permeated the building hit her in a noxious wave of damp rot, stale food and cheap cologne, as she made her way upstairs to knock on Cora's door.

'Who is it?'

'It's me – Rose. Can I come in?'

Cora's heavy tread and the creaking of loose floorboards were followed by a click of the latch and the door opened. 'Rose? What the hell are you doing here?'

'Let me in and I'll explain.'

'It must be important to bring you out in this weather. Trade has been slack for the last few days or you might have caught me in an embarrassing situation.' Cora held the door wide open and Rose could see the usual chaotic mess of discarded clothing, and an unmade bed, overflowing ash trays and a washing line stretched across the width of the room, hung with damp stockings and under-wear.

Rose stepped inside. 'I think I can put Regan behind bars, but I need your help.'

Cora took a tobacco pouch from the mantelshelf and proceeded to roll a cigarette, lighting it with a spill from the fire. 'Go on, girl. I like the sound of that.'

In as few words as possible, Rose told her about Gilroy and her connection with Regan and the men who were occupying the Captain's House.

'I'd like to see them blokes get their comeuppance,' Cora said, exhaling smoke at the blackened ceiling. 'What d'you want me to do?'

'I want you and Flossie to bear witness to Regan's illicit dealings.'

'What does that mean exactly?'

'I'm writing an article exposing Regan, Gilroy and the others. If the editor thinks it's worth printing it will go in tomorrow's copy of the *London Leader*.'

Cora drew on her cigarette and smoke trickled out through her dilated nostrils. 'I dunno, love. Regan would slit me throat if he thought I'd got anything to do with it.'

'The police have been trying to pin something on him for years, so I was told. This should see him arrested and thrown into jail.'

'But what if it don't? And how long would it take the cops to nab him?'

'I can't say, but do you want to live like this for ever, Cora? That man bleeds you dry.'

'No, but I don't want to end up in a wooden box either.'

Rose thought quickly. 'What if I could find you somewhere safe to live? Would you and Flossie agree to testify against Regan then?'

'Depends on what it is? I ain't going in the workhouse.'

'No, of course not. I have a much better idea. I'm sure that my fiancé's half-sister, Maria, would be pleased for you both to reside in her house until Regan is safely behind bars.'

'People don't just invite women like us to stay, Rose. You're living in an imaginary world where folk are kind to all sorts, even pros like me and Flossie.'

'Maria isn't like that and it would only be temporary. You helped me when I was in dire need and I have a chance to repay you for your kindness. Please say yes, Cora.'

Cora tossed the stub of her cigarette into the fire. 'Let me go and ask Flossie. I know she's on her own because she's come down with a stinking cold. Give me a few minutes.'

'I have a cab waiting.'

'Two minutes, then.' Cora waddled from the room and the sound of her bare feet pounding on the stair treads echoed throughout the building. She returned a few minutes later, breathless but enthusiastic. 'Flossie said she'd do anything to get us out of this hellhole.'

'What about you, Cora?'

'If it nails Regan I'm for it. You're right – I can't keep this up for ever, and by the time Regan has taken his cut and the rent, I've barely enough to keep meself in baccy and tea.' Cora scrabbled under the bed and pulled out a threadbare carpet bag. 'Give us the address, and we'll need cab fare. I haven't had a punter for two days and I'm broke.'

'I'll come back for you,' Rose said eagerly. 'Pack your things and get Flossie to do the same and I'll hire a hackney carriage to take us to Great Hermitage Street, but first I have to get the article past the editor and then I need to get the key from Maria.'

'Are you sure she'll agree?'

'Yes. I'm certain she will. I'll be back later, Cora.'

'There it is, Mr Radley.' Rose thrust the piece of paper under his nose. 'If that doesn't put Regan and the others behind bars there's no justice in the world.'

'I admire your tenacity, Miss Munday, but please sit down. You're disturbing my train of thought.' Radley put on his glasses and settled down to read the article that Rose had drafted, wording it carefully and using initials rather than names, but the identities of those mentioned would be obvious to anyone who had any knowledge of the criminal underworld.

Radley read on in silence, accompanied by the ticking of the grandfather clock in the corner of the office, and the rhythmic sound of the printing press from the floor below.

Rose sat on the edge of a hard wooden chair, digging her fingernails into her palms as she waited for his verdict, willing him to approve of what she had written. Eventually he raised his head and gave her a blank stare. Her heart sank and she knew that she was beaten, but then a slow smile curved his lips and travelled to his pale grey eyes.

'Excellent, Miss Munday.'

'Really, sir?'

'Yes, really. This is an article that would not have shamed Eugene. You have something of his style, but with a freshness and lack of cynicism that I find quite appealing. I take it that you have checked your facts?'

'I have witnesses who have promised to attest to their statements, Mr Radley.'

'Are you sure they won't renege on their promises? If Regan puts pressure on them or the gangs get to them they might be forced to withdraw their statements.'

'I'm taking them to a place of safety, Mr Radley. Regan won't find them and I'll make sure they remain under cover until after the trial, if the police arrest Regan.'

'Very well. I'll make a few minor alterations and

this can go to press. You go on now and do what you have to do for your informants. I'll take this to the print room on my way out.'

'What about my job, sir? Do I get it back?'

'I'll give you a three-month trial, Munday. You'll learn the ropes and do exactly as you're told or you will find yourself out of work. Do you understand me?'

'Yes, sir. I most certainly do.' Rose stood up. She knew that she was grinning from ear to ear in a most unladylike way, but she had never felt so proud or so happy in her whole life. But it was far from over, as she realised once she was back in a cab, heading for Pier House. First and foremost she had to persuade Maria to allow Cora and Flossie to stay in Great Hermitage Street until Regan was out of the way. It had been rash to make promises that she might not be able to keep, but it was a desperate situation and London would be a safer place with Regan and his associates locked up for a very long time.

She found Maria in the blue parlour with the children. Sparrow looked up from the game she had been playing with Polly, and frowned.

'Where've you been? I thought you wasn't coming back.'

'I had important things to do,' Rose said evasively. 'I'll tell you all about it after I've had a word with Maria.'

'I've just rung for Izzie. It's the children's supper time.' Maria eyed Rose curiously. 'You were gone a long time.'

'The good news is that Mr Radley has relented and given me a three-month trial at the newspaper. He liked the piece I wrote and it'll be in the morning edition.'

'That's wonderful, Rose.' Maria turned her head at the sound of the door opening. 'Izzie, will you take the children to the kitchen? Jessie will have their bread and milk ready.'

'Yes'm.' Izzie held her hand out to Polly. 'Come on, nipper.' She turned her attention to Sparrow. 'If you're coming you can carry the baby. He bit me last time I tried to pick him up.'

'I don't blame him.' Sparrow scooped Teddy up in her arms. 'I'd bite her too if she handled me like I was a sack of taters.'

Teddy grabbed a handful of Sparrow's hair in his chubby hand and planted a smacking kiss on her cheek.

Polly faced Izzie with a mutinous scowl. 'I want to hold Sparrow's hand, not yours.'

'Be a good girl, darling,' Maria said feebly. 'Mama has a headache, so don't make a fuss.'

Izzie shooed the children out of the room, muttering beneath her breath.

'I'm sorry I left you for such a long time.' Rose pulled up a chair and sat down by the fire, holding her hands out to the blaze. 'But I had several things to do, and one of them was to persuade Cora and Flossie, the women I told you about, to testify against Regan.'

'Will they do it?'

'Yes, but they are in desperate need of a safe place to live.' Rose paused, watching Maria's reaction.

'I can see that. What had you in mind?'

'I was wondering if they could stay in your house for a while. It would only be until the trial is over and Regan is sentenced.'

Maria frowned. 'They wouldn't conduct their business from my home, would they? I mean, I have great sympathy for women who are reduced to selling themselves in order to survive, but I don't know Cora and Flossie. Are they honest and trustworthy?'

'There would be no question of that sort of behaviour, and I would hope they'd respect your property. But without their testimonies I'm afraid Regan will walk free, as well as his accomplices – Gilroy being one of them.'

'If it brings that woman to justice I'll do almost anything. I have no love for my grandmother, but I can't bear to see her lying there like a broken doll, begging for laudanum. She was once a proud, handsome woman, and it was Gilroy who reduced her to that state.'

'So you agree?'

'I do,' Maria said simply. 'I'll remain here for as long as it takes for Grandmama to recover, and I hope you and Sparrow will stay, too.'

'I will, gladly.' Rose reached out the clasp Maria's hands. 'Things will improve, I know they will.'

'There's just one thing,' Maria added thoughtfully. 'If your friends will agree to work here, I think I'll send Jessie and Edna home. They'll take care of my house, and it will put a stop to the discord between Mrs Leary and Jessie. I really don't need to have them at each other's throats.' A wry smile curved Maria's lips. 'Besides which, being a reformed character herself, Jessie will do her best to make your friends repent the evil of their ways.'

'In that case I think you're right, Cora and Flossie should come here every day and take over the cleaning. Your grandmother could pay them for their services.'

'What would Grandmama say if she knew?' Maria said, giggling. 'She was always so fond of telling me what a wicked woman my mother was, and that I was a disgrace. She had no time for what she called "fallen women".'

'I think you're very good to look after her, considering how horrible she was to you when you were a defenceless child.'

Maria shrugged and sighed. 'She's the one who is helpless now. Anyway, my mother should be here tomorrow and I hope she'll take over from me.'

'I'm looking forward to seeing her again. I remember your wedding, Maria. I sat in the pew behind your mother and Freddie, but I haven't seen them since that day.' Reluctantly Rose raised herself from the comfortable seat by the fire. 'I'm afraid I have to go out again.'

'It's cold and dark. Can't you leave it until the morning?'

'I promised Cora that I'd return tonight and take them to safety. I'll need the keys to your house, if you don't mind.'

Maria reached for the bell. 'I can do better than that. I'll send Jessie and Edna there now. They can get the fires going and make the place welcoming for those poor women.'

'I hope Jessie won't start preaching at them the moment they walk through the door.'

'I'll make sure she doesn't. It was a mistake to bring them here in the first place.' She tugged on the bell pull. 'Don't forget to ask your ladies to come here first thing in the morning. I want the house ready for Mama and Freddie.'

'Don't worry, Maria. I'm sure it will all work out.' Rose spoke with more conviction than she was feeling.

Minutes later, wrapped up as warmly as possible, Rose left the house and made her way towards the High Street where she hoped to find a cab, but the pavements were slippery and a frosting of snow covered the iron-hard ground. The gaslight at the end of the terrace cast a golden glow on the chilly scene, but a movement beneath the trees caught Rose's attention and she turned her head to peer into the darkness. She could only make out the stark tree trunks and bare branches, and she told herself it was just her imagination. Even so, she could have sworn that someone was watching her and she quickened her pace.

Chapter Thirteen

Jessie opened the door and stood aside, glaring at Cora and Flossie as they scurried in with Rose following on their heels. Edna stood back, studying the newcomers from a distance and Rose could feel the tension surrounding them as the four women eyed each other up and down.

'What's your name?' Jessie fixed her gaze on Flossie.

'Flossie Boxer, what's yours?'

Jessie's frown deepened. 'Boxer. Are you related to Bertie Boxer from Poplar?'

'He's my uncle. How d'you know him?'

'Well, I never did! He's our uncle, too.'

'By marriage,' Edna added, grinning.

'Over the broomstick, more like,' Jessie said, frowning. 'How is the old goat?'

'Same as ever. You know Bertie.'

'I'm Cora Smith.' Cora stepped in between them. 'And I ain't related to the Boxers in any shape or form.

Jessie looked her up and down, her eyes narrowing. 'I know your story, Cora. I expect you and Flossie to behave proper while you're living here. We got rules and we got standards.'

'Give over, girl,' Flossie said, chuckling. 'We might have had to earn our bread the hard way, but that don't make us sinners.'

Cora dumped her luggage on the floor. 'I could do with a cup of tea. Has anybody put the kettle on?'

'It should be boiling by now,' Edna said shyly. 'If you're hungry we've got some bread and dripping.'

'I'm blooming starving.' Flossie patted her belly. 'Got any chocolate, love? I got a craving for a bar of Fry's Chocolate Cream.'

'You'll have to make do with bread and dripping,' Jessie said firmly. 'But you can give me all the family gossip. They don't have nothing to do with me these days, even though I'm a changed woman. Mud sticks,' she added tersely.

'I know, dear. It's the same for us, ain't it, Cora?'

Rose backed towards the doorway. She had told the cabby to wait and this was costing money. 'I can see you're all going to get along splendidly, so I'll say good night and I'll see you two at the Pier

House in the morning. Jessie will tell you how to get there.' She left them chatting amicably. All was well – at least for the present – but she could imagine that four strong and opinionated women might clash at some point. She opened the front door and stepped outside into a mist of softly falling snow.

Next morning, slightly later than expected, Cora and Flossie turned up for work at the Colville residence. They had toned down their flamboyant attire with varying degrees of success. Cora had wrapped a gaudy red and black shawl around her shoulders in an attempt to cover her décolletage, and she had scrubbed her face clean of powder and rouge, leaving her skin reddened and patchy. Her bleached hair was trying desperately to escape the confines of a greasy mobcap, and she moved in a cloud of cheap cologne. Flossie reeked of tobacco with a hint of gin, and her hair was concealed beneath an odd-looking turban that came down over her eyebrows. Her faded print gown was at least two sizes too small with the buttons on the bodice straining each time she moved.

'What are they wearing?' Maria asked in a whisper as she sent them down to the kitchen to collect dusters and mops. 'It looks like fancy dress.'

Rose shook her head. 'The poor things aren't used to being in service, Maria. Did your grandmother provide uniforms for her servants?'

'I don't know, but I'd better have a look in the linen cupboard. Would you mind sitting with her while I sort things out below stairs? Grandmama is very restless this morning and keeps calling for Gilroy, but I've only given her a very small dose of laudanum. She's getting so hard to handle – I'll be glad when my mother arrives. Maybe she can do better.'

'I'll do my best.' Rose went straight to the drawing room, but as she opened the double doors she felt a gust of cold air. It took her a couple of seconds to realise that it came from one of the tall windows that opened out onto the garden, and a quick glance at the bed revealed tumbled sheets and coverlet, but there was no sign of Mrs Colville. Fearing the worst, Rose rushed out onto the snow-covered terrace and her breath caught in her throat as she saw a slight figure teetering on the wall above the dock entrance. Her arms were outstretched, as if she were a bird about to fly the nest.

'Mrs Colville.' Rose walked slowly towards her, trying to keep calm, but the old woman was dangerously close to a drop of twenty feet or more into the turbulent water. 'Mrs Colville, please come away from there.'

Clarissa Colville turned to give Rose a vague smile and stepped forward – into nothing but thin air.

The scream that escaped Rose's lips was lost in the hoot of a whistle from a passing steamer, and for a moment she was frozen to the spot. It was a nightmare come true and it was hard to believe that such a terrible thing could have happened, but as the mist cleared from her brain she realised that this was not simply a terrifying dream. She moved forward, oblivious to the cold. The noise from the docks and the sounds of the river traffic merged with the greedy sucking of the water below as the tide turned and the river flowed down towards the sea. It took all her courage to peer over the edge and a wave of nausea almost overcame her as she caught sight of a white shape, spread-eagled on the surface of the dark, oily water as Mrs Colville floated effortlessly away on the ebb tide. Finding her voice at last, Rose screamed for help but the cries of the gulls carried more force and her words were borne away by the east wind.

'Rose. What are you doing out here? Where is my grandmother?'

She turned slowly to face Maria. 'I couldn't stop her. I'm so sorry.'

Maria's hands flew to cover her mouth and muffle the cry of despair. 'No. She wouldn't . . .'

'She just stepped over the edge, Maria. I wasn't near enough to do anything.'

Maria stared at her aghast. 'I only left her for a short while.'

Rose hurried to her side and slipped her arm around her shoulders. 'I saw a boat nearby,' she said gently. 'They'll bring her to shore.'

Unresisting, Maria allowed Rose to take her indoors. 'She couldn't have known what she was doing.'

Rose guided her to a chair. 'Maybe she'd taken too much laudanum. Did you leave the bottle with her?'

'No, of course not. I always measure a dose and then I take the medicine back to my room.'

'Is this the one?' Rose went to a small table at the bedside and picked up an empty bottle. 'It says Laudanum on the label.'

'No, I have the bottle here.' Maria pulled it from her pocket. 'This is the one I've been using, but I hadn't had time to put it away. How did that one come to be in her possession? I didn't give it to her.'

'And who opened the window?' Rose stepped outside and retraced her steps, and as she leaned over the wall she saw a limp body being hauled unceremoniously into a small boat. Any vague hope that the old lady had survived was immediately dashed, but it was the footprints leading away from the scene that caught Rose's eye. Despite the bitter wind, laced with sharp particles of ice, Rose followed the trail around the side of the house where they were lost in the trodden snow and then something shiny caught her eye. She swooped on the empty bottle and hurried back to the drawing room with it clutched in her hand.

'Did you see her, Rose?' Maria's voice broke on

a sob. 'Grandmama was a hard woman and she treated me badly, but she didn't deserve this.'

'Don't distress yourself,' Rose said gently. 'This is a case for the police. I think someone else was involved because there are footprints in the snow. They're too small to be those of a man, and I can think of only one person who might have done something so wicked.'

'Gilroy?' Maria whispered. 'Why would she want to harm Grandmama?'

'Revenge maybe, or to cover the fact that she stole from your grandmother. She might not have pushed the old lady, but she must have left the window open, and I found this.' Rose held up a small medicine bottle. 'Chloral,' she said simply. 'That, together with laudanum, might explain Mrs Colville's confusion and irrational behaviour.'

Maria stared at her in horror. 'Why would Gilroy return? I can't believe that it was simply to give Grandmama a fatal dose of these drugs, unless . . .' her eyes sparkled with unshed tears. 'Rose, I can't do it – will you look in that cupboard? There should be a jewellery box on the top shelf. It's where Grandmama kept her valuables.'

Rose did as she asked, but the lid of the ornate brass-bound box was open and it was obvious that the lock had been forced. She placed it on the table at Maria's side. 'It's empty. I'm so sorry, it seems you were right.'

Tears spilled from Maria's eyes and she buried her face in her hands. 'I'm certain it was Gilroy. She was the only one who knew where we kept Grandmama's precious things. Some of the jewels were very valuable.'

Rose turned her head at the sound of running footsteps and Cora burst into the room. 'There's a copper on the doorstep, missis. Says he wants to see you. I thought he'd come after Flossie and me for a moment, but he just give me a funny look and asked for you.'

'I'm not sure I feel up to speaking to the police,' Maria said faintly. 'This has all come as such a shock.'

'Would you like me to see him first, to give you time to compose yourself?' Rose asked anxiously.

'Yes, please do. I'll be all right in a minute or so.'

Rose shooed Cora out of the room. 'You didn't find any plainer gowns, then?'

'I ain't dressing like a dowd just to please her ladyship.'

'Think of it as acting a part, Cora. You're pretending to be a maidservant.'

'I can do that,' Cora said defiantly. 'I'm as good-looking as that new actress they all rave about. Lillie Langtry, they calls her, and I've heard that she's no better than she should be.' Cora shot a wary glance at Rose. 'That's what they say, and she has a royal patron.'

'Never mind that now, Cora. Mrs Colville has had a fatal accident and I want you to go downstairs and break it gently to Mrs Leary. Leave me to deal with the police.'

Cora's eyes almost popped out of her head. 'Really? Was she done in?'

'It was an accident, as I said. The poor lady fell in the river and was drowned. Mrs Barnaby is naturally very upset.'

Cora tossed her head. 'From what I've heard the old woman was a spitful old b—'

'Gossiping again, Cora.' Rose tut-tutted and walked away, heading for the entrance hall where she found the police constable studying the portraits of the Colville family.

He jumped to attention as Rose approached.

'Good morning, Constable. If you've come to tell us about Mrs Colville's tragic accident, we know already.'

'What accident was that, miss?'

'They've just taken her body from the river, Constable.'

'Then it's a case for the River Police, miss.' He stared at her, frowning. 'I'm sorry for your loss, but that's not why I'm here. I'm Constable Palmer, might I ask your name before I go any further?'

'I'm Rose Munday and I'm a friend of the family.'

'Mrs Colville made a complaint against a former servant, by the name of Maggie Gilroy.'

'I don't know how she could have reported the crimes, Constable Palmer. Mrs Colville was an invalid.'

'She sent a servant to report that things had gone missing from the house.' The constable took a notebook from his pocket and flipped through the pages. 'A certain Ada Leary, who is employed as a cook by Mrs Colville.'

'I knew about the thefts, but I didn't know that Mrs Leary had been asked to report them.'

'I need to speak to Mrs Leary regarding a certain article in this morning's edition of the *London Leader*. You wouldn't happen to have a copy, would you?'

Rose shook her head. 'Why do you ask, and what has it to do with Cook?'

'My sergeant drew my attention to it, miss. No names are mentioned, but it concerns a maidservant who steals from her employer, and that said servant is friendly with a man who's repeatedly escaped capture. It seems to match what your cook told us.'

'That could be any household in London,' Rose said warily.

'It goes on to name a well-known fence and the man who runs the sort of establishment that a young lady like yourself would know nothing about, and he's the one we're after.'

'What has that got to do with us?'

'Cora Smith is well known to the force, Miss

Munday. If you'll excuse me saying so, she ain't the sort of person you'd want in the servants' hall.'

Rose thought quickly. The young policeman was no fool, and he had recognised Cora, which in turn would link them to Regan. 'I think you'd better come into the blue parlour, Constable Palmer.'

'I'll need to speak to everyone in the household.'

'Yes, of course.' Rose led the way to the blue parlour, where Flossie had laid a fire earlier. Judging by the lingering smell of tobacco smoke she had stopped to enjoy a cigarette before returning to the kitchen. Mrs Leary would most certainly disapprove of such behaviour and there would be trouble below stairs if either Flossie or Cora were caught smoking indoors.

Rose was about to invite the policeman to sit down when the door opened and Sparrow rushed into the room.

'Is it true, Rose? Has the old lady thrown herself in the river?' Sparrow came to a halt as she spotted the policeman. 'I'm sorry. I didn't know you was busy. I'll go.'

'No, wait a minute. I've seen you before, young lady.' Constable Palmer advanced on Sparrow, giving her a searching look. 'You wasn't so well dressed when we last met, was you, Sparrow?'

'I dunno what you're talking about.' Sparrow backed towards the door. 'I never seen you afore in all me born days.'

'You're Piggin's nipper. I seen you with him and his woman on several occasions. I apprehended you once or twice, too. D'you remember me now?'

Sparrow sent a pleading glance to Rose. 'No, guv. It's slipped me mind.'

'What had you done?' Rose moved to her side and placed a protective arm around Sparrow's shoulders. 'What was she accused of, Constable?'

'Pick-pocketing, miss. Piggin trains street arabs to do his dirty work, and I caught this one in the act of pinching a gent's wallet, but I let her off with a caution. It was Piggin I wanted to nab, not a nine-year-old girl.' Palmer bent down so that his face was on a level with Sparrow's. 'We had a deal, nipper. You was going to keep an eye on Piggin and let me know when he received a big haul.'

'I ain't soft in the head, mister. Piggin would kill me and if he didn't, then she would. I ain't got to my age by being stupid.'

Rose gave Sparrow a hug. 'I think you should leave Sparrow out of this and concentrate on Gilroy. I saw her with Regan, and that's why I brought Cora and Flossie here. They used to work in Regan's establishment, but they've turned over a new leaf, and they want to get away from their old life and start afresh.'

'That's right,' Sparrow added fervently. 'Me, too. Rose took me in and give me new duds and everything. I ain't going back there, not ever.'

'Of course not.' Rose hugged her again. 'You're with me now, Sparrow. I won't let anyone hurt you. Now you can help the constable by asking Mrs Leary, Cora and Flossie to come here one at a time. The constable has some question he wants to ask everyone.'

Sparrow puffed out her chest. 'I'll do that and I'll make sure they do what you say.' She shot a triumphant glance at the constable as she left the room.

'She's had a hard life,' Rose said hastily.

'You don't have to tell me that, miss. I've got sisters and I wouldn't want any of them to have to suffer what that nipper has in her short life, but she must learn to abide by the law.'

'And she will. I'll see to that.'

Palmer laid his notebook on the table. 'Might I ask you a question, Miss Munday?'

'Yes, of course. What is it?'

'Have you anything to do with the piece in the newspaper? You seem to know a lot about the criminals named in it.'

'I wrote it,' Rose said simply. There seemed little point in prevaricating when Palmer had obviously guessed her secret. 'I've only recently started working for the *Leader*. It was the first thing I'd written for them, apart from a review of a Gilbert and Sullivan opera.'

'It's not the sort of story I'd expect a young lady to follow up. In fact, I don't know of any other ladies working in the newspaper business.'

'It came about by a series of mishaps.'

'Would you care to explain? I have a report to write, Miss Munday.'

Yet again Rose found herself going through everything from the moment she stepped off the ship, but this time she was able to make an official complaint about the men who were living in the Captain's House, and she made sure that Palmer wrote it down in his notebook. She had just brought him up to date with the events leading to Clarissa Colville's death when Mrs Leary knocked and entered. Her plump cheeks were flushed and she answered Constable Palmer's questions at length, gesticulating and adding her own opinion until Rose began to feel sorry for the young policeman. All his attempts to stem the flow fell on deaf ears, and, in the end, it was only the arrival of Flossie that put a stop to Cook's denunciation of Gilroy and her thieving, conniving habits.

'And the mistress would still be alive if that woman hadn't crept in and dosed her with laudanum,' Mrs Leary continued, ignoring Rose's attempts to persuade her that it was Flossie's turn to speak. 'That's murder. You need to arrest Gilroy, Constable.'

'Thank you, Cook,' Rose said hastily. 'That was most useful. I'm sure Constable Palmer has taken down every word.'

'Ada Leary,' Cook called as Rose hustled her out of the room. 'Have you got that, Constable?'

'Some people don't know when to shut their traps,' Flossie said, sighing. 'What can I do for you, Constable?'

After calming Maria's worries and having managed to convince her that the police were intent on catching Regan, Rose went off to work. Muffled against the bitter wind that roared upriver bringing with it ice-cold conditions from the north-east, Rose finally arrived. She forced herself to stroll into the main office as if nothing was wrong. Nicholls glared at her.

'What sort of time d'you call this? Mr Radley's been looking for you.'

Rose acknowledged him with a casual nod, and went to knock on the editor's door without saying a word.

'Come in.'

Radley's tone was not encouraging but Rose opened the door and went in anyway.

'Good morning, Mr Radley,' she said brightly. 'Sorry I'm late but I've been dealing with the police.'

'What have you done, Miss Munday? Are you in trouble?'

'No, sir. I witnessed a suicide and it's connected with the woman I mentioned, anonymously, of course, in my article. It all ties in and the police are looking for Gilroy and Regan.'

Radley took off his spectacles and polished them on his tie. 'Write it up and put it on my desk.'

Rose tried to look casual, but in reality she had been expecting a good telling-off, if not the sack for coming in so late. 'Yes, sir. I'll do it right away.'

'Just a minute, Munday.'

'Yes, sir?' Rose hesitated in the doorway.

'I'm afraid I have some bad news.'

Rose could tell by the tone of his voice that this was something out of the ordinary. 'What is it, sir?'

'I had a cable from Alexandria. Eugene is missing.'

'Missing? What does that mean?'

'Apparently he accompanied a party of soldiers into the desert, and they were ambushed by tribesmen. There were fatalities, but Eugene wasn't among them. He hasn't been seen or heard of since.'

Shocked and stunned by the news, Rose hurried through the outer office, ignoring the questions thrown at her by Nicholls. She sat at her desk and forced herself to concentrate on writing the account of the tragic occurrence at Pier House, but she was careful not to mention names. Cora and Flossie would be in considerable danger if Regan were to discover their whereabouts, as would Sparrow. Rose worked diligently until late afternoon, but Eugene was never far from her thoughts, and as soon as she had finished she placed the work in front of Radley. He read it without comment until he reached the end.

'Very good, Miss Munday. Take this to the print room and tell them to put it on the front page.'

'Yes, sir. Right away.' Rose hesitated in the doorway. 'There's just one thing . . .'

Arthur Radley took off his spectacles and sat back in his chair, regarding her with a hint of a smile. 'Yes, you may go now. Give my regards and commiserations to Cecilia, and tell her not to worry about her brother. Eugene is a survivor.'

Cecilia was in the middle of packing, or at least Lindon was doing the work and Cecilia was sitting on the edge of her bed, supervising.

'Rose!' Cecilia stood up, holding out her arms. 'I've been trying to get in touch with you since last evening. I sent Giddings to Great Hermitage Street but you weren't there.'

'I was in Pier House with Maria, and I've only just heard about the guvnor. Mr Radley told me when I arrived in the office. I was late because I had to deal with the police after Mrs Colville threw herself into the river.'

'What?' Cecilia sat down again. 'Are you talking about Maria's grandmother?'

'Yes. I'll tell you everything later, but is there any more news of your brother?'

'None, I'm afraid. I'm leaving tomorrow morning, first thing. I've sent a cable to my parents to let them know.'

'I am so sorry. I wish there was something I could do.'

Cecilia dabbed her eyes with a crumpled handkerchief. 'I don't think I can do this on my own. Come with me, Rose. Please say you will.'

Chapter Fourteen

Rose was torn between loyalties to Maria and Cecilia, both of whom had taken her in without question and treated like family. Now each of them needed her help and support, and it was going to be a difficult choice to make. Then there was Sparrow – how could she abandon a child who had no one to love and care for her?' Lastly there was her job at the newspaper that had been hard won, and would be even harder to maintain, given the misogyny of the men who were employed there.

Rose sat in the cab going through all the arguments in her head, but she was no nearer a conclusion when she arrived at Pier House. Cecilia had been understanding when Rose had explained why it was so difficult to choose, but she must make a decision and make it quickly.

Cora answered Rose's knock on the front door. 'Thank the Lord,' she said, dragging Rose over the threshold. 'You've come just in time.'

'Why? What's happened?'

'We've been invaded by toffs. At least, Maria's mother is all right, but her stepfather is a loony. He wants to paint me with nothing on – in the buff – naked. He said so in front of his missis and she never batted an eyelid. I never heard the like in all me born days.'

Rose controlled a desire to giggle with difficulty. 'I'm sure he meant nothing by it, Cora. Mr Dorincourt is a famous artist. Some of his paintings hang in the National Gallery.'

Cora rolled her eyes. 'Ta very much, but I don't want to be a spectacle for all and sundry to gawp at.'

'I'm sure that won't happen, and you can always say no.' Rose peeled off her gloves and undid the ribbons on her bonnet. 'Where are they now?'

'In the blue parlour with Maria. Izzie's put the little ones to bed, and Sparrow is in the kitchen with Mrs Leary.'

Rose dropped her bonnet and cape onto the nearest chair. 'I'd better make myself known to the Dorincourts before I go upstairs. I was about Sparrow's age when I last met them and I doubt if they will remember me.'

'Good luck, that's all I can say. And watch out

because he'll want you to take your duds off and pose for him. You've still got your figure, but I lost mine years ago.'

Rose was still chuckling when she reached the blue parlour, but she paused outside the door and composed herself before entering. Maria was sitting next to her mother on the sofa while Freddie lounged in a chair by the fire. The years had been kind to both Grace and Freddie, and they looked little different from the memory that Rose had of them. Grace must be in her mid-forties, but, despite her prematurely white hair, she was still an attractive woman with a kindly expression. Freddie, who was probably in his early fifties, had put on weight and his dark hair was streaked with silver, but had retained much of his former panache and the mischievous twinkle in his blue eyes was unchanged.

Maria rose to her feet. 'Rose, dear, come and meet my mama and stepfather.'

'I don't suppose you remember me,' Rose said tentatively. 'I was at Caroline's wedding, and Maria's.'

Grace Dorincourt turned to her, smiling. 'Of course I remember you, Rose. It's good to see you again.' She sent a warning look to her husband. 'Don't embarrass Rose by demanding that she sits for you, Freddie. I've seen that look on your face often enough to know what it means.'

Freddie Dorincourt stood up and crossed the

floor to grasp Rose's hand. He raised it to his lips. 'You've grown into quite a beauty, Rose. Of course I remember you, too, and my wife is right – I would love to paint those lustrous green eyes and silky Titian hair. You have the complexion of a milkmaid and my fingers itch to immortalise you on canvas.'

'That's enough, Stepfather,' Maria said, chuckling. 'You've already scared poor Cora half to death and I don't want you to frighten Rose.'

Freddie shrugged. 'I think it would take more than a compliment or two to alarm this young lady. She has a determined chin and a martial sparkle in her eyes. I know when I am beaten.'

'Freddie,' Grace said sternly. 'Remember this is a serious occasion. My mother has met her death in the worst possible circumstances. We're facing a court case against a former servant, and possible murder trial.'

'I always look on the bright side of things, my love.' Freddie shuffled back to his chair and sat down. 'She was a dreadful creature, and she treated you and Maria shamefully. I refuse to mourn for the woman.'

'Well, she can do no harm to anyone now,' Maria said firmly. 'It's just having all this hanging over us that I find hard to bear.'

'We're here with you now, Maria.' Grace reached out to lay her hand on her daughter's arm. 'Freddie and I will stay with you until everything is settled.' She fixed her husband with a warning look. 'We will, won't we, dear?'

'Oh Lord. Yes, I suppose so. Anyway, it will give me time to visit a few old friends at the Royal Academy, and maybe I'll even pick up a few commissions while I'm in London.'

'Freddie, really!' Grace raised her eyebrows, but her eyes were smiling.

'What about you, Rose?' Maria asked anxiously. 'Is everything all right?'

'I was reinstated at the newspaper, but I have to go away for a while.' Rose glanced anxiously at Maria's parents, gauging their reaction, but they seemed more interested than annoyed.

'Why?' Maria demanded. 'Where are you going?'

'Eugene is missing. Apparently he accompanied a party of soldiers into the desert and they were taken prisoner. Cecilia is frantic with worry and she's leaving for Egypt in the morning.'

'And I suppose she wants you to carry her luggage,' Maria said bitterly. 'That's the trouble with people like her. They expect everyone to drop everything when they so much as crook a little finger.'

Grace shook her head. 'That doesn't seem fair, dear. Is this man Cecilia's husband?'

'No, Mama. They're brother and sister, and I don't see why Rose has to accompany Cecilia. I need Rose here. And there's Sparrow. Am I supposed to look after her? What happens if that awful man comes looking for her?'

'I'll take her with me.' Rose looked from one to the other, her mind made up. She would not leave Sparrow where she was not wanted.

'Don't be silly,' Maria said crossly. 'I didn't mean what I said. Of course she can stay here, Rose. You can't take a child to a war zone.'

'I believe the conflict is settled.' Freddie stretched out his long legs. 'I'd say you have enough on your plate without taking in an orphan, Maria.'

'Sparrow seems a bright little thing,' Grace added hastily. 'I like her, Freddie. Even though I've only spent a short time with her. The child has promise.'

'Stop there, Grace.' Freddie held up his hands. 'I draw the line at adopting an urchin.'

'She must remain here, if you're set on going, Rose.' Maria managed a weak smile. 'I'd much rather you stayed, but I know how fond you are of Eugene, and if your editor wants you to do a story about it, I suppose that would be good for your career.'

Rose stared at her nonplussed. She had not given a thought to her job or what Arthur Radley might say if approached, but Maria might have had a brilliant idea. 'Maria, you're wonderful. I hadn't thought about it like that.' Rose backed towards the doorway.

'Where are you going?' Maria demanded. 'It's only an hour until we dine.'

'I have to find Mr Radley. I've decided to go to Egypt with Cissie. That's if you are sure you are all right without me, and if you don't mind looking after Sparrow.'

'I can see that your mind is made up, but you must tell the child and make things right with her. I don't want a broken-hearted waif left on my hands.'

'I'll speak to her now, and if I'm not back in time for dinner don't wait for me.'

Rose found Sparrow seated at the kitchen table enjoying her supper.

Mrs Leary looked up from the pan she was stirring on the hob. 'If you're looking for Cora she's gone home. She said she didn't want to wait on table with him looking her up and down as if she was a side of beef in Smithfield market.'

'Mr Dorincourt is an artist,' Rose said patiently. 'I think he wants her to model for a painting.'

'I'll be a model.' Sparrow gulped down a mouthful of bread and jam. 'He can paint me, if he likes.'

Rose ruffled her hair. 'Maybe he will.'

'Flossie's outside having a smoke,' Mrs Leary said grimly. 'I won't allow the habit in my kitchen.'

'It's Sparrow I came to see.' Rose pulled up a chair and sat down, taking Sparrow's sticky hand in hers. 'I have to go away for a while, but I will be back as soon as I can.'

Sparrow snatched her hand away and leaped to her feet. 'You promised you wouldn't leave me.'

Mrs Leary sniffed and turned her back on them, muttering something unintelligible.

'I'm not leaving for good, but it's to do with the newspaper and I have to travel to Egypt.'

Mrs Leary dropped the wooden spoon sending a spray of soup over the hob where it bubbled and hissed until it burned away. 'Heaven help us. They're killing each other over there.'

Sparrow's hand flew to her mouth and her eyes filled with tears. 'Don't get killed, Rose.'

Rose reached out to wrap her arms around Sparrow's skinny body. 'The war is over, according to the papers, so it's quite safe.'

'Then why are you going to a foreign country?'

'The man I worked for at the newspaper is missing and his sister has asked me to accompany her to Egypt. I'm hoping my employer will pay me for the story when I return.'

'Take me with you, Rose.'

Rose smoothed Sparrow's tumbled hair back from her forehead. 'I would if it were possible, but it's no place for a child. I'll be back in time for Christmas.'

Mrs Leary stood, arms akimbo. 'That's less than two months away. You shouldn't make promises you can't keep.'

'I'll be back for Christmas even if I have to walk all the way,' Rose said, giving Sparrow a hug.

'Easy to say.' Mrs Leary retrieved the spoon and turned back to the range.

'I believe you, Rose.' Sparrow slid her stick-like arms around Rose's neck, clinging to her as if she would never let go.

Next morning Rose arrived at the house in Tavistock Square to find Cecilia in the entrance hall counting the items in an impressive pile of luggage.

'You came, then,' she said casually. 'I knew you would.'

'And I have Mr Radley's blessing.' Rose tried not to sound too triumphant, but it had been a hard-won victory. It had been sheer luck that Arthur Radley was still in his office when she arrived in Fleet Street and she realised that he, too, was worried about Eugene, despite the off-hand way in which he had treated his cousin. Rose had put her case, expecting to be rebuffed, but eventually he had agreed and had gone as far as giving her money to pay her way.

'I don't know how you managed it, but well done. Maybe Cousin Arthur has a heart after all. I always thought his veins were filled with printer's ink.'

Lindon had been standing at a respectful distance, but she stepped forward. 'Might I say something, Miss Cecilia?'

'Yes, what is it? Have we forgotten anything?'

'There are only two sets of tickets,' Lindon said smugly. 'Unless Miss Munday has managed to book her own.'

'No, I thought I might get mine on the way.' Rose had not given it a thought, but she was not going to admit it in front of Lindon, who was looking at her with a scornful expression in her dark eyes, and it occurred to Rose that the woman was jealous.

'Everything has been booked in detail through Thomas Cook,' Cecilia said slowly. 'There's only one solution. You must stay here, Lindon. Have a holiday – go and see your sister in Skegness, or wherever she lives.'

'But, Miss Cecilia, you can't travel without a maid!'

'I have Rose. She can help me with my hair, and we'll be travelling for days. There won't be any smart social functions to attend to on a boat or a train. We need to get to Alexandria as quickly as possible.'

Lindon drew herself up to her full height. 'I should be accompanying you, not her.'

'Really, Lindon. You forget yourself,' Cecilia said angrily. 'I choose my travelling companion and Rose will be much better company than you, especially when you sulk, as you are about to do now. Be grateful for the unexpected holiday and make the most of it, because I hope to return before Christmas.'

'I've heard that Alexandria was badly damaged

in the bombardment,' Rose added, hoping this might make it easier for Lindon.

Lindon tossed her head and marched off with an affronted twitch of her thin shoulders.

Barely disguising a smirk, Giddings announced the arrival of the carriage and a hackney.

'Is that all the luggage you're taking?' Cecilia demanded, staring at Rose's carpet bag.

'It's all that I need.'

'No matter. I'm sure I can lend you a ball gown or two. There are bound to be some social occasions at the consulate.' Cecilia turned to Giddings. 'The luggage will go in the hackney carriage. Make sure it's loaded properly.' She lowered her voice. 'And be nice to Lindon while I'm away. She is a treasure, when all is said and done, and I don't want to lose her.'

'But you'll have to make do with me in the meantime,' Rose said, chuckling. 'Don't forget that I'm coming in my professional capacity, Cissie. I'm being paid by the newspaper to send back my reports on our progress.'

Cecilia shot her a sideways glance. 'I can see that this is going to be an eventful journey, but it won't be dull.'

The first part of the journey was completed by rail. They caught a boat train from Victoria Station to Dover, and in Calais they boarded a train for Paris.

The night was spent in a smart hotel and they travelled on next day, catching a train bound for Marseilles. Rose would have enjoyed their trip more if she had not been anxious about leaving Sparrow and worried about Eugene. There had been no more news of his whereabouts. Although Cecilia appeared to be calm Rose knew her well enough to sense the tension that she tried to conceal beneath her apparently carefree demeanour. After yet another night in an elegant hotel they embarked next morning for Alexandria.

Rose was used to sea voyages, but to her surprise she discovered that this was the first time Cecilia had spent more than a few hours on the water, and at first she was bored – pacing the cabin they shared like a caged tigress. However, their fellow travellers proved to be amusing and after a day or two Cecilia began to acknowledge this, and held court regularly in the saloon. Rose sat back and enjoyed the scene while Cecilia commanded the attention of the gentlemen passengers, who were in the majority. Their wives seemed to be in awe of Cecilia, and they formed an appreciative audience. Although Rose suspected that behind their fans they were secretly making unfavourable comparisons between the forward behaviour of Miss Sheldon and the more discreet conduct of their daughters.

Rose spent at least part of each day writing a journal, which she hoped might help her when she wrote the newspaper article. She made sketches of the other passengers and the ports where they took on coal and water, and she loved to sit on deck, wrapped up against the chill as she watched the waves and marvelled at the ever-changing colours of the sea and sky. They sailed through storms and rough seas and many of the passengers retired to their cabins suffering from seasickness, but Rose and Cecilia were unaffected by the pitching and tossing of the vessel. Cecilia flirted outrageously with the gentlemen whose wives were indisposed. On one occasion Rose found her drinking brandy and smoking a cheroot in the company of a rather dashing army officer, who was on his way to join his regiment. Rose was highly amused, but it was obvious that some of the more staid gentlemen found such wayward conduct unladylike and shocking. As they edged past a table where four men were playing cards, Rose overheard one of them criticising Cissie's behaviour and she came to a sudden halt.

'Shame on you,' she said angrily. 'Would you begrudge that soldier some innocent entertainment?'

The man choked on his drink. 'Well-bred young ladies don't behave like that.'

Rose leaned over the table, fixing him with a hard stare. 'You are a narrow-minded hypocrite. I saw the way you were ogling her earlier, but she ignored you. Did she hurt your pride, sir?'

'Sit down, young woman.' One of his companions

puffed cigar smoke in Rose's face. 'No one asked for your opinion.'

'Nor I yours, sir. And I would have had the good manners not to blow that disgusting weed in someone's face.' Rose stalked off, head held high, and went to sit next to Cecilia.

'What was all that?' Cecilia demanded.

'Just passing the time of day,' Rose said casually.

The weather improved as they neared the Egyptian coast, and when they landed in Alexandria it was warm and pleasant. Rose was shocked to see the devastation caused by the naval bombardment.

Cecilia stepped off the gangway into the arms of a tall, distinguished-looking gentleman, who bore a striking resemblance to his son.

'Papa, it's so good to see you.' Cecilia held him at arm's length. 'But you've lost weight and you look tired. Has it been as awful as it looks?'

'It's over now, Cissie. We're bearing up.' Desmond Sheldon turned to Rose with smile so reminiscent of Eugene that Rose wanted to hug him. 'And who is this, Cissie? Won't you introduce me to your companion?'

'Yes, of course. I was forgetting my manners in my delight at seeing you again.' Cecilia beckoned fiercely. 'This is Rose Munday, Papa. She works for Gene's newspaper and she's here to write a story about his rescue. Have you any news of him?'

'Darling girl, I wish that I had, but we've heard nothing. Perhaps when we return to Cairo we might be better informed.'

Cecilia hugged him, and Rose turned away, touched by the obvious affection that existed between father and daughter, and their mutual distress, although she herself was suffering equally. All the way from England she had hoped that Eugene would have been found, but hearing that it was not so, she felt her heart sink. She was also desperate for news of Max, but having only just met Mr Sheldon, she did not like to bother him at present.

Desmond turned to her with an apologetic smile. 'I'm sorry, Rose. We're forgetting our manners, but I haven't seen my daughter for a year or more.'

'I understand perfectly, sir.'

He held out his hand. 'Let's get away from all this. We're camping out in what's left of a school, but at least we're safe and well. Your mother has been so brave, Cissie. I'm very proud of her.'

'We Sheldon women are tough,' Cecilia said laughing as she tucked her hand in the crook of his arm. 'Rose and I have just survived the voyage across the Mediterranean with nothing worse than a few bruises, caused by falling against the bulkheads in one of the many storms. But for the most part it was a pleasant voyage.'

'You're here now, and that's all that matters.' Desmond proffered his other arm to Rose. 'Allow me to escort you to our extremely humble and uncomfortable abode, although we're hoping to return to Cairo very soon.' He beckoned to a youth standing by a donkey cart, issuing instructions to load the luggage that the crew had dumped unceremoniously on the quay. 'Jabari will bring your things, but I'm afraid we'll have to walk. It's not too far,' he added.

Rose took his arm and they walked slowly through streets where the army were still clearing away the rubble from damaged buildings. The air was thick with dust and the smell of charred wood. Flies buzzed around their heads and it was so hot that Rose could feel sweat trickling down between her breasts, and there were damp patches forming under her arms. She wished she had worn something lighter, but there was nothing she could do until they reached their destination and she had time to unpack.

'Surely the bombardment couldn't have caused all these fires?' Rose gazed at the ruined buildings, some of which were still smouldering.

Desmond nodded. 'You're quite right. There was a great deal of looting and the perpetrators set fire to what they couldn't take. It's been a horrendous few months since the troubles began. Most of the European inhabitants fled, and only a few have returned, but as you can see there isn't much left of this part of the city.'

'At least you and Mama are safe,' Cecilia said breathlessly. 'But you say there's no news of Gene?'

'No, not yet. The army have sent out search parties, so we can only hope.'

Rose sidestepped a pothole in the gritty surface of the road. 'My fiancé is in the army,' she said shyly. 'I was hoping I might get news of him, too.'

Desmond came to a halt outside a building that might once have been an imposing edifice but was now a crumbling ruin. 'Really, Rose? What regiment is he in?'

'He's Captain Max Manning of the 7th Dragoons.'

'I believe they fought bravely at Tel-el-Kebir, but perhaps you'll find out more when we get to Cairo. The railway tracks were damaged in the fighting – they're being repaired as we speak. Anyway, this is where we've been camping for the duration. Come inside but mind how you go – there's a lot of rubble still to clear away. Jabari will bring your cases.'

Rose followed father and daughter through a narrow gap between the crumbling walls of the ruins, but to her surprise the passage opened out into a sunny courtyard complete with a fountain, which by some miracle of engineering was still working. A tall fig tree with some fruit still visible on its spreading branches partially concealed a doorway in the far wall, and even as Rose peered into the shadow the door opened and a small, dark-haired woman came towards them with her arms outstretched.

'Cissie, darling. At last.'

'Mama.' Cecilia melted into her mother's embrace and they hugged and kissed, laughing and crying at the same time.

Desmond laid his hand on Rose's shoulder. 'They'll calm down in a day or two. My wife and daughter are very emotional people, as you must have realised.'

Rose tried not to feel envious. She had only vague memories of her own mother, who had died when she was very young.

Then, as if sensing Rose's discomfort, Cecilia broke free from her mother's embrace and held her hand out. 'Rose, come and meet my mama.'

Desmond put his arm around Rose's shoulders. 'Elizabeth, this young lady is Rose Munday. She's a colleague of Gene's.'

Elizabeth Sheldon moved swiftly to give Rose a hug. 'I can't believe that a lovely young woman would be involved in the newspaper world, but you are more than welcome, my dear. Although you'll have to forgive the Spartan accommodation. We're just thankful to have survived when others were not so fortunate. Do come inside.' She hesitated in the doorway. 'I suppose Jabari has their luggage. You'd better check on him, Desmond. You know that he wanders off occasionally.'

Cecilia shook her head, chuckling. 'Mama will get everyone organised, Rose. That's her way, so be warned.'

The interior of what was once the kitchen and servants' quarters of the fine house was warm without being oppressive. It seemed dark compared to the brilliant sunshine outside, but upstairs the room allocated to Rose was light and airy. It was quite small, but the white walls made it seem more spacious and there was a single bed, a chest of drawers and a small washstand with a chipped jug and basin. A narrow window overlooked the courtyard, and if Rose leaned out far enough she could pluck a fig from the tree, although they were obviously past their best and not very tempting. Jabari delivered her luggage and bowed out of the room before she had a chance to thank him, but at least she was able to change out of her travelling clothes and put on something lighter and more comfortable. She sat on the bed for a while, giving Cecilia a chance to talk freely to her parents, and herself time to adjust to her new surroundings. It was hard to believe that she was in the same country as Max and Eugene, and the possibility of seeing them again made her heart race. Then she remembered that she was here on official business and she was supposed to be writing an article for the newspaper. She rifled through her case to find her journal and sat for a while, chewing the end of her pencil while she gathered her thoughts. It was hard to know where to begin, but once she started writing she found that the words flowed easily. She had just finished describing the desolation she had seen that day when the door opened and Cecilia rushed into the room.

'You'll never guess what, Rose,' Cecilia said excitedly.

Chapter Fifteen

Slightly dazed by the interruption when her mind had been on her work, Rose stared at Cecilia in surprise. 'I don't suppose I will. What is it?'

'We were just talking about life here, and how hard it's been for the Europeans who did not evacuate, when Papa mentioned that he's planning to visit the hospital tomorrow.'

'That's interesting, I suppose.'

'Don't look at me as if I've gone mad, Rose. Apparently Papa goes regularly to check on the progress of the injured British soldiers and sailors, especially those who are not yet well enough to endure the sea voyage back to England. He showed me a list of names, Rose, and one of them was a sub-lieutenant from one of the navy ships in the harbour, a certain James Manning.'

Rose dropped her journal and it fluttered to the floor together with the pencil. 'Jimmy? It can't be my Jimmy, can it?'

'There's only one way to find out.' Cecilia grabbed Rose's hands and pulled her to her feet. 'Come downstairs, and maybe we can persuade my father to let us accompany him to the hospital in the morning. We've nothing else to do, and I'm sure the wounded sailors and soldiers would be cheered to see two lovely ladies from England.'

'Jimmy might know where Max is,' Rose said eagerly. 'Of course I'll go with you. Nothing would keep me away, and even if it isn't Jimmy, we might be able to make ourselves useful.'

After a long and dusty walk through the derelict streets where skinny feral dogs snuffled in the gutters looking for scraps of anything edible, and beautiful, brown-eyed children played amongst the ruins, the small party eventually reached their destination. The hospital, as Desmond explained, was an old cotton store that had been converted for use by the military. He led them into the building and they were met by a formidable-looking woman, who looked as though her entire body had been dipped in starch. Her dark hair was sleeked back from her shiny forehead and pinned ruthlessly beneath a white cap, and her all-enveloping white apron was so stiff that it would probably stand up on its own.

She informed them at the start that she was Matron Harvey, a Nightingale nurse, and she was in complete charge, something that Rose did not doubt for a moment. Desmond took Matron aside and Rose crossed her fingers. It would be a bitter disappointment to have come this far only to be denied the chance of seeing Jimmy, but Desmond exerted all his diplomatic skills and Matron began to unbend. It was agreed that Rose could see Sub-Lieutenant Manning, but Cecilia would have to wait in the anteroom.

Matron led the way to a ward lined with cast-iron bedsteads, where the white coverlets were tucked so tightly beneath the thin mattresses that the patients looked like parcels ready for posting. The men were in various stages of recovery and Rose received whistles of admiration from one sailor, who had his right arm in a sling and a black patch over his left eye. She gave him a cheery smile and received a scolding from Matron, who accused her of flirting. The sailor was also given a sound telling-off, but the moment Matron's back was turned he winked at Rose.

Matron Harvey stopped at the far end of the ward and pulled back a screen. 'Is this your friend, Miss Munday?'

Rose's hand flew to cover her mouth as she suppressed a cry of delight, but concern for his welfare overcame her pleasure and she moved to the foot of the bed. 'Jimmy?'

James Manning opened his eyes, staring blankly at her with a puzzled frown. 'Rose? Is it really you?'

'You may have five minutes with the patient and not a second longer.' Matron Harvey backed away, leaving the screen open so that both Rose and Jimmy were clearly visible from the nurses' station at the far end of the ward.

Rose moved closer, covering his limp hand with hers. 'How are you feeling, Jimmy?'

'I can't believe you're here, Rose. It must be the fever and you're just a dream.'

She leaned over and dropped a kiss on his brow. 'It is me, and it's a long story, but I really am here. But, more importantly, what happened to you?'

His blue eyes darkened and he shook his head. 'It's not very romantic, Rose. I came through the fighting unscathed, and then I contracted typhoid, so I ended up here.'

'But you're on the mend?' Rose said anxiously.

'So they say. Although I'm as weak as a kitten.'

Rose brushed a strand of fair hair back from his forehead. 'But not as pretty. You look awful, Jimmy,' she said, smiling tenderly.

'Thanks, Rose. You always knew how to make a fellow feel better.'

'You're my brother, and I love you, even if we aren't blood related.' Rose hesitated, hardly daring to ask the question that was burning a hole in her heart.

Jimmy reached out to grasp her hand. 'I saw Max briefly, but that was back in September.'

'Was he well? Did he mention me?'

'There wasn't time to exchange more than a few words. He told me that his regiment was being sent to the barracks at Kasr-el-Nil, on the outskirts of Cairo.' Jimmy's grip on her hand tightened. 'Why are you here, Rose? I thought you were safe in London.'

'Did Max tell you that?'

Jimmy made an effort to sit up, but fell back against the single pillow with a groan. 'Yes, he said that you would be waiting for him at the Captain's House.'

'Max wasn't at the docks to meet me, and I wasn't to know that he'd been sent abroad. I found myself alone and near penniless in London.'

'Oh, Rose, I'm so sorry. I don't know what to say.'

'He hadn't thought to make alternative arrangements,' she said grimly.

'Where was Carrie? She would have helped you.'

'I found out later that she is with Phineas, on a business trip to Australia. Anyway, it's not your problem, Jimmy, but I'll have a few words to say to Max when I see him next. We'll be going to Cairo as soon as the railway lines are repaired.'

'You didn't tell me how you came to be here.'

'You'll hardly credit the things that have happened to me since I arrived in London.'

Rose was in the middle of relating her recent experiences when Matron Harvey pounced on her, making her turn with a start. 'Five minutes, I said, Miss Munday. I can't allow you to tire my patient.'

A quick glance at Jimmy's white face was enough to convince Rose that it really was time to leave. 'I'm sorry,' she said hastily. 'I'll come back tomorrow, Jimmy. If Matron will let me?'

'You may, providing my patient is well enough to receive visitors.' Matron stood aside. 'Time to go, Miss Munday.'

'I'll see you soon.' Rose blew him a kiss and hurried towards the door, ignoring the wounded men who vied in their attempts to gain her attention. It seemed heartless, but she did not want to jeopardise her chances of seeing Jimmy the following day by encouraging them. Then she saw a young man whose head was swathed in bandages that covered the top half of his face, leaving only his nose and mouth visible. He called out to her and she came to a halt at his bedside.

'Do you need the nurse?' Rose asked anxiously.

'No, miss. I heard your voice and you sound like a kind lady.' He held out his hand and his lips trembled. 'Would you do something for me, please?'

Rose moved closer, taking his hand in hers. 'How can I help?'

'They say I might never see again.' His voice broke on a sob. 'But I ain't one to give up easily.'

'No, of course not.' Rose struggled to combat a wave of pity that threatened to overcome her. 'I'm Rose Munday. What's your name?'

'Private Henry Norman, Royal Engineers, miss.'

'What can I do for you, Henry?' Rose tried to sound cheery and confident when all she wanted to do was to give the poor boy a hug.

He leaned closer. 'I want to send a letter to my mum. I know it's a liberty, but would you write it for me and post it when you get back home?'

'Of course I will, Henry. It would be my pleasure.'

'It's Harry, miss. My mum always calls me Harry.'

Rose could see Matron Harvey bearing down on them and she squeezed Harry's fingers. 'I'll bring pen and paper tomorrow and you can tell me what to put, but I'd better leave now because Matron is coming.'

Harry's lips curved in a grin. 'Best not get on the wrong side of her, miss. She's a tartar.'

Rose straightened up as Matron drew near. 'I'm leaving now,' she said hastily.

Cecilia was on her own in the waiting room. 'How did it go?' she asked eagerly. 'It must have been your James Manning or you wouldn't have taken so long.'

'You're right, it was my Jimmy. He's been suffering from typhoid, but thankfully he's on the mend now.'

'That's good,' Cecilia said, smiling. 'What a coincidence that he should be here.'

'I know – I can hardly believe it myself.' Rose sank down on the seat beside Cecilia. 'I'm going to visit him again tomorrow, Matron permitting. She really is a martinet, Cissie.'

'I expect she has to be if she hopes to keep the soldiers and blue jackets in order,' Cecilia said drily. 'Did Jimmy have any news of his brother?'

Rose clasped her hands tightly in her lap. Despite her efforts to keep an open mind she was still angry with Max. 'He's safe and well in the Cairo barracks.'

Cecilia put her head on one side. 'Isn't that a good thing? You look angry.'

'I'm happy to think that he's unhurt, but he must have known that he wouldn't be able to meet me in London. He could have sent a cable to tell me to stay at home until the fighting was over, but Max knew that I would go anywhere to be with him.'

'Maybe that was the problem, Rose. Perhaps you were too eager. I hate to say it, but some men are so sure of themselves that they can take what they want regardless of anyone else.'

'I didn't think that he was like that.'

Cecilia slipped her arm around Rose's shoulder. 'He's a man and he's thoughtless, darling. He should have known better, but luckily you're a strong woman even if you are very young.'

'I'm eighteen, Cissie.'

'As I said, you're very young, but I admire you and so does Gene. I just wish I knew what has happened to him. At least you know that Max and Jimmy are safe.'

'You're right,' Rose said reluctantly. 'When we get to Cairo I'm going to visit the barracks and demand to see Max. I need to know if he still loves me.'

'Or if you still feel the same way about him.' Cecilia gave her a hug. 'You might realise that you're the one who's changed, Rose.'

'I think I've grown up quite a lot since I arrived in London, and I'm much more independent than I was.'

'Gene thinks a lot of you, Rose. He spotted a talent that you didn't know you possessed.'

Rose stared at her, frowning. 'Talent?'

'For writing,' Cecilia added, chuckling. 'And Cousin Arthur obviously agrees with him. You're a modern woman, Rose, as am I. We can change the world if we put our minds to it.'

'I don't know about that, but there are certainly stories to be told. I spoke to this poor young fellow who is suffering from a serious head injury. He asked me to write a letter to his mother.'

'I suppose a lot of them are illiterate,' Cecilia said calmly.

'He had bandages over his eyes and he thinks he might never see again. It's so sad.'

'Poor fellow.' Cecilia glanced over Rose's shoulder. 'Here's Papa. Now we can go. I hate the smell of carbolic.'

Desmond strolled up to them. 'Duty done, but some of those poor fellows are in a sorry state. I hate to send them home to their loved ones with their bodies mutilated and their health wrecked.'

'At least they're going home, Pa.' Cecilia rose to her feet. 'There must be many who won't be returning to their families,' she added, sighing.

'Great heavens, Cissie.' Desmond stared at his daughter in amazement. 'What's wrought this change in you?'

'I don't know what you mean, Papa.'

Desmond met Rose's questioning look with a smile. 'My daughter used to be a social butterfly, with nothing on her mind other than the latest fashions and which invitation she was going to accept.'

'Cissie has been very good to me,' Rose said stoutly. 'I wouldn't be here but for her, and I wouldn't have found Jimmy.'

'It was the same James Manning, then? Excellent.' Desmond eyed her curiously. 'He's on the mend, I hope?'

'Yes, Jimmy seems to be over the worst, but I was touched by the state of some of the men. One of them might be blind for the rest of his days. He asked me to write to his mother. That would be all right, wouldn't it?'

'I don't see why not.'

'Do you think I could interview some of the other patients as part of my article for the newspaper?

The fighting might be over, but these men are still suffering. I wouldn't mention names or regiments, but I think their stories would be of great interest to the readers.'

'I think that's an excellent idea,' Cecilia said before her father could respond. 'Gene would be proud of you, Rose. Anyway, I'm ready to leave this depressing place – my clothes are going to smell of carbolic and putrefying flesh for days.' Cecilia made for the door and Rose followed with a degree of reluctance. It was hard to walk away and leave Jimmy in the hospital, and there was a wealth of information and personal stories to be gained from the wounded men.

Desmond moved swiftly to hold the door open and Cecilia sailed past him, but Rose hesitated. 'Is there really no news of Eugene's whereabouts, sir?'

'None that I can pass on, even to you, Rose. Although I can assure you that everything is being done to free him and the officers he was accompanying. We just have to wait and pray that they will be released unharmed.'

Rose stepped outside to join Cecilia, who had unfurled her parasol in preparation for the long walk back to their lodgings. The armed soldier, who accompanied Desmond as his bodyguard, was standing stiffly to attention despite the heat. Rose could see beads of perspiration running down the unfortunate man's face and his uniform jacket was marked with damp patches beneath his arms. She caught sight of a young girl carrying a water jar and she beckoned to her.

'I wouldn't drink that,' Cecilia whispered. 'You'll go down with typhoid or cholera.'

'It's not for me.' Rose steered the child towards the soldier. 'Miss Sheldon thinks the water might be contaminated, but you look as though you need a drink.'

'I can't without permission, miss.'

Rose turned to Desmond. 'This man looks fit to drop. He shouldn't have been standing in the sun for so long.'

'You have my permission to drink, Private.' Desmond put his hand in his pocket and gave the child a couple of coins.

'Thank you, sir.' The soldier saluted and drank thirstily, handing the vessel back to the girl and then snapping to attention. He shot Rose a grateful smile. 'Thank you, miss.'

'Let's hope he doesn't die from some dreadful illness,' Cecilia called over her shoulder as she walked on.

'That was a kind act,' Desmond said in a low voice. 'Don't worry about Private Cook, he'll survive now, thanks to you.'

'You'd have done the same for someone at home who was so obviously suffering, wouldn't you?'

Desmond adjusted his pith helmet. 'I hope I would, Rose.'

She fell into step beside him, with Cecilia walking on ahead and Private Cook following a couple of paces behind them.

'You know that I'm here to write for the *London Leader*?' Rose began tentatively.

'Yes, you said so last evening, and it was thanks to my son for giving you a chance that most young women would never have.'

'Which is true, and I want to prove him right.'

'What are you trying to say, Rose?'

'I'd like your permission to interview some of the wounded men for my first article.'

'I can't see any objection, as the war has ended, although I'd like the opportunity to cast my eye over it first.'

'Of course,' Rose said hastily.

'But I imagine you'll do it with or without my say-so.'

'I will, Mr Sheldon. But I'd prefer to have your blessing.'

'I can see why my son gave you a job, Rose Munday. However,' Desmond added sternly. 'I won't allow you to wander round the town unaccompanied. You'll have an armed guard wherever you go, and that's an order.'

Private Cook was waiting for her next morning, standing stiffly to attention in the street outside the ruined building.

'Oh, it's you.' Rose beamed at him. 'I was afraid it might be someone I didn't know.'

Private Cook stared straight ahead, saying nothing.

'It's all right,' Rose said hastily. 'You don't have to treat me as if I were a high-up in the army. I'm simply someone trying to do their job, just like you.' She thought she detected a glint of humour in Cook's blue eyes, even though he was gazing into the distance. 'What's your name? If we're to work together I can't keep calling you Private Cook.'

'It's Bradley, miss. If I might be so bold, it would be best if you call me Private Cook – just for the look of things, if you know what I mean.'

'If you say so. Anyway, I'm going to the hospital, but there will be nothing for you to do once we're there.'

'That's all right, miss. I've been detailed to take care of you, and take care of you I will. You saved my life yesterday and I won't forget it.'

Rose stared at him in surprise. 'I saw you were hot and thirsty. Anyone would have done the same.'

Private Cook met her gaze for the first time and his lips trembled. 'It might have been nothing much to you, miss, but it meant the world to me.'

'Tell me about yourself as we walk. I can tell that you're a Londoner.'

'I'm on duty, miss. I have to be on the lookout for snipers or thieves.'

'I'm sure you can walk, talk and keep an eye on

me all at the same time.' Rose shot him a sideways glance. 'I'd say you came from Stepney.'

He fell into step beside her. 'Not far out. I come from Poplar to be exact, miss.'

'Tell me about your family.'

Cook needed no further encouragement, and by the time they reached the hospital Rose knew all about his hardworking mother, who took in lodgers to make ends meet, and his three elder sisters, two of whom were married, and his four younger brothers. Their father, also a soldier, had been killed in a street brawl, and Bradley was now the main breadwinner.

Rose left him waiting outside while she went in and sought permission to visit the ward. Matron Harvey materialised as if from nowhere and accompanied Rose like an oversized shadow as she made her way to Jimmy's bed.

'Five minutes as before, Miss Munday. We mustn't overtire the patient.'

Jimmy pulled a face behind Matron's back as she walked away. 'It's good to see you, Rose,' he said in a low voice. 'Your visit yesterday did me more good than all the horrible medicines they pour down my throat.'

Rose perched on the edge of the bed, but a stentorian voice bellowed her name and she leaped to her feet, feeling like a naughty schoolgirl.

'We don't sit on beds, Miss Munday.' Matron's

departure was accompanied by stifled sniggers from some of the soldiers, and a muffled cheer from the man who had spoken to Rose the previous day.

'You do look much better,' Rose said earnestly. 'Do you think they'll discharge you soon?'

'I hope so, Rosie. I don't think I can stand being stuck in bed for much longer.'

'That sounds encouraging. You must be on the mend.'

'I'll be straight back to duty when they do let me out, so I won't see you again.'

'Perhaps you could spend your next shore leave in London, Jimmy. I'm not sure where I'll be living but we can always find room for one more.'

'Max has a lot to answer for,' Jimmy said angrily. 'He should have made proper arrangements for you, but that's my brother all over. I'm sorry to say it, but Max is selfish and always will be.'

Rose stared at him in silence for a moment. It was the first time she had heard him say anything against his brother, although there had been plenty of squabbling when they were at school in Bendigo. She realised suddenly that she barely knew the boys as adults, and she experienced a sudden cold chill, as if a ghostly hand had clutched at her throat. Was the charming, worldly army officer who had swept her off her feet the same person as the boy she had known and hero-worshipped? She opened her mouth to answer but a stern voice made her turn with a start.

'Time to go, Miss Munday.' The ward sister had crept up on them unnoticed. 'Matron said I was to make sure you didn't tire my patient.'

'But I've only just arrived,' Rose protested.

'Be a sport and let Rose stay a little longer, please, Sister.' Jimmy smiled up at her. 'My little sister is the best medicine.'

The nurse, whose grey eyes were underlined with dark smudges, looked pale and exhausted, but she managed a weak smile. 'You'll get me sacked, Lieutenant Manning.'

'It's Jimmy to my friends, Sister.'

She wagged her finger at him. 'Two minutes and then I must insist that your visitor leaves.' She hurried away to attend to another patient, who was writhing about in his bed and groaning.

'You shouldn't have lied,' Rose said softly. 'I'm not your sister.'

'It worked, didn't it?' Jimmy reached out to grasp Rose's hand. 'You'll be leaving soon for Cairo, won't you?'

'Yes, I think so.'

'I wanted to tell you to be firm with Max when you next see him, Rose. Don't allow him to charm you into doing what he wants regardless of whether it's right for you.'

'What brought this about, Jimmy? I thought you and Max got along so well?'

'We do, as brothers, but I'm fully aware of his

faults, and my own. Max is a charmer who's used to getting his own way, and I very much doubt if he'd approve of what you're doing.'

Rose stared at him aghast. 'What do you mean by that?'

'He wouldn't want his future wife to work in any capacity, least of all as a newspaper reporter.'

'You can't speak for Max. He might see things my way.'

'He'll want you to be a perfect army wife. You'll be there to support him no matter what.'

Rose knew in her heart that what he said was true, even if it was a bitter pill to swallow. She glanced over her shoulder at the sound of footsteps and saw the sister bearing down on them. Rose leaned over and dropped a kiss on Jimmy's forehead. 'I have to go now, but I'm going to speak to some of the other patients, and I promised to write a letter to the blind soldier's mother. The poor fellow might never see again, so it's the least I can do for him.'

Jimmy reached out to clasp her hand. 'Remember what I said about Max.'

'Don't worry about me, Jimmy. I'm sure I can make him understand.'

'You don't know my brother as I do.' Jimmy turned his head away. 'I'm afraid you're in for a shock. Don't say I didn't warn you.'

Chapter Sixteen

Rose sent a cable containing her hastily written article to Arthur Radley. She had no means of knowing whether it was good or bad, but she had obtained stories that would wring the hearts of their readers, and she had not spared the details. The letter to Harry's mother had been sent in the official mail bag, and Rose had had the satisfaction of seeing a genuine smile on Harry's face when he told her that he was to be repatriated as soon as possible. She was planning to return to the hospital to visit Jimmy, and to speak to more of the wounded soldiers, when Desmond came rushing into the house with the news that the repairs to the railway line were complete, and they would be leaving for Cairo later that day. There was immediate panic, with Cecilia and her mother hurrying to their rooms to oversee the packing of their portmanteaux, while Hebony, the Egyptian maidservant, did her best to please both of them. Rose had only to throw a few things in her carpet bag and she was ready, but she insisted on going to the hospital to tell Jimmy that she was leaving.

'I had a feeling that arguing with you would be useless.' Desmond shook his head, but a wry smile curved his lips. 'I've already arranged for Private Cook to take you to the hospital.' He beckoned to Cook, who was standing to attention in the doorway. 'I want you to accompany us to Cairo, Private. My daughter and Miss Munday will need a bodyguard and you've done well so far.'

'Thank you, sir.'

'I've already spoken to your commanding officer and we leave at noon, so no loitering, Rose.'

'I'll be as quick as I can, Mr Sheldon.' She stepped outside to find a ragged boy holding the reins of two donkeys and she turned to Private Cook with a puzzled smile. 'Are we riding to the hospital?'

'It'll be quicker than walking and we're to meet the family at the railway station. It was Mr Sheldon's idea, not mine, miss.' He eyed her warily. 'I suppose you can ride?'

'Of course I can,' Rose said scornfully. 'I grew up in Australia. We rode everywhere on bigger animals than this.' She hitched up her skirts and mounted the donkey, sitting astride regardless of her lace-trimmed petticoats. 'Walk on, donkey,' she said, clicking her tongue against her teeth and flicking the reins. She chuckled with delight as the donkey obliged and broke into a trot.

'Hey, miss. Wait for me.'

Rose glanced over her shoulder and she could see Private Cook sitting awkwardly on the animal, flapping the reins and urging the donkey to move. It was the first time she had really laughed for days and her sides were aching by the time she reached the hospital. She dismounted and waited patiently for him to arrive. He slid off the saddle and she thrust the reins into his hands.

'Wait here for me, please. I'll be as quick as I can.'

'I should come in with you, miss. I was told to keep a close eye on you.'

'I think it's more important to guard the donkeys,' Rose said firmly. 'There might be thieves just waiting for their chance.'

'They can steal the perishing animals as far as I'm concerned.'

Rose could still hear him grumbling as she reached the hospital entrance, and she was smiling to herself as she opened the door and went inside, but when she asked to see Jimmy she was told that he had been discharged earlier that morning and had returned to his ship. The nurse explained politely that there had been a fresh outbreak of enteric disease, and beds were needed for the new arrivals, but when Rose asked if she might speak to some of the other patients her request was met with a firm refusal.

'But Matron Harvey allowed me to interview some of the men who were on the mend,' Rose protested.

The nurse turned her head at the sound of approaching footsteps. 'Here is Matron now. Perhaps you'd better ask her yourself.'

'What do you want, Miss Munday?' Matron Harvey demanded coldly. 'Sub-Lieutenant Manning has been discharged, as I'm sure you know by now.'

'Yes, I was told that, Matron. However, you allowed me to speak to some of the other patients yesterday . . .'

'That was then,' Matron Harvey said firmly. 'The wards are closed to visitors, whoever they are, and no exceptions. We can't risk contagion. You must leave immediately.'

Faced with such opposition there was nothing that Rose could do other than to obey Matron's orders. As she left the hospital she wondered if Sir Garnet Wolseley exercised as much authority over his men as the woman in the starched white cap and apron did over her patients and staff, and that in itself gave her an idea for another article. She found Private Cook leaning against the wall outside, smoking a ragged-looking cigarette, which he stubbed out hastily.

'That was quick. I was expecting a long wait.'

'Cholera,' Rose said briefly. 'Anyway, we'd best get to the railway station as we're leaving for Cairo at noon.'

Cecilia had made a point of sitting in the far corner of the railway compartment when they boarded the train. 'I hope you aren't carrying infection from the hospital, Rose.'

'I'm not a leper,' Rose said crossly. 'Anyway, I wasn't allowed into the ward, and I didn't touch anything or anyone.'

'Don't talk about diseases.' Elizabeth settled her full skirts around her as if making a little nest for herself. 'Who knows what we'll come across in Cairo? It might be in ruins like Alexandria.'

'Not according to the reports I've received.' Desmond folded the document he had been reading. 'The Consulate in Cairo has been closed for several years so I am going to be very busy. It will certainly be a challenge.'

'And you have to find us a decent place to live,' Elizabeth said wearily. 'I'm tired of camping in ruins, and I'm desperate for news of Eugene. He should be your priority, Desmond, or have you forgotten that you have a son?'

'That's not fair, Mama,' Cecilia protested. 'I'm sure that Papa has done everything he possibly can to get news of Gene.'

'Of course I have, Beth,' Desmond said patiently.

'And I'll liaise more fully with the military when we get to Cairo.'

Rose would have liked to question him further, but she did not want to add to the obvious tension that existed between Eugene's parents. She took her notebook and pencil from her reticule and began to write her final account of what she had seen and heard at the hospital, and details of their journey across the desert to Cairo. The mere fact that she was continuing Eugene's work was some sort of comfort, and she was doing something that she hoped would please him, if he ever found out. She pushed such thoughts to the back of her mind.

It was late afternoon when they arrived at Cairo station, and they were reunited with Private Cook, Hebony and Jabari, who had been travelling third class. It took three carriages to transport them and their luggage to Shepheard's Hotel, where they would be staying until Desmond had found more suitable accommodation. Rose could not help but be impressed as she climbed the steps beneath a wide canopy, and was ushered into the grand entrance hall. The air was scented with an exotic perfume and potted palms swayed gently in the breeze created by young boys waving huge palm-leaf fans. The marble floors were scattered with Persian rugs and tall columns supported an ornate ceiling. The grand staircase was flanked by impressive life-sized bronze statues of nubile women clad in ancient Egyptian costumes, and, if there was poverty in the back streets, this was another world, one of privilege and opulence. Rose and Cecilia followed Desmond and Elizabeth as they were escorted to their rooms by immaculate, well-trained servants. Rose was relieved to find that she was sharing with Cecilia, and, as if by magic, their luggage was there, waiting for them.

Rose sank down on a low sofa smothered in brightly coloured satin cushions. 'This is such a grand place. It must cost a fortune to stay here, Cissie.'

'Where else would one stay in Cairo?' Cecilia said casually. She strolled round the large, elegantly furnished room, examining the décor with a critical eye. 'We've been here before, but this time I fear it will be for a short while only, more's the pity. I love luxury, but I suppose Papa will rent a dreary house somewhere away from the city centre.'

'Aren't you worried about your brother? You haven't mentioned him once.'

'Gene can take care of himself.' Cecilia shrugged and selected a bonbon from a silver dish on a side table. 'I'm starving and I would love some mint tea. Let's go down to the terrace and order something to eat and drink.'

'What about your parents?'

'They'll go downstairs when they're ready. I say

we leave Hebony to unpack while we concentrate on enjoying ourselves. I spotted a rather attractive man in the foyer and he smiled at me. I'll have a quick wash and tidy my hair and I'll be ready for anything.' Cecilia paused in the bedroom doorway, giving Rose a critical glance. 'You might do the same, darling. You've got smuts on your nose and your hair is a bird's nest.'

The sofa was comfortable and Rose would have liked to lie back on the cushions and simply take in the unashamed luxury of her surroundings, but she raised herself and followed Cecilia into the bedroom. The colour theme of blue and gold was repeated in the curtains and the upholstery of the gilded chairs and stools. Rose was stunned by the size and elegance of their accommodation, but a cry from Cecilia made her rush into the bathroom. 'What's wrong, Cissie?'

'Hot and cold running water. Such luxury – I haven't even got that at home, at least not yet, but I'll do my best to convince Papa that everyone who is anyone in London must have indoor plumbing.'

Rose peered over her shoulder. 'Such a lovely big bath, and just look at those glass jars and bottles. I wonder what's in them.'

'I'll find out after dinner when I wallow in a tub filled with hot water. This bathroom is pure heaven, and so much nicer than the one I had when I stayed here last time.' Cecilia primped in one of the tall mirrors. 'Hurry up, Rose, there's a dear.'

Refreshed after their dusty train journey, with their hair neatly coiffed, Rose and Cecilia made their way downstairs to the terrace overlooking Ibrahim Pasha Street. Above their heads a colourful oriental canopy flapped gently like the sails of a ship catching the wind, and they were shown to a table surrounded by rattan chairs. Cecilia gave the waiter their order and then sat back, scanning the faces of the other guests as if searching for someone. Rose suspected that it was the handsome man who had caught Cissie's eye, but she held her tongue, knowing that anything she said might be taken as criticism. Left to herself, she leaned over the balcony, taking in the sights and sounds of the busy street below, and was fascinated by the polyglot crowd of people going about their daily business. Dark-skinned men wearing baggy trousers and braided jackets walked side by side with Bedouins, looking picturesque in their flowing white robes and head-dresses secured with braids of camel hair. The poorer native women were clad from head to foot in black and heavily veiled, leaving only their eyes uncovered, while the wealthy women were dressed in bejewelled silk and rode on donkeys that were equally well turned out. In total contrast, beautiful barefoot children with lustrous dark eyes and glossy black hair begged for alms from affluent European visitors, while others offered to carry luggage or touted for business selling sticky sweets dusted with icing sugar or carved wooden camels, designed to catch the eye of travellers who were eager to take home a souvenir of Egypt. Rose breathed in the scent of sugar, oriental spices and the Egyptian tobacco smoke filtered through the hookahs in the café across the street. Other less savoury smells and clouds of irritating flies did nothing to lessen her fascination with this world so different from her own. The contrast between hot, dusty and wonderfully exotic Cairo and the snowy streets of a wintry London was both astounding and exciting.

'Rose. I'm speaking to you.'

'I'm sorry. I didn't hear what you said.'

'I don't know what you find so interesting,' Cecilia said crossly. 'It's a street just like any other except that the people dress differently.'

'It's wonderful.' Rose clasped her hands together. 'I never thought to see such sights, Cissie.'

'You are such a child. Anyone would think you'd never left London, and yet you've lived on the other side of the world. You must have seen places even more exotic than this.'

Rose thought for a moment, and then she shook her head. 'I've seen mining camps and the bush, and I've gone ashore in different countries when the ship sailed into port, but this is quite different.'

Cecilia sat back in her chair as the waiter served mint tea and another hurried up with a plate of small pastries soaked in honey and sprinkled with chopped nuts. She acknowledged their offer to fetch anything they required with a gracious nod of her head and waved them away.

'Try one, Rose. I remember these from my last visit. I think they call them *baklava* and they're terribly sweet, but quite delicious.' Cecilia sipped her tea while Rose sampled one of the pastries.

'You're right. They are really tasty,' Rose said, licking her lips. 'Why aren't you eating, Cissie? I thought you were hungry.'

'I will, in a moment. I'm just looking for that person I saw in the foyer, but I fear he must have gone to his suite, or maybe he was just passing through.'

Rose selected another pastry. 'Maybe you'll see him at dinner. I mustn't eat too many of these or I'll spoil my appetite, as Sadie would have said.'

'Oh Lord, here come my parents. Now I'll have to behave.' Cecilia snatched up a pastry and popped it into her mouth.

'So there you are.' Elizabeth waited for her husband to pull up a chair for her and she subsided gracefully in a cloud of expensive perfume.

Cecilia proffered the serving dish. 'Would you like a piece of *baklava*, Mama?'

'No, thank you, darling. I'm saving myself for dinner.'

'Papa?' Cecilia glanced at her father, who was standing behind his wife's chair.

'No, thank you, Cissie. I have to see the High Commissioner and then, if time permits, I'll start looking for a suitable property. We can't stay in this expensive hotel indefinitely.'

Rose looked from one to the other; the conversation seemed so trivial. Eugene was still missing, and yet Mr and Mrs Sheldon were more concerned with where they would live and what was for dinner that evening, and Cissie was more interested in finding the man who had made such an impression on her earlier than searching for her brother.

Rose excused herself saying that she needed to finish the article she had begun, and she was on her way towards the grand staircase when she almost collided with a handsome, olive-skinned gentleman. He apologised profusely.

'I was admiring the statues,' Rose said with a shy smile. 'I wasn't looking where I was going.'

'It was my fault entirely.' He spoke with a hint of an accent that Rose could not place, and he was handsome enough to be the man who had made such an impression on Cissie.

'I should introduce myself,' he said smoothly. 'Seth Mallinson. I was military attaché to the former ambassador.'

'Rose Munday, I'm here with Mr and Mrs Sheldon.'

'Yes, I saw Desmond and his wife, and I thought I recognised their charming daughter.'

'Yes, Cecilia is here, too. They're on the terrace, if you want to make yourself known to them.'

'Thank you, Miss Munday. It's a pleasure to make your acquaintance.' He clicked his heels together and inclined his head in a bow.

Rose watched him walk off in the direction of the terrace and she smiled to herself as she imagined Cissie's face when Seth Mallinson approached her parents. At least one member of the Sheldon family would be happy.

Cecilia confirmed this when she came to their room to change for dinner. 'He's so charming, Rose, and he was very attentive. He has such marvellous dark eyes, like sloes and they twinkle when he smiles.' Cecilia sighed rapturously.

'Yes, he is very charming,' Rose said equably.

'He's invited us all to dine with him this evening.' Cecilia rushed up to the mirror to peer at her reflection. 'I look such a mess. Where is Hebony? Has she unpacked my clothes? I need to wear something special.'

Rose stifled a chuckle. 'But, Cissie, you don't know anything about this man. He's very handsome, but he might be married with children.'

Cecilia turned to her, shaking her head. 'No, he isn't. Mama told me all about him. His father was a high-ranking officer in the Indian Army and his mother was an Indian princess. They eloped because both families were totally against their union. You know how people are about mixed marriages, Rose.'

'No, not really. I don't remember hearing anything about such things in Bendigo, but life is hard in the mining communities, and everyone just gets on with things the best way they can.'

'Well, that's as maybe,' Cecilia said casually. 'But I think Seth is the most interesting man I've ever met, and he's single.'

'What can I say? You know your own mind, Cissie. Maybe he can help us find Eugene.'

'I hadn't thought of that. Anyway, I'm going to have a bath and put on one of my most alluring gowns.' Cecilia eyed Rose critically. 'I hope you'll make an effort, too. And please don't mention that you're working for a newspaper. Heaven knows what Seth would think of that.'

'I'll only speak when spoken to. Go and make yourself beautiful, Cissie. I hope he's worth it.' Rose eyed the gown that Hebony had laid out for her, reviving memories of the evening she had spent with Eugene and Cecilia at the Savoy Theatre. So much had changed since then and it had all started because Eugene wanted to train someone to use his new-fangled typewriting machine. She sighed as she unbuttoned her blouse and stepped out of her skirt. Tonight she would keep in the background and enjoy the luxury and exotic ambience of her surroundings, but tomorrow she would begin her quest in earnest and her first trip would be to the barracks at Kasr-el-Nil where she hoped to find Max. But the prospect of seeing him again was dulled by past events, and the feeling that he had let her down persisted, despite her efforts to rationalise her emotions.

On the far side of the room Cecilia was hanging on to the bedpost for dear life while Hebony did her best to whittle her mistress's waist to a hand span, tugging on the corset strings until Rose was certain they were going to snap. Eventually a gasp from Cecilia put an end to the torture.

'That's enough, Hebony. I can hardly breathe.'

Hebony tied the strings in a bow and stood back, awaiting instructions. Cecilia released her grip on the bedpost and straightened up, panting as if she had just run a race. 'What we go through for the sake of beauty,' she gasped.

'You won't be able to eat a thing,' Rose said, shrugging. 'Is he worth it, Cissie?'

'Don't be silly, Rose. Of course he is. Seth Mallinson might well rise to consul one day, if the post is reintroduced. He's wealthy in his own right, and I should think that he's ambitious. I like that in a man.'

Rose slipped the gown over her head. 'What would your parents think of such a match?'

'For heaven's sake, Rose, I've only just met the man. I'll worry about that if and when the time comes, although, without being immodest, I have broken a few hearts in my time.'

Rose had no answer for this. She beckoned to Hebony. 'Would you do me up, please?'

Sunlight forced its way through tiny gaps between the curtains. Rose sat up in bed, yawned and stretched. She could tell from the even breathing that Cissie was still asleep, and judging by the amount of champagne she had drunk the previous evening, it was likely that she would not be up in time for breakfast. Rose had watched the interplay between her friend and Seth Mallinson with a feeling of amusement mixed with foreboding. She could see from the change in Desmond's expression that he did not approve, and Elizabeth seemed bemused by her daughter's conduct. Rose wondered how much they knew of Cissie's life in London, where she had been free to do as she pleased, and wealthy enough to get away with behaviour that might outrage the more conventional onlooker. Cecilia Sheldon had enjoyed the freedom to go about unchaperoned usually reserved for married women, and, if she were to be believed, had taken lovers when and as she pleased. Time would tell how deeply she felt about her latest conquest, but Rose suspected that Seth Mallinson was well and truly smitten.

She went into the bathroom and luxuriated in a hot bath before getting dressed. Then, having checked and found that Cecilia was still deeply asleep, Rose decided to go to the dining room in the hope that Desmond and Elizabeth would be there, as she did not fancy breakfasting on her own.

Desmond was seated at the table, reading a newspaper and drinking coffee. He looked up as Rose approached. 'Good morning, Rose. You're up early.'

'Yes, sir.' Rose smiled at the waiter who pulled up a chair for her, and she sat down. 'I want to ask a favour.'

He folded the paper, eyeing her curiously. 'What can I do for you?'

'I want to visit the barracks at Kasr-el-Nil. Max, my fiancé, is in the 7th Dragoons and I've been told that's where they're stationed.'

'I see.' He frowned thoughtfully. 'I'm not sure that one can simply turn up and ask to be admitted. There are protocols for this sort of thing, Rose.'

'What should I do to get permission to see Max?'

'There is much to do to get the embassy running normally again, but I might be able to help although it will take time. It won't be today, and that's a certainty.'

'But I've come all this way, and I've waited so long to see him, Mr Sheldon. Isn't there anyone who could help me?'

'You'll just have to be patient for a while longer. I'm sorry, but I'm more concerned about my son at this moment. Finding out what's happened to Eugene must come first.'

'Of course, I understand that, sir. I'll do anything I can to help find him.'

A wry smile flitted across Desmond's aquiline features. 'Bravely said, but this isn't London. You can't come and go as you please. Private Cook will continue to be your bodyguard and I want you to promise that you won't step outside unless he accompanies you.'

Rose was about to protest, but she could see that Desmond was in no mood to make concessions. She nodded. 'I promise.'

'Thank you, and I'll see what I can do to obtain permission for you to visit the barracks.' Desmond glanced at the waiter who was hovering behind her chair. 'However, I believe in starting the day with a good breakfast. Order what you want, Rose. That poor fellow has been standing there for ages.'

Rose studied the menu, but the neat copperplate handwriting might as well have been in Arabic for all the sense it made. Max was uppermost in her thoughts – she could think of nothing else. He was so near and yet he was still beyond her reach, but that would have to change. She had come this far and her patience was exhausted. She had to see Max, and the sooner the better.

Chapter Seventeen

Rose toyed with the boiled egg she had ordered in an attempt to keep Desmond happy, but she had little appetite. She took a sip of her coffee and wrinkled her nose. It was strong and thick with grounds and it left a bitter aftertaste, although that was the least of her worries. Her thoughts were racing. If she could spend a few minutes with Max she would know instantly whether or not he still loved her, and perhaps more importantly, whether her own feelings had undergone a sea change.

'Rose! Why didn't you wake me?' Cecilia sank gracefully onto the chair pulled out for her by an attentive waiter. 'I opened my eyes and found you gone.'

'Where is your mother, Cissie?' Desmond folded his paper and laid it on the table. 'I left her getting ready.'

'I couldn't be bothered to wait for her, Papa. I went to your room, but she was still fussing about her hair and poor Hebony looked as though she was about to burst into tears.'

Desmond rose from his chair. 'Well, I have to go to the embassy now, so make my apologies to her, Cissie. I hope to see you all at dinner, but don't wait for me. I might be very late.' He patted Cecilia on the shoulder as he walked away.

'You should have waited for me to get up, Rose,' Cecilia said crossly. 'I needed your help with my stays and I had to run to Mama's room wearing little else than my wrap. Hebony did my hair for me, but that was your job. You were supposed to take Lindon's place.'

'I'm sorry, I forgot, but you were sleeping so peacefully that I didn't want to disturb you.'

'Well, I'm reminding you now, Rose. You're free to spend your time as you please as long as you're there to help me to dress and do my hair.'

'I'm sorry about this morning, but I have a lot on my mind.'

'You're on edge, I can tell, Rose. I know you want to see Max, but you won't do anything silly, will you?'

'No, of course not.' Rose looked up and saw Elizabeth approaching with a retinue of servants buzzing around her. 'Your mama is coming, and she's attracting a lot of attention.'

'She always does,' Cecilia said soulfully. 'No one has eyes for anyone else when my mother enters a room. I don't know how she does it, but it's always been like that for as long as I remember.'

Elizabeth took her seat at the table amid a flurry of activity as one waiter held her chair and another poured her coffee, while yet another laid a starched white napkin on her lap. 'Thank you,' she said, smiling graciously. She waved the menu away and picked up her cup. 'Now then, girls, what have you planned for today?' She looked from one to the other. 'Nothing? I thought as much. Well, you'll be pleased to know that I've hired a barouche to take us to Giza. The pyramids are always worth a visit, as is the Sphinx, and Jabari had gone to the kitchen to supervise the packing of a luncheon basket. I thought it would be fun to picnic in the place where the ancients used to do whatever they did in those places. History was never my strong point.'

Cecilia sighed heavily. 'Oh, Mama, do we have to? I've seen the pyramids and, quite frankly, I wasn't impressed. I was rather hoping for a leisurely day with perhaps a tour of the bazaar.'

'No, Cissie. I have it in my head that we will do some sightseeing, and maybe you will feel more enthusiastic about the history of Egypt when I tell you that we are to be accompanied by Mr Mallinson.'

Cecilia and Rose exchanged wide-eyed glances. 'Mr Mallinson?' Cecilia breathed the name as if she were mentioning a deity.

'Seth Mallinson, darling. Last evening at dinner I told him that I planned a little excursion today and he volunteered to escort us. I seem to remember that you had gone to the powder room with Rose, so maybe you weren't aware of the arrangement.'

'And did he accept?' Cecilia asked casually.

'Yes, of course.' Elizabeth eyed her daughter warily. 'I thought you were getting on rather well with him, Cissie. All things considered.'

'What do you mean by that, Mama?'

'He's a well-educated, charming man, despite the fact that he's . . .' Elizabeth leaned forward, lowering her voice. 'He's not exactly one of us, if you know what I mean.'

'No, Mama. I'm afraid I don't.'

'His mother was an Indian princess.' Elizabeth glanced round as if expecting the other guests to be hanging on her every word. 'He inherited a fortune from his grandfather, who was a nabob, but he has mixed blood, Cissie.'

'Of course I knew that,' Cecilia said airily. 'I think it's terribly romantic and he's a charming gentleman.'

'And extremely handsome,' Rose added mischievously.

'Yes, indeed, and I believe he has had a distinguished career in the Indian Army.' Elizabeth's hand shook slightly as she picked up her cup and she sipped her coffee. 'All I'm saying is, perhaps he might not be as well received in society circles at home, so I want you to be careful, Cissie.'

'Shame on those who are so small-minded,' Cecilia said angrily. 'If a man is considered good enough to die for his country, then he should be welcomed anywhere. Don't you agree, Rose?'

'I do.' Rose could feel the tension building between mother and daughter and she decided to change the subject. 'The outing sounds wonderful, Mrs Sheldon, but I wonder if I might be excused.'

Elizabeth turned to her, eyebrows raised. 'For what reason, Rose? Are you unwell?'

'No, not at all. I'm feeling fine, but I have an article to finish and send off to the office in Fleet Street.'

'Surely you could do that tomorrow?' Elizabeth's smooth brow furrowed in a frown. 'You might not get another chance to see such wonders. Besides which, Jabari and Hebony are accompanying us, albeit in another vehicle, and I can't leave you on your own.'

'I'll have Private Cook to keep me company, Mrs Sheldon,' Rose said hastily. She glanced at Cecilia, hoping for support from her, but her friend was staring into space with a dreamy expression on her face. Rose gave her a surreptitious nudge. 'I'll be in safe hands, won't I, Cissie?'

Cecilia turned to her with a start. 'Oh, yes. Most definitely.'

'Very well, but I don't approve of young women trespassing in an exclusively male domain,' Elizabeth said tartly. 'I'm sorry, Rose, but I speak as I find, and I think what you're doing is most unladylike. Goodness knows what your fiancé will think.'

Rose was not going to be dragged into an argument that she had no chance of winning. Mrs Sheldon might appear to be meek and mild when in the company of her husband, but Rose was seeing another side of her and she realised that Cissie's mother was a woman with an iron will, which she managed to disguise beneath sweet smiles and a calm demeanour. Cissie herself seemed to revert to childhood when in her mother's company, and the confident, outgoing society darling was completely overshadowed.

Elizabeth pushed back her chair and two waiters rushed to her assistance. 'I'm going to my room to make myself ready, Cissie. We'll leave in half an hour.' She fixed Rose with a stern look. 'You can still change your mind.'

'You're not planning to visit the barracks, are you, Rose?' Cecilia said in a low voice as her mother glided out of the dining room.

'I'm saying nothing, Cissie. You might succumb to your mother's interrogation and tell her everything.'

'As if I would! I'm perfectly capable of standing up to my mother.'

Rose raised an eyebrow, saying nothing.

An hour later, having seen Cissie and her mother set off together with Seth Mallinson, followed in a smaller carriage by Jabari and Hebony with a wicker hamper large enough to feed a small army, Rose sent for Private Cook. They met in the vestibule and she told him that she intended to visit the barracks at Kasr-el-Nil. She had expected an argument, but to her surprise, he merely nodded.

'I was stationed there before I was posted to Alexandria. Shall I go and find a cab, miss?'

'Yes, please do.' Rose waited while he strode off purposefully, and he returned minutes later.

'Right, miss. Let's go, although I have a feeling I might get into trouble for this.'

'No, you won't,' Rose said casually. 'You're doing as I ask, and I'll stand by that. All I want is five minutes with my fiancé and then I'll be satisfied.'

The journey through the back streets revealed a different Cairo from the one Rose had seen when the Sheldons' carriage had entered the city by a different route. She had seen mansions that resembled small palaces, set in the midst of landscaped gardens, overlooking the River Nile, and then there was the splendour of Shepheard's Hotel. Now all she could see was poverty, dirt and squalor. Domestic animals and people shared crowded accommodation, and the children, although still beautiful, were barefoot, dirty and clad in rags. The stench of human and animal excrement simmered in the heat of the day, and the air was black with flies. Cook sat beside her and she could feel the tension in his body as he remained on the alert, looking to the left and right with his hand on the pistol he wore in a leather holster. They travelled in silence and progress was slow as the cab driver flicked his whip and shouted at the other road users, who responded vigorously. Carts, carriages, camels and heavily laden donkeys all vied for space, and none of them seemed willing to give way to the other. For once, Rose was glad that she did not understand their language, although their meaning was clear.

They arrived at the barracks and Rose was amazed to see such an elegant building. Somehow she had imagined it to be gaunt and austere and prison-like, but this edifice was quite as splendid as any of those sophisticated residences she had seen on the banks of the Nile.

Private Cook leaped from the cab and handed her to the ground. 'If you wait here, miss. I'll speak to the guard at the main entrance.'

'All right,' Rose said reluctantly. 'I suppose that is the best idea, as you're in uniform.'

He nodded and marched off, snapping to attention

and saluting the soldier on duty. The cab driver was gesticulating and holding his hand out for money. Rose took her purse from her reticule and selected a few coins at random, dropping them into his palm, which had the desired effect and he subsided, mumbling. The sun beat down from a placid blue sky and she fanned herself, shifting from foot to foot as she waited anxiously for Cook's return. It seemed like an age, although she knew that it could not have been more than a few minutes before he was walking briskly towards her, but his expression was not encouraging.

'What did he say? Can I see Max?'

Cook shook his head. 'Not without written permission, miss. I'm sorry, I did me best, but the sentry weren't going to go against the rules, and I can't blame him for that.'

'What do I do now? It might take days or even weeks to get the necessary documentation.'

'I've got an idea.'

'I'll do whatever you say, but get me in to see my fiancé. I must speak with him.'

'I know the layout of this place, miss. There's a way in that won't be guarded.'

'Will you take me with you?'

'No, miss. I'll tell the cabby where to take you and you must wait there until I return, with or without your young man. I can't promise anything, but if he's in there I'll find him for you.' He helped her into the cab, giving the cabby instructions in halting Arabic. 'I learned a bit of the lingo. It comes in useful at times like this.' He grinned as he slammed the carriage door. 'Sit tight, miss. If anyone can do this it's me.'

Rose was about to thank him when the cab moved forward and she had to hold on in order to prevent herself sliding off the slippery leather seat. They travelled a short distance and the driver drew his horse to a halt in a street shaded by tall trees. There was nothing Rose could do other than sit and wait. The heat was intense, despite the shade, and she could feel perspiration trickling between her shoulder blades, and there were damp patches under her arms. Her tightly laced stays made breathing difficult and her heart was beating so fast that she felt as if she had been running a race.

After what seemed like an eternity, when Rose was giving up hope of seeing Max, she spotted Private Cook moving swiftly in the shadow of tall trees and palms, and then she realised that he was not alone. Her heart seemed to miss a beat as she recognised the tall, fair-haired officer wearing his dark blue patrol jacket, trimmed with lambskin, and a pill box hat set at a jaunty angle. He came striding purposefully towards the cab.

'Max.' Rose thrust the door open and seconds later she was in his arms, laughing and crying at the same time.

His smile faded and he held her at arm's length. 'I can't believe that you've come all this way to find me, Rose. What made you embark on such a reckless journey?'

She stared at him, momentarily lost for words at the unfairness of his remark. 'You're to blame, not I,' she said breathlessly. 'You weren't there when I arrived in London.'

He dropped his hands to his sides. 'You know why that was, Rose. I was called to duty.'

'You allowed me to travel halfway around the world only to find myself alone and virtually penniless in London.'

'We can't talk here in the street.' Max turned to Cook, who was standing at a respectful distance. 'You shouldn't have brought her here, Private.'

'That's not fair, Max,' Rose said angrily. 'I made him bring me, and if it hadn't been for Private Cook I would not have found you, or at least it would have taken a very long time.'

The carriage driver chose this moment to start shouting at them, but when Max answered in fluent Arabic he subsided in silence.

'Where are you staying?' Max opened the carriage door. 'I'll see you to safety and then I must return to the barracks. You shouldn't have come here, Rose. It was stupid and thoughtless.'

'How dare you speak to me in that tone, Max? I'm here as a guest of Mr Desmond Sheldon and his wife. He is on the Embassy staff and we're staying at Shepheard's Hotel, so it's all perfectly respectable.'

'Nevertheless, you shouldn't be in this country. We've won a victory, but who knows what will happen in the next few weeks or months?' Max lifted her off the ground and deposited her on the carriage seat. 'Private, you can sit up front with the driver. Tell him to take us back to the hotel.' Max climbed in and slammed the door. 'Now, Rose. I want a full explanation of what drove you to such madness. You do realise that I can't be responsible for you while you're here?'

Rose stared at him in horror. This arrogant man was nothing like the charming, carefree young officer who had claimed her heart.

'What's happened to you, Max? You didn't arrange to have me met at the docks. You didn't leave a message with anyone, and when I eventually reached the Captain's House I found it had been invaded by squatters.' She clutched the side of the vehicle as it jolted over the rough road surface with Cook perched precariously beside the driver.

'How was I to know that, Rose?' Max said impatiently. 'It's not as if you were a stranger to London. You lived there for long enough to know your way around. I was sent to Egypt at very short notice, and I told Carrie that you were coming. She was supposed to make arrangements for you.'

'Your sister must have forgotten, and she had left

for Australia, as I found out to my cost. If it hadn't been for Maria I would have been quite destitute.'

'If you knew where to find Maria there shouldn't have been a problem. I think you're making it out to be more than it was in order to get sympathy, and to excuse your unladylike behaviour, Rose. You shouldn't be here now.'

She moved as far away from him as was possible in the confines of the open landau. 'You are an unspeakable prig, Max. I found Maria more or less by accident, and if Eugene hadn't given me a job on his newspaper I might have starved.'

'Who is this Eugene fellow?'

'Eugene Sheldon. That's why I was able to come to Cairo. His parents are here and they're desperate to find him, as is his sister, Cecilia.'

'Sheldon, the journalist who went missing?' Max twirled his blond moustache, frowning thoughtfully.

Rose glared at him, irritated by his attitude and hating the facial hair. 'Why did you grow that silly thing?' she demanded angrily. 'It doesn't suit you.'

He eyed her coldly. 'It's the done thing. In fact it's part of the uniform, and one of the things you'll have to get used to when we're married. You have a lot to learn, Rose.'

'And so have you, Max. I'm not someone you can order around as if I'm in the ranks. You might have paid my fare to London, but you made no provision for me after I arrived, and you didn't even have the decency to leave me a note. Shame on you, Max.'

He sat stiffly, facing forward. 'You've placed me in a very awkward situation, Rose. I'll see you safely to your hotel and then I must leave you, but I'll return this evening and I'll have words with Mr Sheldon. He should not have encouraged you in this mad venture.'

'You'll do no such thing,' Rose fired back at him. 'I came here of my own free will, and I'm earning my keep, I can assure you of that. My articles are appearing almost daily in the *London Leader*, and I have no intention of giving up my career.'

'Career!' Max turned to her, his blue eyes blazing and his generous lips tightened into a thin line. 'Don't talk such nonsense. Whoever heard of a woman having a career? Unless you like to class a domestic servant or a shop assistant as an important position in life.'

'Yes, I do, as it happens. We are all important in our own way, and I seem to have a talent for writing. Eugene spotted it and—'

He raised his hand. 'It seems to me that you've become very friendly with Eugene Sheldon. I was feeling a certain amount of sympathy for him until this moment, but suddenly I've lost my enthusiasm for leading the search party.'

'You're going to look for him?' Rose felt her anger melt away and she clutched his hand. 'When is this due to happen, Max? Do you know where he might be?'

'Even if I did, I wouldn't be allowed to give you that information, Rose.'

'Then let me come with you.'

'What?' Max stared at her in disbelief. 'Don't be silly. I've never heard such nonsense in my whole life.'

'I'm being paid to send news back to London,' Rose said stiffly. 'You seem to have difficulty in accepting that fact.'

His expression changed subtly. 'I'm sure you think that you're very important, my dear. But writing about soirées, marriages and christenings is never going to be headline news.'

Rose sat back, gazing at him and seeing a stranger. 'What happened to you, Max? I don't think I know you now. I wonder if I ever did.'

'You're obviously suffering from the heat or maybe fatigue from travelling all the way from England.' Max patted her hand. 'We'll have a more rational conversation after dinner this evening. I'll have words with Mr Sheldon and we can decide what's to be done.'

Rose turned to him, forcing herself to remain calm. 'I make my own decisions. I've had to grow up since I left home and found myself alone in London.'

Barely waiting for the carriage to come to a halt,

Max opened the door and leaped out. He held out his hand. 'We're here. You need to have a long rest and think about what I've said. We'll talk later, but now I have to return to the barracks.'

'I can manage on my own, thank you.' Rose ignored his offer of help and climbed down to the pavement. She beckoned to Cook, who was standing at a discreet distance. 'Private Cook will see me into the hotel.' She swept past Max without a second glance, the reassuring sound of Private Cook's booted feet close behind her as they mounted the steps of Shepheard's Hotel. She fought against the desire to turn her head to see if Max was watching her, but when she gave in to temptation all she saw was the set of his shoulders and the back of his head as the carriage disappeared into the distance.

'Are you all right, miss?'

Rose shot a sideways glance at Cook, with an attempt at a smile. 'Yes, thank you, Private Cook. I think I might go to my room and finish writing my column.'

'I've got something to tell you that might be of interest, miss.'

'Go on. I'm listening.'

He glanced round as if expecting spies to be loitering amongst the hotel guests. 'Might I suggest we go somewhere quieter, miss?'

'I'm hot and thirsty, and I'm hungry, too.' Rose looked over his shoulder and saw an unoccupied table in the corner of the terrace. 'We'll have luncheon and you can tell me what's bothering you.'

'I don't think that's a good idea, miss. I don't belong with the guests.'

'Nonsense. I don't care what they think, and from now on I refuse to call you Private Cook, unless Mr or Mrs Sheldon are within earshot. Come with me, Bradley, and ignore the stupid people who have nothing better to do than to gossip about others.' Rose headed for the table and a waiter appeared as if from nowhere to pull up a chair for her. He glanced at Bradley's uniform and hesitated, but Rose sent him a warning look and the waiter held out another chair, flicking imaginary dust from the seat.

Bradley hesitated. 'I should have gone to the staff quarters, miss.'

'Regardless of that, you're here now, Bradley. Please sit down and tell me what is so urgent that it couldn't wait until later.'

He slumped down in the chair, but before he had a chance to speak the waiter reappeared and handed them each a menu.

Rose scanned it. 'Mint tea, please, and what I'd really like is a plate of sandwiches. Would that be possible?'

The waiter bowed and smiled. 'Of course, Mademoiselle.' He turned his attention of Bradley. 'Monsieur?'

Rose could see that her friend was ill at ease. 'Will

you share them with me, Bradley? And I expect you'd like a glass of beer.'

'Yes, miss. Thank you.'

Rose handed the menu back to the waiter. 'Make that sandwiches for two, please.' She waited until he had moved away. 'Now, Bradley, when we're alone I'd really like it if you would call me Rose.'

'Yes, miss – I mean, Rose.' He shook his head. 'I'm sorry, I can't be so familiar. I'll call you Miss Rose, if that's all right with you.'

'If you insist, but I'm dying of curiosity. What did you have to say?'

He ran his finger round his starched collar. 'I didn't like the way your fiancé spoke to you, miss. I wasn't eavesdropping, but I couldn't help hearing what he said.'

'I dare say it was the shock of seeing me here, Bradley. He isn't normally like that.'

'It's none of my business, but I feel I ought to tell you that he didn't seem best pleased when I found him and told him that you were here.'

'Again, I have to say it must have been a total surprise, and I suppose I should have remained in London with Maria and the children.' Rose leaned her elbows on the table, fixing him with a hard stare. 'Are you going to tell me this big secret, or not? My patience is wearing thin.'

Chapter Eighteen

Bradley cleared his throat. 'I got into the barracks through a ground-floor window. We all knew about the broken latch, but no one reported it because it was a way out for anyone who fancied a night in town. Anyway, I bumped into an old mate and he told me where to find the captain.'

'That's all very well, Bradley, but I don't see how it relates to me.'

'I'm coming to that, Miss Rose. Stubby – that's my mate Private Stubbs – told me that spies have pinpointed the place where the missing soldiers and the newspaperman are being held captive. Your captain is taking a search party into the desert tomorrow.'

'Max said as much, but he wouldn't give me any details.' Rose put her head on one side, gazing thoughtfully at Bradley. 'Do you know where they're going?'

'No, I don't. That's the sort of information only an officer would have, but I do know that the search party is leaving the barracks at dawn.'

'I want to go with them,' Rose said firmly.

'That's impossible.' Bradley's blue eyes darkened. 'You mustn't even think about it.'

'Oh, but I must. I owe it to Eugene and to the newspaper to do my very best to find him, and if I can be the first to cable the news back to London it will make the headlines.' Rose sat back in her seat as the waiter appeared with their order, and she waited until he had moved away. 'You must take me, Bradley. We'll follow the search party at a safe distance.'

He pushed his chair back and rose to his feet. 'I can't do that, miss. It's out of the question.'

'Sit down, Bradley. People are staring.'

'I should go back to my quarters, I'm sorry, Miss Rose, but I can't oblige you.' He walked away, leaving his meal untouched.

Rose glared at the people who were staring at her and they turned away, but she had a feeling that she was the subject of their muffled conversations, and she could have wept with relief when she saw Cecilia making her way through the maze of tables followed by Seth Mallinson. His darkly handsome looks and confident demeanour attracted admiring stares from both women and men, and Cecilia was positively blooming.

'Why are you sitting here on your own?' Cecilia demanded. 'And you've ordered all this food. You must be hungry.' She sat down, beckoning Seth to follow suit. 'I'm famished.' She seized a sandwich and bit into it.

Seth hesitated, eyeing the glass of beer. 'Are you expecting company, Miss Munday? Perhaps we ought to find another table.'

'No, it's quite all right,' Rose said hastily. 'Please take a seat and help yourself. I'll never manage to eat all this.'

He acknowledged her invitation with a smile and sat down next to Cecilia.

'Who were you expecting, Rose?' Cecilia asked eagerly. 'It must have been a gentleman, so have you got a secret admirer? Might he still arrive? I hope so because I must admit I'm curious.'

'There's no one, Cissie. I was trying to be sociable and I asked Private Cook to join me for lunch, but the other guests made him feel uncomfortable and so he left.' Rose could see that Cecilia was not about to accept this explanation and she decided to change the subject. 'Why are you back so early? I thought you went to Giza for a picnic lunch.'

'It was a disaster.' Cecilia rolled her eyes dramatically. 'Mama developed a headache and then a camel spat at us, and a sudden sandstorm ruined everything. Mama insisted that we return here.'

'There will be other chances to see the pyramids,' Seth said smoothly. 'I am at your disposal, ladies. It would be my pleasure to take you sightseeing at your convenience.'

'How kind of you, Seth.' Cecilia took another bite of her sandwich. 'Aren't you eating, Rose?'

'I'm not as hungry as I thought I was. If you'll excuse me, I think I'll go to our suite and change into something lighter. It is rather warm today.'

'You haven't told us what you were doing this morning.' Cecilia dabbed her lips with a napkin. 'You look tired, Rose. Is there something you're not telling me?'

'Newcomers to Cairo often find the climate enervating at first,' Seth said calmly. 'A short rest is probably all that you need to set you up for the rest of the day, Miss Munday.'

Rose pushed back her chair and stood up. 'I expect you're right, Mr Mallinson. I'll see you later, Cissie.' She hurried off before Cecilia had a chance to question her further. This was not the time to admit that she had been to the barracks, or to raise Cissie's hopes by telling her that Eugene's whereabouts was known to those in authority. One thing was certain, and that was her determination to follow the story to its conclusion, and to be there when Eugene was released from captivity. If Bradley would not take her, she would find another way.

Later that day Rose sought Bradley's company and used all her powers of persuasion to make him divulge what he knew, but he refused to co-operate and nothing she said would make him change his mind. In the end she had to admit defeat, but as a concession he agreed to escort her to the barracks next morning, providing she left all enquiries to him. Rose knew in her heart that it was sound common sense, and that it would be foolhardy to attempt to follow Max and his search party. Any interference might endanger the lives of the soldiers as well as the hostages, and she would have to be patient. It was not going to be easy.

She slept little that night and was up before dawn. Fully dressed and seated by the window, she gazed up at the heavens, waiting eagerly for daylight to chase away the stars. Slowly the sky flooded with opalescence, and she struggled to make sense of a confused jumble of thoughts and emotions. Her reunion with Max had not been as she had envisaged during the long sea voyage from Australia, and his attitude towards her had come as something of a shock. Finding Max had been the reason why she had travelled to Egypt, or that was what she had told herself. Now she was beginning to question her motives. Was it Max or Eugene who was uppermost in her thoughts? Or was it the desire to prove herself as a woman capable of pursuing a career in journalism? For all her brave talk she was struggling to survive in what was definitely a man's world, but to acknowledge the limitations forced upon her by society was both frustrating and humiliating.

The brass clock on the side table ticked away the minutes, but the hands seemed to move more slowly than usual, and in the end Rose abandoned all pretence of keeping calm and went downstairs to the terrace. If the waiter who attended her was surprised to see a young, unchaperoned woman at this time in the morning he did not show it, and he smiled urbanely as she ordered coffee, although he seemed to find it hard to accept that she did not want to order anything from the breakfast menu. He gave her a reproachful glance as he poured the coffee, and left the menu in a prominent position on the table, as if expecting her to change her mind.

Rose sipped the beverage and waited, hoping that Bradley would put in an appearance earlier than they had planned. She was on her own at first and then other guests began to take up places at the other tables and she did not feel so conspicuous. The street below was already busy, and on an ordinary day Rose would have been delighted to sit quietly and view the colourful hive of activity, but she could hardly contain the nervous energy that consumed her. In the end she could stand it no longer and she left the table, following one of the waiters who was taking an order to the kitchen. She had a vague idea that someone in the staff quarters would point her in the direction of Bradley's accommodation, or perhaps she might find Jabari and send him with a message, but she had not gone very far when she came face to face with Bradley.

He grabbed her by the elbow and guided her back into more familiar territory. 'You shouldn't have gone there, Miss Rose. Guests don't go below stairs.'

'I wanted to find you.' Rose pulled free from his grasp. 'It's time we left for the barracks.'

'I was on my way to your room to tell you that there's a carriage waiting for us.'

'I'm sorry, Bradley. I was wrong to doubt you, but I could hardly sleep for thinking about today. I was imagining all sorts of disasters that might occur.'

'You just have to trust the captain and his men.' Bradley proffered his arm as they reached the steps that led down to the street, and she accepted without a murmur. He handed her into the waiting landau and climbed in to sit beside her.

'Is there any point in going now?' Rose asked wearily. 'If we'd left much earlier we might have been able to see the search party leave the barracks, and we could have followed them – at a safe distance, of course.'

'We'd have been spotted and arrested for spying. This isn't a game, Miss Rose.'

'I wish you'd stop calling me "Miss Rose", it makes me feel like an elderly spinster. You and I are friends, aren't we?'

'In a manner of speaking, but I doubt if Mr and Mrs Sheldon would think that way.'

Rose shook her head, but she did not argue. There seemed little point, especially when she knew in her heart that he was right. This sort of nicety did not exist in the mining community where she had spent the last nine years, and she was overcome by a wave of homesickness for Bendigo and the family who had given her so much love. Max seemed to have changed out of all recognition and she wished she could turn the clock back to a time when he had meant everything to her. Now she was not so sure.

'Are you listening, Miss Rose?'

She turned to Bradley, realising that she had barely heard a word of what he had said. 'I'm sorry. I was miles away.'

'I said that it would be best if I find my mate Stubby again. I'll ask him if he's been able to find out anything about the plan of action today.'

'What good would that do? Max and his party will probably be there by now, and who knows what the outcome will be? I really need to know if Eugene is all right.'

Bradley gave her a searching look. 'You like him, don't you?'

'He's a decent man, and I want to get my story

cabled back to London before the war correspond-
ents get hold of it.'

His face split in a wide grin. 'I believe you.'

'It's true,' Rose said defiantly. She folded her hands
tightly in her lap, trying hard to concentrate on
anything other than what might happen when Max
and his party descended upon the desert camp. The
tribesmen were unlikely to give up their captives
without a fight.

Once again, Rose found herself seated in a carriage
outside the barracks waiting for Bradley to reappear,
although the carriage driver they had hired was less
volatile than the one who made such a fuss the
previous day. She passed the time by writing the
opening lines of her article in which she described
the magnificent building, now used as a barracks,
but she was finding it almost impossible to concentrate. Having chewed the end of her pencil while
she racked her brains to think of something to
interest her readers, she looked up and spotted
Bradley loping towards the carriage. She leaned over
to open the door.

'Well?' she asked excitedly. 'What news?'

He shouted a list of instructions to the driver in
Arabic and leaped into the carriage. 'Hold tight,
Miss Rose. We're on our way.'

At a crack of the coachman's whip, the horses
lunged forward, but at virtually the same moment

the barrack gates opened. A cloud of dust preceded the thundering hoofs of cavalry mounts ridden by soldiers in scarlet tunics, the sun glinting off their brass helmets. Rose had to hold on with all her might as the open carriage rocked like a small ship on a rough sea. Her notepad and pencil fell to the floor along with her reticule, and her straw bonnet flew off and was left hanging by its satin ribbons.

There was little hope of the rickety landau, drawn by two underfed and overworked animals, being able to keep up with the expert horsemen and their thoroughbred horses, but the driver seemed to be caught up in the general excitement, and he rose to his feet, encouraging his team to go faster. Rose was both exhilarated and terrified. The carriage seemed in danger of being overturned as they rounded a bend in the road, but by some miracle it took the corner on two wheels and then righted itself. All that could be seen of the cavalry was a cloud of dust on the horizon, and the coachman reined in the sweating horses. He turned to Bradley, shouting something in Arabic, and Bradley answered him.

'What did he say?' Rose asked urgently. 'Why have we slowed down?'

'He said he can go no further and I agreed with him. The wheels would sink into the sand and we wouldn't get far. Better to wait here and pretend to be sightseeing. They'll have to come back this way.'

'But they could be gone for hours,' Rose said warily.

'It's up to you. If we pay him enough he'll be happy to remain here. There's an inn of sorts, and shade amongst the palm trees. Are you prepared to wait?'

'Yes, I am. All day, if necessary.'

The inn was a simple, flat-roofed building covered in crumbling white stucco, but the innkeeper was effusive in his greetings and welcomed them into the premises, offering fruit and dates, as well as wine and water. Rose was hungry and she was also thirsty, but Bradley insisted that the water might be contaminated and she accepted a large slice of melon instead. The interior of the inn was comparatively cool, but it was also dark, and smelled strongly of the droppings left by the chickens that wandered in and out at will.

Rose thanked the man for his hospitality, but she could not stand the suffocating darkness or the stench, and she went outside to sit on a bench beneath the swaying palms.

Bradley joined her. 'We could return to the hotel,' he said tentatively. 'I know you want to get your story, but is it worth staying here all day in the baking heat?'

'I can't give in now, Bradley. That's what everyone would expect me to do, and I want to prove that I can do as well as any man. I want to be sure that Eugene is safe before I leave here.'

'I understand. He means a lot to you, doesn't he?'

'He's been good to me. I don't forget my friends.'

It was too hot to make polite conversation, and they lapsed into silence. The leathery leaves of the palms clattered together in a gentle breeze, reminding Rose of Sadie's knitting needles, clicking rhythmically as her skilled hands worked at speed. The sun rose higher in the pearl-white sky and a heat haze shimmered above the ground. Rose found herself nodding off as heat and exhaustion threatened to overcome her, and she came to with a start as Bradley leaped to his feet.

He raised his hand to shield his eyes against the harsh sunlight. 'I can see a cloud of dust on the horizon. I don't think we'll have long to wait after all.'

Rose was wide awake now. She sat transfixed by the dusty cloud that grew in size until it seemed to fill the sky and the cavalry burst through it at a gallop. She raised herself from the hard wooden seat, covering her nose and mouth with her hands as the tiny particles of sand clung to her skin and hair, covering her clothes in a white powder. She had not intended to draw attention to herself, but when she saw Max she waved and called his name.

He reined in his horse, bringing it to a shuddering

halt. 'Rose? What in hell's name are you doing here?' He turned to Bradley, his lips white with anger. 'You'll be up on a charge for this, Private. You had no right to bring Miss Munday here.'

'It's not his fault, Max,' Rose cried angrily. 'I made him accompany me, and if he had refused I would have come alone.'

'Munday? Is that you?' A familiar voice rang out from a group of riders, who approached more slowly, some of them slumped over their saddles as if wounded, sick or suffering from heat and exhaustion.

Rose ignored Max and threaded her way through the sweating animals to where Eugene was seated on a horse that was large enough to pull a gun carriage.

'Are you all right, Guvnor?' She studied his face, noting a livid scar above his left eye. His cheeks were sunken and he looked pale when compared to the bronzed faces of his rescuers. His normally well-trimmed beard was long and unkempt, but his eyes were bright and his smile undiminished.

'I'm all the better for seeing you, Munday. But what in heaven's name are you doing out here in the desert? I thought you were safe in London, learning to use my typewriting machine.'

'A lot has happened since then, Guvnor.' She turned her head at the sound of Max's irate voice.

He strode up to them. 'Come away, Rose. We have

to get the sick men back to the barracks and you're holding us up.'

'I thought you'd stopped to water the horses, Captain Manning,' Eugene said smoothly. 'I could do with a drink myself, preferably a bottle of good claret, or even a cup of tea. Not the minty stuff the locals drink.'

'I've given the men ten minutes to see to their horses and get themselves a drink.' Max seized Rose by the hand. 'Come with me, Rose. I've instructed the driver to take you back to your hotel. This isn't the place for you.'

Rose snatched her hand free. 'I have enough money to pay the driver, and I'm here on business, Max. If the guvnor has ten minutes he can give me his version of events, and I'll cable my piece to London when I return to Cairo.'

Eugene dismounted, although Rose was quick to observe that he moved stiffly and grimaced as his feet hit the hard-baked ground. 'Miss Munday is working for my paper, Captain. I had no idea that she'd been sent to cover the story, but I know that she's perfectly capable of doing so.' He slipped his arm around Rose's shoulders. 'I might have to lean on you, Munday. Got caught in the crossfire and took a bullet or two, but nothing too serious.'

Rose glanced anxiously at Max and she could see from his tight-lipped expression and knotted brow that he was about to make a fuss. 'Ten minutes,

Max,' she said softly. 'And then I promise you that I'll go quietly. And please don't blame Private Cook. He was detailed to take care of me and that's exactly what he's done.'

'We'll discuss this later.' Max turned away to shout instructions to part of the contingent that had just arrived.

'You might not want to get too close to me, Munday,' Eugene said with a rueful smile. 'We weren't given the opportunity to wash or shave in camp.'

She hooked his arm around her shoulders. 'You do look a bit shaggy, Guvnor. You might have to be smuggled into the hotel through the back door.'

'And I was expecting a hero's welcome.'

'Let's get you into the shade and you can tell me all about it.' Rose beckoned to Bradley as they approached the bench where she had been sitting. 'Be a good chap and fetch some refreshment for Mr Sheldon.' She suppressed a giggle as Eugene lowered himself onto the hard wooden seat. 'Sorry, Guvnor, but you look as though you could do with a cushion.'

'It's not funny,' he groaned. 'Being shot in the backside is no joke, although I probably shouldn't use such crude language in front of a young lady.'

She sat down next to him. 'I'm no lady, I'm a newspaperman.'

Eugene threw back his head and laughed, drawing curious glances from the soldiers who were closest to them. 'I've missed you, Munday. I never thought

I'd say that, but all I could think about in that dirty, flea-ridden tent was the brief time we spent working together. I knew I could make a journalist of you, but you seem to have become one without me.'

Rose reached for her reticule and took out the pad and pencil. 'I am a professional now, so give me a broad outline and I'll fill in the twiddly bits.'

'Only you would say something like that, Munday.' Eugene reached out to take the mug that Bradley handed him.

'I'm afraid it's their rough wine, sir,' Bradley said apologetically. 'It's all they have apart from water, which is probably undrinkable.'

Eugene drained the wine in one long swallow. 'That tasted as good as the finest claret, Private. Perhaps a refill is in order?'

'I need you sober for this interview.' Rose made an effort to sound strict, but she could not stop smiling. 'It's good to have you back, Guvnor, even if you do look like a brigand.'

Eugene leaned back against the rough wall, stroking his hirsute chin. 'I think I might go clean shaven for a while.'

Rose shook her head. 'Your lady friends might disapprove.'

'You don't like the idea of my naked chin?'

'I don't think I do, but that's neither here nor there. I'm supposed to be interviewing you.'

'You're right, Munday. Now where shall I begin?

I want you to make me out to be a hero. That will make my sister sit up and take me seriously.'

'You can tell her yourself. We're staying at Shepheard's with your parents. They'll be overjoyed to see you, and so proud.'

'Really, Munday? Do you think so? If you're right it will be the first time my pa has given me credit for anything. I've always been a disappointment to him.' Eugene accepted another mug of wine from Bradley with a nod and a smile. 'I'm beginning to feel mellow. Now where was I?'

'You'd best be quick, Guvnor,' Rose said hastily. 'Max is getting ready to leave and the men are mounting up. Maybe you could travel in the carriage with me, and Bradley could ride your horse.'

A sharp intake of breath from Bradley made her look up and smile. 'It's a trained cavalry horse, and I'm sure it's much better behaved than those donkeys we rode in Alexandria.'

'Good heavens, Munday. It sounds as if you've had a more eventful war than I did,' Eugene said, chuckling. 'Oh hell, here comes your beloved, and he doesn't look very happy. I'd better climb up on that apology for a horse and ride with the men. We'll continue this chat at dinner tonight. Tell my parents to book another place at table.'

The first thing that Rose did on her return to Cairo was to send a cable to Arthur Radley, informing him that Eugene had been found safe and well. She decided to keep the details for a fuller report, but the main thing was to catch the headlines next day. Her attempts to find Mrs Sheldon were fruitless, and the concierge said he had seen her leaving the hotel with her husband. Cecilia proved just as elusive and Rose had to wait for over an hour seated on the terrace, drinking endless glasses of mint tea, until she saw a carriage draw to a halt on the street below and Seth Mallinson handing Cecilia to the pavement. The tilt of Cissie's head and the way she was smiling up at her escort convinced Rose that her friend was enjoying a flirtation with the dashing colonial officer. And who could blame her? Seth was charming, and his exotic lineage added a hint of danger to their relationship, which would be frowned upon by society. Even so, as she watched them mount the steps, arm in arm, Rose was aware that Cissie was playing a dangerous game. She had been frank about her past affairs, where she had been in control and had abandoned her lovers the moment they began to bore her, but Rose had a feeling that Cecilia Sheldon might have met her match. Seth Mallinson did not look like a man who was prepared to give up easily, and Rose suspected that the attraction was mutual. She stood up and waved to attract their attention, and Cecilia acknowledged her with a nod and a smile.

Seth escorted her to the table and he greeted Rose

with his customary charm, making her feel as though he was genuinely pleased to see her, but when he spoke to Cecilia his tone deepened and his expression changed perceptibly.

'Thank you for a delightful afternoon, Cecilia, but I'm afraid I must leave you now as I have business to attend to.' He raised her hand to his lips, his intense gaze focused on her and her alone.

Rose knew then that she had been correct in her assumption that there was more to their relationship than a passing fancy, and she looked away.

'It was lovely, Seth,' Cecilia said softly. 'The Sphinx will hold precious memories for me now.'

For a brief moment Rose thought he was going to sweep Cissie up in his arms and kiss her on the lips, but he merely bowed and smile. 'Until tonight.'

Cecilia stared after him as he walked away. 'Isn't he wonderful, Rose?'

'Are you falling in love with him, Cissie?'

'Do you know, I think I am,' Cecilia said seriously. She took a seat at the table and beckoned to one of the waiters who was hovering at a respectful distance. 'Mint tea, please. And baklava, lots of it. I'm starving.' She sat back in her chair, smiling happily. 'Did you have a good day, Rose?'

'Have you forgotten why I went to the barracks with Private Cook?'

'No, darling. I know it was one of your journalistic wild-goose chases. Did you learn anything new?'

'Not much, other than the fact that Eugene is a free man.'

'What?' Cecilia's voice rose to a pitch that caused the other guests to turn and stare at her. 'They found my brother?' she lowered her voice. 'Is he all right?'

'He made light of his injuries and he looked tired, but he's in good spirits. You'll see him at dinner this evening.'

'I've invited Seth to dine with us,' Cecilia said, frowning.

'Perhaps it might be better to have a family meal?' Rose eyed her curiously. 'I don't know, but it seems to me that's what your parents would want.'

Cecilia looked away. 'I want Seth to be present. Doesn't that count for anything?'

'You've only just met him, Cissie. Eugene has just been found alive and released from captivity. Are you telling me that this man is more important to you than your brother?'

'I love Gene, of course I do. But I'm nearly twenty-three, Rose. I've done exactly as I pleased all my life because my parents indulged me, and I took lovers and rejected them when I became bored.' Cecilia sat back while the waiter brought her order to the table. She took a sip of mint tea, but shook her head when he proffered the plate of sweet pastries.

'You don't have to tell me all this,' Rose said in a low voice when the waiter moved away to serve another table.

'I'm trying to explain myself to you.' Cecilia lowered her voice to little more than a whisper. 'A year ago I found myself in a delicate condition, which would have been the ruin of me.'

'What did you do?'

'The father was a married man, very wealthy and prominent in parliamentary circles. He arranged for his surgeon to take care of me and that, as they say, was that. I'm not proud of myself, Rose.'

'Does Seth know about this?'

'I told him everything and he says it makes no difference. We talked and talked, and I've never felt so comfortable with a man in my whole life. I want my family to accept him, as he has accepted me. I don't want to go back to the old Cecilia, who didn't care about anyone or anything. It was love at first sight for both of us, Rose.'

'If what you say is true he'll understand why you need to have dinner with your family, Cissie. If he can't allow you one evening to celebrate your brother's freedom then he's not the man you think he is. It's your choice.'

'I suppose you're right, and I will speak to him.' Cecilia gave her a searching look. 'On the other hand, you seem to be very concerned about Eugene. Is there something you're not telling me, Rose?'

'I don't know what you mean.'

Cecilia leaned closer. 'Are you in love with my brother, Rose?'

Chapter Nineteen

Rose was unaccountably nervous as she dressed for dinner that evening. Her fingers shook as she fastened the tiny silk-covered buttons on her gown, but Cecilia seemed oblivious to the feelings of anyone other than herself. Her warbling soprano echoed loudly off the marble walls as she sang in the tub, and steam billowed from the marble-tiled bathroom in heavenly scented clouds. The joyful sounds stopped abruptly and Cecilia appeared in the doorway wrapped in a fluffy cotton towel.

'What time is it, Rose? I don't want to be late going down to the dining room.'

Rose glanced at the clock on the side table. 'You have half an hour to get ready. Unless you want to keep your beau waiting.'

'Oh Lord, I'd better hurry. I'll need you to help

me with my hair, Rose. Where is Hebony? I want to get dressed.'

'You sent her to Mr Mallinson's room with a *billet-doux*.'

'It was not a love letter,' Cecilia said hastily.

'I wasn't criticising you, Cissie.'

Cecilia allowed the towel to fall to the floor and she reached for her silk chemise, slipping it over her head. 'I know you think that dinner this evening should be about family because it's Gene's first night of freedom, but Seth is my guest and he has as much right to be there as you do.'

Cecilia's harsh words hurt, perhaps more so because there was an element of truth in them, and Rose bit back a sharp retort. She had never been so conscious of her tenuous position, being neither friend of the family nor an employee. The family had treated her with nothing but kindness, and she had been pleased to accept their hospitality. Her original reason for travelling to Egypt was becoming blurred in her mind: finding Max had become secondary to rescuing Eugene, and competing for the headlines in London had evolved into a burning ambition. Rose gazed into the mirror with a sigh – she no longer recognised the elegant young woman who looked back at her with a question in her eyes. Rose Munday, the girl who had travelled halfway round the world for love, had been lost somewhere in transit. The experiences of the past few weeks had left her confused, but emboldened. The person she had become was ready to fight for what she wanted, but whether it was success in a field dominated by men, or winning the love of the man who had captivated her thoughts and dreams, was a question that she could not answer.

'Rose, come and give me a hand. I'll have a few words to say to Hebony when she shows her face. I need you to lace me up.'

'Yes, of course.' Rose went to her aid, putting everything else from her mind. Tonight was all about Eugene, and she would sit very quietly and only speak when spoken to.

The atmosphere between Elizabeth and Desmond was tense when Rose and Cecilia joined them in the dining room, but within minutes of his arrival Seth won over Cissie's parents. He included Rose in the general conversation, but she was careful to keep her responses neutral, and she found her attention straying. Eugene was supposed to be there, but he was already late, and she wondered if he had been detained at the barracks for some reason best known to the authorities. The evening would be a complete disaster if the guest of honour did not appear, although neither Cecilia nor her parents seemed to be worried. Cissie was positively glowing and had never looked more beautiful.

'It doesn't look as if Eugene is going to make it

for dinner,' Desmond said casually. He raised his hand to summon a waiter. 'We'd better order.'

Rose was about to protest when a movement in the doorway made her turn her head. Casting dignity aside, she stood up and waved to Eugene, but Max was close behind him and she sat down again. She had seen that disapproving look many times in the past, although mostly it had been aimed at Jimmy and not her. This time she was the focus of his attention and she knew she had embarrassed him. Eugene, however, was smiling as he limped towards them. He embraced his parents and acknowledged Cecilia with a brotherly peck on the cheek, and she responded by introducing him to Seth. Eugene greeted him cordially before turning to Rose with a genuine smile of pleasure.

'You look splendid this evening, Munday. Have you cabled your story to the paper?'

'Yes, Guvnor.' Despite the compliment, Rose felt suddenly deflated. She had not expected an ecstatic greeting, but he was treating her as he had when they first met. The fact that she had travelled all the way to Egypt in the hope of finding him alive and well seemed to matter little, as far as he was concerned. She was just a colleague – and Max was still glaring at her.

'I'm being very remiss,' Eugene said, turning to Max. 'This brave officer led the rescue party that secured the release of myself and the other captives.

May I introduce Captain Max Manning of the 7th Dragoons, a gentleman who has the great good fortune to be unofficially engaged to Munday – I'm sorry, I should say, Miss Rose Munday.'

Desmond shook Max's hand. 'Delighted to make your acquaintance, Manning. I'm greatly in your debt.'

'And I,' Elizabeth echoed, smiling. 'We can't thank you enough, Captain.'

'I hope you'll join us for dinner.' Desmond raised his hand to summon a waiter, but Max shook his head.

'Thank you, sir, but I have to get back to the barracks. I have a report to write and I'm afraid it won't wait.'

'Of course, we understand completely,' Desmond said genially. 'However, you must allow us to entertain you properly when time permits.' He glanced at Rose. 'I expect you'd like some words with Rose in private before you leave?'

'Yes, sir. Thank you.' Max held his hand out. 'Rose?'

She shot a sideways glance at Eugene, but he was chatting to Seth and seemed to have forgotten her existence. She stood up and allowed Max to escort her from the dining room.

He waited until they were in the foyer before coming to a halt. 'I'm sorry, Rose.'

She stared at him blankly. 'What for?'

'I was taken aback when I saw you yesterday, and

I must have appeared to be unfeeling and even callous, but I had a lot on my mind. This is a dangerous place to be, even now.' He took her hand in his. 'I want to say how sorry I am for exposing you to such a trying time in London. I was completely at fault, and I should have made better provision for your arrival.'

This contrite Max was someone she barely recognised. Even as a child he had found it almost impossible to apologise or to admit that he might be wrong, and now he was standing before her, looking devastatingly handsome in his dark blue patrol jacket, black breeches and leather boots. His hair was bleached almost white by the sun, and his eyes were a startling blue in his tanned face. Rose felt herself slipping back into her childhood adoration of Jimmy's older brother.

'You weren't very welcoming when you first saw me,' she said vaguely.

He held her hand to his cheek. 'I know, and I can't apologise enough. You're incredibly brave, not to say foolhardy, but I admire you for it, Rose. Say you forgive me?' He kissed her hand and the soft golden hairs of his moustache brushed her skin like a butterfly's wings.

'Of course I do, Max.' She withdrew her hand gently, but she could still feel the imprint of his lips. 'I saw Jimmy in Alexandria,' she said, gathering her thoughts with a concerted effort.

'Really? What was he doing there?'

'He was in hospital.' Rose tempered her words with a smile. 'But he's all right now, Max. He was on the mend after contracting typhoid. I dare say he's back on board his ship.'

'Trust my little brother to do something stupid.' The old arrogant Max returned for a few seconds, but then he relented. 'Poor old Jim. I'm truly glad that he's all right.'

Rose stood stiffly, clasping her hands together. 'What happens now, Max? What do you want me to do?'

'I want you to return to London as soon as humanly possible. Who knows what's going to happen in this part of the world? I need to know that you're safe, and you don't have to work, Rose. I told Carrie to make funds available to you and she was to hire servants to take care of you until I returned. It seems that she left London without doing as I asked, and I'll have something to say to her when I return home.'

'I enjoy working, Max. I'll return to London, but I can't promise to give up my job at the newspaper. I might be wrong, but I think I'm the only woman reporter in the whole country. My name is in print.'

'I'm trying to understand, but it wouldn't do for you to work when we're married, Rose.'

'We aren't even engaged. Not officially, anyway.'

'But you know that I love you, and when I get

back to London I'll buy you a ring, and then we'll be married. We'll never be parted again.'

There was no doubting his sincerity, and Rose did not protest when he took her in his arms and kissed her in full view of the guests and hotel staff. Someone clapped their hands and Max released her with a rueful smile. 'I'm sorry, Rose, but I couldn't stop myself. I love you and I know you love me. We'll be married at the first possible opportunity, but now I really must go, although I don't want to leave you. You do believe me, don't you?'

Dazed and overwhelmed by the sudden turn of events, she could only nod her head. 'I do, Max.'

'This isn't the place for a woman, and there's a rumour that my regiment will return to England in the New Year, so I'll arrange for you to travel back to London – first class, of course.'

'I feel I should stay here, Max. We need to get to know each other again.'

'There won't be much chance of that, I'm afraid. I have to escort a reconnaissance party into the desert and I'll be gone for a few days, but I'll hurry back as soon as possible. I'm sure I can find someone responsible to be your travelling companion. Leave everything to me.' He bowed gallantly, and then left her standing on her own in the middle of the foyer as he strode out of the hotel with a swagger in his step.

Feeling as though she had been caught up in a

whirlwind, Rose made her way back to the dining room and resumed her seat at the table. Cecilia was absorbed with her new beau and both Elizabeth and Desmond were hanging on every word that Eugene uttered. He acknowledged Rose with a brief smile without interrupting his monologue. The waiters, moving like ballet dancers, delivered their food and then disappeared until the next course was due. Rose ate very little, but as fast as she drank her wine the glass never seemed to be empty, and by the end of the meal she was so light-headed that she could hardly stand.

'Come on, Munday, old thing,' Eugene said, chuckling. 'Let's get you to your room.'

'I'm quite all right, thank you, Guvnor.'

'Of course you are, and it's partly my fault. I should have been looking after you better.' Eugene helped her to her feet.

'Well, really!' Elizabeth's disapproving voice echoed in Rose's head. 'I do believe she's drunk.'

'No, I'm not,' Rose protested. 'I'm perfectly . . .' the word escaped her and she leaned against Eugene. 'You've had too much to drink, Guvnor.'

'That's the trouble with us newsmen,' Eugene said with a wry smile. 'We don't know when to draw the line. Anyway, I'll help you upstairs and you can support me.'

'Stop it, both of you,' Cecilia hissed. 'You're embarrassing me in front of Seth.'

'You're as much to blame, Cissie,' Eugene said softly. 'You've ignored the poor girl all evening, when you could see that she was upset.'

'I'm not upset,' Rose countered. 'I'm very happy. I'm going to London to get married. You're all welcome to my wedding. It's going to be wonderful.' She leaned her head against Eugene's shoulder and her tears created a damp patch on his borrowed dinner jacket.

'I made a complete fool of myself, Cissie.' Rose held the damp flannel to her forehead as she sipped the seltzer that Hebony handed to her.

'Yes, you did,' Cecilia said angrily. 'You were drunk, Rose. What on earth is the matter with you?'

Rose passed the empty glass to Hebony. 'Thank you. That will be all for now.'

Hebony slipped away as silently as she had come. Rose gazed after her as she left the room. 'She moves like a dancer. I wish I were half as graceful.'

Cecilia slumped back against a mound of pillows, covering her eyes with her hand. 'You kept me awake half the night, Rose Munday. You were talking in your sleep.'

'I'm so sorry. What did I say?'

'I can't remember, but you were burbling about Max and then you were talking about Maria and a bird of some kind.'

Rose tossed the flannel aside and sat up straight.

'I must go home, Cissie. You're safe here with your parents, and now you have Seth Mallinson to look after you.'

Cecilia was suddenly alert. 'Do you think he's really interested in me? Or am I just one of his conquests, of which I'm sure there are many?'

'I've never known you to be unsure of yourself. Are you really smitten?'

'I really think I am. Isn't it a laugh, Rose? Cecilia Sheldon in love at last.'

'I think it's wonderful, Cissie.' Rose swung her legs over the side of the bed and stood up.

'He is rather splendid, isn't he? So tall and handsome and utterly charming. Mama was really taken with him, and I think Papa liked him, too.'

Wearing nothing but her fine lawn nightgown, Rose crossed the floor to throw open one of the many cupboards that lined the walls. 'Where is my carpet bag? Do you think your father would send someone to book my passage home, Cissie?'

'You really are serious, aren't you?' Cecilia sat up, staring at Rose with a puzzled frown. 'Why do you want to run away? I thought you came to find Max. Well, he's here and he's the hero of the hour, having rescued Gene. So why do you want to leave?'

'I have to get home for Christmas, Cissie. I promised Sparrow that I would be there, and I left Maria to face everything on her own. I owe it to her to stay away for as short a time as possible.'

'But everything you want is here. Or has Max jilted you? Was that the reason he wanted to talk to you? Is that why you drank so much and lost your senses? Gene had to carry you up the stairs despite his weakened state.'

Rose seized the shabby carpet bag and pulled it out of the cupboard. 'Max didn't break off our engagement. He wants to marry me as soon as he gets back to London.'

'I'm even more confused now, Rose.'

'I told you, Cissie. I came here to find Max and cover the efforts to rescue your brother. There's no point in staying any longer, and I'm needed elsewhere.'

'I think you should reconsider,' Cecilia said, frowning. 'Why not wait a couple of days and think about it.'

Rose shook her head. 'Max and I have settled things between us, and Eugene is safe. My article for the newspaper has been telegraphed to the office in London, and there's nothing left for me to do here. Besides which, I gave my word to Sparrow that I'd be home in time for Christmas and I'll do everything in my power to keep that promise.'

Rose dressed hurriedly and made her way to the dining room, where she hoped to find Desmond on his own. To her surprise she found Eugene seated at their table, but there was no sign of his father.

He stood up as she approached, greeting her with a genuine smile.

'You're up early, Munday. I thought you might sleep until noon.'

She looked away, uncomfortably aware that she was blushing. 'I'm sorry about last evening, Guvnor. I don't know what came over me.'

A waiter rushed over to pull out a chair for Rose and Eugene resumed his seat. 'Don't worry about it, Munday. I've been squiffy on a good many occasions.'

Rose glanced at the waiter, who was hovering at a discreet distance. 'Coffee, please. Nothing to eat.'

'You need food, Munday.' Eugene beckoned to the waiter. 'The young lady will have buttered eggs, toast and honey, and I'd like some more coffee.'

'I'm really not hungry,' Rose protested.

'You'll feel better when you've had something to eat. You hardly touched your meal last evening.' Eugene gave her a searching look. 'Did your fiancé say something to upset you?'

'No, on the contrary. I think I was just tired.'

'So why are you looking so downhearted this morning? I know you, Munday. Something is wrong. You can tell me – I'm good at keeping secrets.'

'You're a journalist, Guvnor. If I tell you anything I'll probably find it in your column next day.'

'That was cruel, Munday,' Eugene said, chuckling. 'You know how much I value you as a friend.'

'If you're my friend you'll help me to get back to London before Christmas. I want to leave straight away.' She raised her eyes to his and was surprised to see a gleam of what might be sympathy in their amber depths.

'That's a coincidence,' he said casually. 'Because I am about to book tickets on the next train to Alexandria, and on by sea to Brindisi. I have a story to write that I don't want to send by cable.'

'You're not just saying that, Guvnor?'

'Of course not, Rose. I have a job to do, and you're my assistant, so you'll travel with me. Unless you've a better plan?'

It all happened so quickly that Rose was left breathless by the speed at which she found herself saying goodbye to Bradley, Hebony and Jabari. Mrs Sheldon was gracious, as ever, but Rose sensed a feeling of relief behind Elizabeth's softly spoken words. Desmond was kind, but slightly distant, and Cecilia was almost tearful, which took Rose completely by surprise. Bradley was perhaps the most upset, and Rose was moved to give him a hug. She thanked him for everything he had done for her and gave him Maria's address in Great Hermitage Street, making him promise that he would call on her when he returned to London.

There was no time to visit the barracks, and the possibility of seeing Max was so slim that it was hardly worth the time it would take. Rose wrote him a letter, explaining that she had taken his advice and accepted the offer of an escorted journey back to London. She did not add that she would be travelling with only Eugene for company – that would keep for later. She knew now that Max loved her, but her own feelings were far from clear – perhaps a sea voyage and the long train journey would serve to make decisions about her future clearer. Her sights were firmly set on returning to London, and the people who had come to rely on her for support.

After a hot and dusty railway journey to Alexandria, Rose insisted on visiting the hospital where Jimmy had been a patient. She told Eugene about the articles she had written involving the wounded servicemen, and he agreed to accompany her. Their passage booked, they had several hours before embarkation and they hired a rickety carriage to take them to the hospital. When she enquired about Private Harry Norman the nurse's expression changed. She said that he was still on the ward, adding in a low voice that the poor young man was very depressed, and had twice attempted to take his own life. Rose was horrified and close to tears when she entered the side ward to find him lying in bed, staring sightlessly at the ceiling.

'Harry. It's me, Rose.' She went to his bedside and laid her hand on his shoulder.

He snapped into a sitting position. 'Rose? It really is you. You didn't forget me.'

She perched on the edge of the narrow bed. 'Of course not, Harry. I had to go to Cairo for a few days, but I'm on my way home to England now.'

'I'd give anything to go with you, miss. They got me lying here day after day with no hope of me seeing again. I'm blind and that's how it's going to stay.'

Rose cast a helpless glance at Eugene, who was standing in the doorway. 'I wish I could help you, Harry.'

Eugene shook his head. 'I know what you're thinking, Munday, but it's simply not possible.'

'Who's that?' Harry clasped Rose's hand. 'I don't know his voice.'

'It's all right,' Rose said gently. 'This is Mr Eugene Sheldon. Do you remember me telling you about him, and how he gave me a job on the newspaper?'

'Yes, but what does he want here?' Harry demanded suspiciously.

Eugene moved to the bedside. 'We're on our way to London, but Rose insisted on coming to see you. Is there anything you need?'

'No, sir. I'm done for. I'll never see home again.'

Rose squeezed his fingers. 'Don't say things like that, Harry.'

'Will you do something for me, miss?'

'Of course. What is it?'

360

'Take a message to Ma in Bow. Tell her I love her, and I'm sorry I let her down.'

'You'll go home when they say you're fit and well,' Rose insisted. 'Are you able to stand and walk a little way?'

'What's the point? I can't see where I'm going. If I return home I'll be a burden to Ma and me brothers and sisters. I'll end up a blind beggar, selling matches on the streets.'

Rose glanced at Eugene and saw that he was also touched by Harry's plight. She grasped Harry's hand even tighter. 'You are going home. You can come with us.'

'Hold on, Munday,' Eugene said hastily. 'This man is a soldier. He has to have permission to leave hospital.'

'No, sir. I've been discharged as unfit for service.' Harry slumped back against the pillows. 'Ta for trying to help me, miss. But as you can see, it's useless.'

'I won't allow that,' Rose said angrily. 'You deserve to have the best possible treatment and a hero's welcome home.' She jumped to her feet, facing Eugene with a determined toss of her head. 'Think of the story, Guvnor. A soldier wounded in the line of duty, returning home to his loving family in time for Christmas.'

'You're not going to give up on this, are you, Munday?' Eugene gazed at her with a mixture of admiration and amusement. 'What do you want me to do?'

'Book another ticket. I'll look after Harry during the journey. By the time we get him home to his mother he'll be a new man.'

Eugene leaned over the bed. 'It's up to you, soldier. Do you feel strong enough to face the journey?'

Tears rolled slowly down Harry's gaunt cheeks. 'I was ready to give up and die, sir. I can't believe this is happening to me.'

'That's a yes,' Rose said excitedly. 'You'll be home for Christmas, Harry.'

Chapter Twenty

The journey home proved more challenging than Rose could have imagined. Eugene had changed his plans at the last minute and booked them a sea passage from Alexandria to Portsmouth, instead of travelling to Brindisi and onward by rail. After a brief conversation Rose agreed that the train journey would be too much for Harry, who had been weakened by the length of time he had been bedridden, and the poor diet he had endured both in the field and in hospital. He had lost confidence in his ability to get around unaided and, for the first few days on board Rose had to lead him by the hand as if he were a small child. However, with good food and plenty of rest, as well as light exercise, he began to improve slowly.

Eugene had taken a liking to the young soldier

and he insisted that Harry must join them in the saloon after dinner each evening. Although Harry contributed little to the general conversation, Rose could see that he was listening intently and when Eugene was at his most amusing he could make Harry laugh. To Rose's ears it was the best sound of all, similar, she imagined, to hearing a baby's first words or watching a toddler take his or her first steps. She took pride in helping Harry to conquer his fears and, even if he could not accept his blindness, he was beginning to adjust to the limitations enforced upon him by his disability. Rose insisted that he must rest every afternoon in order to speed his recovery, and she spent much of that time with Eugene, who was working on his article for the *Leader*. She was able to add some of the stories she had gleaned from the injured men, and she had the satisfaction of knowing that Eugene listened to her, and was prepared to include her observations in his work. This was something new to Rose, having lived for years with Sadie, who had strong opinions on everything.

It had been possible to forget that it was winter in the warmth of Egypt, but they encountered squally weather and violent storms in the Bay of Biscay, which laid Harry low with seasickness and confined him to his cabin. Rose and Eugene kept each other company in an almost deserted saloon. When they were not working Eugene told her stories of his rakish past, but he seemed unwilling to talk about his time in captivity and brushed her questions aside. She suspected that he had endured far more hardship and ill treatment than he was prepared to admit, but she did not press the subject.

On the last evening before they were due to arrive in Portsmouth, Rose and Eugene were in the saloon drinking coffee after dinner. Harry had joined them for the meal, but had retired to his cabin early, and the other passengers had drifted away.

'What happened when you were taken by the enemy?' Rose fixed Eugene with a speculative look. 'You've written enough about it, but I feel you're holding something back.'

He reached for his glass and took a sip of brandy. 'It's not very interesting, Munday. We weren't treated too badly because they wanted a ransom, and for the most part it was tedious. Hardly the stuff to sell more newspapers.'

'But it must have been wonderful when the cavalry rode in to save you. Max was the hero of the day.'

'Of course he was, Munday. Now perhaps you'll tell me why you decided to run away when the fellow had asked you to marry him?'

There was a teasing note in his voice, but looking him in the eye she realised that he was deadly serious. 'I didn't run away, as you put it. Max was leaving for somewhere in the desert and there seemed little point in staying.'

'You'll have to get used to that as a soldier's wife.'

'I know that, Guvnor.'

'So why didn't you stay? Cissie would have liked you to keep her company, and my parents had obviously taken to you.'

'I don't like imposing on people.'

'You weren't imposing – you were a welcome guest.'

Rose pushed her coffee cup away and stood up. 'I don't know why you're going on about it. As I told you before, I promised Sparrow that I would be home for Christmas, and I intend to keep my word. I'll see you in the morning, Guvnor.'

She walked off, leaving him alone in the saloon. Her reasons for escaping from Cairo were her own, and she did not wish to discuss them with anyone, least of all Eugene. It was all due to Max and the sudden change in his attitude. Just as she had convinced herself that they were poorly suited, he had revealed the tender side of his nature and thrown her into utter confusion.

She hurried to her cabin to finish packing. The last items to go into the shabby carpet bag were small gifts she had purchased in Alexandria. There was a pair of filigree earrings for Maria, a glass bead necklace for Polly, a wooden horse for Teddy, and best of all, from the same roadside pedlar, she had bought a beautifully carved camel train for Sparrow. She wrapped them in one of her cotton blouses and laid them on top of the clothes. A sudden wave of homesickness washed over her and she lay down on the bunk, still fully dressed, wishing away the hours until they reached England. Despite the fact that she had left the man she was to marry in Egypt, she had an overwhelming desire to be back in London with the people who had come to matter so much to her.

They disembarked on a bleak December morning with cast iron clouds threatening either rain or snow. It was certainly cold enough for the latter. Rose concentrated on helping Harry down the gangway, leaving Eugene to see to their luggage. The rain came down in earnest just as they were about to board the London-bound train, and the first-class carriage was crowded and stuffy. By the time they reached Waterloo Bridge Station the rain had turned to sleet and a porter rushed out to find them a cab. It was late afternoon as the hackney carriage trundled through the busy city streets, and the lamplighter was already on his rounds. With just a few days to go before Christmas the costermongers' barrows were piled high with oranges and lemons, rosy-cheeked apples and heaps of walnuts and almonds. Mistletoe sellers vied for customers with those selling brightly berried holly, and the aroma of roasting chestnuts wafted into the cab through the ill-fitting windows. There were other smells, less pleasant, but

Rose breathed them in as if they had been the finest French perfume. The cobbled streets were strewn with straw and horse dung, and the gutters blocked with rubbish – it was bitterly cold and the smoke hung in a pall over the city – but she was home, and glad to be back in the city she had come to love all over again.

'Why are you smiling, Munday?' Eugene demanded crossly. 'It's cold and miserable, and I almost wish I were back in Egypt.'

'Was I?' Rose came back to earth and shivered. Eugene was right, of course, but home was home, after all. 'I just realised how much I missed London when I was away.'

'It has its merits, but I still think you ought to have accepted my invitation to stay in Tavistock Square.' Eugene glanced at Harry, who was leaning back against the squabs with his eyes closed. 'There's plenty of room for you and for Harry.'

'He wants to go home,' Rose said in a low voice. 'He wants to be with his family.'

'All right, I know when I'm beaten, but where will you go? You don't even know if Maria is still at Pier House.'

'There's one sure way of finding out,' Rose said, smiling. 'Stop putting obstacles in the way, Guvnor. I know you mean well, but I can manage on my own. If Maria and Sparrow aren't at Great Hermitage Street they'll be at Pier House, which isn't far away.'

Eugene sighed and shook his head. 'Have it your own way, Munday. You'll do what you want whatever I say. We'll take Harry to Bow, but I insist on seeing you safe before I return home. Never mind the fact that I'll be on my own in the big house, with no one to talk to.'

His comical expression of self-pity made Rose giggle. 'You won't get round me that way, Guvnor. You'll have servants to take care of your every need, and if you're lonely I'm sure you can find one of your old flames to keep you company.'

'Munday, I'm shocked that you think so little of me.'

'You told me about your past liaisons in great detail, as I recall.' Rose turned her head to stare out of the window. 'You said that you would find it virtually impossible to remain faithful to one woman.'

'I should learn to keep my mouth shut,' Eugene said with a rueful grin. 'It's not true, of course.'

But Rose was not paying attention. She pressed her nose against the window glass. 'How lovely. I can see a Christmas tree covered in glass balls and tinsel.' She subsided back in the seat. 'We've passed the house now, but it was in the entrance hall. The door was open and I could see every detail in the gaslight. It looked so cosy and inviting.'

'I'm sorry, Munday,' Eugene said softly. 'I've been so wrapped up in my own affairs that I hadn't realised how much you miss having a home of your own.'

Rose smiled valiantly. 'I know I'll be welcome to stay with Maria and the children. That's where I'll go when we've seen Harry safely back with his family.'

'What did Max say about the Captain's House? You did discuss it, didn't you?'

'There's nothing he can do until he returns to London. You know that as well as I do, Guvnor. If the criminals are caught and arrested I might be able to move in, but until that time I'm happy to stay with Maria.' Rose eyed him warily. 'I still have my job, don't I? Mr Radley seemed quite pleased with my efforts.'

'Of course you do – I'll make very sure of that, Munday. I can't do without you now.'

Rose subsided into silence as the cab rattled on, veering from side to side in the chaotic jumble of horse-drawn vehicles as it bumped over the cobble-stones. Harry's home was much further than Rose had anticipated, and they left the brightly lit streets, plunging into the darkness of the poorer part of town. The windows steamed up on the inside, and Rose wiped the glass with her mittened hand, creating a spyhole, but the rain had turned to driving sleet, which was making it difficult to recognise street names or other landmarks. Eugene's face was in shadow beneath the brim of his top hat, and she could not tell if he was awake or asleep. Harry was snoring gently, but that saved her from making conversation. She knew he was nervous about how his family would react when they realised that his disability was likely to be permanent, and her efforts to boost his confidence seemed to have been in vain. She could only hope that a mother's love would overcome the difficulties that would inevitably face the family.

'That's a heartfelt sigh, Munday.'

Eugene's voice from the shadows made Rose sit up with a start. 'I'm sorry, Guvnor. I was just thinking of Harry's mother and wondering how she'll cope. They're a poor family.'

'I've thought of that, so don't worry. The story I intend to write about Harry Norman will bring tears to the eyes of the most cynical of our readers. I shouldn't wonder if a fund isn't set up in his name,' Eugene said calmly. 'I'll have a word with Mrs Norman and put her mind at rest.'

'You will?'

'Don't sound so surprised, Munday. I may be all sorts of things, but I'm not heartless. He's a good chap, and with the right medical care he might regain at least some of his sight. It's not unheard of.'

'Do you really think so?'

'I'll arrange for him to be seen at Moorfields Eye Hospital. Does that satisfy you?'

'Thank you, Guvnor.'

'Munday.'

'Yes, Guvnor.'

'Do you think you could refrain from calling me Guvnor all the time? I have a name, you know.'

'And so do I.' She eyed him speculatively. 'I'll call you Eugene, but only if you promise to call me Rose.' She held out her hand and he took it in a firm clasp.

'That suits me, Rose.'

She was about to respond when the carriage drew to a sudden halt. 'I think we've arrived.' She turned to Harry, giving him a gentle shake. 'Harry, you're home.'

The house was in the middle of a mean terrace of two-up, two-down properties, and judging by the dreadful smell hanging in a cloud over the rooftops, they shared a communal lavatory. The horrible odours emanating from the glue factory and the noxious fumes from the gasworks added to the general stench, but Harry seemed oblivious to such things as he climbed down from the cab.

Rose knocked on the front door and it was opened by a small, thin woman. She uttered a cry of disbelief as she flung her arms around her son. 'Harry, my boy. You've come home.' She dragged him into the front room where four ragged youngsters huddled around an apology for a fire. Two lumps of coal had burned to embers and Rose was quick to notice that the scuttle was empty. The older boy rose to fling his arms around Harry, and the younger children joined in, clinging to their brother.

'Be careful, mind,' Winnie Norman said nervously. 'Harry's got bad eyes. He can't see.'

'They're all right, Ma,' Harry's voice broke on a sob. 'I didn't want to come home in this state.'

'You're alive, son. That's all that matters to me.' Winnie wrapped her arms around the group and they stood there in the middle of the tiny room, hugging and crying.

'Perhaps we ought to leave now?' Rose suggested tentatively.

'Yes, we can return tomorrow.' Eugene was about to open the front door when Winnie broke away from her children.

'Where are me manners? I ain't thanked you for bringing my boy home, sir.'

Eugene took her hand in his. 'Don't thank me, Mrs Norman. It was this young lady who found Harry in the hospital, and she looked after him on the journey home.'

Rose shook her head. 'No, really. It was a joint effort, ma'am. It was a pleasure to be of assistance.'

'I can't thank you enough,' Harry said earnestly. 'But for you, Miss Munday, and the guvnor, I'd still be in Alexandria waiting for a troop ship to bring me home.'

'Think nothing of it, old chap. Miss Munday and

I will leave you and your family in peace, but I'll be back soon to discuss the articles I'm going to write about you, and your return to full health.'

Winnie clutched her hands to her bosom. 'Are you going to be in the newspapers, Harry?'

'Yes, Ma. That's what the guvnor said.'

'Who'd have thought that my boy would be famous one day?' She wrapped her arms around the younger children.

'There will be some money in it for me, won't there?' Harry asked anxiously.

Eugene patted him on the shoulder. 'There most certainly will be a substantial amount, although I can't say how much until I've spoken to the editor.'

Harry's eyes filled with tears. 'There aren't enough words to tell you how grateful I am for everything you and Miss Rose have done, Guvnor.'

Rose managed a watery smile. 'Don't mention it, Harry. We're just happy to help.'

Eugene opened the door. 'The cab is waiting so we have to go now, Rose.'

'Thank you for bringing my boy home, sir.' Winnie shook Harry's hand. 'God bless you both.'

'Take care of yourself, Harry.' Rose raised her hand to touch his cheek. 'We'll be back soon.' She glanced at the wide-eyed children. 'I'll see you again very soon.' She stepped outside into what was now a blizzard.

The cabby leaned over, brushing ice particles from

his caped greatcoat. 'Hanging about here is losing me trade, Guv. This'll cost you double.'

'You'll be reimbursed. Great Hermitage Street first, please.' Eugene handed Rose into the cab and climbed in to sit beside her. 'If Maria isn't there we'll go on to Pier House, and if she's not there, you'll be my guest in Tavistock Square tonight. Whichever it is, I expect you to be at the office on time tomorrow.'

At first Rose thought that the house was deserted, but a second knock was answered by the sound of footsteps on the bare boards and the door opened to reveal Edna, holding an oil lamp.

'Miss Rose, I didn't expect to see you. Come inside quick. It's perishing cold out there and not much warmer in here.' She glanced over Rose's shoulder. 'Who's the toff?'

'Never mind that,' Rose said hastily. 'Is Mrs Barnaby at home?'

'I dunno where else she would be at this time of day. Are you coming in or not?'

'I see you're in good hands.' Eugene hefted the carpet bag into the hall. 'I'll see you at the office, Rose.'

She hesitated, meeting his smile with a frown. 'I think we'd better keep things formal at work. Good night, Guvnor.' She stepped inside and Edna slammed the door.

'You're just in time for supper, but don't expect too much because Jessie has had an argument with the harlot Flossie, and she says she ain't sweating over the range for ungrateful whores.'

Rose bit her lip in an attempt to stifle a chuckle. 'Oh, well. I'm sure they'll sort things out. Is Mrs Barnaby in the parlour?'

'She might be or maybe she's tucking the little 'uns in bed. If you wait in the parlour I'll go and look for her.'

'Thank you.' Rose headed for the parlour and opened the door to find Sparrow seated on the hearth rug, studying a book, but the moment she saw Rose she leaped to her feet. 'Rose, you've come home.' She threw herself at Rose, almost knocking her over.

Rose returned the hug. 'I try very hard to keep a promise.'

'I'm so happy to see you. We read your words in the newspaper, but it didn't sound like the way you speak.' Sparrow plumped down on the sofa, dragging Rose with her. 'Tell me all about it.'

'Let's wait until Maria joins us,' Rose said, smiling. 'Then I can talk to you both at the same time, so why don't you tell me what's been happening while I've been away?'

'Have you brought me a present?'

'You'll have to wait for Christmas Day. It's not long now.'

'I got you something.'

'That's really kind of you, Sparrow.' Rose turned her head at the sound of the door opening and Maria hurried into the room.

'Rose. How wonderful. I was beginning to think you wouldn't manage to get home for Christmas.' She rushed over to the sofa and gave Rose a quick hug. 'Move up, Sparrow. Then I can sit next to Rose and hear about her adventures.'

'More to the point, what's been happening here?' Rose looked from one to the other.

Maria sat down but before she had a chance to speak the door flew open, and Flossie burst into the room, red-faced and furious.

'I ain't going to stay here a moment longer. I'd rather go back to Black Raven Court than put up with that Jessie Spriggs. We may be related but that don't mean I have to put up with her airs and graces and sermonising. You'd think she'd been brought up a vicar's daughter the way she carries on. I'm sick of her calling me names.'

Maria held up her hand. 'That's enough, thank you, Flossie. I know it's difficult for you, but Cora seems to cope. Maybe if you—'

'Don't give me that, missis. I've been patient and all I gets is insults.'

Rose picked up her reticule and took out her purse. 'I'm sorry to find you so unhappy, Flossie.' She took out a few coppers and handed them to Flossie. 'Why don't you and Cora go to the pub and enjoy yourselves? Maybe we can sort things out in the morning.'

Flossie pocketed the money with a reluctant grin. 'Anything to get away from her downstairs. I know she used to be on the turf, just the same as me and Cora, but now she's got religion and she's forever singing hymns and trying to convert us, like she was a bloody missionary and we was savages.'

Rose stood up to give Flossie a hug. 'You're a good woman, and so is Cora. We all have to survive the best way we can, so don't let Jessie upset you. I promise to find a better solution, but I can't do anything until morning.'

Tears rolled down Flossie's plump face, leaving slimy trails on her rouged cheeks. 'You understand, Miss Rose. Ta for that.'

'It's just Rose. You helped me once when I was in desperate need and now I'm going to help you, so go and enjoy yourselves.'

Flossie nodded and sniffed. 'Good night, Rose. Good night, missis.' She shot a sideways look at Sparrow. 'Just be warned, nipper. You don't want to end up like me and Cora.' She waddled from the room, closing the door softly.

'I seen enough of that sort of thing to put me off for ever,' Sparrow said, shrugging. 'I seen things what would make you ladies faint with horror.'

Rose sat down again, slipping her arm around

Sparrow's thin shoulders. 'We know you've had a terrible time, but it's over now.' She met Maria's gaze. 'So what's been happening in my absence? Did the police catch Regan?'

Chapter Twenty-One

Maria shook her head. 'Regan seems to have vanished. But the good news is that some of his gang have been arrested.'

'And what about Gilroy?' Rose asked eagerly. 'I hope she was caught, too.'

'She's disappeared. The officer in charge of the case thinks she must have gone with Regan, and they could be anywhere by now.'

Rose laid her hand on Maria's arm. 'I'm sorry, it must have been a difficult time for you.'

'Grandmama's funeral was the worst. I felt guilty because I hadn't done enough to protect a sick old woman, and even worse because I couldn't mourn her passing, but I had Mama and Freddie to help me.'

'You did all you could for her, and from what

you told me about your childhood it's hardly surprising that you had very little feeling for your grandmother. I wish I'd been here to support you.'

Maria sighed and looked away. 'The funeral was a small affair because quite frankly none of the relations had much time for her, or else they were too old and infirm to travel to London. But she's gone now and the house is shuttered and empty, and it will remain so until Caroline and Phineas return from Australia.'

'But there's no one living in your house now, Rose.' Sparrow bounced up and down on the sofa. 'The bad men were put in prison.'

'Really?' Rose looked from one to the other.

Maria nodded. 'Yes, they were among the ones who were arrested. The police gave me the keys so the Captain's House is yours, to all intents and purposes, but I don't know what sort of state it's in. I let the company know; they should take some of the blame for allowing the house to fall into the wrong hands in the first place.'

'I'm sure Max will have something to say about that when he comes home, although I don't know when that will be.'

Maria put her head on one side. 'You saw him in Egypt?'

'Yes, we met briefly.'

'You don't seem as thrilled as I would have expected, Rose. Didn't it go well?'

'Yes, of course. Max was the hero of the hour. He rescued Eugene and he still wants to marry me.'

Sparrow seized Rose's hand and held it to her cheek. 'You look sad. Don't you love Max?'

'Of course I do,' Rose said with more conviction than she was feeling. 'It was all so different in Egypt, but it will be better when he returns home.'

'You know you can tell me anything.' Maria reached out to grasp Rose's free hand. 'I'm your friend.'

'And so am I,' Sparrow added eagerly. 'I'm your best friend, Rose.'

'I know you are, both of you, and I couldn't wait to return to London.' Rose squeezed their fingers: Maria's were soft and plump and Sparrow's little hand felt small with bones as delicate as the bird after which she had been named.

'Didn't you want to stay in Egypt so that you could be near him?' Maria eyed her curiously.

'I'm confused,' Rose said slowly. 'The Max I met in Cairo wasn't the boy I knew as a child, or even the young man who made my heart sing. I don't know if he has changed, or if it's me. So much has happened since I left Australia.'

'You've been through a difficult time, but I know I'm not the only one who has benefited from your misfortune.'

'I haven't done anything out of the ordinary.'

Maria leaned forward to kiss her on the cheek.

'You rescued Flossie and Cora from Regan's clutches. You saved Sparrow from a terrible existence, and you helped me to face up to my grandmother. I don't know what I would have done had you not been there when Gilroy murdered the poor soul.'

'You did save me,' Sparrow added eagerly. 'Look at me now, Rose. I'm turning into a lady like you and Maria. I ain't a street urchin no more.'

Rose gave her a cuddle, resting her cheek on the top of Sparrow's head. 'You'll be a proper lady when you're older, but don't grow up too quickly.' She released her with a quick hug. 'As to Flossie and Cora, that doesn't appear to have worked very well. They seem lost now they're away from Black Raven Court. Maybe they don't want to change the way they earned their living.'

'It's Jessie's fault. She goads them about their profession,' Maria said, sighing. 'And they retaliate because they know that she was in the trade before she took to religion.'

'Surely that's a good thing?'

'Of course it is, but she keeps trying to reform the other girls and they won't have it. I think they would go back to Regan rather than put up with Jessie's preaching.'

Rose frowned thoughtfully. 'I got you into this mess, Maria, and I'm sorry. I'll do my best to make things right.'

'I took the Spriggs sisters in, so I'm just as culpable.

I might have saved them from a life of poverty and degradation, but Jessie doesn't seem to have much time for those less fortunate, despite her religious convictions.'

'Perhaps it's simply a clash of personalities,' Rose said thoughtfully. 'Flossie and Cora might appear to be brash and overbearing, but their hearts are in the right place. They were kind to me when I was in need.'

'I'll have to ask them to leave, Rose. I'm so sorry, but it's becoming unbearable.'

'If I move into the Captain's House I could take Flossie and Cora with me. I'll go there tomorrow to see what sort of mess those men have left.'

'I'll help you,' Sparrow said eagerly. 'I can scrub and clean. Jessie's been teaching me, and I've been helping Izzie with the nippers. I'm a useful person now.'

'You were always that.' Rose brushed a strand of pale blonde hair back from Sparrow's brow. 'And I'd be grateful for your help. I have to go to the newspaper office first thing in the morning, but if we get up early we can go to the Captain's House and see the damage for ourselves.'

To Rose's surprise she found Cora, Flossie and Sparrow waiting for her in the breakfast room next morning. Armed with mops and buckets, dusters and cleaning rags, they left Maria's house and headed for Black Lion Wharf. The first thing that hit Rose when she opened the front door was the stench of stale alcohol and rotting food. The air was thick with dust, which lay on the surfaces like a grey fur coat.

Cora rolled up her sleeves. 'Let me find the kitchen and I'll make a start. This is the sort of challenge that makes my blood boil. Them filthy beggars should be strung up by their toes and horsewhipped.'

'I agree. Let's get to work.' Flossie waddled off, her pail clanking at her side.

'I'd love to stay and help, but I have to get a cab to Fleet Street.' Rose gazed round, trying hard to remember the house as it was in the old days when Sadie had everything in order and the aroma of baking wafted from the kitchen. She took out her purse and laid some coins on the window seat, which seemed to be the only place free from the rubbish. Broken clay pipes, torn up newspapers, dirty crockery and empty beer bottles littered the floor, and odd socks hung from the mantelshelf. Rose sighed and turned away. 'Sparrow, I want you to be in charge of purchasing. Go out and buy soap, candles, coal and matches, and there should be enough left to pay for food. I've got to go now, but I'll come back later and I'll do my share.'

Sparrow puffed out her chest. 'I'm in charge of buying things.'

'That's right, and with a bit of luck we might be able to move in before Christmas. I haven't time to inspect the bedrooms, but I don't suppose they're in any better shape than the living room. The old captain must been turning in his grave.'

'Was he drowned, Rose?'

'As far as I know he retired from the sea to live here, so I would hope that he passed away peacefully, listening to the sounds of the river he loved. They say that if he's happy he visits the house and you can smell tobacco smoke wafting through the rooms.'

Sparrow clutched her throat. 'He ain't going to haunt us, is he? I don't want to sleep in a place where there are ghosts.'

'No, certainly not. I think the captain was a kind old gentleman, who wants to have nice people living in his old home, and he isn't at all frightening.' Rose leaned over to kiss Sparrow on the cheek. 'Now I must go, or I'll be in trouble with Eugene, and I don't want that.'

Scully was the first person Rose saw when she entered the office building. He grinned sheepishly. 'You've come back, miss.'

Rose shook snowflakes off her mantle, leaving tiny puddles on the marble-tiled floor. There was something in his manner that was different and he did not seem able to look her in the eye. She gave him a searching look. 'Is anything wrong, Scully?'

He backed away. 'No, miss. You'll have to excuse me, I got to take this article to the print room.'

Mystified, and with all her senses alert and ready for trouble, Rose made her way to the main office. There was a sudden silence when she entered the room and the clerks turned their backs on her, but the sly smile on Nicholls' face was enough to convince her that there was mischief afoot. She ignored his sarcastic greeting as she crossed the floor and let herself into Eugene's office without bothering to knock. He was standing by the window, staring out into the swirling snow.

'What's up, Guvnor?' Rose took off her bonnet and was about to hang it on the coat stand when Eugene turned to face her.

'It's no good, Rose,' he said wearily. 'I've tried every trick in the book but I can't make my cousin see sense.'

'Are you telling me that I've been given the sack?' She met his apologetic look with a defiant toss of her head. 'Why? I did everything that was asked of me.'

Eugene walked over to his desk and sat down. 'It seems that the men have got together and threatened strike action. It's not you personally, Rose. They don't want to have any women in the workplace.'

Rose clasped her bonnet tightly in her hands to

stop them shaking. 'But I've done nothing wrong, Guvnor. It's not fair.'

'It isn't, and I agree with you entirely, but my cousin is the editor and owner of the newspaper and Nicholls has put pressure on him. This is a small and relatively new journal, when compared to *The Times* or some of the even older newspapers. If the press stops rolling the paper will go out of business, it's as simple as that. I'm sorry, Rose. I've been arguing the point since I got here this morning, but Arthur is adamant. He doesn't want trouble and I'm afraid you are expendable.'

'I understand,' she said slowly. 'I don't agree, of course, but I've known all along that Nicholls and the other men in the office didn't approve of me.'

'It's not you, Munday. They're afraid to allow women into the workplace because they fear for their own jobs. You're a talented young woman and you deserve a chance to show what you can do.'

Rose shrugged and turned her head to stare out into the swirling snow. 'I have plenty to do. Maria needs my help, and the Captain's House is free now, so I can move in and get things straight. Then there's Harry Norman: I'll have time to visit him.'

'Wait a minute, Munday. I have an idea.'

The eager tone in his voice made Rose turn to face him. 'What is it, Guvnor?'

He rose to his feet, chuckling. 'I've thought of a

way round this problem. Sit down and I'll tell you.'

Rose did as he asked, folding her hands neatly in her lap. 'Go on. I'm listening.'

'You intended to write an article featuring our wounded soldier's return home and his struggle to provide for himself and his dependants.'

'That was my idea, but I can't do it now.'

'Yes, you can, Munday. Do exactly as you planned, but do it under a pen name – a masculine one, of course. Women novelists have been using male pseudonyms for years, so why shouldn't you?'

'I could write the articles, but I wouldn't be able to show my face here.'

'Of course not, and that's where I come in. Bring your work to me in Tavistock Square and no one will be any the wiser. Leave the rest to me, and I'll arrange payment.'

'Won't Mr Radley want to know the identity of this new contributor?'

'Not at all. We have many such people, which means we have no need to employ full-time reporters. I myself am just playing at being a journalist, as you very well know. I thoroughly enjoyed my time in Egypt, even if part of it was spent in a smelly tent with a group of angry captives – that is until your gallant captain rescued us.'

Rose could tell by Eugene's tone that he was testing her, and she looked away. 'Yes, it was a brave deed,' she said casually.

'I expect he'll be relieved to know that you are about to move into the Captain's House.'

'I'm sure he will,' Rose said evasively. 'What male name do you think best suits me, Guvnor? Or should it be something cryptic?'

'What do you suggest?' Eugene leaned back in his chair, his eyes the colour of warm honey and a humorous curve to his lips.

Rose thought for a moment. 'Nomad,' she said firmly. 'I think that sums me up nicely.'

She stood up and was about to leave the room when Eugene called her back. He rose to his feet and moved around the desk, holding out his hand. 'Take this, Munday. You'll need it for expenses.' He pressed two gold sovereigns and some small change into her hand.

'I can't accept it, Guvnor,' Rose protested. 'It's your money.'

'Don't worry about that. I'll claim it off expenses.' Eugene gave her a searching look. 'Did your fiancé take care of you financially, Munday?'

'He offered to pay my fare home, Guvnor.'

'But he didn't make arrangements for you to receive a regular allowance?'

'I saw him briefly, Guvnor. There wasn't time . . .'

'You're making excuses for the fellow. He should have done all that before he left the country.' Eugene held up his hands as Rose opened her mouth to protest. 'Don't worry, Munday. I'm not going to say anything further on the subject, but you must come to me if you need funds. The paper will pay, so you don't need to feel under an obligation to me.'

'Thank you, Guvnor.'

'Do you promise to tell me when you need money?' His gaze held hers and she nodded.

'I promise, Guvnor.'

His stern look softened into a wide smile. 'That didn't hurt, did it? Good luck with the story, Nomad. I'll await the first article with bated breath.' He returned to his seat and picked up a sheaf of notes.

The door to the Captain's House was open when Rose arrived, and as she stepped over the threshold she was enveloped in a steamy cloud smelling of carbolic and furniture polish. The sound of voices was interspersed with gales of laughter and she recognised Flossie's gravelly tones with Cora's smoky voice giving a response. Sparrow's high-pitched efforts were accompanied by Polly's giggles, and then Maria appeared at the foot of the staircase, calling out for quiet because Teddy was taking a nap.

'Maria, what are you doing here?' Rose asked anxiously. 'I didn't expect you to help with the hard work of clearing up after those pigs.'

'I haven't done much, Rose. I came to get away from Jessie, who's driving me mad. She wants to turn my house into a refuge for fallen women, as she puts it. So I wrapped the children up in their warmest clothes and we enjoyed a brisk walk. Polly is so excited about Christmas, that it was a way of diverting her attention to something other than presents and Christmas treats.'

'Where is she now? I thought I heard her voice.'

'She's in the kitchen, supposedly helping Sparrow to make bread under Cora's supervision. They managed to get the range going, which is why the house feels reasonably warm, and Flossie seems intent on scrubbing floors. I think she's upstairs, starting on one of the bedrooms as we speak, although I hate to think what sort of state they might be in.'

'Everything seems so well organised.' Rose opened the sitting-room door and stepped inside. 'Someone has been working hard,' she said, gazing appreciatively at the coal fire roaring up the chimney and the newly scrubbed floor. The sofa and two armchairs were worn and threadbare, but the previous occupants had treated them reasonably well, and although there were ring marks and burns on what once had been a polished oak tea table, it was still usable. 'I thought it would be worse,' she added with a sigh of relief.

'Flossie and Cora thought it best to make one room habitable at a time, but they're adamant they want to move in before Christmas.' Maria went to sit on the window seat. 'I love this house and the view of the river. If I lived here I think I'd sit all day, and watch the boats coming and going, and the cranes working.'

'You really are a romantic, aren't you?' Rose said, smiling. 'But I agree, there's something so vital about the river, despite the mud and the stench in summer. My earliest memories are of Pa taking me out in one of the rowing boats, and the sunbeams skimming the ripples of the water. He used to tell me that they were angels' smiles, and I loved that.'

Maria dashed a tear from her cheek. 'Stop it, Rose. You're making me cry and that won't do. We have to be practical as well as thrifty, but a few bright cushions on the sofa and chairs, and a decent table-cloth to cover the marks will make a huge difference.'

'I suppose I ought to take a look at the kitchen,' Rose said reluctantly. 'I'm not much of a cook. Sadie did all that when we lived in the school house. She used to make the most marvellous gingerbread.'

Maria turned her head to gaze out at the wintry scene. 'I wonder if Caroline and Phineas will give this house to you and Max as a wedding present. You'd be happy here, wouldn't you?'

Rose took off her mantle and draped it over the back of the sofa. She sat down, resting her feet on the brass fender. 'I don't know. I hadn't thought that far ahead. I had a vague idea that we would live in married quarters wherever Max was stationed. He said India was a possibility.'

'Are you sure that's what you want, Rose?' Maria

stared at her, frowning. 'I just have a feeling that something is not quite right between you two.'

'I still love Max. Of course I do. I've been in love with him since I was nine years old, but now I've been given a chance to do something for myself. To be someone in my own right and not just an officer's wife.'

'Go on,' Maria prompted. 'Has this anything to do with Eugene Sheldon?'

Rose looked away, staring into the orange and yellow flames as they licked the soot on the fireback, creating glow fairies. 'Indirectly, I suppose. As a matter of fact I've lost my job at the newspaper because the men don't want to work with a woman.'

'I'm not surprised,' Maria said wearily. 'It's the way of the world, Rose. Maybe in a hundred years or so things will be different, but there are very few professions open to us women.'

'Maybe, maybe not. Anyway, Eugene has asked me to write articles under a pseudonym, starting with Harry Norman's story. No one will know I'm a woman.'

'How exciting. What name will you use?'

'We thought that Nomad was quite suitable. That's what I am, Maria. I've spent my life moving from one place to another, and lived with people who aren't my real family. I'm like driftwood, tossed about on the tide.'

'Not any more,' Maria said firmly. 'Max must

provide you with a home in London so that you have a base to which you can return. He won't be a soldier for ever, so he must think ahead, especially when the babies start to arrive.'

'Heavens above!' Rose said, chuckling. 'I'm not even sure I'm engaged.' She demonstrated by holding out her left hand. 'No ring, although Max did promise to buy me one when he returns to London.'

'And is he supporting you financially? I'm not being nosy, it's just that Max seems to be so casual in his arrangements. How does he expect you to live while he's away?'

'Eugene has given me money for expenses. I'll support myself until we're officially engaged, Maria. I'm nobody's property.'

'I'm married to Theo, but I don't regard myself as being his property. He treats me like an equal, and when he's away at sea I have to be both mother and father to my children.'

Rose stood up again and reached for her mantle. 'I didn't mean to offend you, and I'm not against marriage. I'm just not sure I'm ready for such a commitment.'

'Where are you off to now? You've only just arrived.'

'I'm going to Bow for a chat with Harry and his mother. I want to get the first article written as quickly as possible, so that I can begin work on the second.'

Maria jumped to her feet. 'Won't you go to the kitchen first? Sparrow will be terribly disappointed if you go without seeing her.'

'I think I'll just slip out, otherwise she'll want to come with me, and this is business, not pleasure. I'll make it up to her when I get home. Perhaps we'll go out and buy a huge Christmas tree.'

'Not too large,' Maria said, smiling. 'This isn't Pier House.'

'Killjoy.' Rose gave her a hug.

Outside a bitter east wind slapped Rose's cheeks, making her eyes water as she climbed the watermen's stairs to the main road. She stood on the edge of the pavement, hoping she would not have to wait too long for a cab, and it was a relief when one finally came to a halt at the kerb. She climbed in and huddled in a corner, shivering and wishing that she had the fur-lined cape that Cecilia had given her, but it was still with the rest of the garments in Tavistock Square, awaiting collection. The sleety rain dampened her mantle, and her fingers and toes were numbed with cold long before she reached her destination. As the driver drew his horse to a halt outside Harry's house, Rose fumbled in her reticule for money to pay the fare, which the cabby accepted with a grunt.

'How long are you going to be, miss?' he demanded, scowling at her beneath beetling black eyebrows. 'This ain't the sort of place you'll be likely to find a cab to take you home.'

'If I say half an hour, how much would that cost if you were to wait for me, sir?'

A reluctant smile creased his weathered cheeks. 'Well, for a lady like yourself I'd add an extra florin, considering the distance we've come.'

'That's fair enough,' Rose said gratefully. The thought of wandering the back streets of Bow in search of a cab was too daunting to worry about the cost, especially as it was a legitimate expenditure, and she was certain that Eugene would approve. 'I'll be as quick as I possibly can. Thank you.' She alighted and crossed the narrow strip of pavement to knock on the door.

It opened just far enough for a small girl to poke her head out. 'Who are you?' she demanded. 'You don't look like the tallyman.'

'I came here yesterday,' Rose said patiently. 'Do you remember me now?'

'Your bonnet's ruined, miss. The feathers is all wet and droopy.'

'Who is it, Mary?'

Rose recognised Harry's voice and she leaned closer. 'It's me – Rose. May I come in?'

'Let the lady in, Mary.' The sound of shuffling footsteps grew nearer and the door opened wide. Harry's smile was all the welcome she needed and Rose entered the untidy front room. Nightclothes had been thrown off and discarded over a wooden clothes rack, and crudely carved wooden toys littered the floor. The pervading smell of damp, dry rot and sour milk made Rose recoil, but she forced herself to smile even though Harry could not see her.

'How are you today, Harry?'

'Better for being with my family, but I'm bloody useless, if you'll excuse the language, miss.' Harry felt his way to the battered sofa and sat down, narrowly missing the toddler who was sitting on the floor, chewing a carrot.

'You nearly trod on Daisy,' Mary said crossly. 'You got to be more careful, Harry.'

He pulled a face. 'My little sister bullies me, and she's only five.'

Mary stood very erect. 'Ma leaves me in charge when she's out at work.'

Rose sat down next to Harry, shifting her weight uneasily as one of the sofa springs dug into her flesh. Daisy had finished her carrot and was beginning to whine. Rose scooped her up and sat her on her lap, trying not to grimace as she caught a whiff of a soiled nappy. Daisy stopped crying and amused herself by tugging at Rose's bonnet strings.

'Where is your mother, Harry?' Rose asked as she dandled Daisy on her knee. 'Is there anything I can do to help?'

'We don't need you. I'm looking after them,' Mary said firmly.

'And you're doing a very good job, too.' Rose reached out to stroke Mary's cheek and she was struck by the difference between Polly Barnaby, who was a picture of health and happiness, and Mary Norman, whose sallow skin and stick-thin arms and legs told a very different story.

'Ma goes to people's houses to do their washing,' Harry said apologetically. 'I suppose you're wondering why there's no man of the house, but I never knew my dad. I were only eight when Ma met Clem and they got together, and then come the nippers. It was all going fine until two years ago and there was an accident at the factory. Clem never come home again.'

'I'm so sorry,' Rose said gently. 'But where are your brothers?'

'The boys have jobs in the soap works, and here am I, sitting on the sofa, doing nothing.'

Rose laid her hand on his. 'You were wounded in the service of your country, Harry, and you need time to recover.'

'But I won't, will I? I'm a blind man, Rose. What good am I to anyone?'

Daisy began to struggle and Rose set her down on the rush matting. 'Your story will make the newspaper, and you'll be paid for telling the world what it was like out there in the desert. I'll write down what you say, and then everyone will know what brave soldiers we have protecting us and our interests abroad.' She took out her purse and pressed two silver crowns into his hand. 'That's just the start,' she said eagerly.

'Ten shillings!' Harry whispered. 'Ma don't earn that in a week.'

'If I do my job properly you'll have people offering to help you and your family, and maybe the eye doctors can do something to restore your sight.'

'Do you really think so?'

'I believe there's always hope.' Rose took her notebook and pencil from her reticule. 'We'll start right away – from the beginning, Harry. Why did you join up in the first place?'

Chapter Twenty-Two

Daylight was fading when Rose eventually arrived back at the Captain's House. She had worked on her notes during the cab ride from Bow, and she was satisfied that she had the beginnings of a fascinating story, as told by a man who had seen action in battle and had suffered an injury that would change his life, and that of his family, for ever.

The door was not locked and as Rose entered the house its warmth seemed to wrap itself around her. The aroma of cooking made her stomach rumble and she realised that she had not eaten since a hurried breakfast of bread and jam. Flossie's warbling soprano came from somewhere on the upper floors, and a whiff of tobacco smoke might show approval from the old captain, or it could be Cora having a rest over a cup of tea in the kitchen. Rose smiled as she went into the front parlour where Sparrow was curled up on the sofa with Polly and Teddy, while Maria read them a fairy story.

'Oh, there you are.' Maria laid the book down on her lap. 'You've been ages, Rose.'

'You went without me,' Sparrow added crossly. 'You said you wouldn't leave me again.'

Rose laid her reticule and gloves on a side table. 'I have a job to do, but I'm back now, and there's still time to go in search of the Christmas tree that I promised we'd get.'

'Really?' Sparrow jumped to her feet and danced round the room, which made Polly and Teddy follow suit.

Laughing, Rose picked up Teddy, who was in danger of being trampled on, and set him down on his mother's lap. She shot a questioning look at Maria. 'Are you going home, or are you staying here tonight?'

'I would love to stay here, but that's not possible. I didn't come prepared, and I need to keep an eye on the Spriggs sisters. I'm afraid if I leave them for too long I'll find my home filled with desperate souls, saved from perdition by Jessie.'

'Must we go home, Mama?' Polly asked plaintively. 'I like it here. It's warm and cosy, and Cora cooks nice things.'

Maria shook her head. 'I'm sorry, poppet. This

isn't our house, it's where Rose is going to live. All your things are at home.'

'We could bring them here,' Polly said hopefully. 'We haven't got a tree in our house.'

'Then we ought to buy two Christmas trees, Polly,' Rose said, smiling. 'One for you and one for us.' She glanced out of the window. Darkness was falling quickly, due in part to the lowering clouds that were threatening more sleet or even snow. 'If we go now we might miss the worst of the weather.'

Maria rose from the chair by the fire. 'Polly, I want you to fetch your outdoor things and Teddy's from the hallstand,' she said firmly. 'Perhaps you could help them, Sparrow? Teddy always needs a hand.'

Sparrow hesitated in the doorway. 'Will we get some glass balls and tinsel today?'

'Yes, if we see a shop selling such things.' Rose picked up her gloves and reticule. 'Hurry now, or we'll find that all the trees have been snapped up.'

'I'll get my cape and bonnet.' Maria hesitated, gazing out of the window. 'It looks so cold and miserable outside.'

'Perhaps we could spend Christmas Day here?' Rose said, picking her words carefully. 'I don't wish to interfere, Maria, but Cora is a far better cook than Jessie.'

'That would be wonderful. Anyway, I think Jessie intends to help in the soup kitchen on Christmas

Day. I was thinking we would have to make do with cold pie. Mama and Freddie invited us to join them at Starcross Abbey, but I couldn't face the journey with two small children.'

'Then that's settled. Perhaps I'll invite Eugene to join us. He'll be on his own because Cissie chose to remain in Egypt. Did I tell you that she's fallen in love with a really handsome gentleman whose mother was an Indian princess?'

Maria was about to leave the room, but she came to a sudden halt. 'No. Tell me more.'

The slippery pavements were crowded with late shoppers and people on their way home from work, mufflers flying and gloved hands clenched against the cold. Rose and Maria guided the children to the nearest greengrocer's shop where Christmas trees were lined up like soldiers waiting for their orders. The window was illuminated by gaslight, adding a festive glow to the pyramids of oranges, lemons and apples, and the waxy white fruits and pale leaves of mistletoe were in sharp contrast to the scarlet berries and dark green leaves of the prickly holly. The contrasting bunches hung in rows, suspended on silver wires that twisted and twirled in the draught from the constant opening and closing of the shop door, creating a ballet of shimmering foliage.

Rose had grown used to spending Christmas in

the summer months, but she could see from the rapt expressions on the children's faces that they shared her feelings of excitement and awe, and to them the feathery pine trees must seem like an enchanted forest.

When it came to choosing, Sparrow took the lead and insisted on having the biggest tree that they could carry. Rose was doubtful at first, but Sparrow insisted that she was strong and proved it by hefting the desired fir off the pavement. Polly was also determined to have the tallest specimen possible, and, although Maria protested half-heartedly, Polly and Teddy began to snivel and another equally large tree was purchased. It proved too heavy for Maria and the children to carry, but a passing workman spotted their predicament and came to their rescue. Maria dimpled appreciatively as she accepted his offer of help, and the last Rose saw of them they were headed for the house in Great Hermitage Street followed by the burly man carrying the tree on his shoulder.

Later that evening, after an excellent supper eaten in the warmth of the kitchen, which was now sparkling clean, Sparrow had gone to bed exhausted, and Rose sat by the fire in the parlour writing her article for the newspaper. The scent of pine filled the room and the fir tree took up an entire corner, its topmost branch almost touching the ceiling. There had not been enough time for the purchase of decorations, but Rose had promised to remedy that next morning. She was tired, but happy to be in her new home, and pleasantly relaxed. The words had come easily as she described Harry's struggle to come to terms with his disability, and the difficulties faced by his family. She had just inserted the last full stop when someone rapped on the front door. Rose waited for a moment, hoping that either Cora or Flossie would answer the urgent summons, although she suspected that they had slipped out to the nearest pub for a drink to celebrate their freedom from the Spriggs sisters. She set aside her work and went to see who was hammering on the door at this time in the evening.

She unlocked the door and opened it to find Eugene standing on the top step. 'What are you doing here?' she demanded.

'That's a fine way to welcome an old friend, Munday. May I come in?'

His comical expression brought a smile to her face and she stepped aside. 'Of course. I'm sorry, Guvnor, you took me by surprise, that's all.'

He stamped the snow off his shiny black shoes and shook the snowflakes off his top hat before entering. 'I was on my way home, and, as I was passing, I thought I'd call in and see how it went with Harry this morning.'

Rose closed the door and turned the key in the

lock. 'This is the opposite direction to Tavistock Square,' she said, chuckling.

'A slight exaggeration.' He tossed his hat at the hallstand, and as usual it missed and fell to the floor. He shrugged off his coat and handed it to her.

'I see your aim hasn't improved, Guvnor.' Rose hung up his coat and rescued his hat, placing it out of harm's way. 'Just as well you weren't given a pistol to protect yourself in Egypt – you'd probably have shot yourself in the foot.'

'I'm an excellent marksman, as it happens, Munday,' Eugene said equably.

'Come into the parlour. It's nice and warm.'

He stopped and sniffed. 'Is Cora smoking navy twist these days?'

'The girls are out, so it must be the captain. I think he's happy that we're here.'

'Superstitious nonsense,' Eugene said casually. 'On the other hand, if it is you, sir,' he added raising his voice slightly, 'I am here on a goodwill mission, so there's no need to worry about Miss Munday's safety.' He followed Rose into the parlour. 'Well, this is pleasant. Small and shabby, but homely, and I see you have a tree. Isn't it supposed to have things hanging off it, Munday?'

Rose motioned him to take a seat. 'You know very well it is, Guvnor. Sit down and tell me why you came all this way to see me. It wasn't to admire my Christmas tree, of that I'm certain.'

He perched on the edge of the sofa. 'The springs in this piece of furniture are trying to escape. Maybe it ought to be humanely put out of its misery.'

'I haven't enough money to buy a new one, and as the house isn't mine it would be pointless.' Rose resumed her seat. 'I'd offer you a drink, but there's only tea, and I expect you'd prefer something stronger.'

'I called in to see if you'd managed to finish the first part of Harry's story.'

'I have, and I hope I've done him justice.' Rose handed over the paper she had written in neat copperplate.

'You didn't waste any time. That's excellent.' Eugene settled back on the sofa to read the article. He folded the paper and looked up, smiling. 'Actually, I would love a cup of tea, please, Rose. If it's not too much trouble.'

'I'll make it myself, as my servants are out carousing.' Rose stood up, giggling at the shocked expression on his face. 'I'm sure they aren't misbehaving. It is almost Christmas and the poor things have had a truly miserable time under the thumb of Jessie Spriggs. She's a redoubtable woman, but I've discovered that reformed sinners are very hard work.'

'I'll come and sit in the kitchen, then. I like to watch others work.'

'When did you ever venture into the kitchens at Tavistock Square, Guvnor?'

He raised himself from the sofa and followed her.

'I'm not sure I ever ventured below stairs in our London house. Our housekeeper is as fierce as Medusa. I wouldn't be surprised if she has snakes instead of hair beneath her spotless white mobcap. But when I go to Greenfields, I often descend to the lower regions. Some of my best meals have been taken seated at the kitchen table.'

Rose led the way down the stairs to the basement. 'I think you mentioned it before. How grand to have a house in town and another in the country.'

'I love Greenfields. I spent most of my childhood there.'

'I like the name. Is it as idyllic as it sounds?' Rose opened the kitchen door and the scent of savoury stew still lingered in the warm air. 'Make yourself comfortable, Guvnor. I'll make the tea.'

'Perhaps I'll take you there one day.' Eugene took a seat at the scrubbed pine table. 'So how was Harry? Is he settling in at home?'

The kettle was simmering on the top of the range and Rose busied herself making a pot of tea, which she placed on the table. 'They are so poor, Eugene.' She blinked away a tear at the memory of the tiny house and the barefoot children. 'I doubt if they get enough to eat, and, even including the money we'll pay for his story, Harry isn't going to be able to do much to support his family.'

'Don't upset yourself, Rose. I'm sure that there will be something we can do to help.'

She poured tea into a cup and added a dash of milk. 'I'm afraid there's no sugar.'

'Are you short of money? You must be honest, Rose.'

She smiled as she pulled up a chair and sat opposite him. 'You called me Rose.'

'And you used my name, too.' Eugene sipped his tea. 'I prefer Gene. It's less formal.'

'I'm still your employee.'

He shook his head. 'No, Rose, you're more than that. I'm your friend and you will be a valued contributor to the *Leader*, starting with your article on Harry and his family.'

'Do you like it?'

'It's a good piece, worthy of going to print.'

'Really?'

'I wouldn't say so if it weren't true. You have talent, and you have compassion, but you aren't overly sentimental, which leads you to a balanced point of view. I think we can do something for Harry, and the first thing is to get him seen by a specialist at the Royal London Ophthalmic Hospital at Moorfields.'

'It's Saturday tomorrow, but if we could get him an appointment at the hospital, and if there was a glimmer of hope that he might see again, it would feel like a Christmas miracle.'

'You're right, Rose. What a story that would make, and I think it could happen.'

Rose eyed him over the rim of her cup. Her heart was thudding and she could feel the blood rushing to her cheeks. 'How? Tell me, please.'

'I know one of the surgeons at Moorfields. He's a good chap and he owes me a favour. I can't say any more without betraying a confidence, but leave it to me, Rose.' Eugene downed the remainder of his tea. 'I'll take a cab to his house. Who knows? I might get invited to stay for dinner, if I'm not too late.'

'Oh, I'm sorry. I should have offered you food.'

'I wouldn't have imposed on you, Rose.' He folded the paper and tucked it into his inside pocket. 'I'll call in at the office on the way home and make sure that this goes into tomorrow's edition. It's just the sort of Christmas story that will tug at the readers' heartstrings, and it might encourage a benefactor to come forward; someone who'll be able to help the family. But first we need to get Harry an appointment at the hospital.'

'I can hardly believe it,' Rose jumped to her feet as he left the table. 'Do you really think you can get Harry seen at such short notice?'

'I can have a damned good try, Munday,' Eugene said, chuckling. 'I can swear in front of Munday, but I wouldn't do so if I were speaking to Rose.'

His laughter was infectious and she found herself giggling. 'You are ridiculous, Guvnor. I can poke fun at my boss, but I wouldn't tease Gene.'

He took a small leather pouch from his pocket and laid it on the table. 'Take that as payment for Nomad's first piece. It should see you through the week, Rose.'

'Thank you, Gene.' She hurried after him as he was about to leave the room. 'By the way, I've invited Maria and the children here for Christmas dinner. I'd really love it if you were able to come, too.'

He hesitated in the shadow of the doorway, turning to look her in the eye and his smile faded. 'Would you, Rose? Or are you just saying that?'

'I've said it, and I meant it.' She stood on tiptoe to plant a kiss on his whiskery cheek. 'I like your beard now that you've had it trimmed so neatly. It makes you look distinguished.'

He raised his hand to touch the side of his face. 'I thought you disliked it, Rose.'

'I didn't care for the wild man look, but you are quite presentable now.'

'I'd better leave before you destroy my morale entirely.' He leaned over to kiss her lightly on the forehead. 'You, on the other hand, always look beautiful, like a perfect rose.' He took the stairs two at a time, leaving her staring after him in amazement.

Next morning Rose was up first. She went to the kitchen and riddled the embers in the range, adding kindling and more coal until she had a good fire going. Having filled the kettle she put it on to boil and cut herself a slice of bread. She had money for provisions, thanks to Eugene's generosity, but Cora and Flossie would have to go shopping for necessities. There were other more important things to be done and Rose wanted to be out of the house before Sparrow awakened. The cups and saucers from last evening were still on the table and she picked up the one that Eugene had drunk from, holding it in her hands for a moment longer than was necessary before emptying the dregs and placing it in the stone sink. Eugene had complimented her on her writing and also on her looks, but Eugene Sheldon was a notorious flirt and saying such things came naturally to him. She spread butter and jam thinly on the bread and ate without really tasting it. She drank a cup of tea, and scribbled a note telling the others not to worry, she would be back later.

Having put on her mantle, bonnet and mittens, she left the house without disturbing anyone and set off on her mission to purchase presents for her surrogate family. The snow that had fallen in the night had frozen hard, but the sun was shining and there was barely a breeze as she made her way to the High Street. To take a cab was an extravagance, but the omnibuses were slow and crowded and Rose managed to convince herself that the outlay was justified. She was beginning to question her judgement after several cabs bowled past, and she was thinking of abandoning her plan to shop in Oxford Street when she saw a barouche drawn by a matched pair of bays, and it drew to a halt at the kerbside. She recognised Giddings, who was seated on the box next to the coachman, and he leaped smartly to the ground and opened the door.

Eugene leaned out. 'Where are you off to, Rose? I was on my way to see you.'

'I was trying to get a cab to Oxford Street. I need to get some presents.'

'Then I arrived at the right moment.' He alighted and proffered his arm. 'Climb in, Miss Munday. Tell Simms we wish to visit Oxford Street, Giddings. We're going shopping.'

'But surely you have work to do?' Rose allowed him to help her into the cab and he climbed in to sit beside her.

Giddings closed the door and the carriage moved off slowly at first, gathering speed as it made its way along the High Street, heading towards the City.

'I went in early and did what was necessary.' Eugene handed her a folded copy of the *London Leader*. 'Here it is – today's paper with your article on the front page.'

Rose's hands shook as she unfolded the newspaper and saw the words she had penned put into print. 'It's hard to believe.'

'Cousin Arthur thought it excellent. He didn't even enquire as to the identity of Nomad.'

'I don't know what to say, Gene.'

'You did it, Rose. It's all down to you for bringing
Harry Norman home, and even better, I managed
to persuade my friend at Moorfields to see him this
afternoon. That's why I was up at the crack of dawn
– I was coming to give you the good news.'

'We must let Harry know. I ought to go there instead
of buying presents.'

'There's time for everything. I sent a messenger
to tell Harry to be ready at one o'clock. My carriage
is at your disposal.'

'We're taking him to the hospital?'

'Of course. It's the least I can do, considering the
progress of Private Harry Norman is going to increase
circulation by a huge amount.'

'Why do you make yourself out to be a lesser
man than you really are, Gene? You didn't have to
do this for Harry, and you didn't have to help me.'

'Perhaps I see something in you that others have
missed, Rose. I will bask in your glory when Nomad
is the most popular contributor to my paper.'

'Your paper?'

'Arthur is a wealthy man in his own right and
he's decided to retire. It came as a bit of a shock,
but he's handing the business over to me. Even so,
I'm not sure that I want the responsibility – it means
that I'll have to be a respectable citizen and turn up
for work every day.'

'You don't fool me,' Rose said, smiling. 'You are

a far better man than the person you pretend to be.'

'Tell that to my pa. I doubt if he'll believe you.'

'It seems to me that you've spent so much time acting the part of a libertine that your own family think it's true.'

'But you know differently?'

'Yes, Gene. I do.' Rose reached out to pat his gloved hand. 'You're a good man at heart.'

Eugene curled his fingers around hers, and they settled into a companionable silence as the carriage weaved through the traffic on its way to the West End. Rose was conscious of Eugene's nearness, but it was a comfortable feeling and she was able to relax and look out of the window without feeling the need to make conversation. The snowy streets were crowded with horse-drawn vehicles, while pedestrians thronged the pavements, stopping to stare into brightly lit shop windows, or to pass the time of day. Rose was conscious of an air of excitement and anticipation that she had not experienced since she was a child. 'We're here,' she cried as they approached Oxford Circus. 'Just look at the shop windows – it looks so festive.'

Eugene tapped his silver-headed cane on the roof and the carriage drew to a halt. 'We have plenty of time, so let's enjoy ourselves, Rose.'

There had been so little time for light-heartedness recently that Rose was unable to refuse and she linked arms with him. 'Why not?'

They explored the various departments in Peter Robinson's store, where Rose purchased a lace shawl for Maria and a blue plaid dress with a white lace collar for Sparrow. They went on to Debenham and Freebody in Wigmore Street where, encouraged by Eugene, Rose bought silk stockings for Cora and Flossie. It was a huge extravagance, but Rose knew that her friends would be thrilled to receive such gifts, and after such a generous gesture she could not neglect the Spriggs sisters. She chose a red woollen scarf and gloves for Izzie, and similar sets for Edna and Jessie, although in more subdued colours.

Eugene loaded the packages into the carriage. 'Where to now, Rose?'

She hesitated, standing ankle deep in the snow that had been shovelled to the edge of the pavement, but she was oblivious to the cold. Spending money on others was exciting enough, but sharing the experience with Eugene was quite intoxicating. 'I'd like to take something to the Norman family, but I don't want to offend them, Gene.'

'I know just the thing.' Eugene handed her into the barouche. 'Fortnum's, please, Simms.'

'What do they sell?' Rose moved some of the beautifully wrapped gifts aside in order to make room for Eugene.

'Something we all need, and I'm sure your protégé's family even more so. A hamper of food will surely make their Christmas a great deal more festive.'

'I hope you're right,' Rose said doubtfully.

Rose had never seen anything like the interior of Fortnum and Mason's shop. She wandered amongst the counters and stands, which were piled high with luxuries. The aroma of smoked ham, exotic cheeses and fresh bread made her mouth water. The scent of tea, coffee and spices mingled with the tangy zest of citrus fruit, and bunches of grapes were artistically arranged alongside colourful fruits, most of which were foreign to Rose.

'It so happens that I ordered a hamper for you to share with Maria and the children,' Eugene said casually. He beckoned to a smartly suited assistant, who rushed to his side.

'Your order is ready, Mr Sheldon. It's about to be sent to the address you gave us.'

'Thank you, Burton, but if it's not too much trouble I'd like Miss Munday to see the contents. I'm thinking of ordering another, if you can pack it for us to take away now?'

'Of course, sir. Fortnum's can always oblige.' He scuttled off, returning moments later with a large wicker hamper, which he set down on the counter.

Rose looked inside and was amazed. 'This looks wonderful, Gene, but I don't think the Normans would appreciate game in aspic, caviar and smoked salmon. I'm not sure I know what all these things are.'

'But you would enjoy sampling those foods, wouldn't you, Rose?'

'I think so, but it's too fancy for people who exist on so little.' Rose smiled at the shop assistant, who was visibly anxious. 'I can see that everything is of the finest quality, but would it be possible for me to select the items to go in a second hamper?'

Burton's creased face lightened with a smile. 'Yes, miss. Of course you may. Would you like me to assist you?'

'That would be very kind.' Rose shot a sideways glance at Eugene. 'You don't mind, do you, Gene?'

He shrugged. 'Of course not. I'll leave it entirely to you.'

Rose knew exactly what she wanted, even if her choice of simple food frustrated the salesman in Burton, but he was too well trained to argue with a customer. A large baked ham crusted with sugar and spiked with cloves went in first, followed more mundanely by bread, butter, cheese and bacon, and these were joined by tea, coffee, milk and sugar. Rose added oranges, lemons and apples, an iced Christmas cake and a pound of walnuts. Eugene, who had been following their progress, insisted on adding a bottle of brandy and several bottles of ale. Rose had spotted something on the freshfood counter that intrigued her, and Burton introduced her to Fortnum's speciality, which he called 'scotch eggs', cutting one in half to reveal sausage meat wrapped around a soft-boiled egg.

'Very tasty, miss,' he said, licking his lips. 'And very popular with travellers who want something to eat on a long journey.'

'Better add some to both hampers, Burton,' Eugene said firmly.

'Yes, sir. Is there anything else?'

'I think that's enough,' Rose said, frowning. 'Although I would like to buy some chocolate for Flossie. She loves Fry's Chocolate Cream bars.'

Burton moved closer, lowering his voice. 'There's a grocery shop not far from here where you can purchase them. I know because my lady wife has a sweet tooth.'

'Thank you,' Rose said, smiling. 'That's very kind of you.'

'But please don't mention it to my manager. I could lose my job for sending you to a competitor.'

Eugene patted him on the back. 'Our lips are sealed, but I'd be obliged if you'd have the hampers taken to my carriage.'

'Yes, sir. Most certainly.' Burton hurried off, calling for one of the minions to help him.

'And now I suggest we have some lunch before taking the hamper to Bow.' Eugene proffered his arm. 'Do you fancy the Café Royal?'

'Actually, I'd rather have one of those delicious scotch eggs to eat on the way. It's getting late and I have yet to take Sparrow to purchase glass balls and tinsel for our tree.'

'What a splendid idea.' Eugene summoned another assistant. 'We'll picnic on scotch eggs and champagne, and then we'll take the hamper to Bow, and I know exactly where to go for the decorations.'

'Are you sure, Gene? You must have better things to do so near Christmas.'

'Can't think of any at the moment, Rose. But if something crops up, of course I'll abandon you and go off to do something disreputable.' He tucked her hand in the crook of his arm. 'Food first, then chocolate bars, and then off to Bow, but we'll have to hurry if we're to get our friend to Moorfields for his appointment.'

Chapter Twenty-Three

Winnie Norman was out when they arrived at the house in Bow, and the two younger boys were also at work, leaving Harry on his own with his two small sisters. Mary's eyes opened wide when Giddings strode in carrying the large wicker hamper, and Harry sniffed appreciatively.

'Something smells tasty,' he said eagerly. 'What is it, Miss Rose?'

'Just a few extras for the Christmas table, Harry.' Rose gave Mary a stern look. 'You mustn't open it until your ma comes home. Do you promise?'

Mary clasped her hands behind her back. 'What's in it, miss?'

'Some nice things for all of you,' Rose said, smiling as she remembered the sugared almonds covered in gold foil that she had added at the last minute, and the buttery shortbread that Eugene had casually tossed into the hamper.

Eugene put his hand in his pocket and pulled out a paper poke filled with boiled sweets and a box of chocolates. 'These are to share, Mary. But you mustn't allow little Daisy to have the big sweets because she might choke. Little pieces of chocolate will be fine.'

Rose gazed at him in amazement. 'Goodness, Gene. You sound quite fatherly.'

'I have many faccts to my nature, Rose. But that was simply common sense.'

'Don't I get a sweet?' Harry asked plaintively.

'You'll have to wait until you've seen the eye specialist,' Rose said, chuckling. 'And if you're very good, we might allow you to have a treat afterwards.'

Harry threw back his head and laughed. 'Miss Rose, you're a tonic. I'm feeling better already, and Ma will be so pleased. She's been fretting about what she can give us for our Christmas dinner, and now she won't have to worry.'

'That's splendid, Harry, but we'd better be on our way.' Eugene signalled to Giddings, who was standing to attention by the door. 'We're ready to go now. Tell Simms we're off to the Royal London Ophthalmic Hospital, Blomfield Street.'

Rose sat with Harry while Eugene had a word with the ophthalmic surgeon who had examined Harry's eyes. She reached out to grasp Harry's hand. 'You mustn't worry. I'm sure they can do something to help you.'

He squeezed her fingers. 'It's good of you to go to all this trouble, but I don't hold out much hope.'

'Can you see anything at all, Harry?'

A wry grin twisted his lips. 'That's what the doctor just asked me. I was completely blind at first, but I can see light and shade now, and I can make out the shapes of people and things.'

'That's good, isn't it? What did the specialist say?'

'Not much – I think he wanted to talk to someone he thought was better equipped to handle bad news than me.'

'I'm sure that's not true.' Rose released his hand and jumped to her feet as Eugene came to join them. 'Well? Don't keep us in suspense.'

'He said there's hope because there's been some improvement, but time will tell. There's nothing surgically to be done, but he'll see you again in a month, Harry. You're to take moderate exercise and he advised a spell in the countryside.'

'That's out of the question, sir. I've got to find work as soon as I can, even if it's selling matches on street corners. My family need the money and I'm the head of the house.'

'There might be a way,' Eugene said thoughtfully.

'There's a cottage at Greenfields that hasn't been occupied since my head gardener passed away.'

Rose clutched his arm. 'Would you allow the family to live there, Gene? Perhaps Mrs Norman could help in the house, and the boys could give the gardeners a hand?'

'Do you think your mother would agree to leave London, Harry?' Eugene took the seat next to him. 'I'd like you to think about it and talk it over with her.'

'We've always lived in Bow, sir. I dunno how she'd take the idea, and I ain't no gardener. I wouldn't know where to start.'

'You wouldn't be expected to work until you're fit and well. I have a couple of under gardeners who are quite capable of keeping things tidy, but I'm thinking of expanding my dairy herd, and there's plenty of work around the farm generally. My estate manager could do with some help, and I think you and he would get on well together, if you're prepared to learn.'

'Think about it, Harry,' Rose said enthusiastically. 'All that lovely clean air, and perhaps the children could attend the village school. I'm assuming there is one.'

Eugene nodded, smiling. 'Indeed there is. You'll have to take everything into consideration, Harry. But I need someone I can trust, and I think you're the man.'

'I'd do it in a shot, sir, but Ma has her own opinion about things. She might not be so easy to convince.'

Rose shot a sideways glance at Eugene. 'Leave it to Mr Sheldon. He has a way with women.'

'I'll take that as a compliment, Rose.' Eugene helped Harry to his feet. 'Come on, old chap. Let's get you home.'

Winnie was there before them. She met them at the door and Rose could see by her tight-lipped expression that she was seething with anger.

'Do you know anything about this, Harry?' she demanded, waving her hand in the general direction of the hamper.

'It's a Christmas gift, Mrs Norman,' Eugene said hastily. 'I hope you will forgive the presumption on my part.'

Winnie faced up to him, baring her teeth like an angry terrier. 'I don't accept charity. You can give it to those what do.'

'Really, Ma! There's no need for that.' Harry held his hand out to her. 'It was done out of kindness of heart, and should be accepted as such.'

'I don't doubt it was meant well,' Winnie said huffily. 'But we ain't beggars. Me and the boys can provide food for the table until you're fit enough to work, son.'

Rose cleared her throat nervously. She could see that Winnie was close to tears and had to be handled carefully. 'I'm at fault, Mrs Norman. I chose the contents and if it offends your sensibilities we'll take it away.'

'No, Ma,' Mary cried, grabbing her mother by the hand. 'We're all hungry.'

'It's a shame to let good food go to waste,' Harry added. 'The doctor said I was to have proper meals as well as rest if me eyes was to get better.'

Winnie turned to give him a searching look. 'What else did he say? Will you get your sight back?'

'Maybe. He don't know for sure, but Mr Sheldon has come up with an idea, Ma. He's offered us a cottage on his land where we can live and I'll help around the farm, and the nippers can go back to school.'

Winnie rounded on Eugene, her eyes narrowed. 'I know your game, mister. I seen the newspaper at the house where I was working this morning. You think you can write stories about us to entertain your readers. Next thing you know we'll have people coming here to gawp at us like we was animals in the zoo.'

'That's so unfair, Mrs Norman,' Rose protested angrily. 'I wrote that article to make people realise the sacrifice our soldiers make when they go to war. Harry is a hero and so are his comrades in arms.'

'Fine words,' Winnie said scornfully. 'But I got the sack because of it. Her ladyship at the big house said she didn't want newspapermen nosing around, making up stories about how bad she treats menials like me.'

'That's not what we intended.' Eugene took a leather pouch from his pocket and laid it on the table. 'That's the first of the payments for your story, Harry. There will be more . . .'

Winnie snatched up the purse and threw it at him. 'No, there won't, young man. We ain't for sale – just leave us alone.'

'We'd better go,' Rose said in a low voice. 'I'm sorry if we've caused trouble for you, Harry.'

He held up his hands. 'It's not you, it's Ma, being pig-headed as usual.' He followed them to the door. 'I'm grateful for what you've done, miss, and you, sir. I'll try to talk Ma round, but it won't be easy.'

Rose reached up to plant a kiss on his cheek. 'Merry Christmas, Harry. At least your ma has forgotten about the hamper. Don't let her give it away.'

'She'll come round, especially when my brothers get home and fall on the food. There won't be none left to give to the poor and destitute. Leave Ma to me.'

Eugene shook his hand. 'The offer of the cottage still stands. Talk it over with your mother, and, if she agrees, I'll take you there next week so that she can see for herself.'

'I'm much obliged for everything, sir.' Harry closed

the door, leaving Rose and Eugene out in the cold with soft, feathery flakes of snow falling from a blanket of clouds.

'Oh dear,' Rose said tearfully. 'What have we done, Gene?'

He brushed a snowflake from her cheek with the tip of his finger. 'Winnie Norman is a stiff-necked woman, but she loves her family and when she's had time to think it over I'll bet you twenty guineas that she'll change her mind.'

'If I had that much money I'd accept the wager, but I haven't.'

Eugene handed her into the carriage and climbed in after her. 'No matter. It's a dead certainty anyway. I wouldn't take your money.'

'I'm truly sorry that Winnie has taken it so badly, but I have others to think of now. I promised to take Sparrow to purchase ornaments and tinsel for the tree.'

'We'll collect Sparrow and take her to the Soho Bazaar. You can buy almost anything there.' Eugene leaned out of the window. 'Wapping High Street, please, Simms, and then we'll be going to the Soho Bazaar.'

It was Christmas Eve and the tree stood in all its shimmering finery. Glass baubles danced from the branches and tinsel glittered in the firelight. The finishing touch was a silver star that Maria had made, and Eugene lifted Sparrow up so that she could fasten it to the topmost branch.

'Splendid,' he said as he put her down. 'You've done wonders, Sparrow.'

'I had help,' she said, blushing rosily. 'Polly did the lower branches.'

'And Teddy kept pulling the tinsel off,' Polly added, glaring at her little brother, who was now sitting quietly on his mother's knee, sucking his thumb.

'It's really beautiful,' Rose said, clapping her hands. 'It's the best Christmas tree ever.'

'It is lovely,' Maria agreed.

'It should be,' Eugene said, chuckling. 'I think Sparrow bought up the entire stock of one stall in the bazaar yesterday. If it hadn't been for the offer of an ice cream at Gunter's I might have been bankrupted.'

'Don't exaggerate, Gene.' Rose glanced at the clock on the mantelshelf. 'Heavens, look at the time.'

Maria hitched Teddy over her shoulder. 'This little man is almost asleep. I'll put him to bed, and you, too, Polly.'

'But, Mama, I want to stay and look at the tree.'

'Santa Claus won't visit unless you are tucked up in bed asleep,' Maria said sternly.

'I'll go to bed now, Mama,' Polly said sulkily. 'But I want Sparrow to tell me a story.'

Sparrow yawned, covering her mouth with her hand. 'All right, but I think I might go to bed, too.

Maybe Santa Claus will leave something for me this year.'

'Do you mean to tell us that you've never hung up a stocking?' Rose asked, frowning. 'Surely you were given presents at Christmas?'

'A clip round the head was all I was likely to get,' Sparrow said grimly. 'It were a different world – one you know nothing of.'

'Things will be very different from now on.' Rose gave her a hug. 'I'll come up and tuck you in later.'

Polly took Sparrow by the hand. 'If Santa doesn't bring you anything you can have some of my presents.'

'Ta, Polly. But I think I'm too old for Christmas stockings and all that. What story would you like tonight?' Sparrow and Polly wandered out of the room, discussing fairy stories, followed by Maria with Teddy in her arms.

'Who would believe that a child could be treated in such a way?' Rose said angrily. 'It's a wonder that Sparrow has turned out so well.'

'It's just as well you bought those fripperies in the market when young Sparrow was otherwise engaged,' Eugene said, smiling. 'I dare say they're the sort of thing that girls her age would enjoy.'

'I would have done at her age, so I think Sparrow will love them. We'll have to make this a very special Christmas.' Rose held his gaze for a moment, losing herself in the warmth of his smile, but a sound outside brought her back to reality and she looked away. 'I can't thank you enough for everything you've done for us. You'll stay for supper, won't you, Gene?'

He shook his head. 'I should get home. I told Simms to pick me up at seven o'clock.'

'Of course, but you'll be here tomorrow, won't you?'

'If the invitation still stands.'

Rose was about to answer when the sounds outside grew louder and she realised that someone was hammering on the front door. 'Who could that be?'

'Are you expecting anyone?'

She shook her head. 'I'll go and see. I let Flossie and Cora have the evening off, so I expect they're in the nearest pub.' She left the room and went to open the door. 'Who is it?' She peered into the darkness and her breath caught in her throat. 'Jimmy! It can't be.'

He stepped inside, shaking snow off his cap. 'It's none other, and look who came with me?'

Rose's hands flew to cover her mouth. 'Max. I can't believe it.'

He pushed past his brother, coming to a halt when he saw Eugene. 'What's he doing here?'

'Max!' Rose cast an anxious glance at Eugene, but he was shrugging on his greatcoat.

'Don't mind me,' Eugene said casually. 'I was just leaving.'

Rose rounded on Max. 'That was uncalled for.'

'We mustn't detain you, Sheldon.' Max held the door open. 'Compliments of the season.'

Rose stepped in between them. 'Wait for me in the parlour, Max. I'll see Eugene out.'

'Yes, come on.' Jimmy slapped his brother on the back. 'I need to get warm after that walk from the station.'

With a reluctant backward glance, Max followed his brother into the parlour.

'I'm so sorry,' Rose said hastily. 'I don't know what's come over Max. That was so unlike him.'

Eugene hesitated in the doorway. 'He's jealous, Rose. It's perfectly natural and I dare say I might be the same if I arrived home from war to find my fiancée entertaining another man.'

'You wouldn't behave like that,' Rose said firmly. 'I'll have words with Max to make sure he doesn't spoil Christmas with his childish behaviour.'

'I think it best if I stay away tomorrow.' Eugene took her hand in his and held it in a warm clasp.

'No, that's not necessary. I won't allow Max to upset our plans.'

'Don't worry about me, Munday. I've had many requests for my company – it's just a question of choosing which one I'll accept.' He raised her hand to his lips. 'Merry Christmas, Rose.' He stepped outside into the swirling snow before she had a chance to protest. She stood for a moment, willing him to turn and acknowledge her with a wave, but he disappeared into the darkness.

Rose slammed the door and marched into the parlour to find Max standing with his back to the fire, and Jimmy sitting in the armchair with his booted feet resting on the brass fender. He made to stand but she motioned him to remain seated.

'Why did you do that, Max?' she demanded furiously. 'Eugene Sheldon is my employer and he's also a good friend. You were incredibly rude to him.'

'Why is he always sneaking around you, Rose? You're my fiancée and yet the fellow is always at your side. You followed him to Egypt, and I return unexpectedly to find him here, in my house.'

'Hold on, Max,' Jimmy said abruptly. 'Give Rose a chance to explain.'

'I don't have to explain anything, thank you, Jimmy.'

Max folded his arms across his chest, fixing her with a hard stare. 'The man is a bounder, Rose. He's bought you with promises of a career in journalism, when we all know that it's not a suitable occupation for a woman, let alone someone of your age and background.'

'And what is my background, Max? What is it that puts me above others?'

'Don't play word games with me. You know very well what I mean. You were well educated, thanks to the Dorincourt family, and brought up to be a lady. Eugene Sheldon will drag you down to the level of the gutter.'

'I can't believe you're saying these things,' Rose said slowly. 'What happened to you in Egypt, Max? You weren't like this in Australia.'

'I've seen more of the world since then, and I want my wife to be above reproach. I intend to move up the ranks, and my lady will be expected to mix with the higher echelons.'

'I say, Max, old fellow. You're laying it on a bit thick, aren't you?' Jimmy rose to his feet. 'For heaven's sake, calm down. Let's have a drink and put all this behind us.'

Rose took a deep breath. 'That's a good idea, Jimmy. We've been given a superb Fortnum and Mason hamper from the man you so obviously despise, Max. I left it to Flossie and Cora to unpack, but I believe there's some brandy and maybe a bottle of rum. I'll go and see.' She made a move towards the door but Max stepped in front of her.

'You have servants. Ring for them.'

'I gave them the evening off,' Rose said coldly. 'And for your information, I don't think of Flossie and Cora as servants. They saved my life when I was lost and alone in London, which was largely your fault for not making proper arrangements for me. They took me in and gave me shelter.'

'Who are these women?'

'They're my friends, Max. They've escaped from

a life of brutality and degradation and they're putting the old ways behind them.'

'Do you mean to say that you're sharing my house with common prostitutes? You'll tell them to leave, or I will.'

'Max! That's enough,' Jimmy said angrily.

Rose clenched her hands at her sides. For a wild moment she had been tempted to slap Max's face, but she managed to control herself. 'Cora and Flossie are my friends. If anyone leaves this house tonight it will be you.'

'You can't throw me out of my own property.'

'As far as I know this place still belongs to Caroline, and I think she would agree with me. In fact, I know she would. Your sister is a warm-hearted, compassionate woman. I don't know what the army has done to you, Max, but I don't like it.'

Jimmy placed himself in between them. 'This is getting out of hand. Max, you're being unreasonable. You've upset Rose and I think you should apologise.'

'I come home and find another man in my house.' Max turned on Rose, his nostrils flaring. 'And I haven't forgotten that you seemed more interested in that fellow's welfare after I rescued him than you were in mine, and I'm your fiancé.'

'This is nonsense inspired by jealousy. You should be ashamed of yourself, Max.' Rose turned away.

'I'm going to the kitchen to find you some food and something to drink. Talk to him, Jimmy – make him see sense.'

'Don't bother on our account,' Max said stonily. 'We're leaving.'

'We are?' Jimmy countered. 'Where the hell will we go on Christmas Eve, in the midst of a blizzard?'

'Yes, that's ridiculous,' Rose added. 'You two can share the room you had when you were boys.'

'I know where Phineas hid a set of keys for Pier House. I overheard him telling Caroline that he'd done it in case the old woman had a fall or a fit, or some such thing. We'll spend the night there, Jimmy.'

'But it's been locked up since the murder.' Rose looked from one to the other. 'It will be freezing and the beds won't be made up. Please stop being so pig-headed, Max. You're behaving like a five-year-old.'

'Thank you for that,' he said coldly. 'Now I know exactly what you think of me. Come along, Jimmy. We're leaving.'

'This is madness. Let's have something to eat and a few drinks and remember that it's the season of "peace on earth, goodwill to men".' Jimmy turned to Rose with a wry smile. 'Do you remember the year when Laurence made us learn the poem by Longfellow, and we had to recite it in full or forfeit breakfast on Christmas morning?'

Rose nodded and was about to answer when Max pushed past her.

'Coming here tonight was a mistake,' he said angrily. 'We'll spend the night at Pier House and it will give you time to think things over, Rose. If you still cling to your mindless loyalty to that libertine, then I consider our engagement terminated.'

Rose stared at him aghast. 'I'm beginning to think I was a fool to agree to marry you in the first place. Even so, it's Christmas and I'll expect you both for dinner tomorrow, and we'll say nothing about this, because I'm not going to ruin Christmas Day for the children.'

'Of course we'll join you for the celebration, Rose.' Jimmy slipped his arm around her shoulders. 'Who's staying here with you, tonight? I don't want to leave you like this.'

'Flossie and Cora will be home soon, and Maria Barnaby is here with her two children. Last, but definitely not least, there's Sparrow, a child from the streets who now lives with us.'

'You seem to delight in using my house to shelter undesirables, apart from Maria and her children, of course.' Max headed for the door. 'We'll continue this discussion tomorrow, Rose.' He turned to his brother. 'You're welcome to remain here, if you wish, Jim. This is my business, not yours.'

Jimmy shook his head. 'I don't agree with you, Max, but I'll keep you company. Maybe we could find a nice warm room in one of the pubs. I really don't fancy breaking into a house where an old lady was murdered.'

'Ghosts can't hurt you, Jim.' Max shot a reproachful glance in Rose's direction. 'Only the living can do that.' He marched out of the room.

Jimmy kissed Rose on the cheek. 'I'll try to talk some sense into him, Rose. Maybe after spending a freezing night in a haunted house he'll see things more clearly in the morning.' He followed Max into the hall.

Rose remained standing in the middle of the room, stung by the unfairness of Max's remarks, and angry that he should have behaved in such a cavalier fashion. It was she who had suffered from his thoughtlessness, and yet he had never apologised for dragging her halfway around the world without making any provision for her welfare. What a naïve fool she must have been to undertake such a journey. She spun round at the sound of the door opening but it was Maria who rushed to her side.

'What's happened, Rose? Who was here? I heard raised voices but I couldn't come immediately without scaring the children.'

Rose sank down on the nearest chair. 'You won't believe it when I tell you.'

'You're trembling.' Maria eyed her worriedly. 'I'm certain I saw a bottle of brandy in the Fortnum's hamper. I think we could both do with a tot, and then you can tell me what happened just now.'

Rose was about to follow her from the room when she heard someone knocking on the front door. 'I'll go and see who it is,' she said wearily. 'Perhaps Max has had second thoughts.' She went to open the door.

Chapter Twenty-Four

Eugene brushed past her, sending a shower of snow-flakes onto the floorboards as he took off his hat. He tossed it at the hallstand and this time his aim was perfect. 'I'm done with being a gentleman, Rose.' He wrapped her in his arms and kissed her long and hard.

His face was ice-cold but the warmth of his lips sent fire racing through her veins, and although Rose's first instinct was to push him away, she found herself responding in a way that seemed completely natural. The powdery snow on his greatcoat melted, soaking through the thin woollen fabric of her gown, but she was oblivious to everything other than the achingly familiar scent of him and the strength of his arms around her.

'I'm not going to apologise, Rose,' he said softly,

caressing her cheek with his lips. 'I've held back because I thought you were in love with someone else, but from what I witnessed tonight he's not worth it. I'm a bad lot, but at least I admit my failings.'

Dazed and breathless, Rose gazed into his eyes and saw her own bewildered reflection. 'This is all wrong, Gene.'

'Maybe, but I love you and I know now that you're not indifferent to me, Rose. For once in my life I've tried to do the right thing, but to hell with that. You were meant for me and I'm not giving you into the hands of that stiff-necked idiot.'

'Is that what you came back to say?' Rose broke free from his embrace. 'You never gave a hint of having any feelings for me before now.'

He dropped his hands to his sides. 'That's what comes from trying to do what I felt was in your best interests. I've never met anyone like you, Rose. I've led a completely selfish existence, doing precisely what I wanted with no thought to other people, unless they were likely to make the front page of the *Leader*.'

'But you abandoned me. You went off to Egypt and left me to cope on my own. That doesn't seem like the action of a caring man.'

'I ran away, Munday. I'm ashamed to admit it, but I was scared for the first time in my life.'

'I don't believe that for a moment. I saw how you

handled those costermongers in a fight, and you accompanied an army patrol into the desert. You were captured – that must have been truly frightening.'

'Those were physical things, Rose, and I knew it was only a matter of time before we were rescued, but as for myself – I felt that I'd lost control of my senses, and that was what worried me most. I wasn't interested in my personal safety – all I could think of was a girl with the most amazing green eyes and a mass of flame-coloured curls. Someone who was determined to take on the world all by herself. Your small hands held my heart from the first moment I met you, Rose Munday, and I've been fighting against it ever since.'

Rose took a step backwards. 'Stop there, Gene. I'm more confused now than when you started. You say one thing and then you contradict yourself.'

He seized her by the shoulders. 'I'm very bad at this because I've never told a woman that I loved her and meant it – until now. I need to know if you have the smallest regard for me, Rose.'

'You've taken me completely by surprise. I suppose you're used to women swooning at your feet, but I honestly don't know what I feel for anyone. I thought I was in love with Max, but now I'm not sure . . .'

'Where is he? I'll have it out with him here and now.'

'He left with Jimmy. We had an awful row and he's decided to spend the night at Pier House.'

'Then that's where I'm going. I can't let this rest.'

'What are you going to do?' Rose turned her head at the sound of footsteps and saw Maria standing by the parlour door, clutching a bottle of brandy in her hand.

'What's going on?' Maria demanded. 'I heard you from the kitchen. You'll wake the children.'

'I'm sorry,' Eugene said humbly. 'I'm leaving now. I have important matters to discuss with a military gentleman.' He retrieved his hat from the floor and rammed it on his head.

'No, you don't.' Rose grabbed him by the arm. 'This is madness, Gene. Leave it until morning and we can talk about it then.'

He gave her a penetrating look. 'Tell me that you don't have any feelings for me, Rose, and I'll go back to Tavistock Square and all this will be in the past.'

'I don't know what to say,' Rose whispered. 'This has got out of hand.'

'All right. Let me put it another way,' Eugene said softly. 'Do you love Max Manning?'

Rose cast an anxious glance in Maria's direction, but Maria merely shrugged. 'Tell him the truth, Rose. Listen to your heart.'

'I – I don't feel as if know Max any more,' Rose said haltingly. 'He isn't the man I thought he was.'

'That's what I hoped you'd say, Rose.' Eugene wrenched the door open. 'I'm going to Pier House to tell Max how things stand. I should have done it earlier this evening, but I thought you were still in love with him.'

'What are you going to do?' she asked nervously. 'Don't start a fight because he'll beat you, Gene. He's a trained soldier and Jimmy is bound to take his side.'

'Leave everything to me, Rose. I can take care of myself.' Eugene rushed out into the snowstorm.

'He'll be killed.' Rose snatched Maria's fur-lined cloak from the hallstand. 'You don't mind if I borrow this, do you?'

'No, take it. Go after him, Rose. Bring him back here and talk things over.'

Rose wrapped the cloak around her, covering her head with the hood as she raced after Eugene. 'Wait for me.'

He came to a halt at the foot of the watermen's stairs. 'Go back, Rose. This is between Max and me.'

'I think it concerns me, too. You men seem to think that we're chattels that you can pass from hand to hand, and it's just not so.'

He held out his hand. 'You're right. We'll do this together, and if you decide that he's the one you want, so be it, but don't expect me to give up without a fight.'

*　　*　　*

They battled their way through a fierce blizzard, and it took twice as long to reach their destination as it would have done normally. It was a relief to arrive at Pier House, where lights shone from several of the ground-floor windows.

'At least they made it here,' Rose said breathlessly. 'I can see someone moving about in the morning parlour.' She tightened her grasp on Eugene's hand, dragging him to a halt. 'But that's neither Max nor Jimmy.' She uttered a gasp of horror. 'It looks like Regan, but it can't be. I know that he evaded arrest, but surely he wouldn't be stupid enough to hide out here.'

'Wait here and I'll get a closer look,' Eugene said, pulling her into the shelter of the portico.

Rose waited, hardly daring to breathe as he moved stealthily towards the window. He returned moments later. 'That fellow fits Regan's description and there's a woman with him. Would that be Gilroy?'

'It's possible,' Rose whispered. 'Did you see Max or Jimmy?'

He shook his head. 'If they're in the house they'll be in trouble. Regan will face the noose if he's caught, so he won't take kindly to interlopers.'

'You're not going in on your own, Gene. I won't let you.'

A smile creased the corners of his eyes as he met her anxious gaze. 'Are you worried for my safety,

Munday? My gory murder would make wonderful headlines for the next edition.'

She slapped the back of his gloved hand. 'Don't make a joke of it, Gene. Gilroy really is a murderess, and Regan would slit your throat at the first opportunity.'

'I know it's a lot to ask, but could you make it to the High Street? There'll be drunkards falling out of the pubs, so there should be several policemen on the beat, ready for trouble.'

'I'll go, but only if you promise to stay outside. Don't go into the house, no matter what.'

'I'll be careful.' He drew her into his arms. 'You do love me, or you wouldn't care what happens to me.'

She stood on tiptoe and kissed him on the lips. 'I'll get help, just stay where you are.' She attempted to move away, but he held her close.

'Say it just once, Rose. Tell me you love me as I love you.'

She met his gaze with a tremulous smile. 'I'm not saying anything that will encourage you to risk your life in any way. I'm going to get help, and you'd better be waiting out here when I return with the police.'

'That sound like a threat, Munday.'

She threw her arms around his neck and kissed him. 'That will have to be your answer until this is over, Guvnor. From now on I'm going to be purely professional, as you taught me.'

'I should learn to mind my own business,' Eugene said ruefully.

Rose slipped away, ducking down out of sight of the windows as she left the shelter of the walled carriage sweep and encountered the driving snow. She clutched Maria's cloak around her, grateful for the fur lining and the hood that shielded her face from the worst of the storm. There were not many people on the streets, which was hardly surprising in such terrible weather, but those who had braved the elements were staggering from one pub to another. Doors opened and clouds of tobacco smoke billowed out and were swept away by the wind and snow. Drunken men staggered about crabwise on the slippery pavements, clutching at lampposts or anything they could grab as their legs gave way beneath them. Rose dodged in between them, keeping her head down and ignoring their crude remarks. She had not seen a single policeman and was just beginning to lose heart when she spotted two constables, who were breaking up a fight outside one of the more notorious pubs. She broke into a run, risking her own safety in her desperate need to get help.

They barely glanced at her at first but, having separated the two opponents and threatened the onlookers who were egging them on with prison, the older constable turned to Rose with an air of studied calm.

'What can I do for you, miss?'

'Never mind them,' Rose said urgently. 'Come with me if you want to catch a couple of real criminals.'

'What have they done, miss?' The younger man adjusted his helmet. 'Shouldn't a young lady like you be safe at home, reading the Bible and sipping sherry?'

'That's enough, Carter.'

'I was supposed to have this evening off, Trimble. Now I'm stuck out here in a snowstorm, dealing with drunks who ought to know better.'

Constable Trimble turned to Rose with a hint of a smile. 'Who are these bad people, miss?'

Ignoring his patronising tone, Rose tugged at his sleeve. 'Come with me and you'll see.' She lowered her voice. 'I don't want to say it out loud. Those men might be his friends.'

'On your way,' Carter said, waving his truncheon at the bystanders. 'I won't tell you again.'

The drunks staggered off, grumbling audibly.

'Now then, miss. Can you give me any details of these criminals?'

'Regan and Gilroy,' Rose said tersely. 'Is that good enough for you? They're hiding away in Pier House and I think they've taken two men prisoner. Do you want to catch them or not?'

'Are you sure it's them, miss?' Trimble asked urgently. 'This is a serious matter.'

'Of course I'm sure,' Rose said angrily. 'Follow me.' She hurried off, running as fast she could in the adverse conditions, and she had the satisfaction of hearing their booted feet pounding the pavement behind her. Breathless, but determined, Rose came to a halt outside the gates of Pier House. 'They were in one of the front rooms, but I can show you round to the back of the house.'

Trimble shook his head. 'No, miss. Stay where you are and leave this to us. If you're right and those two criminals are still inside, it's up to us to apprehend them.' He beckoned to Carter. 'Come with me.' They loped off into the darkness, leaving Rose standing on the pavement.

She glanced up at the sky, and, for the first time that evening she could see stars sparkling like diamonds. The snow had stopped falling, but the temperature had plummeted. Ice crystals were forming so that the pristine whiteness of the new-fallen snow reflected the lights from the docks. It was a picture of purity and loveliness, but inside the house anything could have happened. Rose picked up her skirts and followed the constables, keeping at a safe distance.

Moonlight reflected off the snow-covered lawn, turning night into a theatrical imitation of day, and Rose could see that one of the tall windows had been forced open. She entered what had once been Mrs Colville's sick room and a shiver ran down her spine. This was where Gilroy's actions had led to Clarissa Colville's untimely death. Rose stood very still, hardly daring to breathe. At first there was nothing but silence, and then she heard shouts and running footsteps, the door flew open and a female figure hurtled towards her. Acting on instinct, Rose put out her foot and the woman fell headlong onto the polished oak floorboards, where she sprawled on her belly, gasping for breath. Rose threw herself down on the struggling body, straddling Gilroy and pinning her to the floor.

'Get off me,' Gilroy growled. 'You'll pay for this.'

'Not I,' Rose said gleefully. 'I think your days of freedom are well and truly over.' She pinned the woman's arms to her sides. 'I might not be as strong as you, but I have the advantage.'

'I know who you are,' Gilroy muttered. 'You're that stuck-up bitch who stole Piggin's nipper.'

'I rescued that child from a life of crime.' Rose was forced to put all her weight on Gilroy.

'I can't breathe.'

'I'm not falling for that one. You'll stay there until the police come for you.' Rose looked up, uttering a cry of delight. 'Gene, you're all right.' She leaped to her feet, forgetting everything other than the relief of seeing him in one piece, but Gilroy was also quick to rise and she headed for the open window.

Eugene rushed past Rose and caught Gilroy before she had a chance to escape. At that moment Carter appeared, brandishing a pair of handcuffs, which he clipped around Gilroy's wrist. 'Your luck's run out, luv. You're under arrest.' He led her protesting from the room.

'Are you all right, Gene?' Rose asked anxiously.

He placed his arm around her shoulders. 'I'm fine, and so are Max and Jimmy. They're giving the constable their details.'

'And Regan?'

'Handcuffed and tied to a chair, waiting for the Black Maria to take him to the police station.'

'Take me home, Gene. I don't want to stay in this house a moment longer.'

'What about Max? Don't you want to see him first?'

Rose shook her head. 'No, not now – I need time to think.'

'You're trembling. Are you able to walk?'

'I'm cold and wet and I'm shivering. All I want is to get home to the Captain's House and have a nice hot cup of tea and then bed.'

'Come on then, Rose. We'll leave the police to sort everything out. I'm sure that Max and Jimmy can take care of themselves. Let's go.'

Next morning Rose was awakened early by Sparrow, who came bouncing into her room holding a candlestick in one hand and a woollen stocking in the other. Rose sat up and blinked as Sparrow placed the lighted candle on the table at her bedside. 'What time is it?' she demanded sleepily. 'It's still dark.'

'Merry Christmas,' Sparrow cried happily. She sat down on the edge of the bed, peering into the depths of the stocking. 'Are you sure this is for me? It was on my bed, not Polly's, so I guessed it was mine.'

'Yes, it's all yours. Have a look inside.'

Sparrow plunged her hand into the stocking and pulled out a multi-coloured glass bead necklace, followed by a small hand mirror, a tortoiseshell comb, an embroidered handkerchief and a bag of sugared almonds. 'This can't all be for me,' she said as she extricated an apple, an orange and a handful of walnuts. 'I got enough presents here for everyone in the house.'

'No, dear. It's all yours and you'll have more gifts to open later.'

'More?' Sparrow's eyes opened wide and her jaw dropped. 'You're kidding.'

'No, I'm not.' Rose leaned over to give her a hug. 'You've seen the parcels under the tree, haven't you?'

'Yes, but I never thought there was one for me.'

'Why not? Why would you think that?'

'I'm only here because you felt sorry for me.' Sparrow looked away, dashing a tear from her eyes. 'You'll send me to the workhouse when you get tired of having me around.'

Rose sat upright, staring at her in horror. 'That's just not true. Who's been filling your head with such dreadful lies?'

'Izzie said that's what toffs do when they get fed up with helping poor people. Jessie told her so.'

'Well, Jessie is wrong and she shouldn't frighten her sisters with such stories. Maria wouldn't do such a thing, and neither would I.'

'I don't talk proper, but I am trying to learn, and sometimes I forget me table manners. Izzie says I'm a pig.'

Rose moved closer and gave her a hug. 'Now, you listen to me, Sparrow. I'm not going to desert you, no matter what happens, and you mustn't take any notice of what Izzie says.'

'Why do you care, Rose? Why didn't you leave me with Ma and Piggin?'

'I was shocked to see how they treated you, and I saw something in you that reminded me of myself when I was your age.'

Sparrow's anxious expression melted into a grin. 'Am I really like you was?'

'In a way, because my ma died when I was very young and my pa had to look after me. He ran a boatyard in Chelsea and I loved the river, and still do. But we were poor and the boats he hired out were old and he couldn't afford to replace them, so he went back to sea and I came to live here with Sadie and Laurence.'

'This was your home?'

'For a few months it was, and then Sadie and Laurence took me to Australia with them, and they treated me like one of their own, even when their babies came along. So you see, you don't have to be related by blood to be part of a family.'

'Am I like that?'

'Of course you are, and don't let Izzie tell you differently.'

'She's mean sometimes,' Sparrow said thoughtfully. 'Have you got her a present, Rose?'

'Yes, of course. I wouldn't want anyone to feel left out at Christmas.'

Sparrow put her head on one side. 'Have you bought something for Mr Eugene? He's a lovely man.'

Rose stared at her in horror. 'Oh, heavens! I was so busy thinking of everyone else that I forgot Gene, and I've nothing for Max or Jimmy, either.'

'Well, they're grown-ups, so I suppose it don't matter, but I made a picture for Mr Eugene. I borrowed Polly's paint box and brushes. It took ages, but I done it all by myself.'

'That is so thoughtful of you, Sparrow. You make me feel quite ashamed.'

Sparrow studied her presents lined up on the coverlet, chewing the tip of her finger and frowning. 'You don't have to worry, Rose.' She picked up the sugared almonds and handed them to her. 'Give him these and tell them they're from you. I won't say nothing.'

Rose swallowed hard. She knew that Sparrow had a sweet tooth and that giving up one of her most favourite things was a supreme sacrifice. She shook her head as she handed them back. 'That's a lovely thought, but they are for you. I'll think of something, so don't worry.'

Sparrow leaped off the bed and ran to the door. 'I can hear Polly and Teddy. They've found their stockings. Shall I go and help them?'

'What a good idea, and I'll go downstairs and see if Cora has started making breakfast.' Rose smiled to herself as Sparrow raced from the room and her small feet pattered up the staircase, calling out to the younger children. Rose listened to their excited chatter – it would seem strange, and very quiet, when Maria and her little ones returned home. Rose shivered as her bare feet touched the floorboards, and she crossed the room to draw back the curtains. The world outside was blanketed in snow and smoke billowed from chimneys on the other side of the river. Rose went to the washstand and had what Sadie would have called a 'cat's lick' of a wash in cold water.

She dressed hastily and was seated at the dressing table, brushing the tangles out of her hair, when she remembered the events of the previous evening, which cast a pall over the excitement of Christmas morning. It was a relief to know that Regan and Gilroy were locked up and would face justice, but the row with Max had left its mark. Their future together hung in the balance and, not for the first time, Rose was beset by doubts. Maybe it was the adverse circumstances under which they had met in Cairo, or the fact that he had arrived to find Eugene in his house that had caused the rift between them to widen – or perhaps they had simply grown apart. There was another possibility that worried her even more and now a different person haunted her dreams. Her reaction to his kiss had both shocked and enthralled her, but Eugene Sheldon was a self-confessed rake. If only Cecilia were here to give her advice. Cissie loved her brother and made light of his failings, and his mother plainly adored him. Rose frowned at her reflection in the mirror. Whatever his faults, Eugene had treated her like an equal and had given her the opportunity to prove herself as a journalist. They worked well together and it would be better to keep their relationship on a professional level. It was Max who was being difficult, and if her feelings toward him had changed she must tell him so. He was a good man at heart – he would understand.

Rose pinned her hair on top of her head so that it fell in loose curls around her neck, and fastened it with a *paste barrette* that Cecilia had discarded in a box of unwanted oddments. It was Christmas

Day, after all, and a chance to dress up a little. The fact that Eugene would be coming to dinner had nothing to do with the extra care she had taken over her toilette.

She left the dressing table in a comforting jumble of hair pins, ribbons and oddments of jewellery, and as she stepped outside her room she could hear the children's excited shrieks. She made her way downstairs. It was going to be a busy day, and the sooner she put things straight between herself and Max, the better. Suddenly, the prospect of a happy day was cast into doubt. Knowing Max as she did, or had thought she did, would he accept her decision to break off their engagement? And Eugene had also promised to join them for Christmas dinner – it was going to be a difficult meal.

Rose made her way to the kitchen, but there was no sign of Cora or Flossie and the fire in the range had died down to ash with only a hint of an ember. Rose sighed and shook her head. Normally she would have told them off for over-sleeping, but they had been out celebrating last evening, and after all, it was Christmas. But the goose was still lying on the marble slab in the larder, beside a bowl of sage and onion stuffing, and the pudding mixture remained in the bowl. Rose had scant knowledge of cooking, but she remembered Sadie telling her that the pudding took several hours to cook, and nothing could be done until the fire in the range had heated the oven and the cast-iron hob.

The one thing Rose had learned in Bendigo was how to get a fire going, whether it was in the range in Sadie's large kitchen, or in a bush camp, and after a couple of failed attempts she managed to get the flames licking greedily around the kindling. She was about to add lumps of coal when she heard a frantic knocking on the front door, and she hurried up the stairs to the hallway.

'All right,' she called out. 'I'm coming.' She opened the door, half expecting to see a police constable requesting yet another statement, or even Max who had come to apologise, but her visitors were the three Spriggs sisters.

Jessie stepped into the hall without waiting for an invitation, followed by Edna and Izzie, who stamped the snow off their boots on the rush matting.

'Blooming freezing out there,' Jessie said angrily. 'And there's no coal in the cellar at home. The cat ate the chicken we was going to have for our dinner and the plum pudding exploded in the pan. It's spread up the walls and hit the ceiling – you never saw such a mess.'

'That's awful, but what can I do about it?' Rose asked warily.

'You're a good Christian lady, miss,' Jessie said silkily. 'You took two fallen women into your home, so I'm sure you can spare some Christmas fare to us poor starving souls.'

'Yes,' Izzie added, grinning. 'We come to dinner, miss. And we ain't had no breakfast neither.'

Chapter Twenty-Five

Cora and Flossie joined them, apologising profusely, and Rose escaped to the front parlour leaving them to cope with the two elder Spriggs sisters, Izzie having rushed upstairs to reclaim her charges. Rose positioned herself on the window seat, preparing for the inevitable spate of complaints from all parties. Jessie, it seemed, could not resist the temptation to interfere in the kitchen, while Cora was visibly hungover and in no mood to be tolerant. Flossie openly disliked Jessie and Edna, and the feeling appeared to be mutual, despite the fact that they had seemed to be getting on well initially.

Rose turned her head as the door burst open to admit Maria. Her cheeks were flushed and she was breathing heavily. 'It's ridiculous,' she said angrily. 'The goose isn't going to feed all of us and neither is the Christmas pudding. Are you sure that Max and Jimmy are coming for dinner?'

'I had to invite them,' Rose said apologetically. 'And I'm afraid I asked Eugene to join us, too.'

'What are we going to do? I'd send the sisters home, but they have nothing to eat.'

'We'll have to make do. We have the hamper from Fortnum's.'

'That's true, and you're right, of course. It is Christmas Day and everyone should be welcome.

'Even the Spriggs sisters?'

Maria pulled a face. 'I suppose so. Mind you, Rose, I'm regretting my decision to give them a home. It's not their former profession that bothers me – I can accept that some unfortunates have to sell their bodies in order to live – but Jessie's constant sermonising is driving me mad. She would do better to become a missionary in some far-off country.'

'I think you've solved the problem,' Rose said thoughtfully. 'As I told you before, it was Festus Parker who introduced me to Eugene.'

'How might that help?' Maria demanded crossly. 'There's a war about to break out in the kitchen. Cora insists on smoking and Jessie keeps telling her that tobacco and alcohol were invented by the devil, and then Flossie stands up for Cora and Edna puts in her two penn'orth.'

'It's still early,' Rose said slowly. 'Tell Jessie to get ready. We're going to church.'

'What?' Maria stared at her open-mouthed. 'Are you leaving me to cope on my own?'

'Not at all. Cora will take over in the kitchen, and Flossie can help you lay the table. I'm going to find God's work for Jessie and Edna.'

'What are you going to do, Rose?'

'I'm taking the ladies to meet Festus. The Parkers are certain to attend morning service, and all I have to do is find their local church, which shouldn't be difficult. I'll let Jessie speak for herself and hope that Festus will guide her footsteps to the sort of life she yearns for.'

'I hope you're right.' Maria shrugged, shaking her head. 'But anything is better than listening to the squabbling going on in the kitchen. I'll give Jessie the glad tidings.'

'Good. It's time I called on the Parkers, anyway. I need to thank them for what they did for me.'

'As I recall they abandoned you in London with nowhere to go,' Maria said caustically. 'However, if they can take Jessie off my hands I will love them for ever.'

The High Street was eerily silent with very little traffic, and the only pedestrians were those making their way to church. Rose stood on the edge of the kerb trying to attract the odd passing cab, but all were taken and Jessie was beginning to complain. Edna had insisted on accompanying them, but Izzie had been left behind to supervise the children. Rose was glad to be out of the house, and if she were not there to greet Max and Jimmy, at least she had a good excuse. No one could criticise her for attending church on Christmas Day, but getting to Spitalfields from Wapping seemed to be an almost impossible task with so few cabs on the streets. It was with mixed feelings that she recognised Eugene's carriage as it drew alongside the kerb.

Eugene stuck his head out of the window. 'I was on my way to see you, Rose. Where are you going?'

'To church, but we'll miss the service if we can't get a cab soon.'

He opened the door and alighted before Giddings had a chance to jump down from the box. 'Where do you want to go?'

'I don't know exactly, but the Parkers live in Elder Street, so it will be the nearest church.'

Eugene repeated the instruction to Giddings, who passed it on to Simms. 'Allow me.' He handed Jessie and Enda into the carriage and, for once, both were speechless. 'Now you, Rose.' He sat down beside her. 'I didn't know you were religious.'

The teasing note in his voice and the twinkle in his eyes made it almost impossible to keep a straight face, but she managed with a supreme effort. 'I'm a woman of many surprises. Anyway, I thought it was time I saw Adele and Festus, if only to thank them for putting me in touch with you.'

He shot a curious glance at the Spriggs sisters, who were staring fixedly out of the window. 'And who are these ladies? I don't think we've met.'

Jessie eyed him suspiciously and Edna stifled a giggle.

'This is Jessie Spriggs and her sister Edna. They've been looking after Maria's house in Great Hermitage Street, and they're joining us for Christmas dinner.'

'Delighted to make your acquaintance, ladies,' Eugene said cheerfully. 'It's quite some time since I attended church.'

Rose smiled and said nothing, but she crossed her fingers, hoping that Festus and Adele were among the congregation, otherwise this journey would have been for nothing.

The church was crowded with worshippers, and at first, Rose could not see the Parkers. She was beginning to wonder if they had been sent to another mission, but during the first hymn she recognised the unmistakable baritone that could only belong to one person. Jessie sang loudly, mostly in tune, but even she could not drown Festus Parker's heartfelt rendition of every hymn and prayer. Rose tried to concentrate on the service but it was almost impossible with Eugene sitting so close that she could feel the warmth of his body, and his fingers closed around hers during the last hymn.

'Now what?' he whispered as they waited to join the exodus from the church.

'The Parkers were the first to leave,' Rose said anxiously. 'Could you head them off, Gene? I really need to speak to them.'

'Leave it to me.' He slid into the slowly moving crowd and threaded his way to the front.

Rose sighed with relief as she waited her turn to leave in an orderly manner with Jessie and Edna tagging on.

Outside, in the narrow passage between White Lion Street and Lamb Street, Eugene's tall figure and elegant attire made his stand out amongst those who were shorter and less well-dressed. He looked up as if sensing Rose's presence and greeted her with a smile.

'Rose, look who I've just met.'

She hurried to join them. 'Mr and Mrs Parker, Merry Christmas.'

Adele broke away from her husband to give Rose a warm embrace. 'My dear, how well you look. It's lovely to see you again.'

Festus nodded gravely. 'Eugene tells me that you've had an article printed in the newspaper, Rose. Well done, indeed.'

'It wouldn't have happened had you not introduced me to Eugene,' Rose said tactfully. She beckoned to Jessie and Edna, who were hovering a few feet away. 'May I introduce Miss Jessie Spriggs and her sister Edna? Jessie, Edna, this gentleman is Mr Festus Parker and this lady is his wife, Adele. They are missionaries, something that I think is dear to your heart, Jessie.'

Festus acknowledged them with a curt bow. 'Ladies.'

'How nice to meet you, my dears,' Adele said, shaking them by the hand. 'Won't you join us for a cup of coffee?'

Jessie bobbed an awkward curtsey, as if in the presence of royalty. 'Thank you kindly, ma'am. I am thinking of putting myself forward for missionary work, and my sister also, but we have duties to attend to in Wapping. I would not want to let the mistress down, even if it means suppressing my own inclination to accept your gracious invitation.'

Rose exchanged amused glances with Eugene. Jessie was obviously doing her best to impress the Parkers, and judging by the expression on their faces, her humble words had met with approval.

'An admirable sentiment,' Festus said, beaming. 'I understand perfectly, but we are always looking for helpers. If you would like to call on me in a couple of days' time, we can discuss matters over a cup of tea.'

'Oh, yes, sir. Thank you, sir.' Jessie's face split in a wide grin.

Adele laid her hand on her husband's arm. 'We could do with some assistance today, dear.' She turned to Rose with a persuasive smile. 'We're giving a Christmas meal to the poor and needy in rooms above the Pewter Platter in White Lion Street. Mr Fowler, the licensee, has very kindly allowed us the use of his kitchen.'

'Jessie is a keen cook,' Rose said hastily. 'I'm sure we can manage at home, if Jessie and Edna wish to help Mr and Mrs Parker.'

'And that would be an excellent item for the next edition of my newspaper,' Eugene added. 'We're doing a feature on Christmas stories, aren't we, Rose?'

She nodded vigorously. 'And as such I'm sure that the *Leader* would be most generous in contributing to your next venture.'

'We'll stay, Guvnor,' Jessie said eagerly. 'I can roll up me sleeves with the best of 'em, and Edna and me can talk to the unfortunates on their level, so to speak. We've been poor sinners, and now we're saved.'

'Amen,' Edna said vaguely.

'Come, Rose.' Eugene tucked her hand in the crook of his arm. 'We must let these good people go about their business.'

'Of course.' Rose kissed Adele on the cheek. 'I'll see you very soon, I promise.'

Eugene pressed some coins into Jessie's hand. 'This will get you back to Great Hermitage Street when you're finished here.'

'Yes, and don't worry about Izzie,' Rose said before Jessie had a chance to argue. 'She can stay with us tonight. That will save you a double journey.'

'That's settled then.' Festus backed away, motioning Adele and the sisters to follow him. 'We have God's work to do.'

'And we need to get home,' Rose said in a low voice. 'Maria will be coping on her own, but at least it should be more peaceful now.'

Max was pacing the floor in the front parlour when Rose walked into the room. Maria jumped to her feet, frowning.

'What took you so long, Rose? The goose will be cooked to a cinder.'

Jimmy looked up from the newspaper he had been reading. 'I'm sure it will be fine, Maria. Don't fuss.'

'It's all very well for you, Jimmy,' Maria said crossly. 'But I've had hungry children pestering me for an hour or more.'

'Then they'll enjoy their meal even more.' Jimmy folded the newspaper and set it aside. 'The piece you wrote about that family in Bow is very touching, Rose.'

'Never mind all that, Jimmy,' Max said irritably. 'I want a few words with Rose, in private.'

Rose glanced at Eugene, who was close behind her. 'I'm sorry I was out when you arrived, Max, but you might call it a mission of mercy.'

'Where are the sisters?' Maria asked anxiously. 'I hope they didn't rush downstairs to the kitchen. Cora is likely to set about them with a rolling pin if they make any adverse comments.'

'There's no need to worry. They're helping to feed the poor and needy,' Rose said, smiling. 'And I think, if Festus has his way, they'll be fully occupied with good works from now on.'

'Rose, a word, if you please.' Max grabbed her by the arm. 'This is ridiculous. I come home expecting to find my fiancée waiting for me, and it seems that your interests are elsewhere.'

'Steady on, old chap.' Eugene's tone had a sharp edge.

Max rounded on him. 'Keep out of this, Sheldon. I blame you for the current situation.'

'Stop it, both of you.' Rose shook free from Max's restraining hand. 'I won't talk to you while you're in this bullying mood. Everything you say makes me glad that we aren't engaged.'

'You don't mean that, Rose.'

Maria hurried to the door and held it open. 'I'm going to call the children to the table, and that includes you, Max. We're going to have our Christmas dinner in peace and harmony, or I'll want to know the reason why.' She stepped into the hallway, calling the children's names.

Jimmy stood up and stretched. 'I agree with Maria. No more bickering, if you please.'

Max proffered his arm to Rose. 'Allow me.'

She was tempted to walk past without acknowledging his attempt at peace-making, but she knew it would make matters worse, and she laid her hand on his sleeve. 'We'll talk about this later,' she said in a low voice. 'But I'll never speak to you again if you ruin the children's Christmas.'

The meal passed off surprisingly well, largely due to Eugene's efforts. He kept the children amused with accounts of the scrapes he had got into as a boy, and the dire punishments he had received. Sparrow hung on his every word, as did Izzie, who was clearly impressed and rendered speechless. Max countered with stories of his experiences on the battlefield, which made the two older girls stare open-mouthed, until Maria put a stop to a tale that was likely to conclude with gory details. Jimmy was more successful with tales of his misfortunes as a midshipman and junior officer, and his vivid descriptions of dolphins, whales and flying fish. Polly wanted to know if he had seen any mermaids and was quite tearful when he replied that they were only to be found in fairy stories. Eugene saved the situation by telling Polly about narwhals, whose long ivory tusks had been brought back by seafarers in the past, convincing some people that they had come from the legendary unicorn. Then Cora brought in the showpiece, which was a pudding with blue flames licking round it as the brandy burned away. She served generous portions, doused in custard for the children and brandy butter for the adults. There was a brief period of silence while everyone ate, hoping to find one of the silver charms at the bottom of their plate.

When the meal was over Maria ushered everyone into the parlour to give out the presents from beneath the tree. The candles had been lit and the tinsel shivered in the draught and twinkled as brightly as any star. There were cries of delight from the children and Sparrow insisted on rushing upstairs to put on her new frock and the bead necklace. Izzie had tears in her eyes as she opened her gift of a muffler and hat, and Rose had added a bag of sweets, which met with her instant approval. Cora and Flossie were delighted with their gifts and retired to the kitchen saying they were going to wash the dishes, although Rose suspected that they would end up sitting round the table, drinking port and smoking cigarillos. Maria loved her shawl, and her present to Rose was a silver-backed hand mirror and matching comb.

It was time for Rose to confess, but she waited until Izzie had taken the younger children upstairs. 'I'm afraid I have nothing for you, Max and Jimmy, because I didn't know you would be here, and the same goes for you, too, Gene.'

Jimmy sipped his brandy and declared that spending Christmas with the family was a treat in itself, but Max put his hand in his breast pocket and took out a small velvet-covered box. He flicked it open and a large diamond sparkled in the firelight. He seized Rose's hand and went down on one knee.

'My dearest Rose, I know we haven't got off to a good start, but I'm sincere in my regard for you, and this is the ring I promised you all those months ago in Bendigo. I would be honoured if you would agree to marry me.' He took the ring from the box and slipped it on her finger.

'I – I don't know what to say,' she murmured, glancing at Eugene.

Max sent him a triumphant look. 'Can you beat that, Sheldon?'

Eugene shook his head. 'I wouldn't be so crass as to try.'

'Congratulations, Max,' Jimmy said, slapping his brother on his back. 'Rose is a diamond beyond price.'

'Yes, I second that,' Maria added, giving Rose a hug. 'That makes us true sisters, Rose.'

Rose stared at the diamond as it flashed white fire on her left hand, and she was lost for words. To refuse in front of the family would humiliate Max further, and she had loved him once. Eugene could have intervened, but he had refused to say anything and she felt as if she had walked into a huge spider's web and was entwined in its silken mesh, unable to break free.

'Well, Rose, my love. Will you give me an answer?' Max raised her hand to his lips, holding her gaze.

There was silence in the room and everyone was staring at them. Rose was so shaken that all she could do was nod.

'I take that as my answer, Rose.' Max swept her into an embrace that was more possessive than passionate.

'Have we any champagne, Maria? This calls for a toast.'

'Yes, indeed. I think there was a bottle in the Fortnum's hamper. That's if Cora and Flossie haven't drunk it.' Maria made for the door but Eugene forestalled her. 'Thank you for taking pity on a lonely bachelor. I've enjoyed your hospitality, but I must leave now.'

'Won't you stay a little longer?' Rose suddenly found her voice. 'It's still early.'

He shook his head. 'No, but thank you for the offer. I sent Simms and Giddings back to Tavistock Square, so I'll have to find a cab or walk, but I'll see you tomorrow, Rose. I'll need your contribution to Wednesday's edition.' He left the room without a backwards glance.

Rose met Max's triumphant smile with a sudden rush of anger and she wrenched the ring off her finger. 'You took me by surprise and you didn't give me a chance to speak, Max.'

'What's the matter, Rose? You accepted my

proposal in front of witnesses. We've been unofficially engaged for months – isn't this what you were waiting for? You travelled all the way to London so that we could be together.'

'I'm sorry, Max, but I don't feel the same as I did then. If you'd been here to meet me, things might have been different.'

'That wasn't my fault, and you know it. I'm a soldier and I have to obey orders.'

'I know that.' Rose shook her head. 'Please don't make this harder than it already is – I'd like us to part as friends.'

'I have to rejoin my regiment in the New Year, but I think we'll be returning to England in February. We'll get to know each other all over again. I'll bring you flowers and gifts, if that's what you want.'

'No,' Rose said firmly. 'I'm sorry, Max, but I don't want to marry you.' She pressed the ring into his hand and headed for the door.

'You need more time,' Max called after her. 'But I won't wait for ever.'

Maria caught up with her at the foot of the stairs. 'Rose, you're upset and it was stupid of Max to spring it on you like that. Maybe he's right and you ought to give yourself time to think it over.'

Rose shook her head. 'I'll always be fond of Max, but marriage is out of the question. I won't change my mind.'

*　　　*　　　*

Rose sat on the edge of her bed, staring at her left hand, naked now that she had returned the ring to Max. His proposal had caught her off guard and she was annoyed with him for putting her in such an invidious position. Even so, she could have handled the situation better, but she had made her decision and she still had a job to do. Eugene had reminded her that he needed her next piece on the Norman family, and she must put personal feelings aside.

She made herself comfortable and reached for the notebook and pencil she kept on a table at the side of her bed. She started to write, continuing the story with Harry's visit to the ophthalmologist, but it was incomplete – there was no happy ending – there was no Christmas miracle. They had left the family with food for a few days only and then they would be back where they started, unless Winnie Norman had a change of heart. If Eugene fulfilled his promise of finding Harry work at Greenfields, with a cottage for the family, there was hope for them, but everything had been left hanging in the balance. She lay back against the pillows and closed her eyes.

The sound of Maria's voice awakened Rose with a start and she sat up in bed. 'What time is it?'

Maria placed a cup of tea on the table and went to draw back the curtains, allowing a stream of sunlight to filter through the small windowpanes.

'It's nearly nine o'clock.' She turned to look at her with a wry smile. 'You must have been exhausted. You went to bed fully clothed.'

Rose glanced down at the bodice of her best gown and pulled a face. 'Oh, heavens! I was trying to complete my article for the paper and I must have dozed off.'

'Your job means a lot to you, doesn't it, Rose?'

'Yes, I suppose it does.'

'Even more than Max?'

'I'm sorry for making a scene last evening, but Max took me unawares. He shouldn't have proposed in front of everyone.'

'By everyone, do you mean Eugene?'

Rose shook her head. 'I don't know. Please don't say things like that. It makes things even more confusing.'

Maria perched on the edge of the bed. 'Max said he would come back this morning. You two need to talk, Rose. That's all I'm saying.'

'I expect you're right, but it won't make any difference to the way I feel. I'll get up and make myself presentable.'

Maria leaned over to kiss her on the cheek. 'I know I don't have to remind you, but this house belongs to Caroline and she might not allow you to stay here if you've upset her brother. I know it sounds petty, but Max could turn you out if he chose to do so.'

'I suppose so.'

'You're more than welcome to come and live with me, but if you do I'll have to ask for a contribution to the household. I'm sorry, Rose, but Theo isn't a wealthy man, and I could only afford to keep the Spriggs sisters because I paid them so little.'

'Of course,' Rose said earnestly. 'I understand perfectly, and I'll ask Eugene for more assignments. I'll pay my way.'

'Thank you. I hate to bring up the subject of money, but one has to be practical.' Maria rose to her feet and made her way to the door. 'I'm sure everything will work out for the best. You might even change your mind about Max if you spend more time together. Maybe it's all been a silly mistake.'

Chapter Twenty-Six

Rose was sitting on the window seat in the parlour, trying hard to think of a suitable ending for her piece. Outside the sun was shining palely from a cloudless opal sky, and the river looked quite benign at the turn of the tide. Small craft and large boats, barges and wherries were on the move, despite the bank holiday. There were patches of rapidly melting snow in sheltered spots, but the wharf was largely clear. She had a sudden desire to put on her bonnet and cape and go for a long walk in order to clear her head. Her nerves were on edge, and any moment she expected to see Max striding towards the house as if he had not a care in the world. She knew him well enough to realise that he was not one to give up easily, especially when his pride was hurt, and Maria's words had made her understand the gravity of her situation. Supporting herself in London on the money she might earn writing for the *Leader* was a daunting prospect, and one she had not faced until now. The unpalatable truth was that she could neither afford the upkeep of the Captain's House nor the wages she would have to pay Cora and Flossie.

The sound of someone knocking on the front door brought her back to earth, and she jumped to her feet. If it was Max it would be best if they spoke freely without interruption. She hurried to open the front door, but the speech she had prepared went out of her head when she saw Eugene standing on the top step.

'May I come in?'

'Of course.' Rose stood aside, closing the door after him. 'I was in the parlour, trying to complete the article on the Norman family.' She followed him into the room. 'You haven't allowed me much time to get it finished.'

'As a matter of fact I came to collect you, Rose. I don't want to upset your fiancé's plans, but I promised the Normans I'd take them to Greenfields, and today seems as good a day as any.'

'It's all right. I have no plans, other than finishing this wretched piece. I'm stuck – I admit it.'

'Don't worry. It happens to us all at times, and all you need is fresh material. Get your bonnet and cloak, and you'll need gloves and a muffler, too. There's a chilly wind.'

'We're going to Greenfields now?'

'I sent the barouche to collect the family. We'll travel in my Tilbury, but I left a youth holding the horse's reins, so if you could hurry it would be much appreciated, Munday. We have work to do.'

Eugene's casual manner came as a pleasant contrast to the tension she had felt when in Max's company, and she uttered a sigh of relief. 'I'll just tell Maria where I'm going and I'll be ready in two ticks.'

'I'm not taking you away from anything important, am I, Munday?' Eugene handed her into the Tilbury. Taking the reins from the boy who had been minding the carriage, Eugene tossed him a coin and climbed in beside her.

'No,' Rose said airily. 'I had nothing planned.'

'I was afraid your fiancé would object to us working together.'

'I returned his ring. I was taken by surprise when he proposed in front of everyone and I meant to say no, but I found myself nodding. I rectified my mistake.'

'So you're a free woman?'

She smiled. 'I am, and I'm determined to work hard and prove myself to be as capable a journalist as any of my male counterparts.'

'Now there's a challenge, Munday. Perhaps you could start by persuading Winnie Norman that a move to the country would be in their best interests. I'm certain it would benefit Harry and the young-sters, but Winnie is proud and independent. I think you might talk to her on equal terms.'

'You think I'm proud and independent?'

'I'd say that sums you up, Munday.'

Rose sat back, watching him handle the reins with surprising expertise, which became even more apparent when they left the crowded city streets and headed out into the country. The lanes were deeply rutted, and the bare hedgerows were in stark contrast to the snow-covered fields. Rose pointed to a solitary scarecrow that had been abandoned to the mercy of the elements. 'Just look at that poor thing. He looks so sad and lonely.'

Eugene glanced over his shoulder. 'I'm sorry, Rose. I draw a line at rescuing solitary scarecrows.'

'He isn't alone,' Rose said, laughing. 'He has a robin perched on the crown of his hat.'

'That's a relief. I won't have to worry then.'

'If I lived round here I would find the scarecrow a place in a nice warm barn, where he could spend the rest of the winter.'

'I'll make that Harry's first job.'

'Do you mean to say that this is your land?'

'I am a countryman at heart, and yes this is part of Greenfields. We're nearly there.'

Rose leaned forward in order to get a better view. In the distance she could see ornate red-brick chimneys rising from a slate roof with smoke spiralling up into the azure sky. 'Is that your home, Gene?'

'That is Greenfields. It's a sixteenth-century farmhouse with bits added on by successive generations.'

Rose studied his profile as he encouraged the horse to a brisk trot. 'You love it, don't you? I can tell by the tone of your voice.'

He shot her a sideways glance. 'My family have lived and farmed here for over two hundred years.'

'But your father is in the diplomatic service.'

'He wanted nothing to do with the land, although he's happy to accept the income it provides, which is a pittance compared to the fortune my mother inherited.' He reined in the horse and leaped off the box to open a pair of wrought-iron gates. 'Welcome to Greenfields, Rose.'

Having led the animal a little way along a wide drive, Eugene climbed back onto his seat and flicked the reins. 'Walk on.' He turned to Rose with a smile of genuine pleasure. 'We've beaten the barouche so I'll be able to take you on a tour of the house before the Normans arrive.'

'That would be lovely.' Rose took in every detail of the rambling two-storey, half-timbered house and fell instantly in love with Greenfields. As she alighted on the gravel forecourt she felt as if she had come home at last, and yet this was the first time she had set foot on the property. 'It must be so beautiful in the summer,' she said softly. 'I've always wanted to own a house with roses growing round the door.' She came to a halt as she spotted a clump of pure white flowers growing in a sheltered bed. 'Flowers in December – can you believe that?'

Eugene followed her gaze. 'They call them Christmas roses. I've always loved them since I was a boy. Greenfields is noted for them.' He handed the reins to a young boy who had come running from somewhere at the rear of the building. 'Take good care of him, Finn.'

'This is such a lovely place,' Rose said enthusiastically. 'I can't wait to see inside.'

Eugene made a move towards the metal-studded oak door, which opened as if by magic. 'Mrs Cardew – one step ahead of me, as always.'

To Rose's surprise, Eugene gave the small, thin woman a hug and she responded with a giggle and a blush colouring her sallow cheeks.

'Mr Eugene, you're embarrassing me in front of your young lady.'

'No,' Rose said hastily. 'I'm not . . .'

Eugene turned to her with a wide smile. 'Rose, I wanted you to meet the woman who kept me on the straight and narrow during my salad days when I was a wild youth.'

'And you're not too old for a slap on the wrist now, sir.' Mrs Cardew glowered at him, but Rose did not miss the twinkle in the older woman's grey eyes.

'How do you do, ma'am? I'm very pleased to meet you.'

'Well, that goes for me, too, miss. Won't you come in out of the cold?' Mrs Cardew turned on Eugene with a mock frown. 'Where are you manners, sir?'

Eugene stood aside while Mrs Cardew ushered Rose into the stone-flagged hall. The first thing she noticed was the scent of burning pine logs and of lavender, hung in great bunches, from the oak beams. The heat from a fire blazing up the chimney was more than welcome, but Rose had little time to admire the stone mantelshelf or the carved antique furniture. Mrs Cardew led her at speed along a narrow wainscoted passageway and Rose was shown into the drawing room.

'Now then, I'm going to the kitchen to order tea and cakes for the young lady,' Mrs Cardew said, still glowering at Eugene, who had followed them without protest. 'She must be hungry after such a long journey in the freezing cold. Lord knows why you didn't bring her in the barouche, sir. And don't tell me any more about the deserving family of the soldier blinded in battle, because I reserve judgement on whether or not they should be given such open-handed treatment.' Mrs Cardew whisked out of the room, leaving Rose and Eugene gazing fixedly into space, but when the door closed they broke down into laughter.

'You see how I'm treated,' Eugene said, shaking his head.

'I see a woman who clearly adores you, and treats you like a naughty schoolboy. I think it's very touching, Gene.'

'You're right, I suppose, but it does get a little tiresome. However, I wouldn't hurt Cardy's feelings for the world.'

Rose went to stand by the fire, warming her hands. 'This is a delightful room. It has such a lovely mellow atmosphere. It's wonderful to think of the generations of your family who have lived here, and the dramas that must have happened in this very room.' She glanced at the highly polished floorboards, gleaming with the patina of centuries of loving care, and the comfortable chairs and sofas upholstered in handcrafted tapestries. Outside she caught a glimpse of a parterre garden, blanketed in snow, with the occasional stone statue standing naked but oblivious to the cold.

Eugene crossed the floor and took her by the hand. 'Let's escape for a few minutes, and I'll show you the rest of the house. It's not huge, but there are plenty of places to hide, as I discovered when I was a boy.'

'I'd love to see everything, but we mustn't offend Mrs Cardew.'

'Cardy is used to me, Rose. I don't know how I'd manage without her.'

Hand in hand they crept out of the room like a pair of naughty children, and Rose entered the world that belonged exclusively to Eugene. He showed her the gun room, lined with trophies from the past, and the garden room where empty jardinières begged to be filled once again with exotic indoor plants. The still room and the boot room were at the back of the house, as were the kitchen and the larders and store rooms. The servants greeted them with smiling faces, which was a startling contrast to the underlings employed in Tavistock Square, who were trained to avoid eye contact with their superiors and only to speak when spoken to.

From the servants' hall to the rooms upstairs, Greenfields was not luxuriously appointed, but it had a lived-in, comfortable atmosphere. Rose could have spent all day happily exploring, but from one of the attic rooms they saw the barouche drawing to a halt outside, and they raced downstairs to greet the visitors.

Winnie Norman was clutching Daisy in her arms as if afraid to put her down, and Mary clung to her mother's skirts, while Benny and Billy lingered behind, gazing round as if stunned by the size and comparative opulence of their surroundings. Giddings led Harry into the entrance hall with a pained expression on his face.

'Thank you, Giddings,' Mrs Cardew said firmly. 'When Simms has stabled the horses you'll receive sustenance in the servants' hall.'

Giddings nodded and marched off, head held high.

Rose noted that he closed the front door quietly behind him, and she smiled. It seemed that everyone was in awe of the formidable Mrs Cardew, apart from Eugene.

Eugene stepped forward to shake Harry's hand. 'Welcome to Greenfields. I'll show you round the farm and gardens later, but first I'm sure you'd all like something to eat and drink. Mrs Cardew has kindly had refreshments laid out for you in the drawing room, so if you'd like to follow Rose she'll take you there while I have a quick word with Harry. We'll join you in a moment.'

Mrs Cardew bustled to the fore. 'I'd better go first, in case you've forgotten the way, miss. The old house, with its twisting passages, can be confusing. Follow me, children, and don't touch anything.'

Rose realised that she had been put firmly in her place, but she could hardly blame the woman, who seemed to have been Eugene's surrogate mother in his formative years. She followed them, trying to imagine Elizabeth Sheldon living in the old farmhouse and failing. Eugene's mother was a beautiful, charming woman with all the social graces, but she lacked warmth and empathy, and perhaps that explained why her son and daughter had grown up searching for something they had lacked in childhood. Rose reached the drawing room just as Mrs Cardew was leaving. She looked her in the eye and smiled.

'Thank you, ma'am, and don't worry, I'll watch the young ones. I used to help to keep order in my guardian's school, so I know what to expect.'

'Thank you, Miss Rose. That's a weight off my mind. I dare say they mean no harm, but I can't abide sticky fingerprints on the furniture, and some of the family heirlooms are priceless.'

Rose entered the room to find the children lined up on the sofa like dolls in a shop window, their hands clasped in their laps while they gazed fixedly at the plate of small cakes set before them on a low table. Winnie had taken a seat in an armchair by the fire and young Daisy had fallen asleep on her shoulder. Rose decided to take charge. She gave each child a plate with two cakes on it and she poured tea for Winnie, placing the cup and saucer on a table at the side of her chair, and adding a plate of cakes.

'This is a very grand house, miss,' Winnie said in a low voice. 'I should feel more at home in the kitchen.'

Rose pulled up a stool and sat next to her. 'If you aren't comfortable with this you must say so. I know you want to do the best for Harry, but you and the children must come first.'

'Ta, miss. I've hardly slept for worrying. It's kind of Mr Eugene, but I'm a Londoner born and bred, and I don't know how I'd get on in the country.'

Rose patted her on the shoulder. 'See how you feel when you've seen the cottage, and, remember, you don't have to make up your mind today. You can go home and think it over, and you must discuss it with Harry, and the youngsters, too. Although I believe Mr Sheldon said there is a very good village school.'

'I'll bear it in mind, miss.' Winnie gazed longingly at the tea and cake.

'May I hold Daisy?' Rose asked gently. 'Just while you drink your tea, of course.'

Winnie passed the sleeping child to Rose, but Daisy began to whimper. Rose stood up, and was cradling the small child in her arms, rocking her gently when Eugene guided Harry into the room.

'You seem to have a knack with little ones, Rose.' Eugene helped Harry to a chair and placed some tea and cakes within reach.

Rose hitched the sleeping infant into a more comfortable position. 'I had plenty of practice helping Sadie with her babies, and little Daisy seems quite placid.'

'Daisy don't take to everyone,' Harry said through a mouthful of cake. 'And I ain't heard a peep out of the boys since they got here, nor Mary neither.'

'That's because this ain't a farm,' Billy said despondently. 'I ain't seen no animals.'

'That's easy enough to remedy.' Eugene handed the cakes round and eager hands reached out to grab the last of them. 'When you're ready we'll do the tour.' He turned to Winnie. 'And I'm sure you're keen to see the cottage.'

'Yes, sir. But it will have to be as big as the one we rent in Bow, or it won't do. I don't want to sound ungrateful, but we're city dwellers and we don't understand country ways.'

'It will be your choice, Mrs Norman,' Eugene said calmly. 'It will be for you and Harry to decide what's best for the family.'

The sun had disappeared behind a bank of iron-clad clouds by the time everyone was muffled up and ready to go outside. Eugene had sent for Giles, his farm manager, and Giles took Harry and the boys on a tour of the farm outbuildings, followed by a cart ride to see the livestock that were hardy enough to overwinter in the fields. That left Eugene and Rose free to take Winnie and the two little girls to see the cottage where they would live, should they decide to accept his offer. It was easy walking distance from the main house and the cottage was set on a rise, sheltered by a stand of trees. The view from the front door was breath-taking and Rose could have stood all day gazing at the neatly hedged fields sloping down to a silver ribbon of river, where the bare branches of willows dipped into the water.

She clutched Eugene's arm. 'What river is that, Gene?'

'It's the Thames. We're a couple of miles upriver from where you were born, Rose.'

'It's beautiful,' she breathed. 'What a wonderful view.'

'Never mind the view, duck,' Winnie said, shivering. 'This looks like a nice house, but can we go and see the cottage now, sir? Me and the nippers are freezing to death.'

Eugene produced a bunch of keys and opened the door. 'This would be your home, should you decide to make the move, Winnie.'

Winnie stared at him open-mouthed and it was Daisy who toddled into the cottage first, followed by Mary.

Rose gave Winnie a gentle shove and she tottered into the narrow entrance hall, from which a staircase led up to the first floor. Two doors on either side of the hall opened into rooms far more spacious than those of the ground floor of the Normans' present home in Bow.

'You're joking, sir? It ain't fair to tease a poor woman.' Winnie wandered into the living room like a sleepwalker.

'This would be your house,' Eugene said firmly.

Rose looked around with an approving nod. 'It's a nice size, Winnie, and the range seems to be in good condition.'

Winnie trailed her fingers over the dusty cast iron. 'A bit of black lead will bring this up a treat. I ain't had a proper oven since my old man passed away.' She turned to Eugene with trembling lips. 'Are you sure this is meant for us, sir? Is there another family going to share it?'

Eugene shook his head. 'I can assure you that your family will be the only people living here. Why don't you have a good look around? I believe the bedsteads were left behind by the previous tenant, and I'm sure we can find you some furniture from the attics in the big house, should you require it, of course.'

'Ma.' Mary appeared suddenly through a back door. 'Come here. There's a wash-house with a copper, just like the one where you work, and there's a blooming big mangle – bigger than me.'

Winnie hurried to examine the latest treasure, returning moments later with a wide grin. 'There's a stone sink and a pump what works. We won't have to go down the street for water.'

'I'm afraid the privy is out in the garden,' Eugene said apologetically. 'It's built over a stream so it's really quite convenient.'

'Do the people from the cottages lower down share it with us?' Winnie asked anxiously. 'You don't have to come here from the big house, do you?'

Eugene threw back his head and laughed. 'Lord, no! It's all yours, Winnie. No one will bother you if you live here. There's a parlour for your use and there are three bedrooms upstairs.'

Winnie collapsed on her knees, covering her face with her hands. 'It ain't fair to show us this when we won't be able to afford to live here.'

Eugene raised her gently to her feet. 'I need a good man to help Giles, and if Harry is keen to learn, the cottage is yours for a peppercorn rent. The boys will go to school and they can help at harvest time and learn to do odd jobs around the house. Go upstairs, have a good look round and see what you think.'

Mary grabbed her mother's hand. 'I been up there already, Ma. It's like a palace and there are big beds in all the rooms. I won't have to sleep in a drawer now. Come and see.'

Winnie scooped Daisy up in her arms. 'Well, I never! I dunno what to say.'

'We'll leave you to explore properly,' Eugene said, taking Rose by the hand. 'Giles will bring Harry and the boys here, and if you feel like joining them on the wagon ride, please do so. I have a surprise for Rose.'

'What is it, Gene?'

He led her out of the cottage, closing the door firmly behind them. 'It won't be a surprise if I tell you.' Eugene tucked her hand through the crook of his arm. 'I have your Christmas present in the house, and I'm only sorry I couldn't get it for you on the right day.'

'It sounds exciting, but it makes me feel even worse because I didn't get anything for you.'

'There is something I would like, but I'll tell you later.'

'That's not fair,' Rose said breathlessly as she tried

to keep up with his long strides. 'Being mysterious doesn't suit you, Gene. You usually come right out with whatever is on your mind.'

'Not this time. I had to force myself to keep quiet, but not for much longer.'

'Now I am really curious.' Rose gave up trying to speak as the cold air and the fast pace made it virtually impossible, but she managed to keep up with him until they reached the house.

'You're back early, sir.' Mrs Cardew passed them in the hallway. 'I've had a cold luncheon laid out in the dining room. I thought that would be the easiest way, considering we have young children to feed.'

'Excellent, thank you. We'll be in my study. Let me know when the others arrive back from their trip around the farm.'

'Of course, sir.'

Eugene led the way through twisting passages to a small room where a fire had been lit in the grate. 'That woman is a mind reader,' he said cheerfully. 'I didn't have to ask her to light the fire. As usual, she anticipates my wants and needs.'

'She spoils you, Gene.' Rose took a seat by the window. 'Should you ever give up being a bachelor, some unsuspecting woman will take on a real challenge.'

'I'll be careful who I choose in that case, Rose.' Eugene went to his desk and opened a drawer. He took out a shagreen-covered box and laid it on the well-worn tooled leather surface. 'I had this made for you.' He hesitated, eyeing her warily. 'I'd planned to invite you and Sparrow here for Christmas, but events intervened.'

'I suppose by that you mean Max's unexpected arrival?'

'That played a part in it.'

'I'm sorry, Gene. You're speaking in riddles and now I'm even more confused.'

'I'm not sure where I stand with you, Rose. Being your employer complicates matters.'

'I know I'm a bit late with the next article, but I'd have finished it this morning if I hadn't come here with you.'

'That's not what I meant.' Eugene picked up the box and handed it to her. 'I was going to give you this on Christmas morning, Rose. Open it, please.'

She lifted the lid and the diamond centre of the white enamel petals flashed as they caught the light.

'Do you know what flower that is?'

'It's the same as the ones blooming outside your front door.' She looked up, smiling. 'It's a Christmas rose.' She took it from its velvet bed and her smile faded.

'What's the matter? Don't you like it?'

'I love it, but it's obviously very expensive.' She replaced the piece of jewellery in its box. 'I can't accept it.'

'That's ridiculous. It's a gift.'

'A very expensive gift, Gene. It wouldn't be proper.'

'Since when have you worried about propriety? I seem to recall a young woman who left home and travelled on a steamer from Australia to London, with nothing more than a vague idea of where she would meet a man to whom she was unofficially engaged.'

Closing the box, Rose laid it back on the desk. 'I can see the cart bringing the Normans back for luncheon. We'd better join them.' She took a step forward but Eugene moved swiftly to bar her way.

'No, you don't, Rose Munday. You're not going anywhere until we've had the talk we should have had weeks ago.'

'Let me pass, Gene. We need to look after the Normans.'

'They can take care of themselves for five minutes. Damn it, Rose, I should have spoken up before, but I suppose I was afraid you would turn me down.'

'What are you saying, Gene?'

'I'm offering you everything I have, Rose, including my heart. I'm probably making a mess of things, but you must know how I feel about you.'

There was no mistaking the sincerity in his voice or the depth of feeling in his gaze, and she knew she was lost for ever. Their last short but passionate encounter had left her yearning for more, and she made no attempt to push him away as he drew her closer and their lips met.

'Say it,' he whispered in between kisses. 'Tell me that you love me, Rose.'

'I do.' The confession floated on a breath, and she relaxed into his embrace, giving as well as receiving. 'I do.' She drew away just far enough to gain control of her breathing. 'But Max hasn't given up, despite the fact that I gave back his ring. He still thinks I'm going to marry him.'

'Max will have to learn that he can't have everything his own way.' Eugene released her gently, turned and reached for the box. He flipped it open and held it out to her. 'Now will you allow me to give you your Christmas present?'

She dashed a tear from her eyes. 'Thank you, Gene. It's beautiful – I love it.'

He pinned it to her bodice. 'The next thing I buy will be an engagement ring.'

'You haven't proposed.'

Eugene smiled. 'I will when the time is right.' He was about to kiss her again when a sharp rap on the door announced Mrs Cardew's appearance to inform them that the family were in the dining room and had already started on the cold chicken.

They entered the dining room hand in hand to find everyone intent on eating as much as they could stuff into their mouths. Winnie looked up and hooted with laughter. 'I knew it. I told you, Harry, he's been and gone and done it.'

'Hush, Ma,' Harry said in a low voice. 'You'll embarrass Miss Rose.'

Winnie reached for her glass of wine and raised it in a toast. 'Here's to you, sir, and you, Miss Rose. Long life and happiness.' She downed the drink in one gulp.

'It's not what you think,' Rose said hastily. 'We're not engaged.'

Winnie picked up the bottle and refilled her glass. 'Well, it's only a matter of time. I could see it coming.'

Eugene pulled up a chair for Rose. 'You're very perceptive, Mrs Norman. I'm doing my best to win the fair lady, but more importantly, have you come to a decision? Will you accept my offer of employment, Harry, and the cottage that goes with it?'

Billy wiped his mouth on his sleeve. 'Say you will, Harry. I ain't never seen grub like this afore.'

Winnie cuffed him round the ear. 'Mind your manners, Billy Norman. You'll be respectful of the master when we take up residence in that little palace. We would be fools to turn you down, sir. I'll be more than happy to offer my services to the mistress of Greenfields.' She sent a meaningful glance in Rose's direction.

Eugene raised his glass to Winnie. 'You're a woman after my own heart, Mrs Norman.'

'It's Winnie, sir,' she said, blushing. 'I'd be honoured to accept your offer of work and a new home. We all would, wouldn't we, Harry?'

'Yes, Ma.' Harry reached out to hold his mother's hand. 'I'll drink to a new life for all of us.'

'I can hear the children singing carols.' Rose huddled closer to Eugene as he handled the reins on the return journey to London. It was getting dark and she could just make out the bulky shape of the barouche ahead of them, and the sound of the children's voices ringing out in the cold air like carillon bells. 'That was a generous thing you did today, Gene.'

He glanced at her, smiling. 'I didn't do it solely for the Norman family. I wanted to make you happy, and prove that I'm not such a bad fellow.'

'I know you're not,' Rose said gently. 'Perhaps I know you better than you know yourself, and you're not likely to give up the newspaper in order to devote yourself to farming. If – and I say if – we were married, what would become of me? I don't think I could bear to be left at home, tending to the household while you were in Fleet Street, working on the latest edition.'

'You have talent, Rose. I'd be a fool to overlook that, and I suppose I've always thought that we would work together.'

'In what way?' Rose asked suspiciously. 'I don't want to sit in front of that typewriter machine all day.'

He threw back his head and laughed. 'What a

picture that presents. I told you that Arthur has decided to retire, but what I didn't mention because I wanted to wait until it was finalised, is that I'm buying him out. The *Leader* will be ours, Rose. We'll run it together and make it the best-selling daily newspaper in London. What do you say to that?'

She slipped her hand through the crook of his arm. 'That's an offer I can't refuse, Gene.'

He leaned over to brush her lips with a kiss. 'Sort things out with Max, please, Rose. I can't live without you. I want you to know that.'

When they arrived back in Wapping Eugene paid a boy to hold the horse while he saw Rose safely home, but when they arrived at the Captain's House lights blazed from all the windows, and the front door had been left ajar.

'This doesn't look right,' Eugene said grimly. 'I'll go in first.'

Rose was close on his heels as he stormed into the parlour, where he came to a sudden halt.

'Where the hell have you been, Rose?' Max demanded angrily. 'Why are you with him?'

'Hold on, Max,' Jimmy said anxiously. 'Don't jump to conclusions.'

A fashionably dressed young woman rose from the sofa where she had been sitting next to Maria. 'How are you, Rose?'

'Caroline!' Rose gazed at her in astonishment. 'I

thought you and Phineas were on a business trip to Australia.'

'Phineas is still there but I decided to return home with my little ones.' Caroline patted her gently swelling belly, smiling. 'I didn't want to risk travelling nearer to my time.'

Rose threw her arms around Caroline, finding herself close to tears. 'I wish you'd been here when I arrived home, Carrie.'

'Max has told me everything,' Caroline said gently.

'Rose is being difficult,' Max added hastily. 'I've bought her a ring, and I don't know what else I can do to show I'm sincere.' He glared at Eugene, who was standing quietly at Rose's side. 'You're the one who's filled her head with silly notions about a career in journalism. You're just using her.'

'That's enough, Max,' Rose said angrily. 'Leave Eugene out of this. I told you that I don't want to marry you, and I just need you to accept it.' She turned to Caroline. 'Please make him see sense. I know he's trying to be honourable by keeping his word, but it wouldn't work.'

Maria rose to her feet. 'Perhaps we ought to leave you to sort this out in private.'

'Yes,' Caroline agreed, nodding. 'But you need to think very hard before you press her any further, Max. If Rose has changed her mind you must respect her wishes, even if they go against your own.'

Rose shook her head. 'Don't go. There's nothing

I have to say to Max that can't be said in front of his brother and sisters.' She reached for Eugene's hand and clasped it tightly. 'I did love you, Max, or at least I thought I did, but now I realise that it was part of growing up for both of us. You need a wife who will do your bidding and never question your judgement. You need someone willing to put you first and make a home for you wherever your next posting happens to be. That's not me, Max.'

'It's him,' Max said gruffly. 'Eugene Sheldon has turned your head, flattering you and flaunting his wealth.'

Rose was alarmed to see a muscle tighten in the angle of Eugene's jaw, but he gave her hand a comforting squeeze. 'I see Rose for what she is, Max, and I love her with all my heart.'

Caroline and Maria exchanged misty glances and Maria's hand flew to her lips. 'Oh, how lovely,' she breathed.

'Do you hear that, Max?' Caroline gave her brother a warning look. 'Mama always spoiled you, but this time you can't have things your own way.'

'Mama didn't approve of my relationship with Rose, which is why I sent her to England,' Max said sulkily. 'I won't be dictated to.'

'Face up to the truth, old chap,' Jimmy said softly. 'Allow Rose to choose the man she really loves, or not, as the case may be. She's a free spirit – let her go.'

'You know that's the right thing to do, Max.' Caroline laid her hand on his shoulder. 'I want you and Jimmy to stay with me in Finsbury Square for the rest of your leave. You mustn't linger in that sad old house on the pier head.'

'I suppose it belongs to my mother and Phineas,' Maria said thoughtfully. 'It seems a shame to let such a beautiful house go to rack and ruin.'

Caroline turned to her with a sympathetic smile. 'Your memories of it must be very mixed, but I thought I'd take the children to Starcross Abbey and find out what your mama and Freddie have to say about Pier House. Maybe you'd like to come, too. You said that Theo isn't due home for quite a while.'

Maria clapped her hands. 'That would be delightful. I hate London in January.'

Max had barely taken his eyes off Eugene, but he turned to his sister with a persuasive smile. 'The Captain's House belongs to you, doesn't it, Carrie?'

'Yes, it does. Phineas bought it for me because he knew I loved it.'

'Therefore you decide who lives here.'

Caroline gave him a speculative glance. 'If you're asking me to evict Rose, the answer is no.'

'But it's ideal for me and Jimmy,' Max said silkily. 'I'd even take on the two dubious characters who cook and clean. They brighten the old place up.'

'For a start, Cora and Flossie are my friends,' Rose countered. 'And, secondly, they are respectable women and deserve to be treated as such. They'll always have a place in my home, should they wish to stay.'

'But if you're to live with your wealthy employer, married or not, you won't want to take them to your smart town house, will you, Rose?'

'Don't speak to Rose in that tone of voice.' Eugene stepped forward, hands fisted. 'I've put up with this for long enough. Come outside and we'll settle this like gentlemen.'

'With pleasure. I owe you a good thrashing, Sheldon.'

'Stop this at once.' Rose threw herself between them. 'You're behaving like stupid schoolboys. I'm not something you can fight over. I'm not a prize to be won or lost. I'm a person and I have a will of my own.'

Caroline and Maria clapped their hands in unison.

'You're right, and I apologise,' Eugene said humbly.

'The world has gone mad.' Max strode towards the door. 'I'm leaving. You can contact me at Pier House, Carrie.' He fixed his brother with a stony stare. 'Are you coming, Jimmy?'

'I need to see Carrie safely to her carriage and then I'll join you.'

'I'm leaving now,' Caroline said firmly. 'I've said what I had to say.' She embraced Rose, kissing her on both cheeks. 'I wish you well, whatever your choice. Come and see me whenever you have a free moment.

I have messages from home for you,' she shot a glance at Eugene and smiled, 'but that can wait.'

'I haven't asked you how they are,' Rose said hastily.

'They're all well and they send their love. I'll tell you all the gossip when we meet again.'

'I'll come to see you tomorrow, Carrie.' Maria made to follow them from the room. 'But now I really must go and check on the children. Shall I tell Cora that we'll be one extra for supper?'

'I'd love to stay,' Eugene said before Rose had a chance to reply. 'If it's not too much trouble.'

'Of course not.' Maria smiled and left the room, closing the door behind her.

There was a moment of almost complete silence, apart from the ticking of the clock on the mantelshelf and the crackle of the logs on the fire. Rose met Eugene's enquiring look with a weary smile. 'What now, Gene?' She was, as always, acutely aware of his nearness. Warmth radiated from his body and his eyes glowed amber in the firelight.

He took both her hands in his. 'Did you mean what you said when you turned Max down?'

She nodded dully. 'Yes, of course.'

He went down on one knee. 'Rose Munday, I've loved you from the moment I first saw you. Will you do me the honour of becoming my wife?'

Despite the fact that this was no surprise, she realised that she was crying. 'Yes, Gene. I will.'

He rose swiftly to his feet and took her in his arms. 'Now I claim the only gift that I want from you.'

'What is it?' she asked in a breathless whisper.

'A kiss from the woman I want to spend the rest of my life loving and caring for. Kiss me, my Christmas Rose.'

Read on for an exclusive
extract of Dilly's next novel

Nettie's Secret

Coming June 2019

Chapter One

Covent Garden, 1875

Robert Carroll appeared in the doorway of his attic studio, wiping his hands on his already paint-stained smock. A streak of Rose Madder appeared like a livid gash on his forehead. 'Nettie, I want you to go to Winsor and Newton in Rathbone Place and get me some more Cobalt Blue, Indian Yellow and Zinc White. I can't finish this painting without them.'

Nettie looked up from the garment she has been mending. 'Do you need them urgently, Pa? I promised to finish this for Madame Fabron. It's the opening night of her play at the Adelphi, and she must have her gown.'

'And I have to finish this commission, or I won't

get paid and we'll find ourselves homeless. We're already behind with the rent, and Ma Burton isn't the most reasonable of souls.'

'All right, Pa. I'll go, but I thought we didn't have any money, which was why we had nothing but onions for supper last night.' Reluctantly, Nettie laid her sewing aside.

'Food is not important when art is concerned, Nettie,' Robert said severely. 'I can't finish my work without paint, and if I don't get this canvas to Dexter by tomorrow there'll be trouble.' He took some coins from his pocket and pressed them into her hand. 'Go now, and hurry.'

'I know you think the world of Duke Dexter, but how do you know that the copies you make of old masters' works aren't passed off as the real thing?' Nettie pocketed the money. 'You only have Duke's word for the fact that he sells your canvases as reproductions.'

'Nonsense, Nettie. Duke is a respectable art dealer with a gallery in Paris as well as in London.' Robert ran his hand through his hair, leaving it more untidy than ever. 'And even if he weren't an honest dealer, what would you have me do? Commissions don't come my way often enough to support us, even in this rat-infested attic.'

'I still think you ought to check up on him, Pa.'

'Stop preaching at me, Nettie. Be a good girl and get the paint or we'll both starve to death.'

'You have such talent, Pa,' Nettie said sadly. 'It's a pity to squander it by making copies of other people's work.' She snatched up her bonnet and shawl and left her father to get on as best he could until she returned with the urgently needed paints. Everything was always done in a panic, and their way of living had been one of extremes ever since she could remember. When Robert Carroll sold one of his canvases they lived well and, despite Nettie's attempts to save something for the lean times to come, her father had a habit of spending freely without any thought to the future.

Nettie made her way down the narrow, twisting staircase to the second floor, where the two rooms were shared by the friends who had kept her spirits up during the worst of hard times. Byron Horton, whom she thought of as a much-loved big brother, was employed as a clerk by a firm in Lincoln's Inn. Nettie had been tempted to tell him that she suspected Marmaduke Dexter of being a fraud, but that might incriminate her father and so she had kept her worries to herself. The other two young men were Philip Ransome, known fondly as Pip, who worked in the same law office as Byron, and Ted Jones, whose tender heart had been broken so many times by his choice of lady friend that it had become a standing joke. Ted worked for the Midland Railway Company, and was currently suffering from yet another romantic entanglement gone wrong.

Nettie hurried down the stairs, past the rooms where the family of actors resided when they were in town, as was now the case. Madame Fabron had a small part in the play *Notre-Dame, or The Gypsy Girl of Paris*, at the Adelphi Theatre, with Monsieur Fabron in a walk-on role, and their daughter, Amelie, was understudy to the leading lady, Teresa Furtado, who was playing Esmeralda. The Fabrons were of French origin, but they had been born and bred in Poplar. They adopted strong French accents whenever they left the building in the same way that others put on their overcoats, but this affectation obviously went well in the theatrical world as they were rarely out of work. Fortunately for Nettie, neither Madame nor her daughter could sew, and Nettie was kept busy mending the garments they wore on and off stage.

She continued down the stairs to the ground floor, where sickly Josephine Lorimer lived with her husband, a journalist, who was more often away from home than he was resident, and a young maid-servant, Biddy, a child plucked from an orphanage. Nettie quickened her pace, not wanting to get caught by Biddy, who invariably asked for help with one thing or another, and was obviously at her wits' end when trying to cope with her ailing mistress. Not that she had many wits in the first place, according to Robert Carroll, who said she was a simpleton. Nettie knew this to be untrue, but today she was in a hurry and she was desperate to avoid their landlady, Ma Burton, who inhabited the basement like a huge spider clad in black bombazine, waiting for her prey to wander into her web. Ma Burton was a skinflint, who knew how to squeeze the last penny out of any situation, and her cronies were shadowy figures who came and went in the hours of darkness. Added to that, Ma Burton's sons were rumoured to be vicious bare-knuckle fighters, who brought terror to the streets of Seven Dials and beyond. It was well known that they were up for hire by any gang willing to pay for their services. It was best not to upset Ma and incur the wrath of her infamous offspring and their equally brutal friends.

Nettie escaped from the house overlooking the piazza of Covent Garden and St Paul's, the actors' church, and was momentarily dazzled by the sunshine reflecting off the wet cobblestones. She had missed a heavy April shower, and she had to sidestep a large puddle as she made her way down Southampton Street. It would have been quicker to cut through Seven Dials, but that was a rough area, even in daytime; after dark no one in their right mind would venture into the narrow alleys and courts that radiated off the seventeenth-century sundial, not even the police. Nettie stopped to count the coins her father had given her and decided there was enough for her bus fare to the Tottenham Court Road end of Oxford Street, and from there it was a short walk to the art shop in Rathbone Place. She must make haste – Violet Fabron would expect her gown to be finished well before curtain-up.

Nettie spotted a horse-drawn omnibus drawing to a halt in the Strand and she picked up her skirts and ran. The street was crowded with vehicles of all shapes and sizes, and with pedestrians milling about in a reckless manner, but this enabled Nettie to jump on board. As luck would have it, she found a vacant seat. One day, when she was rich, she would have her own carriage and she would sit back against velvet squabs, watching the rest of the population going about their business, but for now it was the rackety omnibus that bumped over the cobblestones and swayed from side to side like a ship on a stormy ocean, stopping to let passengers alight and taking on fresh human cargo. Steam rose from damp clothing, and the smell of wet wool and muddy boots combined with the sweat of humans and horse-flesh. Nettie closed her mind to the rank odours and sat back, enjoying the freedom of being away from her cramped living quarters, if only for an hour or so.

Two hours later, Nettie returned home with the paints and two baked potatoes that she had purchased from a street vendor in Covent Garden.

Robert studied the small amount of change she

had just given him. 'The price of paint hasn't gone up, has it?'

Nettie took off her bonnet and laid it on a chair in the living room. 'No, Pa. I bought the potatoes because we need to eat. I'm so hungry that my stomach hurts.'

'There should be more change than this.'

'I had a cup of coffee, Pa. Surely you don't begrudge me that?'

Robert shook his head. 'No, of course not. I'm hungry, too. Thank you, dear.' He took the potato and disappeared into his room.

Nettie sighed with relief as the door closed behind her father. She reached under her shawl and produced the new notebook that she had purchased in Oxford Street. It had cost every penny that she had earned from mending a tear in Monsieur Fabron's best shirt, and she had supplemented it with a threepenny bit from the coins that her father had given her for his art supplies. Perhaps she should have spent the three-pence on food, but she considered it money well spent, and paper, pen and ink were her only extravagance. Writing a romantic novel was more than a guilty pleasure; Nettie had been working on her story for over a year, and she hoped one day to see it published. But she dare not reveal the truth to Pa – he would tell her that she was wasting valuable time. No one in their right mind would want to pay good money for a work written by a twenty-year-old girl with very little experience of life and love. She knew exactly what Pa thought about 'penny dreadfuls' and he would be mortified if he thought that his daughter aspired to write popular fiction. It was her secret and she had told nobody, not even Byron or Pip, and Ted could not keep a secret to save his life. Poor Ted was still nursing a broken heart after being jilted by the young woman who worked in the nearby bakery; he wore black and had grown his hair long in the hope that he looked like a poet with a tragic past. Nettie had met the love of his life, Pearl Biggs, just the once, and that was enough to convince her that Ted was better off remaining a bachelor than tied to a woman who was no better than she should be.

Nettie hid the new notebook, along with two others already filled, beneath the cushions on the sofa, where she slept each night. She was in the middle of her story, and the characters played out their lives in her imagination while she went about her daily chores. Sometimes they intruded in her thoughts when she was least expecting it, but occasionally they refused to co-operate and she found herself with her pen poised and nothing to say.

She put the potato on a clean plate and went to sit on a chair in the window to enjoy the hot buttery flesh and the crisp outer skin, licking her fingers after each tasty bite. When she had eaten the last tiny morsel, she wiped her hands on a napkin and picked up her sewing. She concentrated on Madame Fabron's gown, using tiny stitches to ensure that the darn was barely visible. Having finished, she put on her outdoor things and wrapped the gown in a length of butter muslin. She opened the door to her father's studio.

'I'm off to the theatre, Pa.'

'The theatre?'

'Yes, Pa. You remember, Madame Fabron needs her gown for the performance this evening.'

'Oh, that. Yes, I do. Wretched woman thinks she can act. I've seen more talented performing horses. Don't be long, Nettie. I want you to take a message to Duke. You'll need to make full use of your feminine wiles because this painting won't be finished today. He can come and view it, if he so wishes.'

'Yes, Pa. I'll be as quick as I can.'

Once again, Nettie left their rooms and made her way downstairs. She was tiptoeing past the Lorimers' door when it opened and Biddy leaped out at her.

'I heard you coming. I need help, Nettie. Mrs Lorimer's having one of her funny turns.'

'I'm sorry, Biddy. But I'm in a hurry.'

Biddy clutched Nettie's arm. 'Oh, please. I dunno what to do. She's weeping and throwing things. I'm scared to death.'

'All right, but I can only spare a couple of minutes.' Nettie stepped inside the dark hallway and Biddy rushed past her to open the sitting-room door. The curtains were drawn and a fire burned in the grate, creating a fug. The smell of sickness lingered in the air. It took Nettie a moment to accustom her eyes to the gloom, but she could see Josephine Lorimer's prostate figure on a chaise longue in front of the fire. She had one arm flung over her face and the other hanging limp over the side of the couch. Unearthly keening issued from her pale lips.

'What's the matter, Mrs Lorimer?'

Josephine moved her arm away from her face. 'Who is it?'

'It's me, Nettie Carroll from upstairs. Biddy says you are unwell.'

'I'm very ill. I think I'm dying and nobody cares.'

Nettie laid her hand on Josephine's forehead, which was clammy but cool. 'You don't appear to have a fever. Perhaps if you sit up and try to keep calm you might feel better.'

'How can I be calm when I am all alone in this dark room?'

Biddy shrank back into the shadows. 'Is she dying?'

Nettie walked over to the window and drew the curtains, allowing a shaft of pale sunlight to filter in through the grimy windowpanes. 'Mrs Lorimer would be better for a cup of tea and something to eat, Biddy. Have you anything prepared for her luncheon?'

'There's soup downstairs on the old witch's range,

but I'm scared to go down there. She'll put me in a pot and boil me for her dinner.'

Josephine groaned and turned her head away. 'Have you ever heard such nonsense? I'm supposed to be looked after by that stupid girl.'

'I'm not stupid, missis,' Biddy muttered.

'Come with me,' Nettie said firmly. 'We'll go down together. Ma Burton may be an old witch, but she doesn't eat people.'

Biddy backed away, but a fierce look from Josephine sent her scurrying for the door. 'All right, I'll go, but you must come with me, miss.'

'We'll be back in two ticks.' Nettie lowered her voice. 'She's just a child and she's scared.'

Josephine's lips trembled. 'I need someone like you – someone capable and caring, not a silly little girl.'

Nettie gave up her attempt to reason with the irritable patient and followed Biddy from the room.

Look out for Dilly's brand
new novel

Nettie's Secret

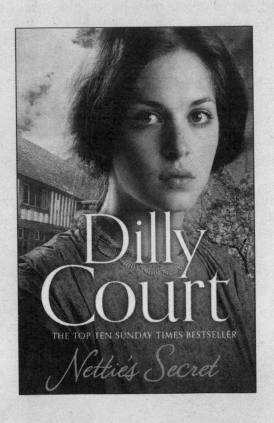

DILLY COURT

THE TOP TEN SUNDAY TIMES BESTSELLER

Nettie's Secret

Coming June 2019